THE PRINCESS FUGITIVE

THE FOUR KINGDOMS AND BEYOND

THE PRINCESS FUGITIVE

A REIMAGINING OF LITTLE RED RIDING HOOD

MELANIE CELLIER

LUMINANT PUBLICATIONS

THE PRINCESS FUGITIVE: A REIMAGINING OF LITTLE RED
RIDING HOOD

First edition published in 2016
Second edition published in 2018 (v2.1)
by Luminant Publications

ISBN 978-0-9806963-8-7

Luminant Publications
PO Box 203
Glen Osmond, South Australia 5064

melaniecellier@internode.on.net
http://www.melaniecellier.com

Cover Design by Karri Klawiter

For Marc
who loves me with his words and his actions

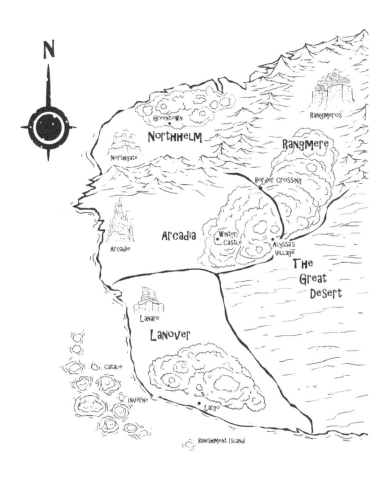

ASSASSIN

*M*oonlight shone through several tall windows, illuminating the large empty room and the lone man slowly pacing its length. He was tall and broad shouldered, and he wore his strength easily, like a well-fitted cloak. He made it all the way across the room and back before raising his head and peering toward a door hidden on the opposite wall.

A second figure appeared and moved swiftly to intercept the first. He was shorter, but a hidden menace lurked behind the taut grace of his movements.

"Is everything ready?" asked the waiting man, his voice low and deep.

"It is. My men are in place."

The tall man nodded, and there was a moment's silence. The new arrival shifted his weight in a subtle gesture of unease.

"What is it, Joran?" asked the tall man quickly, although he kept his voice quiet. "The plan is perfect."

"Of course. We *will* succeed. Have I ever failed?" The unease was in his voice now, though. "Nothing can go wrong. Unless..." he trailed off, apparently afraid to voice his concern.

"Unless what?" asked the tall man, raising his voice slightly with impatience.

There was another pause.

"Unless there's...an intervention."

"An intervention? Oh, a *godmother*? Is that your worry?" The tall man gave a sharp bark of quickly stifled laughter. "You can relax in that case. There hasn't been a godmother in Rangmere for nearly twenty years."

"You're right, as always," said Joran. "But they are known to favor princesses." He directed a significant look at his companion.

"You of all people should know that things are not always as they seem," replied the first. "Godmothers help *deserving* princesses. There may have been a godmother at Princess Ava's Christening, but there's a reason the kingdom hasn't seen one since.

"Ava isn't the damsel-in-distress," he continued. "She's the wolf. There will be no godmother to aid her, I can promise you that."

"Then we are ready," said Joran, "and only await your order."

"Get it done."

PART I
THE FLIGHT

CHAPTER 1

*A*va wasn't sure what had woken her, but something was definitely wrong. She almost never startled so suddenly into wakefulness. She held herself still, assessing the room without opening her eyes.

Only the light of the dying fire leaked through her eyelids, and she could detect no discernible sound. But despite the absence of clues she felt utterly sure that a person loomed over her.

She sighed softly and twitched, using the movement to slide one hand under her pillow. Still the intruder remained motionless. Ava could guess why her unknown visitor had paused. She knew exactly what picture she presented, asleep in her gorgeous canopied bed. Her golden hair, perfectly curled, spread out across the pillow and her dark gold eyelashes rested gently against her perfect, rose-tinted cheeks. Her full lips parted softly, allowing the tiniest glimpse of her straight, white teeth.

Her grandmother had told her that when she slept she looked like an angel, and she suspected she also looked younger than her true age of eighteen.

Innocent and beautiful. Enough to make anyone pause. The

effect was no accident, of course. Her father had taught her that her looks were her greatest weapon.

"Never was there a truer-looking princess than you, my Ava," he had told her as she sat on his knee as a girl. "Your face alone will disarm any opponent."

The memory of his words brought a bitter sting. Her face had not been enough last summer. But she pushed the thought of Arcadia aside. Perhaps her face had not been enough then, but apparently it was sufficient tonight.

As she snapped her eyes open, her hand slashed upward in one fluid motion. By the time she had assimilated the identity of the intruder, the tip of her knife had already penetrated his ribs. She felt a detached pride at the steadiness of her hand and her well-judged aim. But this feeling was soon overridden by betrayal.

"Joran." She now sat bolt upright in her bed. The man had dropped to his knees, his own knife falling into the soft carpet without a sound. He gripped the hilt of the blade protruding from his chest with both hands but didn't attempt to remove it.

He made no reply to his name but looked up and met her eyes. A grudging respect showed through the grimace on his face.

"You called me a fool once," he said, his words labored. "It seems you were right."

"I told you then, I'm always right." Ava was glad to hear her voice come out steady and light. She wasn't squeamish, but she kept her eyes firmly on his face, away from the blossom of blood spreading across his shirt.

"Ah, but you weren't right *that* time, were you?" he asked, mockery in his voice. She stiffened, still not used to the knot of tension she felt at any reminder of Arcadia.

Still her voice remained steady as she replied. "It seems we were both liars on that occasion. I seem to remember you assured me of your loyalty. And yet here we are."

Joran was sagging now, and Ava could no longer ignore the

blood that seemed to be everywhere. She felt her stomach churn and had to call upon her not inconsiderable will-power to keep it in place.

Softly the man crumpled onto the carpet, and she steeled herself to lean over the edge of the bed. His eyes inched open and slowly focused on her.

"My loyalty," he paused as he drew in a burbling breath, "always lay with whoever has the power." His voice trailed off, and this time his eyes closed and didn't open again. A thin trail of blood seeped out of the corner of his mouth, and his chest stopped moving.

Ava sat frozen, watching for signs of life. None came. She slid across the bed and slipped out the other side. Her bare feet sank into the carpet, and she moved silently across the room. Stopping by the fireplace, she reached toward the bell-pull and then paused. Her hand moved instead to pick up a candelabra from the mantelpiece and light it from the fire.

Her thoughts churned, but her face remained still, giving no hint of her emotions. This was another weapon taught to her by her father, and the lesson was so ingrained that she practiced it even now, alone in her room in the middle of the night.

She was glad her father wasn't in the room for many reasons. For one, he was one of the only people still able to read the minute changes in her face, and she suspected he wouldn't like what he saw. While her face remained still, her mind was seething. Her thoughts kept circling back to the corpse behind her, and she knew her father would disapprove of this lack of control.

He had trained her to keep her mind sharp and ordered at all times. He had trained her to be effective and merciless. She admitted to herself now that he had also trained her to be a killer. She knew, somewhere in the back of her mind that she had been responsible for many deaths. *Strange*, she thought now, *how different it is when my own hand did the killing. I didn't expect that.*

For some moments, she dwelt on this thought until horror and self-disgust began to stir within her. As soon as she recognized these emotions she thrust the thought away, burying it deeply, far from her consciousness. She knew she couldn't banish the thought entirely, but *I'll deal with it later*, she decided. Even as she did so, she felt a pang of guilt. Her father would be disgusted at her weakness.

This knowledge brought her back to the far more important reason she was glad of his absence. This was the unwelcome realization that had caused her to move her hand away from the bell-pull. Joran had said his loyalty lay with the power. Once that had meant her, but obviously his loyalties had shifted. And here in Rangmere there was only one power.

She had been waiting all winter to discover the consequences for her failure over the summer. She hadn't expected such a drastic response, but perhaps she should have. Her father had never countenanced failure. The only real surprise was that he had taken this long to act.

Ava saw no choice but to flee. Immediately.

Her face hadn't changed as she processed these thoughts, but with the decision came a new determination that showed only in her eyes and a small tightness around her mouth. She turned away from the fire and moved quickly to a tapestry hanging against the side wall.

She brushed the material aside, revealing a small wooden door. She opened the door without knocking but didn't step through.

A small stone chamber stood exposed. A single candle burned in the room revealing a cot, a chest, and a small washstand. A tall figure lay sleeping in the bed, but at the sound of the opening door he sat up. In one quick movement, he slid out of bed, facing the far wall. As he moved, he seized the hilt of a naked sword lying by the side of the cot. He stared at another door, but it remained firmly closed.

Ava cleared her throat quietly, and the man swung around. She gestured for him to enter her room, but he hesitated. Ava had seen Hans in many different situations but couldn't remember ever seeing him surprised before. And he certainly never hesitated.

But then she had never invited him into her room before, either. She sighed and gestured again before turning and walking back toward her fireplace.

His feet moved as silently as her own, but she sensed him following her across the carpet. After a moment, she heard the sharp hiss of an indrawn breath. She knew without looking that he had cleared the end of the bed and seen what lay on the other side of it. She turned and silently watched him change course.

He knelt beside the dead man and briefly placed two fingers on the man's neck. His observant gaze moved from the hilt of her own knife, still protruding from Joran's chest, to the abandoned knife on the carpet.

It was one of the things Ava liked best about Hans—she never needed to explain things to him.

"Forgive me, Your Highness," he said, his head bowed and voice heavy.

"For what?"

He looked up at that, and although it was hard to read his eyes in the candlelight she thought they held relief.

"It is my job to guard you, and it would appear that tonight, at least, I have failed." There was a strange hardness in his voice that she couldn't quite read.

"There are only two entrances to my room, and you have faithfully guarded the one entrusted to your keeping. The other entrance is locked and guarded from without by my father's loyal guards." She left the rest of the thought unfinished.

The hardness in his voice earlier was nothing to the expression that transformed his face as he pondered her words. His eyes set like granite.

MELANIE CELLIER

She couldn't repress a shiver.

He seemed startled by her small movement, and his eyes softened and focused on her face, assessing.

It took all of her willpower not to blush with embarrassment. Having been with her so long, he was one of the few who understood how shaken she must be to have betrayed herself with the involuntary motion.

She spoke quickly and softly, attempting to recover her poise and sense of control. "We must leave the castle now, tonight. Is there anything you need to pack that isn't in your room?" She gestured toward the hidden doorway which still stood open.

Hans shook his head once, sharply. His own training helped him keep his face steady, but the training of a guard did not compare to that of a princess. Not in Rangmere.

To someone who knew him as well as she did, the shock was painted across his face.

"You are a loyal and skilled guard, Hans," she said with a sweet smile, "but even you cannot protect me against an entire kingdom. We have no other choice but to leave."

She produced the smile without conscious thought. Manipulation came as naturally to her as breathing.

But Hans seemed untouched by it, which was another reason she liked him. He was one of the few who never seemed affected by her beauty.

Her father had taught her how to influence those around her even as she learned her first words. She clung to the sense of control manipulation gave her. And yet, at the same time, she liked knowing that there was one person unaffected by her skills. She had never stopped to consider the strangeness of this dichotomy. Another thought to be pushed down, to be left for another day.

"We'll need horses." His voice snapped her out of her reverie.

She shook her head once to clear it, frustrated at this strange mood that had overtaken her—so different from her normal calm control.

"We must be far from here by morning. Perhaps sooner if someone is waiting for Joran to check back in." Hans had apparently taken her movement as a disagreement.

"No, no, of course. We must have horses. And supplies..." her voice trailed off as she realized this might be more difficult than she had at first envisioned.

"I can find us supplies," said Hans. "I have friends among the kitchen staff, so I know my way around. Everyone will be asleep now."

Friends among the kitchen staff. The words hit another raw nerve, long buried, and Ava marveled at how quickly her life, and mind, had spiraled out of control. With an effort, she forced her mind to resume its usual sharp quality.

"Pack whatever you need from your room and give it to me. I'll pack my own things and meet you at the stables."

"No!"

The sharp retort shocked Ava, who had already turned toward her wardrobe.

"Excuse me!?" she said, ice in her voice.

"I won't leave you alone. I won't fail to protect you again." The intensity in his voice and eyes stripped away her remaining anger.

She moved to him and laid a hand on his arm. "I can take care of myself." She gestured toward the bed and what lay behind it. "I think I've proven that tonight."

Hans didn't reply but instead stared down at her hand. After a moment, he carefully gripped her wrist and removed her hand.

She let it drop and took a step backward, surprised at the hurt that filled her. "I appreciate your concern." Her voice came out harsher than she intended, so she moderated it before continuing. "Right now, all I care about is getting out of this castle alive, and my best chance of doing that is if we split up and move *fast*."

Hans drew in a breath as if to argue and then let it out slowly. "Of course, Your Highness." He turned and strode from the room.

Ava wasted no more time dwelling on the many peculiarities of the night. By the time Hans returned with a small satchel, she had changed into her plainest and most practical dress and had filled a satchel of her own. It wasn't as small as Hans', but then Hans had not emptied an entire jewelry box into the bottom of his.

He gestured silently for her to precede him into his small room and then pulled the tapestry back into place with a swift gesture that allowed him to close his door a half second before the fabric fell into place. Ava didn't imagine it would fool anyone for long, but any small advantage was worth it.

They crossed swiftly to the door in the opposite wall, and Hans gestured for her to step back while he opened it and glanced outside. Another gesture and she followed him into the corridor.

He hesitated, and Ava wondered if he would raise any further objections to their parting ways. Instead he drew a small knife from his boot and handed it to her.

She shook her head and instead of taking it, gently drew the tip of a dagger hilt from her own boot.

With a sigh, Hans handed her his satchel. Then, with a nod, he turned and was gone, quickly swallowed up by the shadows.

CHAPTER 2

*A*va took the opposite direction, both satchels slung across her shoulders. At each corner, she stopped and listened carefully for footsteps or breathing before peering cautiously around. Part of her knew that she was unlikely to be stopped. It was unthinkable that her father would have announced his plans for her assassination. She wondered briefly what story he intended to give the court.

A foreign assassin, perhaps? Another reason to start a war.

A rogue courtier? Another reason to tighten control in Rangmere.

The thoughts were strangely comforting. Cold detachment and logic were familiar friends. The rush of emotions that had overwhelmed her in her chambers was gone, and the underlying fear was tucked away, hidden where it didn't interfere with her functioning.

The familiarity of the dark corridors helped. Ava had always loved the castle. As a child, she had imagined that it had its own personality and consciousness. It was a friendly companion during her many night-time wanderings. After her grandmother's disappearance, it was the most welcoming presence in her often lonely life.

She knew now that such thoughts were foolish, but the old homely feelings still lingered, tinting her adult perceptions. She knew the castle so well that she didn't need light to guide her, and when she finally did hear the sound of quiet steps, she swung around and disappeared into a storage cupboard without needing to consciously think of a hiding place.

She held her breath and listened to the footsteps recede. She then forced herself to count slowly to one hundred before she eased herself back into the corridor. The waiting had increased her tension, and she had to restrain the impulse to hurry and make up lost ground.

When you hurry, you make mistakes. She could hear her father's voice in her mind. Just another one of his endless lessons. *Every action should be deliberate. When you move with speed it should be planned, the result of knowing that, in that moment, speed is your most effective and efficient weapon.* He was big on weapons, the King of Rangmere.

Well, it's backfired on you now, Father, she thought mirthlessly. *You've trained me to be a weapon, and now you're finding I'm not so easy to kill.*

It was actually strangely wasteful, to pour so much effort and training into someone, only to decide they were more useful dead. She could only assume it was a result of her failure in Arcadia. King Josef didn't take failure lightly.

And to think, if it hadn't been for the interference of that infuriating Princess Companion, she would currently be Queen of Arcadia instead of running for her life through her own castle. She had heard that the foolish Arcadian Prince had even married the girl—out of gratitude she supposed. It was sickening really.

But even after all these months, thoughts of Arcadia still made her angry, and she couldn't afford to be distracted by emotion now. She forced her thoughts back to the dark corridor around her.

Two more turns and she was out into the crisp night air. As intended, she'd exited into a small courtyard between the main castle building and the stables. The night was cool, although not as bitingly cold as it had been in winter, and the air was full of the smells of horse and hay and manure.

The horse master's apprentices all slept in a loft above the stable, so Ava moved even more carefully than she had in the palace. As she slipped through a crack in the stable door she listened carefully for any stirrings from above. The stable was full of quiet sounds—the breathing of the horses and the rustle of the hay as several adjusted position—but none seemed human in origin.

Ava moved to the stall of her own mare, Cinnamon. She had been Ava's horse for many years and was older than most other horses in the stable. But she was trusty and true, and Ava wouldn't have considered taking any other horse.

Sensing Ava's presence, Cinnamon looked up, and Ava quickly thrust an apple into her mouth. She had raided the fruit bowl in her room in preparation. Cinnamon gave a snort of pleasure but kept it quiet, as if she sensed Ava's need for silence. Dusty, the gelding ridden by Hans, occupied the next stall, but he slept too deeply to be disturbed by Cinnamon's movements.

Saddling the mare was fast and easy, since Ava had been taught to saddle her own horse before she was taught to ride. She quickly moved toward Dusty's stall but stood for a moment watching him. How would he react to being woken? Perhaps she should find another horse, one who was more awake.

Just as she was turning toward the long row of stalls, a small explosion of noise made her jump. She bit her lip to suppress a gasp. No-one appeared to challenge her, and no sounds other than a sleepy mumble followed by a loud snore emerged from the loft.

As her heartbeat returned to its previous pace, she realized the sound had been a stable cat, cornering and pouncing on a terrified mouse. She decided that if the stable boys could sleep through the cat's night-time adventures, she could risk waking Dusty.

Carefully she eased herself into his stall and stood at his head. She had another apple ready to shove into his mouth as soon as he awoke.

He seemed surprised to see her but satisfied with the treat. Saddling him was a little more difficult than Cinnamon given the regular saddle rather than her own side-saddle, but she got it done eventually.

The most difficult part was leading both horses from the stable without waking anyone with the clatter of hoofs. Thankfully the floor was littered with straw which deadened the sounds of the horses' steps. Still, by the time she emerged from the stable she appreciated the cool night air.

She had told Hans to meet her at the stables, but peering around she could see no sign of him. She had expected him to arrive before she finished saddling the horses. It wasn't like him to be late. Hans was always effective and efficient.

She looked around again. Maybe she had just missed him hiding in the shadows. But he was nowhere to be found.

Just as she was starting to wonder whether she should leave the horses and look for him or take Cinnamon and head off on her own, she spotted a dark silhouette moving into the courtyard.

"What took you so long?" she whispered, her relief making her sharp. Hans gave no reply but began to move toward her more quickly.

He had nearly crossed the small courtyard before she realized something was wrong. The silhouette moved with a choppy stride completely unlike the smooth grace of Hans.

At the same moment her brain assimilated this discrepancy, the figure reached down and drew a long dagger from his belt.

She started back violently, and both horses threw up their heads and pranced in place, picking up her distress and amplifying it around the courtyard.

"Well, well, what do we have here?" The man stopped in front of her.

His back was to the faint light coming from the castle windows, so she couldn't make out his features. But the cold amusement in his voice said he was a part of the plot her father had concocted. And even if he wasn't, saddling two horses, alone, in the middle of the night was suspicious behavior.

Her mind raced faster than ever before, spurred on by her fear rather than hampered by it. She threw back her hood and turned her face toward him, hoping the unshed tears she had quickly summoned were visible in the dim light.

"Oh, thank goodness! You have to help me!" A small detached part of herself applauded. She was sure she had never sounded quite so winsome.

She had carefully avoided looking at his dagger, although her eyes kept wanting to drag her face in its direction. At her words, the man gave a quiet chuckle and lifted the weapon threateningly. With a supreme effort of will, she kept her eyes on the dark shadow of his face.

"My instructions were not to *help*, Your Highness."

"Oh, please, please!" She clasped her hands together and allowed one tear to roll down her cheek. Letting go of both leads, she sank to the ground as if her legs had given way beneath her. She kept her eyes raised to the light, hoping his gaze was fixed on her beautiful, terrified face. Slowly her right hand inched beneath her dress, until she could feel the hilt of the dagger buried in her boot.

She froze for a moment, calculating the distance between them and comparing the time for a thrown dagger to reach him against the time for him to reach her. It was a close call and she hesitated, afraid her blade would catch her dress or her arm would move too slowly.

She allowed her breath to hitch on a small sob, trying to buy herself time. She simultaneously tried to convince herself that the delaying tactic was strategic and not at all motivated by fear. The man took a half step closer, and Ava tensed her muscles to move. If he stepped any nearer she would have no chance at all.

But before she could whip out the dagger, the man jerked and slumped to the ground in front of her. Ava looked up to see a new silhouette in his place. This outline was as familiar as her own reflection. How could she ever have confused the other man for Hans?

"Are you all right?" He spoke roughly and seemed to be breathing hard.

Unable to resist a cheeky grin, she flipped back her skirts just enough for him to see her hand resting on the hilt of her dagger. She knew the playfulness was out of character and out of place, but the relief of a second close escape was making her light-headed, and she knew if she didn't smile, she would cry.

As Hans moved toward her she made out his expression. He was giving her a wry grin even as he grabbed the leads of the horses that had moved several steps away.

"I should have known," he said. "People just keep underestimating you, don't they, Princess?"

"All except for you, dear Hans." She made a sound that could have been a chuckle or a sob.

Hans pretended not to hear the excess emotion as he handed her Cinnamon's lead. "I've been the captain of your guard since you were thirteen, Your Highness. I know you far too well to underestimate you."

His words gave her confidence, and she pulled herself together. Focusing on the rough feeling of leather in her hand, she glanced down at the figure on the ground at her feet. "Is he dead?"

"I don't know," said Hans. "I hit him on the head with the hilt of my sword."

Something about his tone made Ava think he didn't much care either way.

"I recognized his voice," Hans continued. "He's one of Joran's lackeys. And he had guard duty on the side gate tonight. He must have heard you and left his post. Hopefully that means the gate's clear. Let's go, quickly, before someone notices he's gone."

CHAPTER 3

*I*t was a relief to Ava to be free of the capital. They had abandoned subtlety in favor of speed, and the trading road rolled by beneath the galloping hooves of their horses. With the wind rushing past her face and her clothes flapping against Cinnamon's sides, it was easier to suppress the anxiety and the fear and the grief.

The events of the night had tried even her self-control. The cool wind against her cheeks helped numb the tumult inside her.

They had been slow and quiet through the streets of the city despite Ava's concern that they would find every gate of Rangmeros barred against them. Her fears had proved unfounded, however. They left through a small postern gate known to every member of the royal family; no alarm had been raised.

And now at last she could move with a speed that matched her hammering heart. Slowly the distance between them and the capital grew, and Ava tamed her emotions.

The farming land that surrounded Rangmeros gave way to the beginnings of the great forest that stretched across the western half of Rangmere. It was the same forest that touched the southern tip of Northhelm and filled the easternmost part of

Arcadia. Ava wished they had chosen to flee east. They had followed no particular direction, choosing the Western Gate simply because it was closest to the castle. But she hated the thought of traveling toward Arcadia. She wondered, briefly, how transparent it would be if she suggested a change in direction.

By the time Hans signaled a halt, drawing Dusty off the road into the first layer of trees, she had decided against saying anything. Hans knew her too well.

"It'll be light soon," he said. "We should head into the trees away from the road."

Ava looked at him sharply. His words were calm and even, but she detected something else in his voice. She nodded a quick assent but kept a close watch on him as they moved further into the forest. The horses mostly picked their own way between the tree trunks. Cinnamon followed Dusty as she had done on many previous rides, leaving Ava free to focus her eyes on Hans and her ears on the surrounding forest and the road behind them.

Something was making Hans uneasy, and Ava wanted to know what it was. Knowledge is power. Once again, she heard the voice of her father in her mind. Trust is for fools.

Generally, she agreed with him, but Hans she trusted. He had long ago earned her trust with unwavering strength, intelligence, and loyalty. If Hans was concerned about something, Ava was concerned, too.

Still, she bided her time, waiting until Hans found a satisfactory clearing and unsaddled and rubbed down Cinnamon. Then he removed his own saddlebags and rummaged through one until he emerged with a water skin, some bread and some cheese.

When he still said nothing, Ava spoke.

"You haven't unsaddled Dusty."

Hans granted her a brief, tight-lipped smile. "Can't get anything past you, Princess."

Ava felt some relief. Hans rarely made jokes, and if he was

making one now, however small, the situation couldn't be that dire.

"Come on, out with it," she said. "What's concerning you?"

He regarded her silently for several moments and then sighed. "That was too easy."

"Excuse me?" Ava's mind flashed back to the gleam of light flashing against the blade of a knife. "It didn't feel easy in the courtyard."

Hans nodded a brief acknowledgment. "Whoever was behind Joran's attempt, they clearly didn't expect him to fail. Their contingency plans were...sloppy." He paused. "We escaped the castle because we moved quickly. But after that..."

"You think we escaped Rangmeros too easily?" Ava's mind whirled, her relief at the ease of their escape changing all too easily to fear.

"Not just the capital, Your Highness. I've been a member of the Guard for six years and trained with them for two years before that. I know their procedures and protocols. They had time to lock down the city gates before we got there. And we should have seen or heard some sign of pursuit on the road. I expected we'd need to leave the road for the forest long before now."

Ava processed this information silently. Hans was silent also, allowing her the time she needed. His words seemed reasonable, but she had no idea what to make of them. She had never felt so stranded, cut off from all her usual sources of information.

Of course, that was what they needed. Information.

"We need more information." She said it with confidence, certain that Hans agreed. There could be no other reason for him to leave Dusty saddled. "You want to go scouting, but you're worried about leaving me alone. Again."

"I wish I had a few men with me." Hans sounded frustrated. "But most of them I couldn't trust, and I could hardly ask the others to leave their families to flee with us." He ran an impatient hand through his hair and down his face. Ava wondered if Hans felt as tired as she did.

"I hate to leave you alone out here, but we need information."

"You were ready to flee with me at a moment's notice; that is enough." Ava spoke firmly, for once letting her true emotions fill her voice without need for manipulation. "We are both highly skilled, and we will survive. And, for now, what we need is information. So, go, and see what you can discover. I'll be here when you return."

Hans regarded her steadily for several moments and then nodded. "You will survive, Your Highness," he said. "I pledge my life on it."

As soon as Hans and Dusty were out of sight among the trees, Ava sank down onto the ground. Alone at last, she could admit that she was exhausted. Much of the strength she had shown Hans had been a façade. She couldn't remember the last time she felt so physically and emotionally drained.

It had been years since she had felt the comfort of a warm hug but she fantasized about one now. She generally tried to avoid thoughts of her mother or her grandmother, so it felt strange to allow herself to remember the safety of their arms.

She even let herself smile at the memory of the beautiful red cloak her grandmother had given her. Once she wore it everywhere. The last four years it had lain at the bottom of her wardrobe.

After a moment, she shook herself. There was a reason she didn't think of any of these things.

Her mother's mother had hated everything Ava's father had stood for and had been the only adult to comfort Ava as her mother wasted away.

But it wasn't my fault, thought Ava. I didn't want to turn my back on her. Choosing my father's way was my only option. My father may have betrayed me now, but that changes nothing. He made me strong. And that strength is the reason I survived tonight.

Dwelling on this thought helped the old certainty to return.

Dying of a broken heart is ridiculous! I don't believe it's possible, whatever people say. No. Mother was ill long before I ever chose to follow Father's direction. It's coincidence she died so soon afterwards.

The thoughts ran round and round in her head as she tried to stop dwelling on her mother's death, so many years ago now, and the unknown fate of her grandmother.

For a long time, she sat there, staring into the trees but not even noticing the increasing light from the dawn filtering among the trunks. When Cinnamon snorted and stamped her hoof, Ava snapped out of her reverie.

Looking around she registered that it was now full daylight, and she was completely alone. She shivered. She missed the comforting dark; its cloaking presence made her feel safe.

Ava knew she needed sleep, that her mind was beginning to slip, its sharp effectiveness lost to the fog of sleep deprivation. But she wasn't sure she could relax enough to fall asleep without her loyal guard to keep watch over her.

Cinnamon snorted again and tossed her head, making Ava smile.

"I'm not entirely friendless, am I, girl?" Her horse had always been her one weakness. From the first, she had been unable to prevent herself becoming attached to the animal. She had long ago concluded that one small crack in her icy demeanor was an acceptable level of vulnerability. Unlike humans, Cinnamon demanded nothing from her and existed outside of her father's endless quest for power and perfection.

Standing, Ava went over to the mare and took her snout in both hands, resting her head against Cinnamon's silky hair. It was nice to have contact with another living thing, even if it was only a horse. In fact, so much the better if it was a horse. There were no other people here to see her in her moment of weakness and no need to pretend a strength that felt increasingly far away. Yet another reason why she let herself love the animal. Cinnamon was the only one she could truly be herself with.

Finally, Ava decided that she simply had to sleep. Hans will return even more tired than I am now, she reasoned. I need to be rested enough then to keep watch, or he'll never agree to rest himself. She would simply have to trust that if anyone approached the clearing, Cinnamon would be spooked enough to wake her.

Knowing that sleep was her best and most effective strategy made it easier to give in to what her body was demanding. She wrapped herself in her cloak and lay down. Sleep came within seconds.

As she had expected, Cinnamon's movements woke her. She lay still for a moment, assessing the horse's sounds. When a friendly whinny of greeting erupted from the animal, she sat up, looking around for Dusty and Hans.

The pair entered the clearing, both rider and mount looking exhausted.

"You've slept?" asked Hans. He looked relieved to see her nod of agreement and busied himself removing Dusty's tack and cleaning him down.

Ava watched him closely, analyzing his movements and minute facial expressions. Something was wrong. He moved efficiently, but without his usual grace. She had asked him to flee his home and everything he had ever known, and he hadn't hesitated. Yet now he looked like someone whose foundation had been shaken.

It frightened her, but she was determined not to show it.

She waited until he finished every possible activity related to the horse and had turned reluctantly toward her.

"What is it, Hans?" she asked. "Don't try to spare me."

Hans sighed and allowed grief to color his face and voice.

"I'm afraid I have only bad news, Your Highness."

Ava felt her insides clench, but she kept her face impassive and her regard steady.

"I had to go a significant distance back toward the capital before I encountered anyone." Ava could tell Hans was delaying the moment when he would have to impart his news, but she remained silent, allowing him to tell the story in his own way.

"I expected to find troops of guards close behind us. They would have been sent to 'rescue' you from whichever ruffians were being blamed for your abduction, of course. And they shouldn't have been far behind. I found no sign of troops, however." He paused, his eyes distant. After a moment, he shook himself and continued.

"I did pass a royal messenger, riding hard toward the border, but he didn't even spare a glance in my direction. I saw no one else until eventually I came upon a small group of merchants, traveling fast, moving away from the capital."

"By then I was too concerned to consider secrecy. I hailed them and introduced myself as a weary traveler, eager for news from Rangmeros."

"They were clearly reluctant to stop, and no wonder with the news they were carrying." Again, he paused, and Ava began to feel impatient. Despite her best efforts, the tension was rising inside her.

"I'm so sorry, Your Highness. We knew that Joran had betrayed you, but I'm afraid the situation is much worse than that. It seems that Joran betrayed his entire country. Yours was not the only attempted assassination last night. Your brother

Konrad managed to fight off his assailant, although his wife was injured. But your father is dead.

"I'm sorry," Hans repeated, his expression so full of gentle compassion that Ava thought she might break.

Instead, with a great effort, she kept her face impassive. For a moment, it was all she could manage; she had no energy left to process his words or form a response. Eventually, however, a name floated to the surface of her mind.

"My uncle," she said, and it wasn't a question.

"The only identified assailants were killed in the attacks. There is no immediate indication of who is responsible. Or, if there is, the information is not being shared with the city at large." Nothing in Hans' voice indicated agreement or disagreement with her statement. He had schooled his face back to the appropriate blank expression of a guard, although compassion lingered in his eyes.

"As my guard, you spent almost as much time around my father as I did," said Ava, impatient with Hans' silent refusal to affirm her speculation. "If he was afraid of one thing, it was his brother returning and attempting to take the throne. I'll admit I always thought him overly paranoid. After all, my father banished my uncle before I was even born. But it seems that my father was right, after all."

"I will admit," said Hans, "that the possibility had occurred to me."

"So, a royal messenger has been sent to seal the border, and my brother begins the hunt. My uncle made a fatal flaw when he failed to kill Konrad."

Unlike Ava, who worked hard to achieve her detached, rational state, Konrad had been born with their father's natural coldness and logic. And unlike her father, he had also been born with a cruel streak that, if whispers from the servants were to be believed, had come from Ava's maternal grandfather.

Her father's harsh acts, even his attempted annexation of their neighbor, Arcadia, had always been dictated by reason. Reason fueled by a love of power. Her father's actions were always calculated to bring him the greatest advantage, regardless of the effect on others, good or bad. He had succumbed to sentiment only once, in his youth, when he banished rather than killed his brother. He spent the rest of his life regretting that one weakness and resolved never to allow emotions to interfere with his decision making again. It was a lesson he frequently attempted to ingrain in his children.

Konrad also loved power but seemed to derive a sick pleasure from carrying out even the most callous of his goals. While he was as intelligent as their father, Ava was convinced that it was cruelty, not reason, that drove him. In this instance, however, the two parts of his nature would come together and make him relentless in avenging their father and eliminating their uncle.

Ava wondered why the thought gave her no pleasure.

"I suppose we had better return to the capital, then," she said, her voice sounding dull in her own ears.

"I'm not so sure," said Hans grimly, snapping Ava back into the present.

She looked at him with a sharp question.

"The merchants also reported that you had been assassinated."

Ava's mind quickly filled in the rest.

Hans nodded his agreement to the conclusion he could read on her face. "The state in which we left your room should leave no doubt that an attempted assassination was foiled, and that you had fled. The absence of our horses from the stable would confirm that conclusion."

"So, my brother has chosen not to pursue me, but instead to spread the word that I am dead." Ava found that she felt no great surprise. "My brother has clearly decided I am an inconvenience he can do without. A threat rather than an asset. My uncle almost did him a favor."

"Yes," said Hans, his voice dark with an emotion Ava couldn't quite identify. "After all, here is proof, if ever he needed it, that your father's lesson was right. Siblings are best eliminated."

Ava could see the sense of his words, but they opened a yawning chasm before her feet. She had given not only her life but her whole self to Rangmere, changing herself into the person her father had assured her Rangmere needed. And now she was to be cast out, adrift, aimless? On the run with two deadly enemies after her?

It wasn't right!

Her anger felt good, strong, purposeful! She was a princess of Rangmere, and she would not be cast aside. She was not defenseless. She had tools at her disposal, and she was entitled to use them.

"My godmother!"

Hans started violently at the outburst of sound.

"You have a godmother, Your Highness?"

"Of course I have a godmother." Ava looked at him scornfully. "I'm a princess! All princesses have godmothers.

"I'll admit," she continued graciously, "that your confusion is not entirely unmerited as I've never actually called on mine before. But I've been assured she attended my Christening. And my grandmother taught me the words to call her."

The memory made Ava pause. She would gladly have called on her godmother and offered anything the godmother wanted in exchange for curing the lingering illness that claimed the Queen's life. But Ava suspected her mother had guessed as much and so never told her daughter about her godmother or about the words that would call her.

That task had been left to her grandmother. She taught them to Ava the night before she disappeared, and it was the one thing that gave Ava hope that maybe her grandmother had fled the palace.

At least, that's what she told herself. It was better than believing what most of the court did: that her father had done away with his mother-in-law once his wife was out of the way. Her father's belief in the necessity of killing off threatening relatives was no secret. And Ava's grandmother had always disapproved of everything about him, from the way he ran his kingdom to the way he raised her grandchildren.

Ava shook the thoughts off. Both her grandmother and her mother belonged to another life and another Ava. One who had been drowning in the fear and grief and anger that came from watching one parent slowly die, while always failing to meet the expectations of the other. She'd said goodbye to those feelings a long time ago and had never missed them.

Squaring her shoulders and clearing her voice, Ava said the words.

Nothing happened.

CHAPTER 4

*A*va tried to suppress the disappointment and ignore Hans' confused gaze.

"I'm sure those were the right words," she muttered.

"Oh, they were," said a new voice from the edge of the clearing.

Ava and Hans both whipped around toward the newcomer, Hans taking a protective step in front of Ava.

Ava had expected to see a motherly woman with wings. But the gray in the hair and wings of the being before her gave off more steel than softness.

Ava stepped around Hans. She wasn't intimidated, she knew her rights.

"I have been wronged," she started grandly.

"Excuse me?" said the godmother, cutting her off.

"I have been wronged," repeated Ava, a little less sure. "My uncle has attempted to kill me, and now my brother is apparently banishing me from my own kingdom. You have to help me."

"I have to *what?*" said the godmother.

"Help me!" said Ava, starting to get angry. "I'm a princess, and

31

you're a godmother. Your job is to help me, to serve me. And now I'm commanding your assistance."

"Commanding, is it?" The steel was in the godmother's voice as well now. "It seems you've got a few things muddled up, missy."

Ava bristled at the impertinence and opened her mouth to put the godmother in her place.

"I don't serve you, Your Royal Highness," the godmother said before Ava had the chance to speak.

Her words shocked Ava into forgetting what she had meant to say.

"What do you mean?" she asked.

"Precisely what I just said, young lady. I...don't...serve...you."

"But, all the stories..." Ava reeled from this new blow to her foundations. "All the stories say that godmothers are there to help princes and princesses. That's their job."

Her godmother regarded her with something approaching amusement. "Is that what they say?" She turned to Hans who had been watching the exchange in silence, his hand on the hilt of his sword. "What do you think, young man? What do the stories say?"

Hans coughed and looked at Ava uncomfortably.

"Sorry, I didn't hear you," said the godmother, her amusement visibly growing.

"They say that godmothers are there to ensure that true love always reigns over the kingdom," said Hans, his hand leaving his sword to tug at his jacket. "They help deserving princes and princesses but also deserving woodcutters and the like." He threw an apologetic glance at Ava.

"Ah, yes." The godmother nodded. "I see that someone was listening."

She turned back to Ava. "And I'm afraid that a princess you may be, young lady, but deserving you are not."

Ava gasped in outrage and straightened as tall as she could go.

"And who decides who is and is not deserving?" she spat at the godmother. "You?"

"Of course not!" The godmother seemed genuinely surprised at Ava's response. "We serve the High King. He is the one who determines who receives our help."

"The High King?" Ava and Hans exchanged equally bewildered looks. "Who's he?"

"Who is the High King!?! Only the ruler over the Four Kingdoms, and the lands beyond. Who indeed!"

Hans and Ava continued to look confused, and the godmother shook her head darkly. "Degenerate times we live in, degenerate times."

Ava shook herself out of her stupefaction. "And where does this 'High King' live?" she asked skeptically.

"In the Palace of Light, of course."

"And you say he has decided that I am unworthy of your assistance?"

The godmother nodded.

"Then I demand an audience with him."

The godmother actually laughed at that. "Foolish child! You don't seek the High King, he seeks you. You could no more find the Palace of Light than you could fly."

"I will see this High King," said Ava through gritted teeth. "And hear from his own lips what gives him the right to set himself up in judgment over me. And I'll do it with or without your help."

The smile on the godmother's lips faded, and she cocked her head as if listening to something Ava and Hans couldn't hear.

"Well, well, well," she said after a long pause. "It seems you are to be given your chance."

"He'll see me?" asked Ava.

"You'll have to find him yourself," warned the godmother,

"and I don't quite see how you're going to do it. But, apparently, you're to be given the opportunity. And even a little assistance." She shook her head wonderingly.

Moving with a nimbleness that belied her gray hair, the godmother stepped closer to Ava and touched the top of her head.

"This will help you stay out of your brother's clutches long enough to attempt your quest."

Ava returned her regard steadily, but the godmother made no attempt to give her anything.

"But don't bother calling for me again. I won't come. It's on you now." The godmother stepped away from the princess. In the next moment, she was gone.

Ava turned to Hans in confusion. He was staring at her with wide eyes.

"I thought she said she was going to assist with avoiding my brother," Ava said.

Hans gave no reply but pointed at Ava's head.

"What? What is it?" She touched her head and face. Nothing felt different.

"Your hair," said Hans at last.

Ava pulled one of her long curls forward to examine it and gasped. She was holding a long, wavy length of dark brown hair.

"And your eyes," Hans continued. "They're brown."

Ava gasped again, and her hands flew to her eyes as if she would be able to feel the difference in color. She tried to conjure up a mental image of herself with wavy brown hair and brown eyes. Slowly a smile spread across her face.

"So that stupid godmother did something helpful, after all," she said, in delight. "I'll warrant Konrad himself wouldn't recognize me like this."

Hans looked much less sure about the change. "You're not upset?"

"No, of course not. It's brilliant! A strategic move I could never have pulled off on my own. Now I just need to think about how best to put it to use…"

Her mind was already moving. After a long moment, a soft sigh reminded her of her companion. Looking up, she met his eyes.

"You're exhausted, Hans," she said in the gentlest voice she had used since awakening in the palace. "I slept while you were gone. Now you sleep and I'll keep watch."

Hans opened his mouth to protest and then shut it again. Instead he nodded tersely.

"Wake me if you hear or see *anything*." He waited for her willing assent before wrapping himself in his cloak and lying down in the middle of the clearing.

Ava positioned herself on the opposite side of the clearing to the horses, reasoning that together they were covering the different approaches, and sat with her back against a tree. Drawing her knees up and wrapping her arms around them, she stared blankly into the forest.

With the evidence of the godmother's power on her head, she could hardly doubt her words regarding this High King. *How strange,* she mused, *to wield so much power and authority and yet be willing to be unknown and unregarded.* It was a mentality completely unlike the one her father had modeled to her.

Uncomfortably, the godmother's words came back to her. *"… deserving you are not."* She considered all her actions since Joran had appeared beside her bed. She analyzed what her father would think of her responses.

And then, with a surprisingly sharp pang, she remembered that her father was dead. That he would never know about the attack, let alone her response to it. It was a hard thought to fathom. A world without her father.

And strangely, it was also a freeing thought. A world without her father.

She tried to think instead of what *she* thought of her recent actions. But she found her mind drifting back further. To last summer, to her attempts to trick her way into becoming the Queen of Arcadia. To the various stratagems she had used to weaken Arcadia and make it ripe for annexation. To the deeds she knew Joran had carried out in response to her vague commands. Her father had approved it all. Except for her final failure, of course.

But what did she think of her own actions? The thought had never really occurred to her before. It was hard to ignore now, though, in the light of the godmother's assessment. No, the *High King's* assessment, she reminded herself.

Uneasily, she asked herself, for the first time in five years, what her mother would have thought of her actions.

Slowly she felt the old feelings of guilt and grief and anger and shame build inside her.

No! She cried, clamping down on the emotions. *I did what I had to. I did it for Rangmere. I was strong. I will not be weak again.*

Slowly she bore down on her emotions, bringing her will to bear against them. It was difficult, but she was able to repair the wall that had locked them away for so many years.

The effort left her spent and exhausted, but she was determined to come up with a plan. To be strategic. She would find the High King, and she would make him understand that there were good reasons for all her actions. He *would* help her.

The godmother had given no indication of the location of the Palace of Light, but she had specifically mentioned the Four Kingdoms, so Ava called up a mental map of Rangmere and its immediate neighbors.

After long consideration, she decided that the deep forest was the only reasonable option. There was simply no way a palace could be concealed anywhere else. She looked more closely at the trees around them. They could always strike off into the woods at random, but it would be slow going and likely fruitless. She needed a better plan...

~

When Hans awoke, Ava had already retrieved some food from their saddlebags and was waiting for him. He woke like a soldier, instantly alert, his gaze taking in every relevant detail of their surroundings. She waited for him to relax and then handed him some bread.

"I have a plan."

Hans actually laughed. The light-hearted sound was at complete variance with the somber mood that had gripped him before his sleep.

"You always do, Your Highness."

Ava nodded a gracious acknowledgment of this fact but rather spoiled the effect by grinning back at him. She had spent the last several hours working on her new character, and although she didn't doubt her acting skills, she was determined to begin practicing immediately.

"You're going to have to start by losing the 'Your Highness' business," she continued. "I'm just Anna now."

"Anna, Your Highness?"

Ava glared at him.

"Apologies." He grinned again. "Anna, Your Worshipfulness?"

"Hans!"

"All right, all right, why am I calling you 'just Anna'?"

"I've been thinking hard, and I just cannot believe that my father wouldn't have explored every bit of his kingdom. The Palace of Light can't be in Rangmere. Which means we need to get across the border."

"Ah," said Hans.

"Ah, indeed. As we have already surmised, the border is almost certainly closed while Konrad searches for our uncle. But if there's one thing that makes traveling merchants edgy, it's having borders closed to them. I'm sure there's a mass exodus currently underway, with those merchants you ran into only the beginning. And the more merchants who amass at the border, the more pressure it will put on my brother. Eventually he'll have to reopen the border. And when he does, we'll be there."

"I'm not sure…" Hans stopped and glanced at her brown hair.

"Indeed. Thanks to my new disguise and my new role, we'll be hidden within one of those caravans." She was feeling too light-hearted to disguise the triumph in her voice. It felt good to cast aside the burdens of Princess Ava and instead assume the care-free persona of Anna.

Hans still looked a little skeptical, so she outlined the rest of her plan. "I become Anna, the daughter of a traveling merchant. I stayed behind in Rangmeros to visit with family when my caravan moved on to Arcadia."

Hans raised his eyebrows at the mention of their western neighbor, but Ava just shrugged. "It's the closest border."

"When the king was assassinated, my older cousin, Harry," Ava gestured at Hans, "became nervous and decided it was time to escort me back to my father. Now all we have to do is find a sufficiently large caravan where our presence won't cause too much of a stir. The bigger, the better in fact. Bigger trains will have more clout and will probably be the first ones through the border."

"So, just like that we're Anna and Harry," said Hans. "Traveling merchants."

"Just like that," agreed Ava. "Once we're past the border, we'll part ways with our new merchant friends and head off into the forest. Arcadia seems like the sort of poorly run place that might have failed to notice a giant palace hiding in their forest."

A tinge of bitterness had crept into her final sentence, but she quickly shook it off and pasted another smile on her face. *Anna is excited to be going to Arcadia*, she reminded herself. *Anna's family is waiting for her there, and Arcadians are just so nice.*

Even in her head it rang false, but she determined to work on it. By the time they found the right group of merchants, Anna would be perfect. Not even Hans would recognize the brunette merchant's daughter as the golden-haired princess she used to be.

CHAPTER 5

*A*s it turned out, Ava had five days to perfect Anna before they encountered a caravan she deemed suitably large. During that time, she completed one test run in a small town where they stopped to purchase supplies.

She insisted on buying a particularly brilliant red cloak, reminding a disapproving Hans that they were no longer trying to avoid attention. "Why should we? Anna and Harry have nothing to hide."

She didn't tell Hans the real reason she had been drawn to the cloak. It reminded her of a different red cloak that she hadn't worn for years. And, more importantly, it reminded her of a different, lighter Ava. One who knew how to feel and to love. The cloak lent her the final something she needed to fully slip into the role of Anna.

The town had been buzzing with news of a large merchant caravan that passed through the day before. So, when they camped for the night, Ava was confident it would be their last night on their own.

"Go ahead, test me," she challenged Hans as they sat on the bedrolls they had purchased in the town and which they had carefully laid out on opposite sides of their small campfire. "You won't catch me out. I'm Anna now."

"All right." His eyes narrowed. Ava could guess what was going on behind the calculating expression. For Hans, this was just another part of his job, part of keeping her safe.

"I'm surprised we've never crossed paths before, what did you say your name was?" asked Hans, in an almost uncanny impression of the most suspicious shopkeeper they encountered. Ava felt glad to know that she wasn't the only one able to pull off an assumed role.

"Anna," she replied in character. "I haven't traveled with my father much. Most of my time has been spent with relatives in Arcadia and Rangmere. My father's name is Wilhelm." It was a safe choice. It was likely the merchants they encountered would know several Wilhelms.

"I have relatives in Arcadie and Rangmeros." Hans named the capital cities of Arcadia and Rangmere. "Where do yours live?"

"In Arcadie, they live on Hawkers Boulevard," said Ava. The longest street in the Merchant's Circle was a safe choice. "And in Rangmeros, they live in the Green District." Once again this was a densely-populated area of the city.

Hans nodded approvingly.

"And what about you, Harry?" Ava asked, turning the tables with a mischievous expression. "Are you a merchant as well?"

"Of sorts," said Hans without missing a beat. "I'm trained as a caravan guard. I'll be signing on with my uncle's caravan, once I've safely delivered my young cousin."

Now it was Ava's turn to nod appreciatively. "That's a good thought. You're too much of a guard to pass as anything else." She regarded him thoughtfully in the flickering light of the campfire, trying to pin down exactly what it was that made him seem so indisputably a soldier.

His wavy chestnut hair was on the long side for a soldier, and the stubble on his chin—a result of their current exile—was decidedly not regulation. Maybe it was the eyes? The blue gray of his eyes always managed to convey a deadly strength that seemed fitting for a guard.

"I think it's your bearing," she finally announced. "You always hold yourself as if you're poised to spring into action. And you're graceful in the way that only really good dancers or sword fighters are."

Hans, who had endured the scrutiny with a smile, laughed at her last point.

"How do you know I'm not just a really good dancer?" he asked.

Ava raised her eyebrows.

"Why, Harry! Don't tell me you've been holding out on your poor young cousin! Here I am, trying to master all the required steps, when I've unknowingly being sharing the house with a dancing master. You could have offered to share your skills, you know." She pouted and tried to look as endearingly offended as possible.

Hans let out another bark of laughter and then looked slightly guilty.

"Fine, fine, I surrender." He held up his hands. "You're better at this staying in character thing than me. When we actually meet up with this caravan tomorrow, you shouldn't test me so hard." He chuckled again. "The idea of you needing dancing lessons from me." He shook his head. "Considering how many times I've stood guard at balls and seen you dance, how could I take that with a straight face?"

"Don't underestimate yourself," said Ava, also slipping out of character. "I had no idea you were so skilled at playing a role."

Hans regarded her, and the dark intensity of his gaze kept her silent. After a minute that seemed to stretch into an hour, he turned his head away.

"It's not only princesses who have to hide their true selves, Your Highness."

Ava blinked twice in rapid succession, but he wasn't watching her. Instead he slid into his bedroll and rolled to face away from the fire.

Ava waited for a moment, but it was evident he had nothing more to say. When she slid into her own bedroll, she faced toward the fire and stared at the back of his head. It had been five years since Hans had become her personal guard. He had become such a fixture in her life that it had never occurred to her that there might be more to the man than he had let her see.

With only the two of them, they traveled much more swiftly than a whole caravan, so it was still early morning when they caught sight of the merchants' camp. The merchants seemed to be in the final stages of packing up in preparation for the day's travel.

Hans pulled up and turned to face Ava. "Are you sure you want to do this, Your Highness?" He was wearing his most serious expression with no sign of joking Harry.

Ava nodded with determination. "It's the only way."

"You'll have to let me lead," Hans warned. "As your older cousin and escort, it will be expected. And I won't be able to show you any deference."

Ava's second nod was a little more reluctant. She had thought it would be her guard who would be uncomfortable with abandoning formality, but it dawned on her that she had become accustomed to wielding her royal authority.

"I'm certain, Hans. I'm actually looking forward to being Anna. I'm rather sick of all the troubles currently burdening Princess Ava."

To her surprise she realized that there was some truth in her words. The realization helped her straighten her back, put on a smile, and let go of the sting that came with relinquishing her authority to a mere guard. She was Anna now, and Anna was fun-loving and carefree. Anna's biggest worry was getting across the border, so she could re-join her doting father.

"Come then, Anna," Hans said. "It looks as if we've found a merchant train to join." Spurring his mount forward, he trotted into the camp, hailing the first person he saw.

"Greetings!" he called. "Can you point me to your leader?"

The man, who was harnessing his horses, looked up only long enough to point them toward the largest of the wagons. Two shiny chestnut geldings were already harnessed to it, and a friendly looking woman was about to climb up onto the seat. She paused at the sound of their arrival and watched them make their way across the camp.

Ava gasped, a sharp sound that was lost in the bustle of the merchants.

Hans, as attuned to her as ever, caught the sound and glanced at her in concern.

"I know her!" whispered Ava. "It's Ariana, she often stopped by the palace with her wares when I was a child. I haven't seen her in years, but she used to know me well."

Both of their horses had slowed to a crawl, but they were already approaching the lead wagon. Hans reached out and placed his hand over hers where it gripped the reins. "Don't worry, Anna," he said with steady reassurance in his voice, "you have changed much since you were a girl." His eyes, which were holding a warning, flicked toward her hair, and Ava remembered the changes wrought by the godmother.

"Oh, of course," she said, giving him a smile. "As always, you are right, cousin."

They had now reached Ariana, and the woman smiled, somehow making the expression both a welcome and a question.

"Greetings!" said Hans. "My name is Harry, and this is my young cousin, Anna. I am escorting her to join her father, a traveling merchant who is currently at the Arcadian capital. Anna had intended to spend the summer with her relatives in Rangmeros, but…" He made a face at the merchant. "Her family would prefer she re-join her father, and I would prefer not to be traveling the roads with just the two of us. I'm trained as a wagon guard and would be happy to offer my services if you would allow us to travel to Arcadia with you."

"Well, now," said Ariana, "that's a generous offer." She seemed to weigh them both with her eyes. Finally, she gave a decisive nod. "It can never hurt to have an extra guard in unsettled times like these. Besides, I'm a mother myself, though my children are all grown, and I'd hate to see two young things such as yourselves traveling all alone. So, welcome to Caravan Hargrove!"

"Oh, thank you! You're so kind." Ava smiled at Ariana, her confidence slowly rising when she saw no hint of recognition in the face of the older woman.

"That's a beautiful mount you have, my dear," continued Ariana. "Do you prefer to ride her, or would you like me to find you a place in one of the wagons?"

"Oh no, thank you. I'll ride," said Ava. She examined the other woman's face for hidden meaning. Did she recognize Cinnamon and Dusty as royal horses? It now seemed obvious that they should have put some effort into dirtying the animals' coats at least.

"She is beautiful, isn't she?" Ava did her best to look young and pampered. "My father said only the best for his family, so he purchased both horses for me from the royal stables. I prefer Cinnamon though. She's the best mount I've ever had, even if she is a bit old." She stroked Cinnamon's mane.

"You have a loving father, indeed," said Ariana. "And a fine horse. As you can see we're nearly ready to ride out for the day. You're welcome to ride beside my wagon, Anna, and exchange some pleasantries for a while. Harry, you can go and let my Guardsmaster know I've signed you on as an extra guard. He'll be glad to hear it and will let you know where he wants to place you." She pointed toward an older man who sat astride a horse, giving instructions to a group of mounted guards.

Hans looked at Ava, clearly reluctant to be parted from her so soon. She gave him a small glare and waved him away. With a small nod, he rode off toward the Guardsmaster.

"He's a protective one, isn't he?" Ariana chuckled. "I can imagine the family's given him all sorts of dire warnings should he let any harm befall you."

Ava smiled confidingly. "I'm afraid my father is a little overprotective, and all the rest of the family lives in fear of him."

"Oh, aye," said Ariana. "I know the type. Well, don't you fear. No-one's ever yet come to harm in my caravan. I'm famous for it." She straightened her shoulders but then seemed to deflate a little. "Well, there was one time…" She laughed, apparently at herself. "But even that turned out for the best. It was a minor mishap and had me right worried, but it all came out better than anyone could have dreamed!"

Ava had no idea what Ariana was talking about but smiled encouragingly anyway. After all, Anna was friendly and loved to listen to other people's stories.

By the time Caravan Hargrove got underway, Ava had no extra information about the single mishap that turned out for the best, but she did know the names of each of Ariana's children and the many virtues of each of her grandchildren. As she slipped deeper and deeper into the role of Anna, she even began to find herself interested in the people Ariana was describing. None of the woman's children were part of her caravan, and there was something fascinating about this glimpse into the lives of the middle class. A little wistfully she thought that it sounded like they were a happy, if far flung, family.

She only felt nervous once, when Ariana confessed that Ava reminded her of someone.

"She's someone I knew a long time ago, and I always wanted to help her, but I never had the opportunity and won't ever have now," the older woman said. "So it makes me feel good to help you."

She laughed, misinterpreting Ava's unease.

"I know it doesn't make much sense, but there you have it. You'll have to indulge an old woman and her whims." And she let the matter drop.

Ava worried about it for the next hour but eventually decided that there was no reason to be nervous. She had no way of knowing if it was herself that Ariana was thinking of but, either way, the caravan leader believed Princess Ava to be dead and was unlikely to have any true suspicion of Anna. Worrying about it wouldn't help.

Hans didn't have a chance to check in with her until lunchtime when the train stopped to give the horses a break.

"He's a good man, the Guardsmaster," he told her. "Really knows his stuff. He's been riding with merchant caravans since he was a lad, and from what I can gather from the other men, working for Ariana is a privilege. She has the best kept and most successful caravan in the Four Kingdoms. You have to work your way up before you earn a place guarding her train We're lucky she took us in!"

"I'm sure it's you that we have to thank for all her friendliness," said Ava. "Uncertain times always make merchants a bit edgy, and there's nothing like extra guards for relieving their minds."

"You might be right. How did you go talking with her?"

"She's exactly as she appears." And then lowering her voice, "And exactly how I remembered. She stays out of politics, but she has some clout. I'll wager this train will be the first one across the border."

Hans grunted an acknowledgment and began to prepare her lunch. She stopped him with a playful hand on his arm.

"Really, Harry!" she said, her voice back at full volume. "That's very gallant but entirely unnecessary, I assure you. I know how to prepare my own lunch."

Hans froze at her touch, but she punctuated her final words with a sharp reminder pinch that caused him to unfreeze and offer her an easy smile.

"Just making sure you put in a good word for me with my uncle," he said, relinquishing the food to her.

"Oooh, I wish my cousins were half so considerate," said a merchant girl who had strolled over to join them, lunch in hand.

"I'm Sarah." She held out her other hand to shake each of theirs. "My family's wagon is the second down from Ariana's."

Ava deduced from the pride in the girl's voice that the wagons were arranged in order of seniority, and that third place was a matter of some honor.

"I'm Anna," she said with a friendly smile. "And this is my cousin, Harry."

"Oh yes, I know." Sarah's words tripped over each other in a somewhat giddy fashion. "It's all up and down the caravan that we have two new members. There's not too many of us young ones, so it's always exciting to have some fresh faces. I'll introduce you to the rest tonight. Most of them have to stay with their horses now."

Something about the girl's enthusiasm was infectious, and Ava found her warm smile slowly becoming genuine.

"I'd like that," she said. "We both would."

CHAPTER 6

S arah was true to her word. No sooner had Ariana called
a halt to the day's travel, directing the train into a large
clearing just off the road, than Sarah came rushing up to Ava.

"My sister was married this winter," she said, panting for
breath, "and my parents have said you can have her place in our
wagon, if you like." She looked at Ava expectantly and smiled
when Ava began to express polite acceptance.

"Oh, it's no trouble," she said, cutting off Ava's words. "It's a
relief, in fact. You'll save me from being stuck alone in there with
my mother." She made a face.

Ava looked around for a glimpse of Hans. What would he
think of this sleeping arrangement?

"And don't worry about your cousin," said Sarah, correctly
interpreting Ava's searching glance. "Ariana told us how protective your father is. Your cousin can sleep with my father at our
campfire. He'll only be a few feet away." She smiled in satisfaction
at her perfect arrangements, and Ava marveled at how often
Sarah's expressive face held a wide grin. She flitted between
twenty other expressions as she spoke, but her resting expression
seemed to be a smile.

Ava, so used to keeping her emotions hidden and her face carefully blank, found it exhausting to watch her. Of course, none of these thoughts showed in Ava's own expression.

By the time Sarah had led Ava to her family's wagon and convinced Ava to let her father take Cinnamon down to the nearby creek with their horses, most of the wagons were settled into their overnight spaces. Watching them all, it was obvious that they were well practiced at setting up camp and that each person knew their assigned place. Ava felt grateful that Sarah had sought her out so eagerly.

It was a further relief to see Hans making his way toward her and to realize that he had already accepted their sleeping arrangements.

"I'm about to go care for Dusty," he said. "I just wanted to see you first. I'll check in with Cinnamon, too, if you like."

"Yes, thank you," said Ava, relieved.

"Are you happy with this arrangement?" Hans watched her closely. Lowering his voice, he added, "If you'd rather we slept on our own, I can talk to Ariana. But as a guard, I'll have to take some night watches, and I'd feel more comfortable knowing you're not alone when I'm on shift."

"Oh, no." Ava matched his quiet tone. "This is great. We blend right in, just what we were after."

Hans nodded, relieved, and turned to leave. Ava watched him go with a smile, sure that the slight twitch of his hand was an aborted salute. *Oh well, if he does forget one of these times, we'll just pass it off as fun between cousins, I suppose.*

"You are so lucky!" exclaimed a voice she recognized. "Not only is your cousin polite, he's also dreamy." The last comment was followed by a sigh and then a loud snort.

Turning around Ava saw that Sarah was approaching her again, this time with another girl in tow. The second girl, who was clearly the origin of the snort, looked positively grim next to Sarah's cheerful animation.

"This is Evelyn," introduced Sarah.

Evelyn nodded in Ava's direction but didn't hold out her hand to shake Ava's.

Sarah continued on as if Evelyn's unfriendly behavior were perfectly normal. "Is he spoken for, do you know?" She was apparently still thinking about Hans.

"Um, no?" said Ava, thrown off balance.

"For goodness sake, Sarah." Evelyn sounded exasperated.

"What?" asked Sarah. "A girl can dream!" She grinned mischievously. "And come on, Evelyn, even you have to admit that he's the best looking new arrival we've had in absolutely ages!"

"He does seem to be extremely competent," Evelyn agreed reluctantly. "It wouldn't surprise me if the Guardsmaster offers him a permanent job once we arrive in Arcadia."

"Oh, Evelyn," said Sarah, "You're so unromantic." Then turning to Ava, "Evelyn is one of the caravan guards, the first female guard we've had in forever." Sarah seemed equal parts exasperated and proud.

Evelyn rolled her eyes and otherwise seemed to ignore Sarah, but Ava noticed a similar gleam of appreciation in her eyes as she watched Hans disappear among the crowd of merchants.

Overall, however, the two girls seemed so different that she wondered how they had come to be friends.

"We're cousins," said Sarah, as if she could read Ava's mind. "Don't let her gruff exterior fool you. She's nice once you get to know her."

Ava examined the two girls, looking for a family connection. She hadn't noticed it before, but they had the same coloring, including light brown hair, streaked with gold highlights. On top of that, although their eyes were different colors, Sarah's a warm brown and Evelyn's a cool blue, they were the same shape, and both girls had the same nose. Their demeanors and expressions were so different that they masked the physical similarities.

That and Evelyn was nearly a foot taller than either Sarah or Ava and was dressed in the breeches and leather vest of a guard. But still.

I used to be more observant, thought Ava. *I'll have to watch out that Anna doesn't swallow me up completely!*

Evelyn's family had the wagon behind Sarah's, and the two families shared a cook fire between the two vehicles. It struck Ava as incredibly humorous that Sarah's parents were as reserved and dour as Evelyn, while Evelyn's parents were as warm and lively as Sarah. She could see her own amusement reflected in Hans' eyes whenever she happened to glance his way.

She had seen more of his sense of humor since they had fled Rangmeros than she had in the five years he had been her guard. It reminded her of his words from the night before. How much more of himself had Hans hidden away when he had dedicated his life to her protection? Did he have friends who saw this side of him? Did he even have time off? She realized she had never wondered about his personal life before.

Later, as she lay in the back of the wagon next to Sarah and her mother, she found herself dwelling on the girls' words. First, she considered Evelyn's surmise that the Guardsmaster would offer Hans a job. She didn't waste more than a moment's thought on this idea. Hans would never abandon her. But the second part of their conversation occupied her for a surprisingly long time.

She had never really considered Hans' physical attractiveness before. She called up a picture of him in her mind. With surprise, she realized that Hans was an unusually attractive man. Especially when his eyes were alight with amusement, or when he smiled at some joking sally. How had she never noticed it before?

Because before he was always a part of the furniture, she thought. *A very loyal and competent piece of furniture, but furniture all the same.*

Ava's life consisted of duty, and no part of a princess' duty involved making eyes at a guard. It had simply never occurred to her. Plus, under her father's tutelage, Ava had always understood that looks were deceptive. While she used her own perfect princess appearance to her advantage, she tried to look past the image other people portrayed. After all, it might be just as misleading as her own.

She spent a slightly longer moment worrying about what it would mean if Hans returned the interest of one of the girls from the merchant camp. But this thought, too, was rejected with relative ease. She was Princess Ava of Rangmere. Hans would no more leave her service for the sake of a merchant girl than he would leave it for a guard position.

It was a comforting thought, and sleep came quickly after that.

~

It was three days later, not long after the evening meal, that Ava heard Hans' voice calling for her.

"Anna? Anna?" His tone was beginning to creep toward worry.

"Over here!" she called back, not leaving her precarious position.

He'd been busy with his guard duties, so she hadn't seen him since the morning, but she didn't even consider turning around to greet him. His voice had come from the row of trees that blocked the creek from the campsite, and she assumed that he would find her easily enough once he took a few more steps.

"There you are, I've been looking for you everywhere..." His voice gradually tapered off as he got a good look at her, and then he threw back his head and laughed.

"Don't laugh at me!" she said. "Help me!"

Still chuckling, he came over to where she crouched beside the running water. Kneeling down, he removed several of the items that were threatening to slip from her fingers and disappear downstream.

"Looking at you, anyone would think you'd never washed a dish before in your life." His eyes danced with mischief.

"Really, Harry! What a thing to suggest." Her light-hearted tone didn't match the glare she was giving him. 'Harry' had taken rather well to their reversal of stations and often took the opportunity to poke gentle fun at his young 'cousin'.

"And it's such an easy job, too, with a clear, shallow creek like this." He pretended to miss the warning she was transmitting with her eyes. "If you're not careful, you might slip in."

It was exactly what she was worried about, and the reason she had got no further than holding the dishes in the direction of the water. Whipping around to give him another glare, she slipped and would indeed have fallen into the stream if she hadn't instead thrown herself backward. She fell into the grass growing along the bank.

For a moment, she considered taking out her frustration on Hans, but lying there in the grass she found that she couldn't be bothered. Instead she felt a chuckle build inside her until it exploded out in a sound that was part laugh, part snort, and part gasp.

"Well, that was inelegant," she said, when she recovered her voice.

Looking up at the sky she began to trace shapes among the clouds, simply enjoying the sensation of lying still after yet another day's riding.

A shadow covered her face, and Hans sat beside her. He placed a stack of dishes on the grass. Ava eyed them warily, but they appeared to be clean.

"It's easy, you know," he said. "Just do them one at a time. Find a good, solid bit of bank and kneel instead of squatting. Then use some sand from the riverbed to scrub them clean."

When she narrowed her eyes at him, he smiled good-naturedly and added, "For next time. In case I'm not around to rescue you."

His words reminded her that washing dishes was no more a part of a guard's role than it was a princess'. It made her wonder about him all over again.

"Thank you," she said, and he glanced at her with raised brows. "For rescuing me," she clarified. "How do you know so much about washing dishes, anyway?"

"My sister used to work in the palace kitchens," he said, and Ava remembered that he had mentioned friends in the kitchens once before. This was the first time she had ever heard him mention a sister, however.

"Was she a scullery maid?" asked Ava, curious. She had spent some time in the kitchens herself as a child, though it seemed like another life now. As a princess, she had possessed few friends of her own station and had loved to sneak down to the kitchens to watch the hustle and bustle of food preparation and to pinch a bun when the pastry chef wasn't watching. Idly she wondered if she had seen Hans' sister on one of her many visits. Perhaps she had even spoken to her.

"No." His voice was curt enough that Ava didn't want to press him. Perhaps his sister had died, or perhaps there had been a falling out. Either way, the conversation was closed. Sighing, she struggled to her feet and picked up the stack of dishes, ready to lug them back to the wagon.

"Good morning!" After a week's travel, Ava had become used to Sarah's chirpy morning greeting.

"Good morning," she returned, markedly less enthusiastic.

Sarah just laughed at her. "It *is* a good morning, Anna! Don't forget that it's a rest day today. No bouncing along on the wagon, or horse, in your case. And tonight, we'll have a dance." Her eyes positively shone when she said the word 'dance'.

"You know Ariana's only doing it cause everyone's so tense about the assassination and wondering if they'll let us across the border, right?" Evelyn poked her head into the back of the wagon and glared at her cousin. Ava hid the pang she still felt anytime she heard someone mention her father's murder.

"Who cares?" Sarah said before turning back to Ava. "Ignore her, you'd think she'd have gotten over her morning grumps, what with all the strange guard shifts she has to do. She's still a positive ogre in the mornings, though. And it doesn't matter if she's only just woken up or right at the end of a shift, either."

"The only wonder is how you can be so endlessly cheerful in the mornings," said Evelyn. "That and how your mother hasn't killed you for it yet," she added as an afterthought.

"My mother finds me delightful," said Sarah loftily, but her point was somewhat undermined by her mother's snort.

"I'll find you a great deal more delightful if you'll stop mooning over the dance tonight and help me pack up these sleeping pallets."

Ava moved quickly to assist her and earned a grateful smile. Once they were finished, with some intermittent help from Sarah, her mother summarily dismissed them.

"Now be off with you. You can get out from underfoot and make yourselves useful by gathering some water from the creek for breakfast. And find a good spot for washing. If we're having a day's break, it's a good opportunity to get the clothes and linens washed."

"Oh no, not washing." Sarah groaned. "It's supposed to be a holiday!"

"This evening will be holiday enough," said her mother without sympathy. "You know that rest days are wash days. Now get off with you."

The three girls each grabbed a couple of buckets and headed

off toward the small stream running behind the campsite. Sarah dragged her feet and cursed the washing under her breath for a few steps but then seemed to regain her usual good cheer.

"The wash will only take a few hours, after all," she said to the other two, neither of whom had complained at the prospect of doing it. "There'll still be plenty of time to get ready for the dance. I'm going to wear my best dress. The golden one that mother embroidered with green flowers for my last birthday." Ava had already seen the dress since Sarah had showed it to her the night before, and she thought it would match the lively girl's coloring well.

"I'm planning to wear my ice blue dress," volunteered Evelyn. Ava hadn't even been sure Evelyn owned a dress, but she was sure the tall girl would look striking wearing a color that sounded like an exact match for her eyes.

"Oh excellent!" said Sarah. "You haven't dressed up for a dance in ages. I wonder what's inspired you this time, hey?" She accompanied the words with a sly smile and a jab at her cousin's midriff. "A certain someone's cousin, perhaps," she added, in case either of the others had been unsure of her meaning.

"I bet he'll ask me to dance first, though. I've been hinting for the last two days," Sarah admitted shamelessly, taking any sting out of her words.

Evelyn just rolled her eyes, but Ava noticed a slight flush to her cheeks. The whole conversation made her think of Hans' jokes about his dancing abilities. She assumed they would dance together, and she found the idea more appealing than she would have supposed. She discovered she was curious to see how well Hans could dance.

"What do you think, Anna?" Sarah asked, startling her out of her reverie. "Who will Harry ask to dance first? Care to make a wager on it?"

Her suggestion only made Ava laugh.

"You're such a merchant, Sarah," she said, "always looking

for a way to make an extra coin. But you won't be making it from me. My limited funds are staying safely in my purse. Besides, I'm sure I wouldn't have a clue who Harry would ask first."

"Really?" asked Sarah. "He hasn't breathed a word to you?"

"Well," said Ava, drawing the word out long and assuming a reluctant expression. "He did mention…"

"What, what? Tell me!" said Sarah, her eyes wide and voice even more breathless than usual.

"He mentioned a certain blonde-haired, brown-eyed merchant girl… Renee, I think her name is?" Ava assumed a look of confused innocence.

"Renee? Renee?!?" spluttered Sarah, apparently too outraged for words.

But Evelyn gave Ava a small, amused smile and her cousin a sharp poke. "She's teasing you, Sarah, you idiot. Anna knows perfectly well who Renee is. We only listened to you go on and on about her two nights ago."

"Oh," said Sarah, breathing again. "That was a good one, Anna!"

Ava was relieved her attempt at a joke had been so well received. "I will admit, your ongoing feud with your arch nemesis has come to my attention," she said, keeping her expression grave.

Evelyn actually gave a short bark of laughter at this pronouncement, and Ava felt a small stirring of pride.

It hadn't taken Ava long to realize that a merchant train was a miniature village in its own right, and even a train as well managed as Caravan Hargrove had its fair share of alliances and rivalries.

Sarah's and Evelyn's mothers were sisters, and their family seemed to have a long running rivalry with the family who owned the three wagons directly after theirs in the train. Apparently, the order of the wagons was determined by annual revenue, and it was only in the last two years that Sarah's and Evelyn's families had moved ahead of Renee's.

Evelyn and Renee maintained a polite but distant tone, but Sarah seemed to have thrown herself as enthusiastically into the family conflict as she did into everything else. Ava suspected she did it for entertainment as much as anything since her general demeanor was one of cheerful friendship toward everyone. And, so far, Ava had failed to observe Renee in any particularly offensive behavior. In fact, the girl had been quite friendly toward her, despite Ava's position in Sarah's family's wagon.

After fuming for several minutes about Renee's general perfidy, Sarah once again bounced back to her usual levels of enthusiasm. Sometimes the girl's moods were so volatile, Ava wondered how she could keep track of them herself.

"What about you, Anna?" asked Sarah. "What are you wearing?"

This was actually a question that had been causing Ava some concern. She had packed the most practical of her gowns when she had fled the palace, but they were still much too fine for a merchant girl. So, they had all remained safely hidden in the bottom of her saddlebags. Instead she had been wearing the practical merchant style gowns she had purchased in the town the day before they joined Ariana's wagon.

Unfortunately, she had not foreseen a dance and had not purchased any party gowns. Anna would undoubtedly own such garments, however. It was a dilemma.

"I'm not sure," she said after the pause grew too long.

"Oh, did you have to leave all your nicest gowns behind?" asked Sarah. "It sounds like your family sent you packing as soon as the news broke about the king. I suppose you had to leave most of your clothes in Rangmeros."

"Yes," said Ava with relief. "My cousin wouldn't let me bring any evening dresses with me." She sacrificed Hans without hesitation, merely making a mental note to let him know of his new harsh attitude toward ladies' wear. She wouldn't put it past Sarah to chide him on it.

"He said I had enough waiting for me in Arcadia." She made a face, as if offended by this perspective.

"We'll find something for you," said Sarah with determination. By now they had reached the creek and were filling their buckets.

"I'm sorry," said Evelyn. "There's no way you'll fit into any of my dresses." She looked genuinely apologetic about not being able to help. But since she was both taller and broader at the shoulder than Ava, none of her clothes would have a hope of fitting the much more petite princess.

"Mine will be a better fit," mused Sarah, assessing Ava with narrowed eyes as they made their way back toward the wagon. "You're a little slimmer at both the bust and waist than I am, but we're a similar height so it should work." She began a complete verbal inventory of all the party dresses she owned, and Ava wondered at the number. Clearly her parents were more indulgent than their gruff manner suggested.

"The silver one," said Evelyn eventually, cutting off Sarah's rambling monologue. After a moment's silent consideration, Sarah nodded her agreement.

"You're right, as always, Evie," she said, earning a satisfied smile from Evelyn that quickly became a glare at the use of the hated nickname.

"You wouldn't think it, considering what she usually wears," said Sarah, "but Evelyn has an amazing sense of style. I'm always telling her she should put more effort into her outfits."

"I'm a *guard*," her cousin reminded her with a shrug. "Most of the time I'd rather be comfortable than stylish. Plus, it's hard enough getting respect as a female guard without making myself conspicuous with impractical clothing."

Sarah sighed but seemed to accept this argument as reasonable, letting the topic drop.

CHAPTER 7

When the first strains of music permeated the wagon, Ava realized they were going to have to give up on a perfect fit.

"It will have to do," she told Sarah who was standing behind her and intermittently pulling on the laces of the dress Ava was wearing.

"I think, if I just…" the strain in Sarah's voice gave Ava a half second of warning before all the air was expelled from her lungs by an overly enthusiastic tug.

"Eeep," she managed, the sound squeezing out with the air. The whole dress immediately loosened as Sarah let go.

"You might be right," Sarah said, circling her with a dissatisfied air. "Evelyn knew what she was talking about, the coloring is perfect on you, but it just hangs there." She pulled a face.

Ava had an inspiration. "Get a couple of pegs." She dove toward her saddlebags.

Sarah raised an unconvinced eyebrow but rummaged around until she found several wooden pegs.

"Peg me up." Ava presented her back to her friend.

"Are you sure?" asked Sarah. "It'll look great from the front but from the back..." Even as she voiced her concerns, her hands were busy pegging the other girl into the dress.

When Ava could feel that the dress was a snug and flattering fit, she pulled her hand out of her saddlebag, her fingers clutching her red cloak.

"Voila!" she exclaimed, proudly.

"Oooh," said Sarah, instantly grasping the idea. "That'll be perfect! And it's still cool enough in the evenings that no one will find it overly strange for you to wear a cloak. Good thinking."

Ava had almost forgotten about the red cloak she had insisted on purchasing and was glad now that no one had seen her wearing it. She let it fall open at the front so that the silver dress could be seen and faced toward Sarah.

"Ready?"

"Ready," Sarah said with a smile. "Now let's get out there before Evelyn steals a march on us."

Both girls tumbled out of the wagon and rushed toward the sound of a fiddle and pan pipes. The musicians who had previously been tuning their instruments had just launched into the strains of their first dance number. Couples were beginning to step onto the large area of cleared dirt that had been left open in the middle of the circle of wagons.

The space had been enclosed by a ring of logs, and behind the logs was a second ring, this one made up of campfires. Many of the older members of the caravan were sitting on the logs, warming their backs and smiling at the dancers. Ava noted a surprisingly large number of faces that she didn't recognize.

"Where did all these people come from?" she asked Sarah.

"Oh, didn't you hear? Another large caravan set up camp just down the road late this afternoon. Ariana rode over and issued an invitation for any of them who wished to join us. This'll be the best dance we've had all year!"

For a brief moment Ava felt all the excitement of a girl

attending a dance and knowing she looked her best. And then she remembered who she was.

New people were unknowns and therefore represented a potential danger. She looked around a little wildly for Hans. She couldn't see him in the crowd of people, and she began to feel nervous. The circle of firelight was throwing out unusual shadows, and the wagons loomed over her in a threatening manner. A flicker of darkness to her left made her flinch and peer into the gloom between two wagons. Was someone there?

"Anna? Anna!" Sarah had continued several steps before realizing her companion had stopped, but she now doubled back and grabbed the other girl's arm. "Come on! What are you waiting for?"

She dragged Ava between two fires and into the circle of the logs.

"Can you see Evelyn anywhere?" Sarah was standing on her toes and peering around the dancers.

Safely ensconced inside the circle, Ava felt her heartbeat subside and even felt amused at her previous fear. She didn't normally scare so easily! Anna was starting to consume her.

Before she could get caught up in her own thoughts, she spied Evelyn in a gap created by the twirling dancers. The tall girl was standing talking with Hans, and the sight of him erased the last of Ava's fear.

"Over there!" she yelled into Sarah's ear, and this time she was the one dragging her friend along. Evelyn was looking stately and elegant in her long ice blue gown, and she and Hans made a beautiful, if deadly, looking pair. Looking at them, Ava felt a pang at her own short height. It was the first time she had ever considered herself wanting in physical appearance, and she didn't like the feeling.

Sarah pulled herself from Ava's grip and ran up to her cousin, exclaiming loudly about her dress and hair. Ava took the opportunity to turn toward Hans.

Hans was standing completely still and staring at her, and she felt suddenly self-conscious under his gaze. She thought again of how short she was compared to Evelyn.

"There are so many new people," she blurted out, attempting to bridge the awkward moment and then wincing internally. She didn't think she'd said anything so gauche since she was a child. What was happening to her?

Hans didn't seem to notice, however. Her words had snapped him out of his daze, and he stepped forward to greet her, reaching out to grip her upper arm.

"Don't worry," he said, leaning down to whisper the words into her ear. "I went over to the other camp with Ariana."

"What?" asked Ava stupidly, struggling to focus on his words. *This is the first time I can remember him choosing to touch me*, she thought.

"I volunteered to accompany Ariana when she went to issue the invitation to the other merchant caravan." His words penetrated the fog that seemed to have descended over Ava's mind.

"Oh?" she asked, the word sharp and questioning.

"Ariana knows the caravan well, and she didn't seem to notice anything amiss. She was looking sharply, too. These are troubled times, after all, and you don't get to be leader of the most well-regarded caravan in the Four Kingdoms without paying attention.

"I looked them over closely, too. There was no one I recognized from Rangmeros."

Ava felt herself sag a little in relief, and Hans squeezed her arm reassuringly.

"I guess we have nothing to fear, then," she said. "That was quick thinking. Well done."

Hans nodded an acknowledgment of her praise and then quickly stepped away from her, letting his hand drop. Sarah turned toward them eagerly and demanded both Hans and

Evelyn's admiration of the effect they had produced with Ava's dress.

"Sarah's just been telling me how you got it to fit so well," said Evelyn. "It looks great."

Ava smiled and felt some of her earlier good spirits return.

"Well, are we going to dance, or are we just going to stand here?" she asked the other girls.

"An excellent idea," said Hans, surprising her.

"Would you like to dance?" he asked, turning toward Evelyn. She looked surprised and flattered and quickly took his offered hand. In the next breath, they were both swept up into the mass of moving bodies.

"That answers that question," said Sarah, and for once her cheerful tone sounded forced.

Her friend's disappointment pulled Ava out of her own chagrin. She had found the joking competition between the two cousins amusing, but she had secretly assumed that Hans would ask her to dance first. She was his princess, after all, even if no one else knew it.

But hearing the emotion so clearly in Sarah's voice embarrassed Ava. She wasn't some merchant girl, hoping for a sign of Hans' favor. She was the Princess of Rangmere, and he was her guard.

"I'm sure it doesn't mean anything," Ava said. "He'll probably ask you to dance next. Evelyn was here talking with him first, after all. I'm sure he's just being polite."

This thought seemed to cheer Sarah up, because she glanced at Ava mischievously.

"And in the meantime, there's no need to wait around," she said. "Harry isn't the only newcomer here tonight as it turns out." She threw her glance toward a group of unfamiliar young men and put on a bright smile.

Two of them seemed to notice the girls, who were now

standing alone, and broke away from their own group to approach them.

"Would you like to dance?" a tall, dark-haired young man asked Sarah, bowing over her hand with exaggerated grace.

She smiled flirtatiously and nodded an agreement.

"And you?" His friend held out his hand toward Ava. When she also nodded, both boys led the girls into the dance.

Both caravans must have freed the majority of their guards to attend the event since there seemed to be a never-ending supply of fit and graceful young men anxious to dance with Ava. She soon lost track of her friends, although she caught the occasional sight of them as they flashed past on the temporary dance floor. The constant shift of the dancers and the flickering light from the fires made it hard to see amidst the crush of bodies, and she quickly gave up looking for them.

Instead she gave herself over to the enjoyment of the dance, allowing all thoughts of Princess Ava to drain out of her head. She had always loved to dance, so she was determined not to allow this opportunity for simple pleasure to be marred.

The dances were slightly different from the ones she was used to dancing in the ballrooms of palaces and noble residences. They were easy to pick up, however, and there was little variation between them, so she soon had the feel of it. Many times, throughout the evening, she was complimented by her partner for her grace and the lightness of her feet. She drank in the praise and allowed herself to become giddier and giddier.

The dresses of the dancers were much simpler than the ones that usually filled ballrooms, but they were bright in color and the many full skirts filled the dance floor with swirling material. In the uneven light of the fires, the dresses flashed brilliantly, and she decided that she preferred this dance to any that she had previously attended.

There was no one watching her, no one measuring and judging, looking for weaknesses or opportunities to exploit. Instead there was the rhythmic melody of the traditional caravan music, the whirling movement, the flash of firelight on happy faces and an endless stream of enthusiastic young men who grasped her hand or her waist as the music required and swung her easily through the dance. It was intoxicating.

Once she saw Sarah and Hans swing past her, and she flashed a quick thumbs up at Sarah who grinned in response. Ava was interested, but not particularly surprised, to note that Hans was a graceful dancer.

Usually an excellent judge of the passage of time, she quickly lost all sense of the hour. She had no idea how much time had passed when she finally collapsed onto a log. Waving away two young men who approached her, she instead accepted a cup of water offered by an older lady from Caravan Hargrove.

Downing it in two gulps, she fanned herself with her hand and wished she could remove her cloak. Watching the remaining dancers whirl past had a strangely hypnotic effect, and she began to feel fatigued. Looking around for Sarah, Ava wondered if the dance would soon be winding down.

Before she could muster the energy to act on her thoughts, Ava was distracted by a discordant sound, coming from the other side of the dance floor. Slowly the sound of conflict and of loud angry voices rose above the sound of music. First the pan piper and then the fiddler stopped playing. The dancing couples slowly revolved to a stop, and then the dance floor erupted into pandemonium as people began to call out in fear and push in every direction.

Ava leaped to her feet, attempting to see past the mass of bodies to the cause of the disruption. Climbing onto a log, she peered above the heads of the crowd and was met with a familiar sight. Men wearing the light armor of the Royal Guard.

CHAPTER 8

*A*va quickly dropped back to the ground and looked around wildly, wondering where she should run. Before she could make up her mind, Hans materialized out of the crowd. He grabbed her hand and without a word pulled her between two fires and into the darkness beyond.

Running at nearly full pace, Ava twice tripped and would have fallen but for Hans' steady grip. They were quickly through the wagons and into the surrounding forest. He didn't pause but led her on until they were out of sight of the caravan. Only the faintest glow from the fires reached them.

Finally, he stopped and took up a position between her and the distant wagons, his hand on the sword hilt at his waist. Ava hadn't previously noticed his sword but felt relieved that he had thought to include it in his dancing outfit.

For a moment, there was silence except for her gasping breaths and the distant sound of shouting from the caravan.

"How, how did you find me?" she finally managed to get out.

Hans swung his head around to look at her. Her eyes had adjusted sufficiently to the low light for her to make out his expression. He looked confused.

"What do you mean?" he asked.

"It was chaos at the dance," she said, "even before the guards arrived. I couldn't have found you if my life depended on it."

His face tightened in a wince, and Ava wondered if it was possible her life had depended on it.

"I never lost track of you," said Hans simply.

Ava shook her head in wonder. The man had an uncanny sense where his job was concerned. She could only be grateful for it.

The more time that passed without any sign of pursuit, the more Ava felt herself relax. It was unlikely anyone had seen them flee, and they had no way of knowing what the guard was even doing at Caravan Hargrove. There was every likelihood it had nothing to do with her.

Hans, however, remained tensed. His eyes stared back through the trees, and his hand clenched and unclenched on his sword hilt.

Eventually the sound of conflict quieted. Ava began to stir restlessly, anxious to know what was going on, and Hans glanced back at her. She could see from his gaze that he was torn.

"Not this again," she said. "Go, find out what's happening. I'll be fine." When he didn't move, she bent down and flipped back the hem of her skirts. The tip of her dagger could be seen above her boot.

"I never go anywhere without it."

"Stay here," he said. "I won't be long."

He moved so quietly through the trees that Ava wondered when he had received forest training. It definitely hadn't been in the five years he had served as her personal guard.

In the long minutes they had spent waiting in the forest, neither of them had voiced the question that must have been foremost in both of their minds.

What was the Royal Guard doing interrupting the dance of a

prominent merchant caravan? For that matter, what were they doing so far from the capital at all?

She wondered if they had reason to believe her uncle was near. Or worse, did their presence mean her brother was here? The thought made her shiver.

~

It seemed a long time but was likely only minutes before Hans returned. Ava could see immediately from his posture that he was bringing good news.

"The Guard is gone," he said, and Ava gave a long sigh of relief. "Officially they were here investigating your father's and your assassinations. They were asking about any recent additions to the caravan." He gave Ava a significant look, and she reached almost unconsciously to pat her brown hair. "Unofficially, the rumor is that they're shaking down all the merchant caravans fleeing for the border. Luckily for us, Ariana is furious.

"I didn't actually speak to anyone, but I overheard several different accounts of her face off with the captain of the guards. They were in complete violation of international law, of course, which put them at a disadvantage. Apparently, she's made it clear that if another Royal Guardsman steps foot within ten paces of her caravan without due process, she'll be invoking a merchant's ban against Rangmere."

Ava's eyebrows rose steeply toward her hairline. "Wow, that's serious." She pondered for a moment. "This whole thing should work to our advantage then. They won't dare come near Caravan Hargrove again."

Traveling merchants were bound by their own set of complicated laws that were administered by the caravan leader and, occasionally, by a council comprised of the merchants' most senior leaders. The treaty that permitted them free passage through the land and freedom from persecution was one of the oldest treaties in existence. Violation of the treaty could result in a merchant ban being implemented against an entire kingdom, none of which could afford to do without the services of the traveling merchants. Not even the smallest or greediest of caravans would consider coming to a kingdom under a ban. And, if they did, the merchant council would be swift to deal with them.

Ava vaguely remembered that any member of the merchant council could invoke such a ban, and she was unsurprised to think that Ariana wielded such authority. The merchant must have been extremely angry to make such a threat, however.

She could see that Hans agreed with her assessment. His entire demeanor had changed. He was relaxed and even smiling at her. Slowly she felt her own mouth smile in response.

"A pity that the party was interrupted," she said, the smile evident in her voice. "Sarah's probably frantic with worry about me, though. We should probably get back."

"Yes," agreed Hans, but he stepped toward her rather than back in the direction of the caravan. She looked at him inquiringly.

"I'm sure Sarah and Evelyn will have noticed that we've both disappeared," he said. "We'll need a reasonable explanation for our absence."

He closed the distance between them, and Ava found herself a little short of breath. He was looking down at her with a burning intensity that was softened by the smile on his lips.

Slowly he brought one of his hands from behind his back, and she saw that he had been concealing a red rose. She had no idea where the flower had come from, but its color perfectly matched the red of her cloak.

Carefully, he reached out and brushed back her hair, sliding the stem behind her ear. For a long moment he stood frozen there, his hand against the side of her face.

Ava stared up at him, caught by the strength of his gaze, her skin burning from his touch. Her mind had gone numb, and she didn't even try to process the new emotions boiling through her. Slowly, slowly he lowered his face toward hers, and for one charged moment she expected to feel his lips press against hers.

Instead she felt the whisper of his breath against her ear. "You look beautiful, Anna," he said, and she felt a rush of disappointment at the sound of her pseudonym. "So beautiful I didn't even notice a commotion coming from the camp."

Suddenly Ava realized what he meant. She took a quick step backward, putting distance between them and hoping that he hadn't seen the flush of embarrassment on her face.

"I'm sure we weren't the only couple to slip away for a moonlight stroll through the woods," he said. "From what I can gather, 'walking' is the main form of courtship among the merchants as well as among those of the towns and cities."

Ava was vaguely aware of the practice, but it wasn't used among the royalty or nobility where arranged marriages were more common than love matches.

"Of course," she said, finding her voice. "We were 'walking.'"

Firmly taking her hand, Hans led her back toward the wagons. Neither of them said anything, and Ava concentrated on keeping her face blank and trying to ignore the way her emotions roiled at the feel of Hans' fingers twined through hers.

Back inside the ring of wagons, people milled around and talked with agitated voices despite the lateness of the hour. Several glanced toward Ava and Hans, but when they noticed their clasped hands they threw them amused glances, calling out the news to the newcomers.

When they reached the shadows behind Sarah's family wagon, she pulled her hand out of Hans' grip. Sarah paced in front of the wagon, and Ava stepped toward her, opening her mouth to call to the other girl. But Hans reached out and halted her, recapturing her fingers.

Leaning in close, he whispered into her hair, his breath a caress against her cheek. "You really do look beautiful, Ava."

Her own breath caught at the sound of her true name.

"But not as beautiful as you look with golden hair."

And then he was gone, and Ava was left staring into the darkness with wide eyes.

When she turned around Sarah was standing in front of her. The other girl's face was filled with relief but also with curiosity.

"I'm so glad you're all right." She looked significantly in the direction of Hans' disappearance. "But it looks like you've been holding out on me."

Ava stared at her, trying to make sense of her words. Her mind had been scrambled, and she couldn't form a coherent sentence. She was sure she had experienced more emotions in the last hour than she had allowed herself to feel in the last five years.

"The morning," she finally managed to get out, and luckily Sarah seemed to understand her meaning.

"You must be as exhausted as I am," she said, squeezing Ava's arm. "We'll sleep first—but don't think you're getting out of telling me *everything* tomorrow!"

Ava nodded her agreement, glad to have escaped an immediate inquisition.

Once inside the wagon, she changed into her nightdress without conscious thought, her mind still malfunctioning, caught on the last words Hans had said to her.

When she slipped into her bedroll, she remembered the flower in her hair. Carefully she removed it and after a moment's indecision placed it beneath her pillow.

"It's a very beautiful rose," said Sarah, reminding Ava that she was not alone. "He must have bought it from the other caravan, no one in our caravan grows ones with such a vibrant color." There was a sly grin in the girl's words, but Ava was far too tired to dissect any hidden meaning.

Instead she fell into the clutches of sleep and dreamed that she was being chased by a wolf. She ran from him, her red cloak flapping behind her, but she was never more than one step ahead. Hans appeared to one side, an ax over his shoulder, and called to her, offering to save her. She considered turning toward him but was too afraid that the wolf would catch her if she veered off course. Instead she kept running, the wolf snarling at her heels.

CHAPTER 9

*E*veryone overslept the next morning, a combination of
fatigue from the dance and excitement from the run in
with the Royal Guard. Ava had expected that they would camp
for another day after the chaos of the night before, but Ariana
seemed grimly determined to press on.

The leader of the caravan that had joined them for the dance
rode over to consult with Ariana first thing in the morning. The
result of their conference was that the second caravan attached
itself to the back of Caravan Hargrove, making them a much
bigger group for their last few days' journey to the border.

Finding places for so many wagons to camp at night would be
difficult, but everyone seemed to feel the benefits outweighed the
inconvenience. Everywhere Ava went around camp she passed
small huddles of merchants, talking in concerned voices. The
light-hearted mood of the dance had been completely destroyed
by the invasion of the Guard. There was no longer any chance of
forgetting that they were traveling through a country overset by
regicide.

Ava was almost savagely glad for the change of mood since it
was a better match for her own inner turmoil. She did not,

however, enjoy having to shield herself against the constant shock of overhearing the names of her father and brother. It was a good thing she was so practiced at hiding her responses, or she would have been walking around camp with a near constant twitch, so often were they mentioned.

Surprisingly she heard little mention of Princess Ava beyond the occasional comments on her beauty and the savagery of the attacker to target a young princess. She couldn't help but feel a little resentful knowing the hard work she had put in to rival her brother in her father's eyes.

Of course, that was the point, she reminded herself, *my strength was always in subtlety and the power of the unexpected. I wasn't* supposed *to be known as anything but a beautiful princess.* The logic was sound but it stung just the same.

She had avoided Sarah by slipping from the wagon before anyone else was awake. She needed solitude to recover from the strange emotional agitation left by her dreams, brought on, she was sure, by the tumultuous emotions of the night before.

She kept thinking of her father and of the large wolf pelt he had always kept draped over his throne. Was it still there or had Konrad removed it? The appearance of the wolf in her dreams, along with Hans, in the persona of a woodcutter, seemed like a clear indication of how unbalanced she had become.

She still wasn't sure what Hans had meant to communicate in their strange interactions, and she wasn't sure how she should respond when faced with him again. She had no time to formulate a plan, however, because she bumped into him almost immediately.

"Good morning," he said, his usual solid calm marred by only the slightest expression of unease. "I hope you haven't been too disturbed by all the strange happenings."

His eyes flickered to the group of merchants closest to them who were discussing the current state of Rangmere in loud voices. Ava understood by this that he meant the advent of the

Guard and the sudden increase in interest in her family as opposed to his own confusing behavior of the night before.

"No indeed." She matched his light tone. "Although I confess I'll be glad when we're past the border." His eyes locked on hers, and she carefully kept her face neutral.

"I, too, look forward to that day."

She noticed that the knuckles of his right hand were white where they gripped his sword hilt. So, he wasn't quite as relaxed as he appeared, then. The thought gave her some satisfaction.

Apparently, he intended to continue as if the night before had not occurred. She was glad of it, since she had no idea how she should respond to the strange events. Not when she couldn't even decide how she felt about them.

"They've called all the shifts to active duty," he said. "I'll be busy guarding the caravan all day." There was concern now in his eyes where they rested on her. "I've rearranged the placements, though. I'll be riding near Sarah's wagon. Would you consider giving Cinnamon a rest for the day and traveling in the wagon instead? I would feel more comfortable knowing you were safely tucked away out of sight."

For the second time in as many days, Ava found her hand plucking a little desperately at her false brown hair. And before she had even made up her mind, her head was nodding agreement. Hans looked relieved, and the sight made her nervous. If he felt so strongly about it, he must have good reason to believe more trouble could be coming their way.

"I have to get to my post." He lifted his hand as if he meant to grip hers. She pulled her hand quickly out of reach, and he let his own fall to his side.

"Stay safe," he said, his voice low and intense.

"I will." Her own voice was hardly more than a whisper.

After he was gone, she realized that riding in the wagon all day meant keeping company with Sarah.

"No avoiding it, then," she said to herself with a small sigh and turned her steps back toward the wagon.

～

Sarah greeted the prospect of a traveling companion with delight. There wasn't room for all four of them at the front of the wagon, so the two girls would have to ride inside. Ava noticed that Sarah's parents seemed relieved to have the excuse to send their daughter inside, and it only increased her feeling of tension. Despite Ariana's authority and her threats, Hans wasn't the only one worried about further trouble. She wondered what new developments had prompted these fears and ground her teeth at the knowledge that as a newcomer and a mere teenage girl, she would be the last to hear any news.

The wheels of their wagon were barely starting to roll when Sarah turned to Ava with eager eyes. Before she could get out a question, though, they were both startled by someone pulling open the wagon and leaping in beside them.

Ava's hand had already gone to the hilt of her knife before she realized it was only Evelyn. She quickly let her skirts fall back into place, hoping neither girl had noticed. When she glanced up, however, Evelyn was staring at her ankle with a look of surprise. Ava returned the look with a stony gaze, and the young guardswoman gave a slight shrug and let her gaze fall.

"What are you doing here, Eve?" asked her cousin, having missed the brief interchange between the other girls.

"The Guardsmaster wants a guard stationed in every wagon," said Evelyn. "But no one's allowed to be in their own. So here I am." She gave a rare grin, and Ava couldn't help but admire the very specific way in which she had interpreted those limitations.

"That's excellent!" said Sarah. "We couldn't be cosier." She seemed determined to remain cheerful in the face of everyone's rising tension.

"Now settle in," she added, "we're about to hear all about Anna's moonlit stroll, last night."

"Oh, yes," said Evelyn, settling herself with easy grace. "Do tell."

Ava thought she looked slightly less enthusiastic than her cousin but then that was hardly an unusual occurrence.

"Well, there isn't really much to tell," said Ava, calling a false blush to her cheeks and casting down her eyes in an attempt to look demure. "I wasn't sure…I thought you might be angry with me," she added in a rush, raising pleading eyes to the other two girls.

"I know we seem like an odd pair," said Evelyn seriously, "but Sarah and I have been best friends since before we could walk. Neither of us had serious intentions toward your Hans because we would never truly pursue the same man. Sarah just likes to add excesses of enthusiasm to everything. Even the things she doesn't really take seriously." She directed a reproving look toward her cousin who didn't even attempt to look abashed.

"I always suspected there was something between the two of you," said Sarah with great relish at being proved right. Apparently, her rather shaky claim to this foreknowledge in no way reduced her triumph.

Ava rolled her eyes in smiling disbelief.

"It's true!" Sarah insisted. "You can see it in the way he looks at you."

"I know you well enough now to know that you can see whatever you want to see, Sarah," said Ava.

"No, she's right," said Evelyn, surprisingly coming to Sarah's defense. "I noticed it, too. It's not that he's always watching you exactly. It's that he's always aware of you; as if some part of him is always aligned toward you. And when he does watch you there's an intensity in his gaze that's…compelling." The usually stoic guard seemed a little embarrassed at this assessment. "I admire him as a guard tremendously, but none of us have ever given you any real competition."

Ava was impressed at the way both girls were so willing to release any potential jealousy or resentment. And she couldn't help but feel touched at the way they were trying to reassure her of her supposed sweetheart's loyalty.

In truth, though, their words only increased her unease. There were so many layers to her relationship with Hans that they didn't understand. And yet, despite this, it was impossible to dismiss their words entirely.

The best she could do was muster a smile and several more blushes and express her thanks in glowing enough terms to satisfy Sarah that she was a typical young girl in love. She longed to be free of the wagon and riding Cinnamon. Not at the sedate trot required by the caravan but at a headlong gallop.

"What's the news?" Sarah asked Evelyn, pulling Ava's attention back to the conversation in the wagon. Sarah spoke with unusual gravity, showing that she was more aware of the current climate of the caravan than she appeared to be.

"We've had reports about other caravans being examined, so the Guard's arrival last night wasn't entirely unexpected," Evelyn said. "But Ariana was furious that they would show up in the middle of a dance. The Guardsmaster thinks they timed it purposely since we had a minimum number of guards on duty. They came in with a big show of force, trying to cow everyone, but when some of them tried to start turning out the wagons, Ariana confronted them. They clearly didn't expect her to take such a strong line, but she's the most senior merchant in Rangmere at the moment. She's already had multiple envoys from other caravans expressing their unhappiness with the situation, so I think she knew a reminder of our independent status was going to be needed sooner rather than later."

Ava was yet again impressed with the young merchant girl-turned-guard. She was skilled or she would never have won such a male-dominated position, but it was now evident that her skills extended beyond physical combat. There was no way the Guardsmaster had shared all this with his guards. Clearly, she was observant and also giving them the benefit of her own insight.

"We were all hoping that would be the end of it," continued Evelyn, "at least until we hit the border. But our scouts reported that the guards only retreated a short distance and that they are giving every indication of planning to follow us. They may merely intend to tail us to the border, but everyone's on edge. And understandably so. Prince Konrad seems to have thrown the full force of the kingdom into tracking down whoever is responsible for murdering his family."

"Hardly surprising," chimed in Sarah.

Ava remained silent, but she was listening intently and was ready to ask some well-placed questions if the conversation seemed about to wander off track. She had been able to glean only bits and pieces of news from Rangmeros, and she was desperate for more information.

"No, it's not surprising," said Evelyn. "He's even delayed his coronation. He's vowed that he and the country will remain in mourning until his father is avenged. It seems a bit dramatic, but I think he's probably doing it to sway public opinion in his favor. He wasn't overly popular before, but the populace is still feeling sympathy toward him after his tragic loss and his own near escape. I suppose it makes sense to milk that for all its worth."

Inwardly Ava agreed with this rather cold reading of the situation and cheered Evelyn's perspicacity. It was a relief to think that not everyone was blind to her brother's true nature.

She was interested to learn of the delay to the coronation. Rangmeran tradition held that the old monarch was mourned for fourteen days at the end of which the new monarch was crowned. No wonder Konrad was so tirelessly pursuing their uncle. By setting such an extension to the mourning period, he was also potentially delaying his coronation indefinitely.

She suspected that if her uncle didn't materialize, he would begin to talk of the need for stability and for the kingdom to turn their eyes to the future. She could almost hear the perfect mix of sorrow and hope that he would use when he delivered the speech. She wondered how long public opinion would remain on his side.

"Prince Konrad has always scared me." Sarah wrinkled her nose in an expression that seemed more displeased than afraid.

Evelyn raised a skeptical eyebrow.

"What?" asked Sarah. "I saw him once! When I went with Mother and Father to hear the public address he gave on his eighteenth birthday."

"I see," said Evelyn drily. "I didn't realize you'd had so much contact with him."

"He scares me, too," said Ava, surprising herself by voicing her opinion aloud. "I've always thought that Princess Ava must have been glad not to be born a boy." It felt strange to refer to herself in the third person.

"Yes, I wouldn't want to be facing him at the Trials," agreed Evelyn, and Sarah shivered dramatically.

Unlike the other kingdoms, Rangmeran succession wasn't determined by birth order. During the period of mourning, all sons of the deceased monarch were given the opportunity to register as formal claimants to the throne with the Head of the Magistrate's Guild. The brothers then competed in the Monarchy Trials, ensuring that the strongest was crowned king. The fate of the losers was left in the hands of the victor.

It had been thirty years since Ava's father had defeated his two younger brothers in the last Trials, but people still talked of it. One of them had been so badly injured he later died of his wounds, and the other had been banished to the outer lands.

"But why is he targeting the merchants?" asked Sarah, less interested than Ava in the broader politics of Rangmere.

"He's closed all the borders." Evelyn crossed her arms. "But he knows he can't keep them closed to the merchants for long. I suppose he's worried that whoever is behind the assassinations will slip out with us."

"You don't think he'll actually try to prevent us leaving, do you? Once we're all assembled, I mean." Sarah cast a worried glance toward the wagon wall that separated her from her parents.

"That's what we don't know," said Evelyn grimly. "But if he does, we'll be ready."

CHAPTER 10

When it reached late afternoon, no one talked of stopping. Already they had covered more ground than usual, but still the enlarged caravan pressed on. It wasn't until the sun had actually set that Ariana finally called a halt.

Ava remained in the wagon as everyone rushed to set up camp while there was still some light. It was unusually chaotic due to the presence of the additional caravan, and she was sure she would only get in the way.

Hans ducked his head into the wagon and wholly endorsed this perspective.

"I'm still on duty and will be until after midnight. Half of the guards are catching some sleep now, and the rest of us will get some later tonight. I think the Guardsmaster resents the fact that we need rest at all." He smiled briefly. "But even he knows we can't keep going forever."

"And the Royal Guard?" asked Ava.

"They've been following us pretty closely, but they've made no other move as yet. We'll see what happens tonight. When I get off duty later, I'll lie here, at the entrance of the wagon. If you hear anything, slip out to me and we'll be off, just like last night."

Ava nodded, wondering how she would get any sleep at all.

In the end, however, not only did she fall asleep, but the camp remained undisturbed throughout the night. Regrettably, she herself was not so fortunate.

She awoke constantly, drenched in sweat and shaking from the same dream that had plagued her the night before. As in the original dream, Hans was there, standing to the side. Sometimes he was armed with a bow and arrow and sometimes with the ax, but he was always there, offering his help. But as before, Ava was too frightened to turn and run to him.

The most terrifying moments were when Ava woke up, gasping and panting, and realized that this time she had been the wolf. On those occasions, even when awake, she could still feel the hunger and the desperate need to finally consume the girl fleeing before her. But regardless of whether she was girl or wolf, the flapping red cloak always remained just out of reach of the snapping jaws.

It wasn't until the early hours of the morning, well after Hans had finished his shift and lain down at the wagon door, that she finally slipped into a deeper sleep, free of dreams.

The caravan began to stir at the first signs of dawn. Ava knew she must look terrible, but no one commented on it. Pack up was completed quickly, and they were on the road before it was fully light. The harder pace of travel and the constant state of alert was beginning to take a toll, and there was little talking to be heard.

Evelyn didn't join the girls in the back of the wagon, and even Sarah had little to say. Instead she alternated between dozing, her head resting on a small box, and staring at the wagon wall separating her from her parents.

Ava also tried to nap but without much success. Instead she tried to think about the next step in her quest to find the High

King. She had been so focused on blending in with the merchants and making it into Arcadia that she had given little thought to what would come next.

Unfortunately, the more she thought about it, the more her mind became a blank. They could travel between the various small villages scattered throughout the deep forest, seeking rumors of the Palace of Light, but that seemed like a long shot at best. At worst, she would be old and gray before she found the palace home of the godmothers.

So instead, Ava practiced holding herself still and calm, allowing no sign of her inner frustration to show on her face. It was an old game, one she used to play when she was thirteen and fourteen. Back when she was still learning how to block her emotions and be the cold strategist her father demanded. She hadn't needed the exercise for many years.

Whenever the tension grew too high to control, she would peer out of the wagon at Hans, riding beside them. Something about the sight of his alert, strong figure reassured her.

She felt weak, though, for needing the reassurance. She had never needed it before.

The third time she looked for him, he seemed to sense her gaze, and he returned her look. He didn't smile at her or wave, but something in his calm face expressed silent support. She pulled back quickly, overwhelmed by a memory.

It was from one of the first times she had played the game and the first time her father had allowed her to join him at a state dinner. The inclusion was a mark of his trust and pride in her accomplishments, and she was desperate not to let him down.

But Konrad had resented her presence and had constantly needled her, belittling her in front of the visiting dignitaries. Her father did nothing to shield her, and she knew this was yet another test. Just when she had thought she would fail and allow the anger and humiliation to break through, she had looked at Hans, standing guard against the wall. He hadn't been her personal guard for long, and his own face had maintained the look of passive disinterest required of a guard, but something in his eyes had transmitted the necessary strength to her. She had held and had never come so near to breaking again.

Perhaps I've never done it on my own, she thought, and the idea frightened her. *Perhaps I have never been as strong as I imagined.*

The thought continued to plague her throughout the day, and her night was again disturbed by the dreams in which she alternated between terrified prey and hungry predator.

When she awoke the next morning, she was relieved to hear that they would reach the border that day. Whatever awaited them there, at least this unbearable tension would be over.

Ava obviously wasn't the only one glad to be nearing Arcadia at last. The longer they traveled, the more bubbly Sarah became until Ava had to use considerable will power to restrain herself from snapping at the other girl.

"Do you think we're nearly there yet?" asked Sarah for what must have been the twentieth time. Luckily for Ava's self-restraint, Evelyn jumped into the wagon just in time to hear the question.

"What are you, a child?" She rolled her eyes in Ava's direction. Ava allowed herself one subdued smile.

Sarah, oblivious to the criticism, leaped to her feet in excitement.

"Well? What's going on out there? We should have reached the border an hour ago."

"We've had to slow down a bit since there's a fair amount of traffic heading in the same direction. Most people have been getting out of our way once they see how big our caravan is, but it still slows us down. We can finally see the border crossing, though.

"There's a contingent of guards blocking it, and we're not the first caravan to arrive. Hopefully now that we're here, the merchants will have the critical mass required to push the issue. No guarantees, of course."

"What's the plan, then?" asked Ava.

"Ariana's given the order to pull up in the middle of the road. There's simply nowhere left to camp in the area. I have to get back out there, but you both hold tight. We'll know more soon."

She didn't give either girl a chance to respond, instead exiting the wagon as quickly as she had entered it. Sarah stared at Ava with wide eyes, and Ava tried to think of something reassuring to say. Nothing came to mind.

"Ariana will sort it out," said Sarah after a long pause.

Somehow waiting in a stationary wagon was infinitely more frustrating than waiting in a moving one. The thirty minutes it took for the negotiations to take place felt more like two hours. But eventually the time passed, and word was passed down the caravan that Ariana had returned from talking to the border guard. They were to be let through.

Both Evelyn and Hans popped their heads in to pass on the good news, but Hans accompanied it with stern instructions to Ava to stay where she was. With reluctance, she agreed.

They had only just begun to move again when the wagon jerked to a halt, nearly throwing both girls from their seats. Before they could even regain their balance, there were several loud shouts quickly followed by the ringing clang of steel meeting steel and several high screams.

Sarah gave an echoing scream, but Ava ignored her, dropping instinctively to the ground. Crawling to the back of the wagon, she thrust open the door so she could see what was happening outside.

As soon as she did so, the sounds of conflict increased dramatically. She could hear the shouts of the guards and the clash of sword against sword, the whinnies of frightened horses and the curses of the wagon drivers as they attempted to control their animals.

With the wagons arranged in a long line, it was hard to get a sense of what was going on, but Ava could see several of the caravan guard battling with men in the light armor of the Royal Guard. She could only assume they had been attacked. The Royal Guard must have been desperate at the prospect of the caravan escaping across the border.

In the heat of the moment, she felt no fear, just a furious rush of thoughts as she attempted to analyze the situation. Peering cautiously around the end of the wagon she tried to work out what was happening at the border.

The crossing had already been opened, and the border guards were watching the conflict in stupefied amazement. They were certainly making no effort to join the Royal Guard.

The merchants on the other hand seemed much more unified, and Ava suspected they had planned for this eventuality. All the smaller caravans that had gathered at the border were swiftly launching into action. Their wagon horses were being pushed to extraordinary efforts, practically galloping the wagons across the border. Meanwhile, the guards from these other caravans were streaming toward Caravan Hargrove to assist in holding back the Royal Guard

Leaping from the back of the wagon, Ava climbed onto the stationary wheel to get a better view. She could see Ariana standing on the bench at the front of her wagon and waving her arm above her head, gesturing for the other caravans to hurry across the border. Clearly, she meant to keep their larger caravan in place until all the smaller ones had escaped.

The Arcadian guards on the other side of the border had formed into two troops on either side of the road and looked ready to deal with any Rangmeran guards who attempted to harass merchants who made it across into Arcadia.

Ava had only a few seconds to take this all in before the fighting reached their wagon. Leaping from her vantage point, she crouched down to retrieve her dagger. When she stood back up, she found herself face to face with a royal guard whose hand gripped a blood-streaked sword.

For an endless second they both froze, eyes locked. With horror, Ava realized she recognized him. He was one of her brother's favored bodyguards.

From the widening of his eyes, she could tell that he recognized her as well. She gasped and fell back a step but found herself pressed against the back of the wagon.

He also stepped back, twisting around to look for back up. Seeing two mounted soldiers, he waved wildly.

"It's true," he called loudly. "She's here! I've found her."

His words seemed to echo in Ava's head. They confirmed all her worst fears. They weren't searching for the assassin, they were here for her. Konrad had obviously lost patience with the search for their uncle. He was clearly determined to eliminate at least one threat while he had the opportunity to do so.

But Ava had been trained for this situation, she thrived under pressure. If she could just buy herself a few seconds, she could come up with a strategy.

Darting forward while the bodyguard was still twisted away from her, she drove her dagger into his right arm. He screamed and dropped his sword, staggering away from her. The two mounted men moved forward, but she leaped back into the wagon, dragging the doors shut behind her.

Inside the wagon, Sarah was staring at her, her eyes wide with fright and shock. Ava rushed toward her friend, tugging at the strings of her red cloak. She was relieved that she had chosen to wear the distinctive garment that morning. Ignoring Sarah's stutters of confusion, she draped the cloak around the other girl's shoulders.

Stepping back, she decided that, at a quick glance, Sarah could be mistaken for the new brunette version of herself. Sarah seemed too astonished by Ava's actions to respond, so Ava grabbed her wrist and tugged her back toward the wagon doors.

Before Sarah could protest, Ava shoved open the doors and jumped to the ground, pulling the red cloaked figure with her. Sarah fell to her hands and knees, and Ava abandoned her, crawling beneath the wagon and emerging out the left side. Glancing back, she saw that Evelyn had appeared and was battling with the two soldiers. They had both dismounted and were attempting to reach Sarah.

Peering around one of the large wheels, Ava finally located Hans. He was in the middle of dispatching a third royal guard who was attempting to join the fight at the back of the wagon.

"Hans!"

He spurred his horse toward her, his eyes wild with relief. She stepped away from the wagon, and he reached an arm down to meet hers, swinging her up in front of him on his horse. Once she was secure, he spurred Dusty toward the border.

"I couldn't find you anywhere." His voice was almost lost in the sounds of the battle. "Why is Sarah wearing your cloak?"

Ava didn't attempt to answer. Instead she clung to Dusty's mane and marveled at how easily Hans had seen through her small subterfuge. She was only glad the soldiers were less familiar with her appearance.

Looking back, she saw that Sarah's mother was controlling the horses of their wagon, and that her father had joined the fight. He was wielding a large ax with surprising skill. When she looked back again, as she and Hans neared the border, she saw that more and more of the guards from both sides were congregating at Sarah's wagon. With so many bodies between them, she could no longer see the red cloaked figure, and for the first time she wondered, uneasily, what had become of Evelyn and Sarah at the center of the conflict.

In another moment, they were through the border. With a battle raging behind them, the border guards of both countries simply waved them through. The last of the smaller caravans appeared to have made it across, and the first wagons of Caravan Hargrove were beginning to slowly move forward.

Hans did not stop, however. Gripping Ava tightly around the waist, he spurred Dusty onward. When they had passed all of the merchants, he broke into a canter. Ava clung on, desperately trying not to slip from her precarious position.

When they were out of both sight and sound of the border, Hans slowed his horse and veered off the road, pushing into the trees. Only when they were well out of sight of the road did he stop and help Ava to dismount. When her feet hit the ground, her legs crumpled beneath her, and she would have fallen if Hans had not caught her.

CHAPTER 11

*H*ans gently placed her on the ground, and then the two of them remained there, frozen in place with his hands gripping her shoulders.

Somehow, Hans' face managed to express terrified relief at the same time as he transmitted a gentle reassurance. The overwhelming concern he directed toward her was too much, however; it threatened to overset her fragile control. She lowered her head to stare at the ground instead.

"They were after you." His voice was angry, and it shook her, even though she knew the anger wasn't directed at her.

"I know."

"So, it seems we were right. Konrad intends to honor your father's memory by following his strategies—in the most brutal way possible. Starting with eliminating any siblings. I would have thought he would consider finding your uncle a higher priority."

"Clearly my uncle is proving more elusive than we are." Ava's voice was small, and she kept her head lowered.

"It wasn't your fault…"

Ava cut off Hans' reassurances with a violent shake of her head.

He tried again.

"Ava..." She stopped him with a raised hand. The single word reminded her vividly of the only other time he had said her name without her title. She was suddenly unable to bear the rush of emotions threatened by his proximity. Pushing herself shakily to her feet, she began the simple actions of setting up camp.

After a moment's pause, he accepted her unspoken command and began to strip Dusty in preparation for a rub down. In the rush of their escape, they had abandoned Cinnamon, and somehow that thought managed to pierce the fog around Ava's heart and deliver a stinging blow. She pushed it away.

They had only the meager provisions from Dusty's saddlebags, so setting up camp didn't take long. Hans had prepared for the worst and had packed the most essential items with him, but there was only so much one horse could carry. Ava was just glad he had thought to pack her a spare cloak.

By the time she found herself with nothing left to do, Ava was surprised to see that the sky was darkening. She wondered where the day had gone.

Working together, they prepared a simple dinner, still without speaking, and Hans fetched them water. The stream that followed the road had branched off into multiple tributaries, and Hans had followed one of these into the woods.

They ate, still in silence, and Ava pretended to ignore the worried gaze that followed her every movement. Eventually the food was gone, and there was nothing left for Ava to distract herself with.

For the first time, she allowed herself to wonder what had happened to her friends. *No,* she corrected herself, *what had happened to Anna's friends. I am clearly incapable of friendship.*

"Ava," said Hans, worry in his voice.

"No," she cut him off sharply, raising one hand as if she could physically ward off his words. Now that she had finally let her thoughts free, she found that they wouldn't stop. There was a certain satisfaction in thinking such unthinkable things.

"My father was a monster," she said, going the next step and saying them out loud. "And I'm glad that he's dead."

She waited, but there was no outraged protest from Hans. There wasn't even a gentle denial. Looking up at him she saw a fierce agreement in his eyes. It shocked her more than her own words. If he felt that way about her father, what must he truly think of her? What kind of man could show such unswerving loyalty to someone he detested?

Feeling the catharsis of saying the words out loud, she continued. "And I am my father's daughter through and through. I am a monster, too."

Years of denial and of willful blindness to her own actions rushed over her, and she felt the truth of her words seep in. She felt sure she would break beneath the weight of her own horror, but instead Hans spoke.

"I've been the captain of your guard since you were thirteen years old." His voice was fierce. "From the beginning, I could see something in you. Something more than your father."

"How can you say that?" cried Ava. "Everything I am came from him. He created me."

"No, he tried to. And last year, in Arcadia, I thought he might have succeeded. I know you have never wanted to hear it, but the failure of that marriage was the best thing that ever happened to you." He turned away and continued so quietly she could hardly catch the words. "And the best thing that ever happened to me."

For a moment, she wondered what he meant, but then rage consumed her. It was a relief to direct the loathing at another target, anyone other than herself.

"How can you say that?" She almost screamed at him, remembering only at the last moment to lower her voice in case someone was searching for them. "Everything began to fall apart after Arcadia. I lost everything because of that..." She struggled to think of a fitting word as anger and humiliation choked her. The emotions were familiar, inescapably intertwined with the face of the girl who had foiled her Arcadian plot. But for some reason, this time, the face looked strangely like her own.

"If she were here right now, I would kill her." She wished desperately for some outlet for the anger and hate.

"No, you wouldn't," said Hans quietly, "not really. And that knowledge is the only reason I'm still with you."

Hans' words doused the fire in Ava's mind as effectively as if he had poured his cup of cold water over her head. She stared at him in shock, but he had already turned away. Her mind was spinning in a new direction, and she couldn't get it to stop. After all, what was there to anchor to? Hans had just implied that he might leave her. That, after all, there were conditions to his blind obedience and loyalty.

She opened her mouth to say something but was gripped with uncertainty. What could she say? Evidently, he hadn't seen her actions during the battle. He thought better of her than she deserved, that much was clear. What if her words revealed her true nature? Would he leave? Better to be silent.

She wrapped her cloak around her and lay down with her back toward him. She focused all her energy on breathing as if she were asleep, but in reality, she had never felt so far from peace and rest.

Ava was woken the next morning by the sound of distant voices. Looking around she saw that Hans was already loading their few supplies onto Dusty's back. His face was grim and his movements quick. Taking a moment to listen, Ava was unable to discern if the voices were coming from the road or from potential pursuers within the woods.

Climbing to her feet, she rushed to prepare herself for departure. By the time Hans had Dusty ready to go, Ava was also ready. Without discussion, Hans gripped Ava around the waist and threw her onto the horse's back. Taking the reins, he led them deeper into the forest.

They traveled for hours, slowly making their way through the trees and the thick undergrowth. Occasionally, Hans would leave her and Dusty and double back to conceal their trail. Neither of them spoke.

Ava's head hurt from straining to hear any pursuit, but the trees threw sound in strange directions, and she couldn't be sure where any of the noises she heard originated. Eventually several hours passed in which they heard no sounds but those made by themselves and the forest itself.

When they hit a small clearing, Hans reached up to help Ava down. Rejecting his assistance, she slid down on her own, relieved to be on her feet again. Riding Dusty, outfitted as he was with a regular rather than a side saddle, was extremely uncomfortable, and her back ached.

When they set up camp and prepared another cold meal, she realized that an entire day had passed without either of them speaking a single word. The situation could not continue indefinitely. She'd had her first glimpse, riding in the wagon the day before, of how much she relied on Hans' silent strength. Now, after a day of tormenting herself, she knew she couldn't live with the strain of wondering if the next word she spoke might be the word that drove him away.

Better, she thought, *to rip the bandage off cleanly.*

"Hans," she said, and he looked up, startled, at the sound of her voice. "Why did you come with me?"

"What do you mean?"

"For five years you have been head of my guard. In all that time, you have been unswervingly loyal. I always assumed it was loyalty to Rangmere, to my family. But now I'm asking you. Why are you loyal to me?"

It was a heavy question, and she had expected him to take some time thinking on his answer. She hadn't expected a flush to creep over his face.

"The truth, Princess, is that I have no loyalty to your family. My loyalty is to you alone."

"But why?" asked Ava, desperately hoping to hear something that would put her mind at ease. "Why are you loyal to me?"

"My family," said Hans, unexpectedly. "My family is the reason I became your guard in the first place. In particular, it was my sister."

Ava stared at him, unable to understand what his sister could have to do with her.

"I don't know if you remember her, but her name is Hanna," he continued, and Ava gasped.

Hans was Hanna's brother? It was unthinkable and yet…not so strange. Many families lived within the confines of the palace walls and sent all of their children into service with the royal family. Was it so surprising that a kitchen maid and a guard would be siblings?

Still, Hanna had been her closest friend and had never mentioned a brother called Hans. If it was true, though…Did that mean Hans knew about what Ava had done the day Hanna had been forced to flee Rangmere?

"Your father unjustly punished my sister, and he lost my loyalty that day," said Hans. "And you gained it when you rescued her. Thanks to you she is living safe and well in Northhelm."

Ava felt a sort of horror rushing over her, turning her numb. His loyalty was based on gratitude for her rescuing his sister? If that was the case, his loyalty was based on a lie. Hanna was the first in a long line of people that Ava had wronged.

Once, Hanna had been Ava's best friend. And Hanna had been a rising star in the kitchens of the palace, about to start a prestigious apprenticeship that was almost never awarded to a girl. And then Ava had convinced Hanna to join her in a harmless prank that had gone wrong. It had all been Ava's fault, but when her father discovered them, it was Hanna who took the blame. It was the sort of selfless thing she never hesitated to do.

The worst thing was that Ava's father had known it, too. But he had chosen a harsh punishment anyway. Ava had understood his message. It was a familiar one. Princesses didn't have the luxury of friends or feelings.

Hanna's future in Rangmere had been ruined, and Ava had finally realized that there was no point resisting her father. The only way forward was to shut off all emotions and become the cold and clever daughter he so desired.

Hanna had been an innocent casualty of that lesson. Certainly Ava had mitigated the punishment as much as she could. But Hanna had still been forced to give up her entire life and flee for something that had been Ava's fault. And Ava had sent Hanna away for her own sake as much as anything; friends were a weakness she could no longer afford.

Hans didn't know the whole story, and Ava could imagine she had Hanna to thank for that. It was painful to know her friend had remained so loyal.

"I didn't know," said Ava at last, a little stupidly.

"No," said Hans, "there was no reason you would have. Hanna always called me Alfie." He smiled reminiscently. "My middle name is Alfred, and she thought it was so funny. I used to hate her calling me that, so of course it stuck."

Now that he mentioned it, Ava could remember Hanna talking proudly of her brother Alfie and how well he was doing in his training as a guard. She had never given Hanna's brother much thought, and after Hanna had been sent away, Ava avoided the kitchens.

She also remembered Hans' words on the night they escaped about having friends in the kitchens. She wondered how many of the staff had known Hanna and resented Ava for causing her to be sent away. Had Hans defended her to them?

"I'm glad that she's well," said Ava eventually. "Haven't you ever considered joining her in Northhelm, though?" She waited with bated breath for his response.

Now Hans did hesitate, and his flush deepened. He shook his head and looked away from her.

Ava's brow crinkled in bewilderment. Hans never showed confusion.

"What is it, Hans?" She stepped toward him. "Tell me." Without even realizing she was doing it, she reached out and placed her hand on his arm.

He drew in a sharp breath and stared at her hand for a moment. After another long pause, he looked up and met her eyes.

"When Hanna first asked me to protect you, to watch over you, I resented it. And I didn't really know how I could do it. But then I was given the opportunity to become the captain of your guard. I had nothing left in Rangmere but my job, so I dedicated myself to it night and day."

He paused again, and then the words burst out of him, flowing faster and faster.

"We're not stupid, us guards, though we're taught to act like statues. We still have eyes and ears. I could see what your father was doing to you. How hard he pushed you and how hard you tried. I could see the hurt you were hiding, even from yourself. And I admired you. You were just a child, no older than my sister, but you were strong. And every day you became stronger. I could see you had the kind of strength Rangmere needs, even if your father did his best to twist it. I used to wish you had been born a boy so that one day you could stand up to your brother and challenge him for the monarchy.

"And then, last summer, your father sent you to conquer Arcadia using your wits and your beauty. I felt sickened at what you were doing in his name, and I was afraid that you truly had become the person he wanted you to be. I hated every moment we spent there." His voice was deep and impassioned.

"But it was only when I saw you dancing the other night that I finally realized the truth. Realized why I had felt so sick at the sight of you with the handsome Arcadian prince." He paused and shook his head. "I was almost glad when the Royal Guard arrived, and I had an excuse to grab you away from those merchant guards. It was the first time I knew my own heart, and I hated the sight of you dancing with them. I felt like I was losing you."

He gave a short and bitter laugh. "It's ridiculous, of course, because you were never mine to begin with. So how could I lose you?"

Somehow, while he had been speaking, they had traded positions. Now it was Hans who gripped her, his fingers strong and sure on her arms.

She wanted to be shocked at what was clearly a declaration of love, but some part of her had wondered ever since he had given her the rose. She had never seen another guard so loyal and so dedicated.

His words warmed a part of her heart she hadn't known was cold. She felt elated and victorious. There could be no stronger tie to bind him to her, after all. If he loved her, she needn't fear his abandonment. And if someone like Hans could love her, it was justification for her actions. She hadn't known that being loved could feel so good or so affirming.

Without thinking about it, she leaned into his arms and tipped her face up to his, invitingly. For one long moment, he stared hungrily down at her, and then his arms were around her, crushing her to him, and his lips came down hard on hers.

For one breathless moment, Ava felt safe and loved and desirable. But the kiss ignited a fire that burned through her, and as it went, it unleashed the torrent of emotions that she had been keeping in check ever since the night of the dance. The emotions were confusing, but much worse, they felt uncontrollable. Ava wasn't sure how she truly felt toward her guard, but she knew, instinctively, that she could not trust herself to let go. To find out and, perhaps, to fall. She could not lose control.

With a gasp, she broke off the kiss. For one moment Hans still held her, breathing roughly and staring down at her with longing and confusion. Then comprehension filled his eyes, and he stepped back, releasing her so quickly that she staggered and nearly fell.

"Your Highness," he said, shame filling his voice. "I don't know what came over me. I didn't mean...I would never...Please forgive me and believe that I will never do such a thing again." He turned and paced the short length of the clearing, returning to stand in front of her.

"I know that you are not for me; I have made my peace with that. Protecting you, being your guard, will be enough for me. It *must* be enough."

The last sentence was said quietly, as if to himself, and for a brief second Ava wondered which of them was more scared of their own emotions.

Taking a deep breath, Ava tried to control the flush of embarrassment that now raged across her cheeks. Her own loss of control was far more inexcusable than his.

"This journey has been taxing on us both," she said at last. "We'll feel better when we've rested."

She knew she was ignoring something that could not be ignored forever, but for now it was the best she could do.

Hans seemed relieved to let the matter drop, and when he set up their bedrolls, he positioned his as far from hers as was possible within the confines of the clearing. She crawled into bed, and for the second night in a row, lay down with her back toward him.

CHAPTER 12

$\mathcal{T}$he night before she'd been sure she wouldn't sleep, but she'd been wrong. Eventually sleep had found her, plagued though it was by bad dreams. This time, no matter how she tried to empty her mind, she could not calm herself enough for rest.

Eventually she gave up trying and faced the fear that had so quickly replaced the elation of Hans' confession. She had thought, in those first heady moments, that his love would be the tie that ensured he never left her. But with further reflection came doubt. Only that evening he had admitted that his feelings for her were based on a lie of kindness told to him by his sister. He didn't love *her*, not truly. Like so many others before him, he had constructed a fantasy to go with her beautiful face. The princess he loved did not exist.

And one day, something would happen to shatter the false image he had created. No illusion could last forever. The more strongly he loved now, the more disgust and revulsion he would feel when the truth was revealed. And the more Ava herself relied on him, the weaker she would be when that day came.

The more hours that passed, the clearer it became. She had no choice. She would have to leave and leave now. For years she had prided herself on her strength. She would not fail this test.

At first Hans had also only been feigning sleep—she could tell from the complete absence of sound coming from his still figure. But eventually, his breathing grew louder, and his limbs twitched in the small movements of slumber.

Carefully Ava eased herself out of her bedroll, keeping a closer eye on Dusty than she did on Hans. Fortunately, the horse seemed as deeply asleep as his master. There was no way she could take the horse without waking Hans, and she wasn't sure how easily she could mount or dismount on her own, either. She would have to rely on her own two feet.

Without a horse, she couldn't hope to carry her bedroll, but she did recover a small shoulder satchel from one of the saddle-bags. Into this receptacle, she placed half of the food that Hans had packed and one of the water skins. After some consideration, she added an extra knife to complement the one she had already requisitioned for her boot, and a flint.

Fortunately, the moon was mostly full, and some light managed to filter through the branches. At first, she made fairly good progress, buoyed on by the relief of physical activity. After an hour or so, however, fatigue began to overtake her, and her pace slowed. She found herself stumbling over fallen branches and fumbling as she pushed bushes out of her way.

At one point, she followed a small creek, wading in the shallow flow of water. She had seen only glimpses of Hans' tracking abilities, but she was certain they far exceeded her own.

After several hours, she had well and truly left the clearing behind and couldn't have found her way back to it if she tried. In her desperation, and still unable to come up with any sensible plan for finding the Palace of Light, she had struck out into the depths of the forest rather than back toward the road. She had no more desire to run into the phantom pursuers who had chased them during the day than to be found by Hans. That he would search for her she never doubted.

After another hour, she began to question whether she could go on and to think longingly of rest. *I am well and truly lost*, she thought to herself, *surely no one will be able to find me here. It can't do any harm if I rest for a while.*

She hadn't seen or heard any sign of animals, so she felt no fear of being attacked while she slept. Concluding that she needed sleep, she looked around for a small clearing that would allow her to lie flat.

And looked and looked and looked.

The changes had been so gradual that she had somehow failed to notice the forest becoming denser. The trees stood much closer together, and the undergrowth and bushes grew so thick, she couldn't find a single flat space large enough for her body. The moon had also set as she traveled, so that she could see no more than a few feet in any direction. She felt an irrational surge of fear.

Shaking it off, she pushed onward, hoping to make it to a clearer section of forest. But the further she went, the thicker it became until she needed to tread carefully with every step. Still she pushed doggedly on.

When she struggled past a particularly dense bush, only to be confronted by another even thicker one, she let out a grunt of frustration. But there was no good stopping in the middle of a bush. She simply had to push on.

As she wrestled her way free of the second bush, she was jerked backward. Turning, she saw that her cloak had caught on a long thorn. Staring at it, she felt a shiver work its way down her body. She had never seen this sort of bush carry thorns before, and she was sure that the thorn had not been there earlier. Turning and glancing around her, she was sure she saw a branch move, shutting off a small opening between two trees.

Fighting down panic, she pushed forward at a faster pace.

Everywhere she turned, her path was blocked, and she began to wonder if she was hallucinating in her exhaustion. She had heard tales in her childhood of forests that had a will of their own, but she could not believe that such a thing was happening here. If she was being directed down a particular path, there must be some other hand at work.

And then, although no wind had picked up, she heard a peculiar whooshing sound around her. It seemed to swoop past her head, and she ducked, cradling her face in her arms. As the sound grew louder it began to come from all around her. She tried to convince herself it was just the sound of rustling leaves, but it sounded far more like whispers. Ghostly echoes that swirled around her and bounced back at her out of the shadows.

Panting for breath, she kept going, pretending she didn't see the thorns that now sprouted from every bush or the way the trees leaned menacingly toward her. At some point, she had dropped her satchel, but she didn't even give it a second thought, glad to be free of anything that hampered her flight.

"Stupid girl." She whirled around but couldn't see anyone through the gloom. Her heart had already been hammering at superhuman speed but, impossibly, it managed to pick up a notch. She stumbled and nearly fell over a fallen branch that lay twisted into a shape of agony. Her breathing hitched and broke as she found her footing again and then, completely panicked, she started to run.

She ran blindly, her arms out in front of her to ward off the branches and bushes that seemed to spring into her path. The voices followed her.

"Fool."

"Why do you even bother?"

"No one could ever truly love you."

"Don't you know?"

"You're already dead. Dead. Dead. Dead. Dead."

The last one seemed to echo in her mind until she felt it

surrounding her, clawing at her. Pulling at her clothes and climbing in through her nose and eyes and ears and mouth.

At last she couldn't take it anymore and poured all her energy into a final, desperate scream. It was a broken sound, and she wasn't sure if it was a cry for help or a final surrender to the darkness and the voices.

She began to fall but was consumed by blackness before she touched the ground.

PART II
ASYLUM

THE GUARD

When Hans was fifteen years old, his life fell apart. In the years that followed, he often thought about the suddenness with which everything unraveled.

By fifteen, he had already earned a reputation among the guards. The captain had taken him under his wing, and there were rumors he was being groomed to fill the role when the older man retired.

Hans' father was a groom and his mother a general servant so his rapid advancement was a great honor for the family. With Hans' younger sister starting to make a name for herself in the palace kitchens, his father often boasted that he had the two best children in the kingdom.

And then it all came crashing down.

Everyone knew the queen was dying, had been dying for years. And everyone agreed that the king was a harsh man; court was a cold place without his wife's influence. But the king was also intelligent, and Rangmere's economy still prospered.

Some of the older folk muttered that the kingdom wasn't as safe as it used to be and predicted a dire future for a kingdom so lacking in love. The most cautious folk moved away, resettling in Arcadia or Northhelm or even the more southern Lanover.

But most people stayed, and if they kept their sons and daughters a little closer to home they figured it was worth it to avoid the disruption of uprooting. Hans' aunt and uncle had been among those who chose to leave, establishing themselves in Northhelm, but his parents hadn't even considered joining them. Not when Hans and Hanna were doing so well.

And then one day Hanna had come home in tears. She was leaving that night, she had announced. The princess had arranged passage for her with a merchant caravan leaving for Northhelm. All chance of an apprenticeship to the pastry chef was gone, and if she didn't leave that night she would be subjected to a public flogging the next morning.

In growing outrage, Hans had listened to her story and realized that the king was responsible for this crime against his sweet sister. His sister who had never done anything but support the royal family.

His first thought had been to accompany her, but his parents had vetoed this suggestion.

"You are committed to the guard," they had reminded him. "If you leave now, they will consider you to have abandoned your post. They would pursue you both. Hanna's best hope of escape is without you."

He had been forced to acknowledge the wisdom of their words.

"We will pack up our belongings and follow you with the next merchant caravan," his parents had promised Hanna.

And so, with one fell swoop, King Josef had deprived Hans of his entire family.

Of course, Hans was rather inclined to place some of the blame on Princess Ava's shoulders. After all, it was the princess who had led Hanna into the prank she was being punished for. But Hanna had pleaded with him not to blame her friend.

"You don't understand," she said. "She's grieving for her mother, and her horrible father hounds her to death. I'm scared for her. I don't know how she'll cope without me. I saw it today when her father threatened me: she shut herself off, and she's going to lose herself entirely. I won't be the cause of that. You can't let her father win!"

"What am *I* supposed to do?" the young Hans had asked, resenting this suggestion that he extend his protective instinct to cover the princess.

"Guard her, of course!" Hanna had said. "Keep her safe!"

Reluctantly Hans had agreed. And with all his family gone and his loyalty toward the king in tatters, he found himself glad of a cause.

It was only two months later that the princess was attacked. The attackers had been hired by the king to test her personal guard. Princess Ava was unharmed, but only because the attack had been a test. Her guard had failed, and King Josef had responded by executing the man.

The Royal Guard had been in an uproar with none of the senior guardsmen willing to take over the position. Some even began to mutter about taking their families and joining the general exodus. Hans, however, had seen his opportunity and stepped forward. It was both a significant promotion and a significant risk, but he had more than proved himself capable. The captain of the guard, reluctant though he was to lose his protégé, could do nothing but agree to the request.

That had been five years ago, and many things had changed since then. Only one had not. Hans would do whatever it took to protect Princess Ava.

His first thoughts of the day were usually about her location and security, but when he awoke in the early hours of the morning after their kiss, he was assaulted by a bewildering array of emotions.

He had been reliving their embrace in his dreams, and he

could still feel and taste her as he became aware of the world around him. But the joy of the dream was immediately soured by a certainty that something was wrong. All the anguish of loss and shame from the night before rushed over him. He had been weak enough to give in to his feelings, and it made the burden of his hopeless love harder to bear. For a moment, he thought it was this harsh reality that he sensed. But seconds later he was sitting up, staring around wildly, his heart pumping with fear.

The moonlight illuminated an empty clearing. Ava was gone.

Her bedroll remained, and there was no sign of a struggle, nothing to indicate she had been dragged from it unwillingly. He leaped out of his own bed but forced himself to wait, listening carefully in case she had merely stepped out of the clearing to relieve herself.

He could hear no sound of movement in the surrounding forest, and he was able to force himself to wait and listen for only a minute before he launched into action. With great rapidity, he considered and rejected several impossible explanations for her disappearance. The fear he felt at losing her was greater than any he had felt before. The only exception had been several moments during the height of the battle between the merchants and the guards when he had been unable to locate her. But on that occasion, it had been two minutes at most before he heard her calling for him. And already he could feel his panic escalating beyond the fear of that occasion.

A close examination of the clearing revealed their supplies had been tampered with. Kneeling beside the saddlebags, Hans quickly identified what was gone. Given what had been taken, there was little doubt that Ava had packed a bag and taken off into the forest.

Hans was immediately swamped with guilt. The situation was his fault. He had allowed himself to be overcome and had acted recklessly, and now Princess Ava had fled from him. If anything happened to her, he would be doubly responsible.

Hans had no illusions about the girl he loved. He was aware of the way she had locked her emotions away. He had admired the strength that allowed her to do it even while he cursed her father for making it necessary. He had watched over her for years, even before his feelings had transformed into something stronger. No one knew Ava better than he did.

As a commoner toward his princess, his actions had been treasonable; as a guard toward his charge they had been unprofessional and irresponsible. But worst of all, his actions had recklessly endangered the emotional wall with which she protected herself. And he had done it at a time when they were both vulnerable and unable to afford any distractions.

He had to find her and find her quickly.

It wasn't hard for Hans to locate Ava's trail. She had headed into the deeper forest, and with regret, Hans was forced to unhobble Dusty and leave the horse to fend for himself. He could only hope the animal would be waiting for them when they returned.

Their supplies he left in a small hollow on the edge of the clearing, covering the bags with several branches. He took only the remaining water skin since he needed to move as fast as possible. Bending almost double, he confirmed the direction of Ava's tracks and set out after her.

He was able to pursue her swiftly, and he felt confident he was gaining ground until he lost the trail in a shallow creek. He wasted valuable time picking it up again, hampered as he was by the waning moonlight. The whole time he tortured himself with thoughts of the many disasters that could befall her, alone in the forest. Two knives seemed little defense against the dangers conjured up by his imagination.

Thankfully, the trail became easier to follow after the creek since the undergrowth thickened considerably. Signs of her progress were everywhere, and he could even smell the sharp aroma of leaves crushed by her passage.

At last he heard a grunt emerging from the bushes ahead of him. It was a frustrated sound, but it was sweet in his ears. He had caught up to her at last.

But as he attempted to push forward even faster, he found his way blocked. He stared in astonishment at the branches and plants visibly lengthening in front of him. Before he could do more than marvel at the strange sight, he heard the sound of struggling and then of pounding feet. His relief gave way to fear, and he pulled out his sword, hacking desperately at the foliage.

It was slow going and his muscles burned, aching to move freely and swiftly. But gradually he made progress, and he was hopeful that he was nearly through when he stopped, pierced by the sound of a desperate scream.

His blood, which had seemed to freeze, now began to boil, and he hacked madly at the greenery in front of him. During his momentary pause, it had grown thicker, and it now resembled a hedge, covered in long, unnatural thorns.

The desperate tension growing in his core was almost unbearable, and his sword moved with frantic speed. One particularly wild lunge opened a small gap in the leaves, and through it he saw Ava, sprawled on the ground, her skirts fanned out around her. She was completely still, and he told himself that she was merely sleeping. If he could just get through the forest of thorns, he would awaken her.

But the more he struggled to reach her, the thicker the hedge became until, at last, he fell to his knees and bowed his head in despair. He could do nothing. She would continue to lie there, asleep or dead, protected by a hedge of thorns. Felled, he couldn't help but feel, by a single kiss.

CHAPTER 13

*I*t took Ava a long moment to process the light around
her. And a longer moment to remember the darkness
that had come before it. She struggled to recall the fear and
despair. Had it been real or just a dream? It seemed hard to
believe that such darkness could exist when she was surrounded
by such a blaze of light.

She covered her eyes for a moment and gave them a chance to
adjust, slowly lowering her hand when she was ready to start
absorbing the vista around her.

The forest was gone; she could see no sign of the dark trees
and tangled branches in any direction. The golden light from the
sun was warm, and she threw off her cloak, the better to feel its
rays.

She was lying in the middle of a green, verdant valley, and the
grass beneath her was thick and luxurious. A small stream
gurgled beside her and, before standing up, she leaned over to
scoop some water into her mouth. It was cool and clean and
easily the most refreshing water she had ever drunk.

Standing, Ava gazed around in every direction, the view
confirming her suspicions. This was a magical place. Every shade

of green was in evidence, and the plants glowed and reflected the light as if they were made of jewels. A myriad of bright flowers punctuated the grassy expanse before her, and the vibrant colors were so intense they would normally have made her eyes hurt. Yet she felt no discomfort. In fact, she had never felt so comfortable in her life.

She shivered. She had a strong suspicion that she knew where she was, and it wouldn't do to be lulled into a false sense of complacency. This wasn't a place where people like her were welcome.

Abandoning her cloak—it was impossible to imagine being cold in such a place—she ascended the gentle slope before her. When she reached the top, she found a deep valley and, shining in the center of it, a palace.

It wasn't just any palace though. It was far bigger and far more beautiful than any she had ever imagined. The soaring towers looked impossibly fragile and incredibly graceful. If any part of her had doubted her location, all uncertainty was now removed. The palace reflected the golden rays of light so that they bounced in every direction, as if the entire building were carved from a single, giant diamond.

Somehow, she had found her way to the Palace of Light.

Ever since the meeting with her godmother, Ava had been practicing the speech she would deliver to the so-called High King. The one in which she demanded he recognize her rights and restore her to her position as Princess of Rangmere.

Standing in his enchanted realm and seeing his shining palace, her remaining certainty drained away. This High King had every bit of the power the godmother had credited to him. It was no longer a surprise to her that the godmothers wielded so much influence in the Four Kingdoms. Her own country would rise or fall on the smallest part of the power that sustained this place. And her own position of princess suddenly seemed a lot less authoritative.

Still, she had no other option than to press on.

When she reached the great door of the palace, three times her own height and glowing with an iridescent sheen that reminded her of a pearl, she hesitated again. Finally, taking her courage in her hands, she knocked firmly on the great expanse.

The noise reverberated loudly throughout the valley, and the door began to slowly open. She took several involuntary steps backward, distancing herself from whatever was about to appear.

When both sides of the entry had opened, she saw a figure standing before her. He was tall and emitted a faint radiance, but it was his face that drew her attention. His expression was stern, and she had never seen anyone with such natural authority. Any lingering doubt regarding the legitimacy of this High King fled, and she found herself kneeling as her father's subjects did when they came to pay homage to him.

She felt deathly afraid. The memory of the darkness that had led to this bright place returned with a rush. She could hear again the voices echoing around her. She had come to challenge the right of this man to judge her. Instead she found herself agreeing with the godmother's assessment. She had been born with all the advantages of a princess, but she had not been deserving. The thought left a bitter taste in her mouth, and she wished she had simply accepted her godmother's words rather than seeking out a higher authority.

The darkness that festered in both her kingdom and her heart were thrown into stark relief by the brightness of this palace and its ruler. She wondered what words she could say to extricate herself from the situation alive.

Before she could speak, she was addressed.

"Rise, Princess Ava," said the High King. His voice was both musical and strong, and something inside her resonated at the sound of it. Like his face, it seemed at once both old and young.

Looking up, she saw that an incredible transformation had occurred. The terrifyingly stern expression was gone, and instead she found herself looking at a face so warm, so open, and so friendly that she felt instantly as if she had known the High King for years. Her grudging, irresistible deference immediately turned into a warm and steadfast loyalty. Smiling joyfully, she rose to her feet and accepted the royal kiss of greeting he placed on her cheek.

The coldly analytical part of her brain marveled at the power of this man.

Here was someone truly deserving of her allegiance. His power was indisputable, and the godmothers clearly wielded only the smallest part of it. Any ruler who aligned themselves under him was sure to prosper.

Even while she was marveling, speechless, at the turn her emotions had taken, the High King tucked her hand into his arm and led her into his palace. Everywhere she walked was some new marvel of grace and beauty, but she was unable to properly take it in. She felt as if she were walking arm in arm with the sun. It was hard to look away from his brightness.

As they walked, they passed several godmothers going about their mysterious business. They seemed utterly at home in the palace, and none of them even glanced at Ava, although each bowed to the man beside her. She didn't see her own godmother and was rather glad of it.

After traversing a seemingly endless number of corridors and passing at least six godmothers, they came out into a large internal courtyard. The courtyard was overrun with the same vibrant growth as the slopes of the valley, but she could see several large benches and even a simple fountain. Open walkways surrounded the courtyard on every side and blended seamlessly with the corridors of the palace.

They sat on one of the benches, and for several minutes a companionable silence reigned. Ava watched the occasional godmother pass by along one of the walkways, and slowly her earlier unease returned. Surely, any minute now, the High King would remember that he had deemed her *undeserving*. He would remember all the people she had wronged, and he would cast her out of his beautiful domain. She wondered, for the first time in hours, if Sarah and Evelyn had survived the merchant battle, and she felt sick to her stomach.

Unable to bear the suspense of waiting, she opened her mouth and spoke first.

"My godmother said you rule over the Four Kingdoms and the land beyond, yet I have never heard my father speak of you. Do the other kingdoms offer you their allegiance?"

"The royal family of Arcadia serves me, certainly," he said, "although they have never seen me. My servants aid them as needed." Ava's eyes flashed to a godmother who was drifting down the hall past the garden.

"And Northhelm...well, there is a darkness there that lies in wait. The time will soon come when those of power in Northhelm will have to choose their side." He paused. "But I did not bring you here to talk of Northhelm."

"No," she said, her voice heavy with the same dread that filled her insides. "You came to talk to me of Rangmere."

"I have something to tell you that will bring you pain." He seemed genuinely saddened by his words. "But truth is an anchor that should never be discarded. It's about your father's death."

"What is it?" she asked, more sharply than she had intended.

"It was your brother."

"Excuse me?"

"Your brother is the one who assassinated your father and sent Joran to murder you."

Ava stood abruptly and then, just as abruptly, sat back down. She felt as if all the breath had been knocked out of her. She had always known her brother was cold and cruel, but somehow it was still unimaginable that he could kill his own father.

"But...but my uncle!" she said, bewildered.

"Your father's fear of your uncle was never more than his own paranoia. Your uncle sailed away from The Four Kingdoms long before you were born, and he has never looked back."

"I still don't understand," said Ava. "Why would Konrad do it?"

"Power," said the High King. "He could not wait to be king."

Ava shook her head in silent rejection of the idea, but even as she did so, she was already accepting it. In fact, the more she thought on it, the less surprising it seemed.

"Why have you brought me here, and why are you telling me this?" she asked.

"Your brother is leading your kingdom into darkness. Already he is planning reprisals against those who were loyal to your father. Your people will suffer unless someone rescues them. You asked for your rightful place back. I am giving you the knowledge you need to fight for it."

"I can't do it," said Ava. The confidence that had disappeared in the forest had not returned, and she trembled at the thought of facing her brother.

"You are divided," said the High King, simply. "Your father did his best to shape you after his own image. He created a predator. A wolf, if you will. And ever since then, the creature that he formed has been masquerading as a princess and attempting to devour the rest of you. The real you."

Ava's eyes widened, and she wondered if he could somehow see into her dreams.

"But a part of you has been fighting," he said, "because the wolf hasn't yet succeeded. You can still emerge from this whole."

"But how?" Ava struggled to believe his words of hope.

"You must reject the wolf," said the High King as if it was the simplest thing in the world. "Reject what your father turned you into, and pledge your allegiance to me instead. I will help you reclaim your true self."

"Just like that?"

"It won't be easy," he cautioned. "You've locked yourself away behind a wall, and if I break it down you will have to deal with the emotions that are released." He paused, assessing her with his eyes. "It will be worth it, though."

Ava stared down at the ground and tried to remember what the 'real' Ava looked like. She remembered a child who used to slide in her stockings up and down the royal ballroom, shrieking with laughter and tumbling into her mother's arms. She remembered sneaking down to the kitchen for pastries and games of make believe with her best friend, a kitchen maid. But all of that was so long ago. She wasn't a child anymore.

She shifted restlessly.

And then she remembered what it felt like to be Anna. To lie in the grass and stare at the clouds, to whirl around and around and around to the sound of pan pipes, and to laugh with Hans and Sarah and Evelyn at some shared joke. Wasn't Anna just another facet of herself in the end?

"I am strong," she said, taking a deep breath and looking into the High King's ageless eyes. "I will do it."

"Even you are not strong enough for this, princess. But I do not abandon any of my subjects. I will give you the strength you need. And I will bring others to help you also. Do you pledge your allegiance to me?"

"I do," she said, and for just a moment she felt incredibly light and unbelievably happy.

And then the storm hit.

For the second time that day, Ava felt herself falling into blackness. Only this time, there was no welcome oblivion. Instead she descended into a maelstrom of fear and anger and grief, of guilt and rage and inadequacy.

Once again, she inhabited her fourteen-year-old body and stood at the front of the throne room, gazing down at her mother's still face, framed by the cold stone coffin. At the time, she had been tearless and impassive, her emotions safely locked away. Now, however, she found herself sobbing in great, messy gulps that shook her frame so badly they hurt. Her grandmother should have been there, but she had disappeared the night before. Her allies, the only two people who had truly loved her, were gone, and she wasn't sure she could survive the loss.

Suddenly the tears were gone, although the grief still burned hot, and she found herself sitting at a diplomatic table, her eyes cast down and her curls pinned perfectly in place. Her brother was speaking, his voice friendly and jovial but his words barbed darts designed to pierce her. Her face remained calm, however, a demure smile firmly in place and no flush of humiliation on her cheeks. She was the beautiful princess, the perfect diplomat, the cold statue.

While she sat there, unmoving, her brother drew a dagger from his belt and, circling the table, he began to stab their father. His movements were cold and brutal although Ava knew that it hadn't happened like that in real life. The horror of it, however, was all too authentic.

Leaping to her feet, her face burning, she heaved the table toward her brother. Striding over to him, she screamed wordless fury as she hit him again and again and again. When this scene also faded she carried the blazing anger into the next one.

Now she faced her father. She was young again, and the look of disappointment on his face was clear. He didn't even bother to lecture her at her repeated failure. Instead he merely turned away in disgust. She felt herself shrivel and fall to the ground, drowning in her own inadequacy.

Before she had a chance to recover from her father's rejection, she found herself whirled through a series of scenes that went by so fast she barely recognized them. And yet, there she was: sending away her only friend after that friend had taken responsibility for Ava's mistake; turning her back on the family of Rangmeros artisans who had begged that she intercede with her father on their behalf; ordering Joran to weaken Arcadia in any way possible in preparation for annexation; locking the Arcadian Princess Companion away and plotting how she could be used to control the Arcadian prince; tying her own cloak on her trusting friend and thrusting the girl out into the middle of a battle to take the fall in Ava's place. Each act seemed more despicable than the last, and the guilt and shame were overwhelming.

"I'm sorry!" she called to each scene, but it was over before anyone could register her words.

The new emotions built on the previous ones until she was drowning in overwhelming pain. Crying out for help, she reached out her hands blindly. She felt each of them clasped in a firm grip. From one side, she felt the already familiar glow of the High King. And from the other she felt a comforting, well-known strength.

Holding to these anchors, she rode the wave of emotion and allowed herself gradually to float to the top. She emerged into another vision. She felt like herself, but when she looked down her arms were covered in thick fur and her hands were claws. Despite the High King's promise of rescue, she was inside the wolf. Looking up in horror, she saw that he was standing across from her looking at once infinitely sad and boundlessly gentle.

Reaching out, he gripped a handful of fur and pulled. She expected to feel pain, but instead she felt only a soft tugging. Slowly, the pelt of the wolf peeled away as if it was a layer of skin she could simply shed.

Looking over in gratitude she saw that it was the High King's face that was transfigured with pain. She opened her mouth to cry out in protest, but it was over. With a great tearing sound, the last of the wolf pulled free, and the High King discarded the empty shell of the animal, his face free of suffering and suffused with victory. She was free.

Examining every part of her body that she could see, Ava realized her hair had been returned to its normal golden curls. She looked questioningly at the High King.

"The time for disguise is past," he said. "If you are to claim your birthright, you must do it as yourself. I have set you free of the wolf inside you, but you must still deal with the consequences of your actions. You will find the help you need in Arcadie."

She sucked in a horrified breath, unable to believe that he would send her to her greatest enemies.

"But, the Arcadian royal family hate me. And they have good reason to."

"Then you must go to them and ask their forgiveness," said the High King calmly. "You must help them see the justice of your cause."

"I don't know if I can do it," she said, wishing she could have back the certainty and strength that had come with her old coldness.

"You will not be alone," he said and, over his words, Ava heard the sound of another voice. It was desperate and anguished, and it was calling her name over and over.

She realized that her eyes were closed, and when she opened them she saw the face of Hans, leaning over her as she lay on the ground.

CHAPTER 14

The first thing Ava registered was the relief on Hans' face. The second was that she was back in the forest. Except there was moonlight again, and the undergrowth seemed to have subsided to a normal density.

"You're alive!" There was lingering concern in Hans' voice. "What happened to you? The forest was acting strangely—I couldn't get through." Ava could still hear an echo of his urgency, and the sound triggered her guilt. It had been foolish and selfish to run away and cause him so much trouble. Instinctively she began to suppress the emotion, and then she remembered. The wall was gone. For good or bad, she would have to face her emotions from now on. She waited a moment and was pleased when the guilt didn't overwhelm her.

"I'm sorry," she said, and now it was Hans who looked startled. She gave a wry chuckle. "That might be the first time I've ever said that to you. But a lot has changed. Help me up, and I'll tell you all about it."

Gently Hans placed an arm behind her back and helped her into a sitting position. As soon as she was stable, he dropped his arm as if she was hot. Rocking back, he squatted beside her and continued to rake her up and down with his eyes, as if he didn't quite believe she was safe and was waiting for a wound to spring into existence.

"I'm fine, truly," she said. "Please sit back, you're making me nervous."

Reluctantly he settled himself onto the ground, resting his back against a tree trunk, one leg stretched out in front of him. The other, he kept bent, poised to spring into action. She decided it was the best she could hope for.

Drawing a deep breath, she launched into her story.

"I don't know quite how it happened, but I went to the Palace of Light."

Hans' eyes sharpened, but she ignored him and continued.

"I saw the High King, and he told me something." She hesitated briefly but then pushed on. "It was Konrad."

Hans tilted his head in a silent question.

"The assassin, it was Konrad. He killed our father, and he sent Joran to kill me."

"That worm," said Hans in an angry growl. "I've never trusted him—not with the way he treats you—but I'll admit I never suspected him of something like this."

"No, no one did," Ava agreed. "That's why it was such a brilliant plan. He has all the sympathy of a grieving son and brother and the perfect excuse to tighten control over the kingdom. Apparently, he got sick of waiting around for our father to die."

"It's despicable!" Hans actually looked a little sick, and Ava couldn't disagree with him.

"We can't let him get away with it."

Hans started to nod his agreement and then paused, his eyes narrowing.

"And what exactly does that mean, Princess?" he asked. "Because if you think I'm letting you get anywhere near your brother now..."

"Hans." Ava cut him off with a stern look. "You can't stop me doing the right thing."

He raised his eyebrows at her, and she flushed with embarrassment.

"I told you a lot has changed," she said and proceeded to fill him in on what had passed between her and the High King.

"I wish you could have seen the palace," she said at the end. "It was beautiful."

"I have seen it," he said, and she jerked her head toward him.

"It is definitely a wondrous and enchanted place. I, too, traveled there and spoke with the High King, but I saw no sign of you."

"And I saw no sign of you," said Ava in amazement. "Clearly it is not a place one can reach by any normal means of travel. I understand now why my godmother laughed at me when I claimed I would find it."

"Yes," agreed Hans. "The High King told me that the Palace of Light can only be reached through your deepest fears."

Ava considered this for a silent moment and then looked at Hans quizzically.

"And what personal demon did you have to brave, Hans?" she asked.

He looked away, gazing into the forest for so long that she thought he was refusing to answer.

"There was a wall of thorns," he said, finally. "And you were lying behind it. Dead or asleep, I couldn't tell which. I hacked at the branches with all my might, but it made no difference. Eventually I ran out of strength and despaired. And then, miraculously, the branches parted before me. But you and the forest were gone, and instead I found myself on a grassy hillside beside a magnificent, shining palace." His voice trailed off as he relived the incredible memory.

"After I had spoken with the High King, he told me that you had need of me, and I found myself back here, kneeling beside you. You thrashed and screamed, but I couldn't wake you. I feared you truly had fallen into an enchanted sleep, but then you went still. And when I called to you, you woke up."

Ava gazed at him, a slight flush warming her cheeks. No matter which way she turned, there he was, steadfast in his devotion. In her darkest moment, he had knelt beside her, and she had felt the clasp of his hand. Now that her emotions were freed, she no longer felt afraid of the idea of love nor did the reaction he evoked in her confuse her the way it had before. But she was still unsure what her emotions meant, and she was still afraid of losing his love and, therefore, his loyalty.

At some point, she knew she would have to tell him the truth about how she had treated Hanna, and she knew when that day came, she would lose him. That thought had lost none of its sting.

I can't tell him now, she thought, *we have a nearly impossible task to accomplish, and I need his help. It's not for me, it's for the people of Rangmere.*

And perhaps, her mind added, *I can use the time to work out exactly what it is I feel for him.*

~

It took a great deal more conversation, including invoking the High King's authority several times, before Ava convinced Hans that they had to head for Arcadie. He was still grumbling about it when they found their way back to the clearing where they had left their supplies.

They saw no sign of her discarded satchel during their return journey, so she was glad she had so few of their provisions. Thankfully, she had woken in the forest wearing the cloak she had abandoned by the enchanted stream. She was grateful to the High King for considering this detail. It would have been too much to hope that Hans had a second spare cloak for her in his saddlebags.

Amazingly, Dusty was still there, calmly grazing as if they had been gone for mere minutes. The look he gave them when they reappeared seemed to say, 'Oh good, there you are. Are you ready to stop fooling around and get on with things?' Ava felt a rush of affection for the horse and a pang of sadness at the loss of Cinnamon. She reached out and gave him a hug. Dusty responded by huffing into her hair and then returning to the patch of grass he had already partially devoured.

When Ava turned back to Hans, he was watching her with sympathy.

"Whatever they may think about us, Your Highness," he said, "the merchants will treat Cinnamon well."

She nodded, grateful for his sympathy and that he refrained from commenting on all these new displays of emotion. She was still adjusting to the changes in herself, and her emotions felt fresh and raw.

Thankfully she had plenty of time to find an emotional equilibrium in the two weeks it took them to reach Arcadia's capital city. Hans still had the gold and jewels she had brought with her from Rangmeros. In her hurry to flee she had forgotten to pack them in the satchel, and they purchased a second horse and a side saddle from the first town they encountered. It had been slow going until then, but they were able to pick up the pace considerably once they were both mounted.

They didn't push themselves, however. Although neither said it out loud, it was obvious they both felt apprehensive about the possibility of catching Caravan Hargrove before it reached the city. They were certain the caravan would have made it across the border and equally certain that they would be greeted with anger and hostility if they ever met again. Ava's hair and eyes had returned to their natural coloring, but Hans looked the same as he always had, and Ava suspected many in the caravan would recognize her even with the changes.

But there was one familiar face that Ava wanted to see. As they journeyed through Arcadia, she couldn't stop herself from closely examining every white-haired lady they encountered. If her grandmother had fled, Ava believed she would have hidden herself in the Arcadian forest. She had always rather liked Arcadia, and she loved the forest.

Now that Ava had been transformed, she longed to see her grandmother again: to have the opportunity to tell her she was sorry, and that she'd changed. But there was no sign of Ava's missing family member.

It was a full fifteen days after they emerged from the forest before they saw the distant walls of the capital. Ava had been projecting a confident front for Hans' sake, but she felt a shiver of unease when she saw the city come in to view. An even deeper shiver rocked her when they actually passed through the great gates. Glancing back over her shoulder, she wondered if she would ever be given the opportunity to return through those portals. It was quite possible the Arcadians would simply throw her in the dungeon without hearing anything she had to say.

Or worse, her mind whispered, *they might wash their hands of the whole affair and turn you over to your brother.*

Before her fear could build, she felt a steadying hand on her elbow. Looking over, she saw that Hans had pulled Dusty in close beside her and was squeezing her arm reassuringly. *I will protect you,* his eyes seemed to say, and she felt grateful for his support.

The sight of him also reminded her of the past. She couldn't have counted the number of times she had felt his silent presence behind her as he stood guard during some diplomatic meeting.

You can do this, she reminded herself. *You've been trained for exactly this sort of situation.* She knew her brother would never have attempted to kill her unless he saw her as a threat. It was a strangely reassuring thought.

They rode up the broad Palace Way, passing crowded row houses that gradually grew into more and more spacious homes as they traveled through the Merchant's Circle and into the Noble's Circle. They were making directly for the palace, and Ava felt even more of her confidence return the closer they got. The gracious estates of the Noble's Circle felt familiar—among royalty and nobility she was on home turf.

When they reached the main gate in the palace wall, they were stopped by a guard who asked them to state their business in a bored tone. Ava's first instinct was deception. Her mouth opened to tell him she was Anna, a merchant's daughter, but before she could speak, she remembered the High King's words.

The time for disguise has passed. She knew in that instant that whether she succeeded or failed, she would do so as herself. No disguises.

"I am Princess Ava of Rangmere," she announced and felt herself grow taller and stronger as she said the words. "This is my personal guard, Hans. We have come to claim political asylum."

The guard seemed dumbfounded at her words. He had stiffened at her name, so he was obviously aware of at least some of what had passed in Arcadie the year before.

"I seek an audience with King Henry and Queen Eleanor," she said when he didn't speak. "Call for your captain if you must."

He greeted her last suggestion with relief and, looking across the courtyard beyond the gate, he signaled several other guards to join him. Leaving three men to watch over them, he disappeared toward the guardhouse.

When he returned, he was accompanied by a tall, commanding man whom Ava remembered as Markus, the captain of the palace guard. She had marked him out as one of the first targets during her intended coup, and the memory made her uncomfortable. It took all of her training to keep her face and manner impassive.

"I am Princess Ava of Rangmere," she repeated, but the captain cut her off.

"I know who you are." His voice and eyes were cold. "What I don't know is what you're doing here, unannounced and without an escort. It seems unusual behavior for a princess."

Officially she had visited Arcadia last summer to discuss a marriage alliance and had departed on amicable terms when the union had fallen through. Of course, both Ava and Markus knew that she had come with much less friendly intent and had only been narrowly thwarted. Unfortunately for Markus, Ava was still a princess, so despite their history, he would be hesitant to overtly threaten her. All he had were barbed words, and they were something she had long since learned to ignore.

"My guard and I have narrowly escaped Rangmere with our lives. We have come seeking political asylum." Her eyes challenged him to contradict her. "I wish to place my claim in person with their majesties."

The request was within her rights as a royal, but she couldn't think of a single instance in the last two generations when such a thing had been required. Markus regarded her for a long moment with narrowed eyes, and then jerked his head in agreement.

"Of course, Your Highness," he said. "I apologize for the delay. I will *personally* escort you." Ava didn't miss the emphasis or the intended warning. She nodded gracious agreement and signaled to Hans to help her dismount. Once a groom had run forward to take their horses, she allowed the captain to lead them toward the palace.

Markus signaled an entire squad of guards to form up behind them, although they stayed far enough back to be out of earshot. Hans seemed tense, and she knew he was weighing the odds of getting her out safely if things turned ugly. Ava herself felt unbothered by their presence. If anything, she felt amused and rather flattered that Markus considered the two of them to be such a threat. She hoped that this meant progress, emotionally speaking, and not that she was falling back into her old ways.

CHAPTER 15

*M*arkus led them to a small reception room and ushered them inside while the guards were instructed to wait in the corridor. The space was designed to host royal meetings that were too small to warrant the throne room, and it was decorated in an elegant and slightly intimidating way, all white marble and gold. It featured an extremely large and obviously new portrait directly across from the door. Prince Maximilian and his bride made a beautiful couple and the feature piece was imposing, but Ava's father had long ago trained her not to respond to such subtle manipulations.

Casting a quick glance around the room, she was confronted by the sight of the actual prince and princess. She had been expecting to see the king and queen, and the sight of Max and Alyssa was such a shock that she took an involuntary step backward. The vivid memory of the last time she had seen them overcame her. It had been one of the few occasions when her calm control had given way to an embarrassing display of emotion, and it made the bitterness of humiliation even more potent.

It had been Hans who had rescued her then, just as it was he who stepped forward now and placed a reassuring hand on the small of her back. The touch reminded her that she was a different person now. She was no longer her father's puppet, and she was determined to make the rulers of Arcadia realize that.

"I'm sorry," she said, finding her voice. "I was expecting to see King Henry and Queen Eleanor."

"Their majesties are away on a tour of the kingdom," said Markus, speaking up from behind her. "Their highnesses have regency in their absence." He sounded a little smug, and Ava was savagely sure that he had meant her to be shocked by their presence. She straightened her spine.

"Yes, we have been given complete authority in all matters such as these," said Max and, while his tone was level, his eyes were blazing at her from across the room. "And you'd better give me one good reason why I shouldn't have you arrested right now!"

"Max," said Alyssa, her voice a gentle reproof. "Ava has requested asylum, and the laws on such matters are clear. We must give her full opportunity to make her claim." She placed her hand on her husband's arm, and slowly his clenched fist relaxed.

He shot her a look that was both affectionate and amused.

Ava couldn't help but feel a grudging swell of respect. When they had met the summer before, Alyssa had been merely the daughter of a woodcutter, although she had the role of Princess Companion to Max's younger sisters. She would never have addressed a foreign princess by her first name. Although she was speaking to the prince, Ava recognized the subtle power play in her choice of words. She was asserting her authority and reminding Ava that, unlike in the past, they were now on even footing.

Not even, Ava thought wryly. Alyssa's gentle words and gracious manner only emphasized that she was the one in the position of power. Apparently, Prince Maximilian was inclined to ignore international conventions in his anger at her past behavior. Ava's safety depended on Alyssa's forgiving attitude and respect for the law. This knowledge burned a little, but Ava tried to tamp the sour feelings down.

She truly had changed when she had chosen to give her allegiance to the High King, and she wanted to be different. But looking at Alyssa, so beautiful and so confident in both her new role and new husband, Ava felt off balance. The other girl sparked a storm of emotion in her, and it took her some time to register the strongest feeling. But when she did she was surprised.

Respect. While Ava would never be the sweet, fun girl that Alyssa was, there were other ways she could learn from her. Ava wanted to be someone who could use political savvy within the confines of the law. Someone who could be at peace with herself. And as she watched Max gaze down at Alyssa, his eyes shining with love, she acknowledged to herself that she wanted love. To love and be loved. She was sick of being alone, she wanted to have friends and family again, true family.

It was a lot to take in, and Ava was aware that she was standing rather stupidly in front of the other royals. Max had turned his loving eyes away from his wife and their expression had turned cold and hard. She swallowed and tried to think of something to say.

"Alyssa is right, of course," he said, breaking the silence. "We shall do all that the law demands of us." The import of his words was clear. They would do no more.

He sat down on one of the hard lounges arranged around the room and gestured for the others to be seated also. Markus and Hans took up posts on either side of the closed door, each eyeing the other warily.

Ava felt a burst of amusement at the sight. It was so similar to what she herself had been doing with the other royals not moments before. The momentary lightness was a welcome release of tension, and she felt her hard-won equilibrium return. She could do this. She had to be able to do this.

"I'm afraid I have to report a grievous crime, Your Highnesses," she said, falling back on the formality that had been missing from their exchange so far. "My father has been assassinated, and an attempt was made on my own life."

"We had heard these tidings although it was reported to us that you had also been killed," said Max. He cast a quick glance down at Alyssa as he spoke, and Ava could read in his eyes that he hadn't been sorry at the news.

"You're right," said Ava, "you had every reason to rejoice at my death."

Max looked up at her, slight embarrassment in his eyes at being so easily read.

"No!" said Alyssa. "We would never rejoice over death, whatever wrong you have done us."

"I acknowledge that I wronged you," Ava said, relieved that at least one of her audience was willing to receive her with some softness. She paused, her eyes flitting to Markus, and Max broke the solemnity of the moment with a laugh.

"And I acknowledge that I felt no sorrow at the news of your demise," he said. "But I confess, now that my surprise and anger have subsided somewhat, I'm incredibly curious to know how it is that you're alive. And why you would come here of all places. So, let's call a momentary truce. I promise not to call down the guards on you, at least not until you've had your say. And I'll try to lower my hackles, too." He gave her the charming grin for which he was famous. "And, in return, you can stop with all the games and tell us what you're here to say."

Alyssa threw him an approving look and nodded her head in agreement.

"Thank you," said Ava and realized that her gratitude was sincere. "It's a long story, and I appreciate the chance to tell it fully. You see, to understand what has happened in Rangmere in the last few weeks, I will have to give you some account of what it has been like in our kingdom for the last twenty years."

As concisely as possible she filled them in on the cold, power-hungry approach of King Josef and the long, lingering death of the queen. She told them of the differing personalities of her brother and herself and the ways in which their father bent them to his will.

The more she talked, the more Alyssa leaned forward, captivated by her account of the royal dynamics of Rangmere. But when she got to the night of the assassinations and her brother's role in them, the other girl sat back, her eyes wide with horror and disgust.

Quickly Ava skimmed over the rest of the story, of fleeing with Hans and joining Caravan Hargrove and of their narrow escape across the border.

"My brother was attempting to prevent my escape," finished Ava. "We took advantage of the confusion to flee and made our way here alone."

"Ah," said Alyssa, as if Ava's words cleared up a matter of some confusion for her. "Ariana. That explains a lot."

"Does it?" asked Ava, warily.

"The caravan arrived in Arcadie several days ago. They had moved quickly from the border and had a strange tale to tell. Although Ariana spoke of a girl with brown hair and brown eyes…?"

"You've spoken with Ariana?" asked Ava. She knew Ariana was a senior leader among the traveling merchants, but they were usually unaffiliated with the royalty of the kingdoms they traveled through. She hadn't expected the Arcadian royals to have such a firsthand account of the events at the border. She wondered uneasily if she should have disclosed her own role more fully. The memory of the fight brought back the old, sick feeling in her gut.

"Ariana and I are old friends," explained Alyssa. "In fact, she was the one I traveled with when I left my home to come to Arcadie."

"Not that you traveled with her for long," joked Max, lightly elbowing his wife.

She laughed. "No, that's true."

Looking across at Ava, she elaborated. "I went out for a walk one evening and got lost. When a storm came up, I sought shelter at the Winter Castle. The rest, of course, is history." She was smiling, and her words triggered a memory in Ava.

"Oh! Ariana mentioned that she had only ever had one person suffer a mishap in her caravan. I didn't realize she was talking about you." It was strange to think of that conversation, only a few short weeks ago, and how much had changed since then. Knowing the other woman spoke of Alyssa would have enraged Ava at the time.

"She was glad to hear good news of me and to know her record remained unblemished. We've maintained contact ever since, and she often brings bits and pieces of news to the palace. Nothing of this import before, however." Alyssa's expression turned serious. "We have been discussing what to make of it ever since her report. It is a serious business, indeed."

"The official word from Prince Konrad is that it was a rogue squad of guards who were overly zealous in their search for the missing assassin," said Max. "He has issued a formal apology to the merchants, and they have called for a council of caravans to discuss their reply."

Ava raised her brows. It had been years since there had been a formal council of caravans. They were taking the incident extremely seriously.

"The council is to be on the border of Arcadia and Northhelm but Caravan Hargrove won't be leaving until tomorrow," said Alyssa. "I'll send a messenger to let Ariana know that you're safe."

Alyssa's bright eyes weighed Ava for her reaction, and she resigned herself to a confrontation with the merchant. Clearly Ariana had given Alyssa a detailed report, and there was nothing to be gained by protesting.

"You must tell me," continued Alyssa, "how you managed to change your appearance so thoroughly. It seems like the kind of skill that might come in handy."

She was looking at Ava with curiosity, but Ava wondered at the feelings the other girl must be suppressing. If she was friends with Ariana, then she had more recent offenses to count against Ava than the events of last summer.

"I'm afraid it's not something I could repeat. It was my godmother."

"Your godmother?" Max's eyebrows rose up his forehead.

Swallowing her immediate feeling of offense, Ava nodded. "I know that I'm not what most people would call deserving, but the High King decided to give me a chance."

"The High King?" Max looked confused for a moment, and then his brow smoothed. "Ah yes, our mysterious overlord and the commander of the godmothers. So, he's involved in all of this, is he?"

Ava couldn't help but admire his calm acceptance of a higher authority and wonder how different her life might have been if her own family had been able to feel the same way instead of constantly craving more power.

"I suppose you could say he's central to everything," she said, somewhat hesitantly. Glancing at Hans, she received an infinitesimal nod of support and launched into the second, and more incredible, part of her story.

When she got to her own painful transformation and rescue, she slowed. It was uncomfortable to bare herself so completely to these people who were at once both strangers and old enemies. She kept that part of the tale as brief as possible while still conveying the reality of her changes.

"And so, I'm here," she said, at the end, "to ask for your forgiveness and your assistance."

There was a long silence while Max and Alyssa looked at each other. Markus cleared his throat quietly and adjusted his weight where he stood by the door. He had been so silent and still that Ava had almost forgotten he was there. She was sure the movement now was no accident and, looking into his cold eyes, she was sure his vote would still be for the dungeon.

After a long, silent communion between the other two royals, Max stood.

"By your own admission, you have been an enemy of Arcadia," he said, and Ava braced herself for his next words. "But what you've told us today has the ring of truth. I don't believe that even you would be so foolish as to falsely claim that you have the support of the High King. And how can we go against his wishes when he provided my mother with such an excellent magic pea?"

He grinned down at his wife.

"And more importantly," said Alyssa, rolling her eyes and pulling him back down to sit beside her, "it seems there is someone out there more dangerous than you. We may find ourselves with a common enemy, and if it doesn't make us friends, it at least makes us allies."

Ava fought off a shiver at the mention of her brother. She was more relieved to have allies against him than she was to have escaped the dungeons. For the first time, she wondered if perhaps she truly had a chance of saving Rangmere, after all.

"Thank you. It is more mercy than I expected."

"There is one thing, however," said Alyssa, and Ava's heart sank. "We can speak only for Arcadia, but it is not only Arcadia that you have wronged. If Ariana wishes to take you to the council of caravans to face their justice, we cannot stop her."

CHAPTER 16

"*B*ut don't worry overmuch," said Alyssa, when she saw Ava's expression. "Ariana is wise, and we'll speak to her on your behalf. She may dislike you, but she has an even greater reason to dislike your brother. I'm confident she'll see that you're our best chance of checking his ambitions." She turned toward the door. "Markus, send one of the guards to request Ariana's presence at the palace as soon as possible."

Markus looked like he wanted to argue, but Max shot him a loaded look, and the man gave a small bow and left the room. Ava wondered if his biggest issue was Alyssa's promise of support or leaving the royals alone in a room with Ava and Hans.

"Thank you again," she said to Alyssa. After a moment, she decided she couldn't resist continuing. "I have no desire to change your mind, but I can't help asking, why are you so ready to forgive me?"

Alyssa looked at her thoughtfully. "I find it hard to trust you, certainly. But being a ruler means putting aside your personal feelings and considering what's best for your kingdom. Rangmere is large and powerful, and I have no wish to see a monster like your brother poised at our border. You have chosen to reject the path of your father. A little late, it's true, but you got there." She smiled cheekily at Ava before sobering again. "Your brother, however, has only pursued cruelty and power. Yours is not the first account we have had of him, and I admit that it has made me nervous to know that he will soon be king in Rangmere."

"Everything you say is true, of course." Ava wondered why she couldn't just let the matter be. "But it's more than that. You just don't seem very..." She paused, searching for the right word. "Angry, I guess."

Alyssa laughed. "Believe me, I was plenty angry when you locked me in your closet. And when you came within a hair's breadth of marrying Max." She threw a fond glance at her husband who was watching her with an amused smile on his face. "But truthfully, I can't help but feel that you unwittingly brought us together. It's hard to hold on to the anger when everything worked out so well, and I'm so happy." She shrugged. "So, consider yourself forgiven and, as far as the trusting business goes, you're on probation. If you attempt to betray us, well, I'll just have to find a way to defeat you again." She laughed as she said it, and Ava felt sure that Alyssa would manage to do it, too.

For the first time, Ava felt no pang of humiliation or anger at the thought of her failure and of the triumph of the girl before her. She felt instead a strange relief at having escaped the path her father had set. Involuntarily her eyes flew to Hans, and she wished she could read what was going on behind his impassive face.

Following her gaze, Alyssa smiled conspiratorially and lowered her voice. "Who knows, maybe you'll get your happily ever after at the end of all this as well." She waggled her eyebrows at Ava suggestively. "I always did think he was a remarkably handsome captain of the guard."

"Alyssa!" said Max and Alyssa laughed again.

"Second to you, of course," she assured him with a pat on the knee. He laughed as well and tweaked one of her loose waves of hair, but Ava noticed he then put a possessive arm around her shoulders. With difficulty, she restrained herself from looking at Hans.

~

Before the moment could get too awkward, the door to the room was violently flung open, and two small blue blurs rushed into the room. The one in front came to a sudden stop, and the one behind crashed into her.

"Lily!" complained the one who had been behind, rubbing her nose where it had collided with her twin's back. Lily ignored her.

"Alyssa! Max! Why are there so many guards outside the door?" Her words came to a halt when she finally noticed Ava. Her sister—Sophie, if Ava recalled correctly—let out a startled gasp.

"What are you doing here?" asked Lily.

"Lily!" said Alyssa reprovingly.

"What?" asked Lily. "I don't have to be polite to *her*. She locked you in a cupboard!"

"She is a princess, though," Sophie chipped in doubtfully. "So, we're probably still supposed to be diplomatic."

Lily turned reproachful eyes on her sister but subsided. The two girls went to stand next to their brother and directed two identical, cold gazes toward Ava.

"Princess Ava is here seeking political asylum," said Max repressively. The look he directed toward his sisters was the kind of superior look that big brothers were supposed to give their kid sisters. And it was nothing like the looks Konrad had always given Ava. She felt a little sad watching this family interaction.

"Why don't we adjourn this conversation to lunch?" asked Alyssa before the twins could object to Max's lofty manner. "It's well past regular lunch time and I, for one, am starving."

This suggestion found great favor with all three of her family members, so she was able to corral them all out of the room and down the corridor. Hans fell into close step behind Ava, and the squad of Arcadian guards fell into place behind him. Clearly Markus had left them instructions to remain with the Rangmerans.

Once they were all seated at a lavish lunch, Ava looked around the table and shook her head in wonder. It was hard to believe that she was back here, having an amicable meal with this particular group of people. When her gaze passed Hans, standing as always at attention, she realized with a jolt that he also hadn't eaten since their early breakfast.

"Your Highness," she said tentatively, and all four of her table companions looked up. She couldn't help but laugh.

"Sorry, I should have been more specific. Prince Maximilian, since this is an informal meal, would it be possible for the captain of my guard to join us?" She gestured toward Hans. "We have been on the road since early this morning, and neither of us has had a chance to eat."

"Oh, of course, no problem," said Max easily, gesturing for Hans to join them.

He didn't move.

Ava raised a questioning eyebrow at him, but his own expression remained impassive.

"I don't think it would be appropriate, Your Highnesses," he said when the others also turned questioning faces toward him.

"Don't be silly," said Alyssa, briskly. "When I arrived at the Winter Castle, I was nothing more than a woodcutter's daughter, and the royal family gladly welcomed me to their table."

Since there was nothing Hans could possibly say to this, he dipped his head in begrudging acceptance and took a seat across from Ava. She smiled at him encouragingly, but he refused to meet her eyes while he quickly and unobtrusively filled his plate.

While the Arcadians chattered between themselves, Ava tuned them out and focused on her bodyguard. He ate with the same quiet grace that characterized all his movements and, if it wasn't for his clothing, he would have looked at home among the table of royals.

Just as she was thinking this, he looked up and caught her gaze with his piercing gray eyes. She barely stifled a gasp. His expression remained stony, but his eyes burned with passion and longing. She understood instantly what had triggered his emotions.

Even she had been swayed by this casual meal, by the promise held out by the couple sitting at the table with them. The possibility of royalty and commoners finding true love together had never seemed so real as it did in that moment.

If she, unsure of her feelings toward him, had felt it, how much more must this tantalizing glimpse of love fulfilled be taunting him? She had set herself the task of determining what, exactly, it was that she felt for Hans, and for a brief, heady moment she felt sure her feelings could easily turn to love. Surely it would be possible now that she was free from her emotional blocks. She had certainly never wanted love as much as she did now.

But in another second, reality came crashing back down. Hans was a strength she relied on. And his love for her was still built on a lie. She remained determined to wait until after they had faced Konrad to tell him the truth. It was selfish, perhaps, but she needed him. She also understood, however, that the longer she concealed what she had done, the worse his reaction would be.

He was a truly good person, and it wouldn't be right to toy with him now. To hold out the hope that she might love him back, all the while knowing that she would soon be crushing all his dreams of her.

And feelings aside, Rangmere was a different kingdom from Arcadia. They expected their rulers to be strong. It would be hard enough convincing them she was a worthy successor to her brother without appearing like a love-struck princess mooning after her guard.

She would need allies, and that would be far more easily achieved if she remained single. Noble families with nothing to gain under Konrad would be more likely to support her if they thought there was a chance she would choose one of their sons to be her king. Even foreign alliances were a possibility. Both Northhelm and Lanover had princes around her own age.

No, she didn't have the luxury of allowing herself to feel anything but determination.

The thoughts had passed through her mind in the space of only a few moments, but something of her conclusion must have shown in her face because the fire was extinguished from Hans' eyes. She saw the briefest glimpse of anguish hidden behind stoic acceptance before he returned his gaze to his plate and continued eating.

She felt as if the breath had been knocked out of her, and it took a full minute to regain her calm and pick up her own fork. Before she could take a bite, however, her attention was recalled to the conversation at the table.

"What do you think, Ava?" asked Alyssa.

"I'm sorry, what?" asked Ava, thrown off balance and scrambling to recall what they had been discussing.

"We're wondering how you're planning to take your kingdom back from your brother," supplied Sophie helpfully.

"What?" asked Ava again, feeling even more bewildered. Had she seriously missed that particular topic of conversation? And was she really supposed to have this discussion with a child?

Her eyes swung wildly toward Alyssa, and the other girl grinned at her discomfort.

"The twins turned twelve since you were last here," she said. "They need to study their trade just like any other apprentice, and this is an excellent learning opportunity."

Ava looked around the table at five pairs of expectant eyes.

Even Hans had looked up at the question, his emotions safely tucked away again.

"I...I don't know," she said at last. "I hadn't really thought that far ahead."

"That's understandable." Max chortled. "You probably thought we were going to throw you in the dungeon. I have to admit, it was rather brave of you to show up here. I'm afraid the same plan isn't going to work in Rangmere though. From the sound of things, your brother will do worse than send you to the dungeon." His voice had turned dark, and his words offered an overwhelming reminder of the suicidal nature of her quest to defeat Konrad.

"I don't suppose you're planning to lend me an army," she said glumly.

"No, I'm afraid not," he said. "In fact, I don't see how Arcadia can overtly support you at all. We've taken enough risk already by receiving your request for asylum. We're still getting back on our feet after a rough few years, and we can't afford a war with Rangmere."

Ava nodded. It would have been her own response if she'd been in his place. But the stress of the day seemed to have drained all creative thought from her brain. She couldn't think of a single suggestion to make. Before she could come up with some words to break the heavy silence, Alyssa broke it for her.

"The library!"

Now it was Alyssa's turn to have five pairs of curious eyes trained on her.

"We'll find an answer in the library, I'm sure we will."

"Great." Lily rolled her eyes. "More books."

"You'd be surprised how many things you can learn from a book," said Alyssa, but Lily just sighed.

"I really don't think I would be," she muttered. "I think you might have ruined that surprise."

Ava couldn't help smiling in sympathy with Lily. She had

forgotten how much time Alyssa had spent hidden away in the library on her last visit. Ava would have had as little patience for it at twelve as the twins seemed to have.

"In fact," said Alyssa, briskly, "we should get started right away. The faster we find a solution, the faster we can get you safely on your way back to Rangmere."

With that she got up and sped out of the room, leaving Ava blinking at the closing door.

"Safer for us, she means," said Max wryly, casting a fond glance after his wife. "You two seem to have finished, so you should go with her." The last comment was directed at the twins.

"Do we have to?" Lily groaned.

"Yes, you do," Max said firmly, and both girls got slowly out of their chairs with lots of scraping, banging and sighing.

"I'll go and consult with some of my advisors," Max said when the girls had disappeared. "One of them may have a suggestion on how to handle the situation."

"Don't worry," he added when Hans threw him a piercing look. "I'll keep the circle of information small. I'd rather as little of this as possible gets back to your brother."

Ava could see from his eyes that despite his many light-hearted contributions to the conversation, he was wearing his responsibilities heavily. She felt doubly glad that he had decided to accept her request for asylum.

"I'll have a guard show you to some guest rooms," he said. "You might as well get some rest until Ariana comes."

His words shocked Ava. She had completely forgotten that she was still in danger of being arrested and dragged before the council. *Great,* she thought, *there goes any chance of rest.*

CHAPTER 17

*A*s it turned out, Ava was only left to pace her luxurious guest suite for an hour before a footman appeared to inform her that she had visitors. Hans had refused to rest, instead standing guard outside her door, so the servant led them both down the wide corridor.

Ava was almost trembling with fearful anticipation by the time he stopped at the same receiving room where she had confronted Max and Alyssa. She wasn't sure if she was more afraid for her own fate or for the news she was about to receive about the welfare of her two friends. Nothing had tormented her since leaving the merchant caravan like the look on Sarah's face when Ava had thrust her out to confront the Rangmeran guards.

In this second area at least, her suspense was short lived. When the footman announced her and she entered the room, her eyes scanned the occupants, and she almost collapsed with the relief of seeing both Sarah and Evelyn, present and unharmed. The feeling quickly gave way to shame and embarrassment, however. She hadn't expected to have to confront the two people she had most wronged.

Evelyn was looking at her with the cold anger Ava expected. Sarah, however, was staring at her in wide-eyed astonishment. Ava quickly latched her eyes onto Ariana who looked more intrigued than angry. The caravan leader was flanked by her second-in-command, a man Ava had never actually met.

"Well," said Ariana slowly, once the door had closed behind Ava and Hans. "I can't say I expected to see you two again. You're looking a bit different now, of course, but I can see why you looked so familiar when you joined the caravan."

So, it *had* been Ava herself that Ariana had been thinking of when she had looked at 'Anna'. It was strange standing in front of the woman now and wondering which history to bring up first— her history with Anna or with Princess Ava.

"Thank you," she found herself saying, her mouth making the decision for her. "Hans tells me that you delivered Hanna safely to Northhelm. You never came back to the palace after that, so I never had the chance to thank you."

"Hanna?" asked Hans, stepping forward from his usual position by the door. "That was you?"

Ariana seemed a little bemused at the direction the conversation had taken, but she nodded in response to Hans' question.

"It was a pleasure to travel with her, she's a quick-witted and kindly girl. I still stop by to see her when I find myself in the vicinity of the Northgate palace kitchens. And she always has a tasty treat to reward me for my effort," she added with a reminiscent smile.

"But what is she to you?" she asked Hans curiously, and then realization brightened her face. "Never tell me you're that Hans!"

"I am," said Hans with a smile. "And my family cannot thank you enough for what you did for my sister."

"Your sister?" asked Sarah. "I remember Hanna, we were great friends." She smiled at the memory before her shoulders slumped. "For a few weeks anyway, as always happens." Ava could imagine how lonely the life of a traveling merchant must be, always moving on to new people and places. It made Sarah's readiness to welcome a new friend that much more admirable, and Ava's own betrayal of the friendship that much more unforgivable.

"So, you're a princess now?" Evelyn's harsh voice suggested that she found Ava just as culpable as Ava herself did. "And one we all thought was dead."

"It certainly explains a few things that were opaque before," said Ariana, directing a quelling look at the guardswoman. "Princess Alyssa's message only said that she had found our missing travel companions. But there are a few more questions I'd like cleared up."

Evelyn looked mutinous, but Ariana held her gaze with steely strength.

"There's more going on here than just your concerns, Evelyn," the older woman said. "I'll get the answers I need for council before we consider justice for our caravan. But don't worry, I wouldn't have brought you along if I didn't mean for you to have your chance."

Ava felt both glad and sorry for the reprieve. She could feel Evelyn's glare like a weight, but she hoped that the other girl might be softened by Ava's story and apology. She desperately wanted to make things right with both of her old friends.

Telling her story was easier the second time. The words, and the apologies, came more naturally than they had previously. When she recounted the state of affairs in Rangmere for most of her childhood and youth, Ariana nodded her agreement.

"True enough," she said. "It's the reason you didn't see hide nor hair of me after I took Hanna in. I didn't like the direction things were taking in Rangmere and figured there was plenty of gold to be made in the other kingdoms for a while. Some of the other merchants convinced me to go back, but given how the trip turned out, I would have been better off listening to my instincts."

Sarah, who seemed to have recovered from the shock of discovering that her friend was a golden-haired princess, listened with rapt attention. Her exclamation of disgust when Ava revealed her brother's role in the assassinations was the loudest, and her expression seemed to be moving toward pity. When Ava reached the fight at the border, however, her face tightened again.

"I'm so sorry, Sarah," said Ava, directing her comments at the other girl. "I know there's no excuse for it really. I should never have endangered you like that, and I've been tormenting myself with it ever since. The truth is that when I was your friend, I was only acting a part. When I behaved with cold strategy to save myself—regardless of the cost to you—that was the real me. The person my father trained me to be. But it's not the person I want to be, and it's not the person I am now. I've truly changed. And if you're willing to listen, I'll tell you how."

She held her breath waiting for the response. Ariana remained quiet also, seeming to think this decision was Sarah's alone. The merchant girl sat for nearly a minute, assessing Ava with her eyes. While she waited, Ava fought to keep her eyes on Sarah. She was acutely conscious that she had glossed over this part of the story when she had told it to the Arcadian royals, so Hans had never actually heard what she'd done to Sarah during the attack. She felt almost as nervous about his response as she did about Sarah's.

"I appreciate your honesty," Sarah said at last. "I would like to hear the rest of your story."

Evelyn gave a small sound of disgust, but Ava breathed a sigh of relief. Risking a quick glance at Hans, she saw that he was giving Evelyn a cold stare. She could only assume from this behavior that he remained on her side. A small part of her dared to hope that he would have the same non-reaction to hearing about what she had done to his sister. She didn't believe it, though.

As she told the rest of her tale, she kept waiting for someone to exclaim in disbelief. No one did, however. When she reached the end and cautiously expressed her astonishment, Ariana just shrugged.

"We traveling merchants have long allied ourselves with the godmothers. We often serve the High King in our travels. If he's the one who says your brother is guilty, then I don't doubt it. He's uncannily aware of everything that goes on in his domain. And, somehow, I'm not surprised he thinks you might be the one to fix things. You always did have a fire in you; I saw it when you were a child. I figured maybe your father had snuffed it out, but I'm happy to be proved wrong. I'll take your tidings to the traveling merchants, and they'll be sure to enforce a merchant's ban on Rangmere now."

Ava was glad for the news. It was another tool in her arsenal and would be likely to sway a few more of the Rangmeran nobles to her side. A merchant's ban was a serious business and would cripple Rangmere's economy.

"Don't tell me you're all going to forgive her, just like that!" Evelyn crossed her arms and challenged the other merchants with her stare. "Sarah could have been killed!"

"Princess Ava's behavior toward Sarah was certainly inexcusable," Ariana said calmly. "But she has apologized for it, and it is for Sarah alone to determine how she wishes to respond. As far as the caravan is concerned, I am convinced that Her Highness had no idea that she was endangering us when she joined our ranks. Her disguise was unfortunate but understandable in the circumstances."

Evelyn turned her angry gaze on Sarah, silently communicating her preference for revenge and justice over forgiveness.

Sarah looked back at her cousin, but her face was already twisting apologetically.

"I'm sorry, Eve. I know you're only being defensive on my behalf, but I'm tired of being angry." She swung back around to face Ava. "And I've never had a princess for a friend before." Her voice had returned to its usual levels of enthusiasm.

Ava found herself grinning back.

"It's been a long time since I've had any friends at all. But I'd be glad to have one now." She held out her hand and shook Sarah's with mock solemnity.

"Hello. My name is Ava, and I'm the Princess of Rangmere, it's very nice to meet you."

"Hello, Ava." Sarah tilted her head inquisitively, waiting to see if she would get a response to dropping the princess' title. When no one protested, she continued. "It's nice to meet you, too. You look remarkably similar to an old friend of mine. Her name was Anna, so I hope you don't mind if I sometimes slip up and call you by her name."

Ava was relieved to see the mischief back in Sarah's face. Before she could get too elated, however, she caught Evelyn's eye and remembered that only one of the girls had forgiven her.

"So, what's your plan?" asked Ariana, extinguishing any lingering cheer from Ava.

"I don't know," she admitted. "I haven't got that far yet."

Before she could elaborate, the door of the room swung open and a tall, slim man walked in. He looked a little surprised to see them all and halted on the threshold.

"Oh, hello," he said mildly. "I got a note asking me to come here…" He trailed off in confusion when everyone looked back at him blankly. "I'm certain it said the south reception room," he muttered to himself, consulting a balled-up piece of paper in his hand.

While he was still talking to himself, another figure strolled up to the doorway and gave him a gentle shove into the room.

With the doorway clear, Ava could see that it was Max who was following him into the room.

"So, you've been summoned, too, have you Aldric?" asked Max, cheerfully, clapping the other man on the shoulder. "And no sign of my lovely wife, I see. Typical!" He grinned around at them all.

"Oh, you got a note, too, did you, Your Highness?" asked Aldric, appearing relieved to see a familiar face. "I wasn't expecting to see so many people."

"Well, we all know Alyssa doesn't do things by halves." Max disclaimed responsibility with an easy shrug. "I'm sure she'll be along with an explanation any minute. This is Ariana from Caravan Hargrove and," he squinted at the other merchants, "her retinue."

"Oh, I see," said Aldric politely as if this made the matter perfectly clear. "The princess I recognize, of course." He gave a polite bow in Ava's direction. "And the estimable Hans."

Ava was impressed. Lots of people at the palace would have seen and remembered her from her previous visit, but it was unusual for someone to remember the name of her guard. And she didn't recognize the man at all. She nodded at him politely and bent an inquiring eye on Max.

"Oh, sorry," he said. "Everyone, this is Aldric. He's a diplomatic attaché to the Northhelmian ambassador."

Before Ariana could introduce the other merchants, the door, which had been closed behind the prince by a footman, was thrust open in a violent manner. Alyssa rushed into the room with Lily and Sophie hard on her heels. All three appeared to have been running through the palace corridors. Ava couldn't imagine doing such a thing in Rangmere and wondered if Arcadian princesses had always behaved so informally or if it was the woodcutter influence.

"I found it!" Alyssa collapsed onto a lounge. Looking around, she smiled. "Oh good, you're all here. I told the messengers they had to hurry, but I still thought I might beat you."

"That was quick," said Max, admiringly.

"It's the fastest I've ever found something," said Alyssa with a glow of pride. "I'm definitely starting to get the hang of where everything is in the library."

"She went right to it," said Sophie. Both twins were grinning with excitement, and Ava couldn't help but wonder how much of their good cheer was due to the unexpectedly early reprieve from the library.

A quiet throat clearing drew Alyssa's attention to Aldric.

"I hope you don't mind my asking, Your Highness, but what exactly is it that you were looking for?"

"A way for Princess Ava to defeat her brother."

Aldric blinked several times in quick succession and turned to look at Ava.

"I have to admit, the matter isn't entirely clear to me, yet," he said. "In fact, I'm still recovering from the news that her highness is not, in fact, dead."

"Sorry, Aldric," said Alyssa. "The rest of us have heard the story already." She proceeded to give him a lightning quick rundown of Ava's tale.

For a moment, Ava felt herself stiffen. Then she forced herself to relax. She hadn't said anything about keeping her story a secret and, as much as it went against the grain, she had to trust Alyssa, Max, and the merchants to use their own judgment when sharing it.

"Hmmm," said Aldric at the end of the account. "That is indeed an unacceptable situation. My king and queen will not be happy to hear that their neighbor is being ruled by both a regicide and a patricide. It sets an unhealthy sort of precedent." He gave a wry grin.

"Not that they have any concerns," he hastened to add in

response to Max's amused eyebrow raise. "They have excellent relationships with both of their children."

"Exactly!" said Alyssa, a little obscurely.

"So, what is it you've found?" asked Max, and Ava was thankful to have her own burning curiosity voiced.

"The Monarchy Trials!" said Alyssa triumphantly, and she waved a book at them all.

Ava deflated instantly. "That's no help. The Monarchy Trials are only for princes, and I only have one brother."

"Ah," said Alyssa, "that's where you're wrong."

"I have another brother?" asked Ava incredulously.

"What? No!" Alyssa gave a small head shake. "It's tradition that says only princes compete in the Monarchy Trials. There's nothing in the law to forbid a princess from entering. And," she said, on a flourish, "I found a precedent." She looked around eagerly, waiting for their answering enthusiasm.

Aldric and Ariana looked intrigued, Evelyn pleased and Hans horrified. Ava was carefully keeping her face blank, but inside she felt the same shock she saw plastered across Sarah's face. Only Max actually responded.

"Well done," he said. "That's the perfect solution."

"Is it?" Ava cleared her throat self-consciously when the words came out a little squeakier than she had intended. "You know that people die in the Monarchy Trials, right? Some women may be able to compete against the men physically," she nodded respectfully toward Evelyn, "but I don't think I'm one of them."

"Except not all the trials are physical," pointed out Alyssa. "And 412 years ago, one of your distant relatives, a Princess Clotilde, competed in the Trials. She found an ancient law that allowed a competitor to make use of champions. The law she used has never been repealed, and it states that the royal competitor need only personally complete a minimum of two out of the five trials. And you don't even have to use the same champion for the other three."

"But if that's possible," said Ariana, "how come none of the princes ever use champions? Goodness knows some of them could use them."

"I think I can explain that," said Ava as she worked her mind around this new information. "Rangmere is a kingdom that values strength. If a prince used a champion, he would risk appearing weak. We're trained from birth never to show weakness; I don't think any prince would see it as an option. And that's assuming they even knew about it. I've certainly never heard of that law."

"It's ancient and obscure," Alyssa said, "but no less legal." She looked pleased with herself, and Ava was starting to feel a little impressed. Perhaps she should have spent more of her own youth reading, after all.

"Won't the same issue apply to you, Ava?" asked Sarah. "About appearing weak, I mean."

"I don't think so," said Ava. She flashed a smile at her friend. "One of the advantages of being a princess is that there aren't the same expectations about physical strength. It's one of the useful things my father taught me. How to take people's expectations and use them to my advantage. As a princess, I show my strength through will and cunning and intelligence. So, using champions may well demonstrate exactly the traits I need."

"This Princess Clotilde," said Hans, speaking for the first time. "Did she win?"

"Well, no," admitted Alyssa. "She was defeated by her younger brother and subsequently banished from Rangmere."

Ava felt her budding optimism die.

"Doesn't mean it can't be done though," said Ariana. "It's the chance to compete that matters, and if Alyssa's sure of her historical sources…"

"I am," said Alyssa.

"Then it seems to me that it just might be the best opportunity. It doesn't matter if Princess Clotilde won or not, as long as Princess Ava does."

Ava felt a little buoyed by the merchant's vote of affirmation. Her eyes met Hans', and he shook his head at her, his expression grim. She returned his look steadily, trying to convey her determination without words. Because in the end, it didn't really matter whether or not she could win. She had to try.

CHAPTER 18

*O*nce Ava had made up her mind, the rest of the group soon began to show more enthusiasm for the idea. Only Hans remained cold and aloof. Ava was glad of their support since there were still several issues to overcome.

"My brother has already shown that he wants me dead, and he's willing to use unscrupulous means to achieve that end," said Ava. "What's to stop him simply having me killed before I get the chance to register my claim to the throne?" It was a good point, confirmed by the number of nodding heads in the room.

Surprisingly it was Aldric who suggested a solution.

"I think Princess Alyssa must have had some sort of instinct for this problem and its obvious resolution," he said. "Otherwise she wouldn't have sent for me. The answer is quite simple, really. You need witnesses." He looked around the room and, when no one else chimed in, he continued.

"International witnesses, royal representatives who can stand with you and show Konrad that the Four Kingdoms are watching. He's still consolidating power and has already angered the traveling merchants. He won't risk Northhelm and Arcadia claiming he rules illegitimately. He will be angry, I'm sure, but from all reports, he will also be certain of his victory in the Trials. I would recommend not making any mention of champions until after you've registered, and he has accepted your claim."

"You are brilliant, Aldric," said Alyssa. "I knew we needed you here."

Aldric smiled modestly and declaimed any particular mental prowess. "It's all this time as an attaché. I'm actually starting to think like a diplomat."

"Aldric was originally a medical intern," Alyssa said for the others' benefit. "He was transferred to his current role as a diplomatic attaché at the end of last summer."

It seemed like a strange sort of transfer, and Ava suspected there was more to that story.

"It's a good idea," said Ariana. "And I'm willing to send a couple of men to stand with you. On behalf of the traveling merchants. I'd take the whole caravan along if it wasn't for the ban and the upcoming council. I can spare two men, though, and I'll send along formal papers confirming their position as official representatives, too. Only as witnesses, mind, I can't volunteer someone to risk their neck on your behalf."

"She won't be needing any champions." Hans crossed his arms, and Ava sighed.

She opened her mouth to tell him that she was determined to see this through, but he continued speaking. "I will be her champion, of course."

She looked at him in wonder. Knowing that he disapproved of the whole plan only increased her gratitude.

Ariana nodded her approval. "My Guardsmaster gave a very good account of you, Hans. Just make sure you don't get killed. I'd hate to have to take the news to Hanna."

Her words sobered Ava, and she wondered uneasily if she should forbid Hans from standing in for her. His family had already sacrificed enough for her sake.

"Well," continued Ariana, "now that's sorted out, I need to be going. The caravan will be leaving in the morning, and there are various preparations still waiting. I'll pick two trustworthy men and send them your way before we leave."

She and her second-in-command stood to leave, but Sarah remained in place.

"No," she said.

"Excuse me?" asked Ariana.

"I'm the one who's Ava's friend." Sarah looked up at the caravan leader fearlessly. "I want to go and bear witness."

"Sarah, no." Evelyn tried to pull her cousin to her feet, but Sarah resisted, her face taking on a mulish look that Ava recognized.

"I agree with Evelyn," said Ava. "It's too dangerous for you to come."

"I wouldn't be at any greater risk than you would be," Sarah said. "Less, in fact, since you have a target on your back whereas I would be going as a representative of the traveling merchants. With the ban under discussion by the council, I can't imagine your brother would risk hurting me."

Reluctantly Ava had to concede that Sarah made good points.

"If I want to come," Sarah said, "it's no one's decision but mine."

"Your parents might disagree with that statement." Ariana raised one eyebrow.

"I'm old enough to be considered an adult by merchant tradition," said Sarah.

"Well, if you're determined, I won't gainsay you," said Ariana after a moment's consideration. "You can even help me pick the other representative, if you like."

"There's no need." Evelyn shot a venomous look at Ava. "If Sarah goes, I go. I promised our mothers years ago that I'd keep her safe, and I'm not stopping now."

Sarah looked up at her cousin, her face a mix of gratitude and guilt.

"Thank you, Evelyn," she said, "you won't regret it."

"We'll see," said her cousin dourly.

With that decision made, it was a simple matter to confirm the final details. Ariana would provide each girl with a mount, and they and their horses would return to the palace when the caravan departed the next morning.

When the four merchants had left the room, it seemed empty.

"According to reports, Prince Konrad is beginning to talk of his coronation," said Aldric. "It appears he has lost patience with the search for the assassin." His words held a gentle irony. "He has begun talking of the need for stability."

Ava nodded. It was all too predictable.

"Given this circumstance, if the plan is to work, the princess must leave for Rangmere tomorrow and make as much haste as possible. She has to arrive in Rangmeros before the coronation. There will not be time for me to consult with my own monarchs. Given that, and since it was my idea, I think I should be the one to go as a representative of Northhelm."

"Are you sure, Aldric?" asked Alyssa.

"I am certain it is what they would wish me to do," he said. "I will consult with our ambassador here, but he won't raise any objections. He'll have a message sent off to Northhelm immediately, and we can request that an official endorsement of both the Trials and my position as observer be sent to the Northhelmian ambassador in Rangmeros. The relay-messengers should be able to get a message to Northhelm and then on to Rangmere in time for our arrival."

"In that case, I'll give Mathilde the option of going, too," said Alyssa.

"That's his wife," she added for Ava and Hans' benefit. "They were only married at the beginning of the winter, and I would hate to see them forced to separate so soon."

"If Mathilde does go," said Max, "she can carry a message to the Arcadian ambassador in Rangmeros instructing them to join the Northhelmian ambassador in supporting the Trials. And we can grant her international observer status or some such thing. The smaller the group, the faster you'll travel."

"That makes sense," Alyssa agreed. "We'll give her a temporary promotion to junior diplomat."

"I want to go," said Lily. "It sounds exciting."

"You are definitely not going." Max laughed at his sister's enthusiasm. "Can you imagine what Mother and Father would say when they got back? Absolutely out of the question."

Alyssa announced she was off to talk to Mathilde, and she and Aldric escaped the room. While the three siblings argued about the twins' participation in the quest, Ava signaled to Hans that she was also ready to go. They slipped quietly out of the room, leaving Max still attempting to talk his sisters down.

"I know you don't like it, but I have to do it," Ava said to Hans as they made their way back toward the guest quarters. Several guards trailed behind them, apparently still under instruction from Markus, but she spoke quietly so they wouldn't hear.

"It doesn't matter what I think, Your Highness," said Hans woodenly.

Ava sighed in exasperation.

"Don't be silly, Hans. You're much more than my guard these days. Think of yourself as Second-in-command and First Advisor all rolled into one. I value your input. But in this case, I know you're just trying to protect me."

"He'll kill you if he thinks he can get away with it."

"I know," said Ava. "Which is why we need to make sure he knows he can't get away with it. And then, of course, we have to win."

"We will," he said, surprising Ava. "You're stronger than Konrad in every way that truly matters, and I'm stronger than him physically."

His calm confidence impressed her and allowed her to voice her insecurities for the first time.

"I know I was strong before," she said. "But I'm not sure I can be strong enough now that my walls are gone."

Hans looked at her with so much understanding that she felt a little uncomfortable. She still wasn't used to being vulnerable and exposed.

"Emotions aren't weaknesses," he said. "If you let them, they can even be strengths. I know my own are."

He looked at her significantly, and she knew which emotions he was referring to.

Is it true? she wondered. *Is he better and stronger because he loves me?* It was something she wasn't sure she had the answer to, but she knew it was something she wanted to consider further.

"Thank you, Hans. I know there's no way I could even attempt this without you."

"It's my job, Your Highness," he said as they reached her room.

She paused and looked up to meet his eyes.

"And even if it wasn't, I would do anything to protect you." His words were low and earnest, and they made her shiver. She wasn't ready yet to deal with the intensity of his emotions, and she felt the old familiar guilt burning inside. She was supposed to be a new person, a better person, but she was still using him. Just like the old Ava would have done.

"I know, Hans," she said finally. "And that is why I'm thanking you." It was nowhere near enough, but she still couldn't bring herself to say more. Instead she turned and fled into her room.

here were eight of them who met in the courtyard of the palace early the next morning. Max and Alyssa had both come to see them off, but otherwise there were just the six travelers. Max had sent a missive requesting that Sarah and Evelyn be at the palace before first light.

"It's the twins," he said. "I want you packed up and gone before they're even awake. They talked of nothing but your quest at our meal last night, and I don't want them getting any ideas. They're devious those girls, and I wouldn't put it past them to find some means of stowing away."

His dire predictions amused Ava, especially since there was no possible way two twelve-year-old girls could stowaway with a group of six adults traveling on horseback. She appreciated the effort he was making to keep the tone of their farewell light. Every member of their traveling band was aware of the real reason for their early departure.

The fewer people who saw them leave the better. If Konrad thought Ava was in Arcadie, he wouldn't be looking for her on the road to Rangmeros. Once they were in the Rangmeran capital, her witnesses would serve as her protection. But if a band of travelers was attacked by brigands on the road, it could be chalked up to an unfortunate accident. They would have to travel both quickly and inconspicuously.

Mathilde turned out to be a friendly girl who instantly hit it off with Sarah. Within minutes they were trading outrageous stories of life as a traveling merchant and life as a palace servant.

"I'm not actually a servant anymore, though," said Mathilde. "Even before my recent temporary promotion." She grinned at Alyssa. "I'm an apprentice nurse."

"Oooh," said Sarah, with appropriate levels of appreciation. "You'll be a handy person to have around then. I can't stand the sight of blood, myself. I have to lie down or I risk going off in a faint."

"That's after she's thrown up, of course," said Evelyn, apparently finding pleasure in pointing out this less romantic aspect of her cousin's aversion. "Basically, she's completely useless, and I've got no idea why anyone is letting her come on this quest." Her scowl returned with her final words.

"Evelyn!" said Sarah in disgust.

"That's so mean," said Mathilde, indignant for her new friend of ten minutes. "Sarah seems like a useful sort of person to me."

Ava hoped that Evelyn would soften toward Sarah soon. She hated seeing the cousins bickering and knowing that it was her fault. She also wasn't sure if she could bear listening to so much inane chatter all the way to Rangmeros. As soon as she had the last thought, she retracted it. She had enjoyed the conversation of both Evelyn and Sarah when they had last traveled together, and she was determined not to let stress turn her back into a cold person without friends.

"Sarah is extremely useful," she said, attempting to live up to this resolution. "Just not when it comes to anything involving injury. For things like that, Evelyn is your girl."

"Aldric tells me you're a guardswoman," said Mathilde to the merchant. "However did that come about?"

Evelyn seemed pleased to have her strengths recognized and even bent a slightly less angry scowl on Ava, which the princess saw as positive progress. When Evelyn began relating her story of growing up in a merchant caravan and always gravitating toward the guards, Ava took the opportunity to join the other royals.

"I appreciate what you're doing for me more than I can say," she said to Max and Alyssa. "I promise that if I win the Trials, there will be nothing but friendly cooperation between Arcadia and Rangmere for the duration of my reign. And I will do everything in my power to ensure that your people return to you safe."

"You'd better," said Alyssa lightly. "Mathilde was my first friend when I arrived at the Winter Castle, and she still keeps me updated on all the servant gossip."

Alyssa's words reminded Ava of her own childhood friendship with Hanna, and her eyes moved involuntarily to Hans. He was holding the bridles of both of their horses and looking back at her with an expression that made her think he was pondering the same thing. Only he had no guilty knowledge eating him up. She looked away quickly.

After a quick round of general good byes, it was time to mount up. Hans gripped Ava lightly around the waist and threw her up into the saddle. He didn't maintain the contact a second longer than the action required, but Ava felt the phantom sensation of his touch lingering long after he had let her go.

Dawn still hadn't broken as they made their way down the cobblestones of Palace Way. A few people were up and about on early morning business, but the street was mostly empty. Ava was wearing a new cloak, supplied by the Arcadians, with the hood pulled up over her head, and she kept her eyes fixed on her horse's ears. When Sarah and Evelyn had arrived, they had brought with them a gift. Cinnamon.

Ava was ridiculously glad to be reunited with the horse, and she felt as if she had now had two old friends returned to her. She would just have to keep working away at Evelyn. One way or another she would earn back the other girl's good opinion.

As soon as they were out of the city, they broke into a gallop. They rode single file down one side of the wide road, leaving room for the small trickle of farmers who were already making their way toward the capital with goods for the various city markets. *How strange,* Ava thought, *only yesterday morning I felt so nervous to pass through those gates, and now I feel almost equally nervous to leave.*

She wondered briefly if the emotional freedom was worth the weight of nerves and anxiety that seemed to come with it. Then she remembered the feel of Hans' hands lifting her effortlessly into the saddle, and she decided that it was. Regardless of how impossible the two of them were together, she couldn't wish away the sense of excitement and possibility that she was starting to feel around him.

After a while they reined in their horses to a more moderate pace. They needed speed, but they also needed their mounts to last the distance.

They were a motley group, so Ava was pleased at how quickly they fell into a traveling routine. Ordinarily she would have been forced to admit that she was out of her element and of no use when it came to camping. However, she had been on the road for weeks now and had picked up a number of practical skills along the way.

Evelyn seemed determined to treat her as just another member of the group, and a despised one at that, but the others kept attempting to wait on her. Mathilde, in particular, seemed to find it hard to set aside her years of service.

"Enough, Mathilde," said Ava, at last. "When we arrive in Rangmeros we'll need all the pomp and ceremony we can muster. But for now, speed is paramount, and we can't afford to be carrying dead weight. I'll do my part."

Mathilde seemed to accept Ava's words, and Ava was pleased

to note that Evelyn seemed mildly impressed. None of her protestations were enough to move Hans, however. He insisted that the night watch duties be shared exclusively between him and Evelyn.

"It's not just a matter of staying awake," he said, "and, in the middle of the night, even that requires training. I won't risk having us taken by surprise because a sleepy, untrained civilian is 'keeping watch.'"

"But if we're attacked, we'll be relying on the two of you to keep us safe. And how will you do that if you're sleep deprived?"

It was a good point, and Hans had no argument for it. The matter remained at an impasse all through the first evening as they prepared food and set up camp. But then Hans and Aldric went to collect water from a nearby stream together, and when they returned, Hans announced that Aldric would also be a part of the watch rotation. With this compromise Ava had to be content.

It only raised her curiosity about the Northhelmian man, however, and left her more certain than ever that there was more to his story than she had yet heard. He certainly didn't look like someone who had ever been a guard, but Hans seemed convinced of his competency.

Traveling at speed, the group made it to the Rangmeran border in a week. It had taken Hans and Ava twice that time to cross the same distance on the way to Arcadie, but they had been moving slowly on purpose. The journey through Arcadia had been uneventful, but Ava once again found herself feeling nervous as they approached the border. In Rangmere they would be in much greater danger.

And, on top of that, the border itself brought back a host of unpleasant memories. She could almost hear the shouts and the ringing of blades, overlaid by the frightened whinny of the horses. She glanced quickly at the two merchant girls and saw that Sarah's face was unusually blank. Evelyn on the other hand, looked downright stormy. Ava was afraid that she had lost the small bit of ground she had made with Evelyn in the preceding week.

At the border crossing, Ava and Hans hung at the back of the group while Aldric and Mathilde took the lead. They chatted in a friendly way with the border guards on both sides while their royal papers were examined. The group was claiming to be a diplomatic convoy heading to Rangmeros for the upcoming coronation. Max and Alyssa had provided all the necessary documents, so they were passed through without a hitch.

As Aldric waved them across, Ava allowed Cinnamon to brush up against Dusty's side. Reaching out, she placed her hand on Hans' where he gripped the hilt of his sword. His eyes had been fixed on the Rangmeran border guards, but at her touch he started and glanced down at her. She gave him a reprimanding look, and he smiled at her, allowing his hand to relax and drift away from his sword.

With a start, Ava realized how long it had been since she had seen Hans smile with real amusement. Not since she had first proclaimed her determination to take on her brother. Her discovery of his humorous side was so recent that she hadn't noticed its loss at first.

Now that she had, however, she wasn't sure if she could bear it. How much more would she take away from her most loyal supporter?

She had been too internally focused to pinpoint the change in his demeanor during their journey to Arcadie. And in the last week she had been distracted by the good-humored chatter of Sarah and Mathilde. All she had noticed was a lingering darkness and heaviness that had been absent during their time with the merchants.

It now seemed obvious that the missing ingredient was Hans' smile and joking sallies. She immediately determined to do everything in her power to bring back his good humor.

Her first opportunity came that night as they sat around their small campfire in a clearing just off the road. Sarah was joking about life in a merchant caravan and was even managing to elicit small smiles from Evelyn who kept insisting it was nothing like as interesting as Sarah was painting it.

"Interesting or not, it definitely wasn't the life for me," Ava said, entering the conversation for the first time. "I made a truly terrible merchant!"

"You weren't that bad," said Sarah.

"Oh, come on." Ava grinned at her. "Surely you wondered why I was so clueless."

"Well..." Sarah smiled back at her, "I just figured you must have had the most indulgent father in the world. One who never made you lift a finger."

Ava laughed a little bitterly. "My father was anything but indulgent. On the other hand, it's true that I didn't have to do many everyday tasks. In fact..." She turned to Hans. "You should tell them about the time you found me by the stream."

"Are you sure?" asked Hans. She gave him a glare, and he held up his hands in mock surrender.

"If you insist." Already his wicked grin was starting to resurface.

Ava felt a surge of satisfaction.

Hans resettled himself against a log and put his arms behind his head in a relaxed storyteller pose. Everyone else was watching him curiously, and he remained silent, apparently enjoying the suspense he was creating.

"Get on with it!" Ava threw a pine cone at him.

He glanced at her with a mischievous twinkle.

"Whatever you command, Your Highness." He turned to the rest of the group. "I'm sure you've all washed many a dirty dish while traveling."

They all nodded. Even Aldric.

"Well, someone made the mistake of asking 'Anna' to wash the dishes one evening on our way to the border."

"Oooh, I remember that," said Sarah. "I wondered why you looked so reluctant, Anna. I mean Ava," she corrected herself quickly. "We were camped next to the perfect stream, so it was an easy job."

"It was the perfect stream," said Hans. "And when I came looking for her, she had found the perfect patch of sand…" He paused, and Ava knew that he was giving his listeners time to make the obvious assumption about sand and washing dishes. She reminded herself that she had volunteered for this mocking.

"…to stand on," he finished with a verbal flourish.

"What?" asked Mathilde. "She was standing on a sandy portion of the stream bank?"

"Yep," said Hans with satisfaction, and Ava actually felt her cheeks burn as the other members of the group smiled in her direction.

"She was perched on the sandy bank and was trying to clean the dishes by dipping them into the water," said Hans.

"Did she fall in?" asked Evelyn, and Ava got the distinct impression that a dunking would improve the story from the guardswoman's perspective.

"She would have, if I'd breathed in her direction." Hans grinned again. "And I came very close to doing it, too."

"Hans!" said Ava, horrified and unable to help herself.

"Sorry, sorry," said Hans, his laughing eyes belying his words. "It, of course, never occurred to me in any way to impinge on the dignity of Your Worshipfulness."

Ava threw another pine cone at him which he deftly caught before it could hit his chest.

"But the dishes all came back clean," said Sarah. "And I'm sure she never managed it with that method." She was taking as much delight in the story of her royal friend's incompetence as her cousin was. Although for kinder reasons.

"I, a highly trained guard, had to lower myself to wash them." Hans looked around for sympathy.

"It was kind of you to show her how," said Mathilde. Ava knew she meant it sincerely. Her history as a servant would have given her a comprehensive understanding of the rigid hierarchy that usually existed in the lower ranks of a palace.

"Oh, I didn't show her how," said Hans. "She lay on the grass and gazed at the sky while I did the work."

"Ava!" Sarah gave her friend a light blow on the shoulder. "That's terrible!"

"It is kind of terrible, now that he says it like that," said Ava. "I must have picked something up, though, because I managed to do it myself the next time I was asked. First, I scooped up some sand from the stream bed, then I found a nice, solid, grassy patch of bank to kneel on, and I scrubbed each dish one by one." She actually felt a little proud of this accomplishment and looked around the group for affirmation.

For some reason, however, the others found this contribution the funniest part of the whole conversation and began to howl with laughter. She turned her gaze on Hans, and he immediately assumed a mock solemnity.

"That's very impressive, Princess. You'll be rivaling the rest of us soon." And then he couldn't seem to keep his amusement in either, and he began to chuckle, his whole body shaking with the movement.

Seeing him reminded Ava of why she had brought up the incident in the first place, and she began to laugh as well, although she still didn't quite understand what they were all laughing about.

Her willingness to put herself forward as an object of humor seemed to please the rest of the group, and soon they were all following her example, each vying to put forward the most embarrassing story.

It was the longest they had ever sat up talking, and when they finally separated to climb into their bedrolls, Ava felt a glow of satisfaction. It seemed she was learning a new type of leadership.

CHAPTER 20

*C*aravan Hargrove had been pushing itself at full speed in its final rush to the border, but even at its fastest pace, a large group of wagons couldn't compete with the speed of six people on good horses. They passed the campsite where the dance had taken place not long into their second day in Rangmere.

Ava felt pleased with their progress, but it didn't stop her from wishing they could reach the capital more quickly. They didn't dare stop and talk to any travelers they met, and they skirted around every village they passed. Since their primary goal was to remain unnoticed, they couldn't risk stopping for news about the planned coronation.

Throughout each day, they alternated between a canter and a walk, covering as much distance as possible while giving the horses adequate time to rest. When they walked, Ava often found herself riding beside Hans and conversing with him. They talked about what they could expect to find at the gates of Rangmeros, the likely attitude of the court and city toward Konrad and their own strategy. Ava wasn't surprised to find that Hans had a detailed understanding of Rangmeros, from the state of the

179

guards to the attitude of the populace. He had plenty of sensible suggestions to make as well, and the two were able to theorize for hours about their best strategy for countering Konrad. Ava found it useful to talk through her ideas out loud and wished she had thought of doing it years ago.

It would take the Magistrate's Guild a little bit of time to prepare the Trials once she registered her claim. She would use that time to her advantage. Together they agreed on ways to approach several key nobles.

It took them a week to come to a spot within a day's travel of the capital and, by that time, Ava was beginning to feel mildly optimistic about their chances. It helped that they had been moving at a good pace and had seen no sign of danger.

They made camp for the last time knowing that they would reach the city by the noon meal the next day. The mood around the fire was more somber than any of the preceding nights, and they were all quick to move toward sleep. Hans insisted on taking first watch, giving the second watch to Evelyn, and the third to Aldric.

Ava lay in her bedroll and watched him where he sat by the dying fire, his posture alert. As always, his aura of strength had a comforting effect on her, and she fell into sleep faster than she had expected.

She slept deeply, not even stirring, until she was roughly awakened by a familiar sound. It was the whoosh of a flying arrow, followed by the thwack of it hitting the ground. She came instantly awake, rolling out of bed and into a crouch while her eyes searched for the arrow's landing place. It was buried in a pack that had been lying next to her head, and it stood out starkly in the light of the almost full moon. She shivered.

Taking quick stock of the clearing, she could see no sign of Hans. At first, she assumed he must still be on watch, despite how late it felt. But a second glance showed that his empty bedroll had been slept in at some point.

Moving at a crouch, she went to each of her companions and shook them before rushing on to the next person. It was only when she poked Mathilde that she realized Aldric was also missing.

Evelyn was the fastest to wake and seemed to take in the situation almost as quickly as Ava. She gestured silently, offering to go after the archer, but Ava shook her head. If Evelyn left, the remaining three girls would be virtually defenseless. They still had no idea how many attackers there were or what had happened to the two men. All they knew was that since their assailants had chosen arrows over bullets, they favored stealth and accuracy. Guns were becoming more popular among certain circles, but they were too prone to malfunction and inaccuracy. Assassins still favored bows and arrows.

Assassination. Ava shook her head to clear it. She had known what this was from the first moment of seeing the arrow. It was best not to dwell on it, however.

She motioned for Sarah and Mathilde to saddle the horses, and the two girls moved as quickly as they were able, still shaking off sleep and giving the lone arrow a wide berth. Evelyn remained on alert, her sword drawn, and Ava moved to take up a position at her back, the knife from her boot in her hand. Evelyn glanced at her once, taking in the blade with begrudging respect, before returning her attention to the surrounding forest.

For several long moments, there was only silence. It was broken by a sudden flurry of sound and movement. Before Ava could do more than note the direction of the noise, an armed figure erupted from the trees. After the briefest of pauses, he leaped toward the princess but was halted by Evelyn's raised blade. He lunged wildly at her, but she parried him easily and, with one clean stroke, ran him through the heart.

He seemed to fall in slow motion, but Ava forced herself to tear her eyes away, scanning for other assailants. Mathilde was hiding between two of the horses, her eyes wider than Ava had ever seen them, and Sarah had her hand clasped over her own mouth although a whimper still managed to escape.

Ava opened her mouth to suggest the other girls move closer, where she and Evelyn could more easily protect them, when two more figures burst into the clearing. Evelyn spun to meet them, her reddened blade raised in challenge, but a second later she lowered it, a soft sigh of relief on her lips. The newcomers were Hans and Aldric, and both were breathing hard as if they had been running fast or fighting hard.

Aldric moved straight over to the horses and took Mathilde into his arms. Ava couldn't hear the soft words he was murmuring into her hair, but she could see the relief in his eyes. Hans paused for half a second, his eyes meeting Ava's with a similar relief, before his gaze skimmed across the arrow and dropped to the dead man in front of Evelyn.

"Apologies," he said, his voice hard. "That one got away from us. We've taken care of the rest, but we need to move, *now*. Our only chance is to be at the gates of Rangmeros when they open at sunrise."

His words snapped Ava out of the temporary paralysis brought on by her relief, and she rushed to help Sarah with their horses. Unfortunately, just as Evelyn had promised, she found the other girl retching in the bushes. She moved toward her, but Sarah waved her weakly away. Torn, Ava hurried to finish saddling their mounts. By the time she had finished, Sarah had emerged looking shaken but resolute, and Evelyn had cleaned and sheathed her blade and gathered up their waiting packs. When she moved toward their bedrolls, Hans shook his head.

"Leave them," he said, "we won't be needing them again."

Evelyn nodded once and swung herself up onto her horse. The others followed suit, and they were out of the clearing and pounding down the road before Ava had the chance to catch her breath.

They galloped their horses for as long as they dared but eventually were forced to reduce their pace to a walk. They were moving down the middle of the deserted road, unwilling to risk the verge in the light of the moon.

Ava knew she should feel sleepy, but instead her mind and body were buzzing with leftover energy from the fight at the campsite. She had to refrain herself from kicking Cinnamon back into a gallop before the horse was sufficiently rested.

Despite her impatience, the pace they set was blazing, and the first rays of the sun were only beginning to creep over the horizon when she saw the distant walls of Rangmeros rising from the fields.

PART III
THE TRIALS

THE GUARD

$\mathcal{D}$espite the absence of trouble, Hans remained on high alert as he kept watch over his sleeping companions. It was their last night on the road, and their proximity to the capital made him uncomfortable.

Thankfully, years of guard duty had taught him how to maintain vigilance while still allowing part of his mind to wander free. It was a necessary skill in a job that was otherwise mind-numbingly boring.

But, as was so often the case, it was a struggle to keep the free part of his mind from dwelling on the princess. Unacceptably often he found his gaze drifting toward her sleeping face. She looked so peaceful in sleep, in a way she rarely did when awake. She had made significant progress since her encounter with the High King, though.

The thought brought up the memory of his own interaction with the man. He had been everything Hans had always desired in a ruler, everything that King Josef had never been. Swearing fealty to him had been an easy decision.

It hadn't been so easy to accept that the High King was sending Ava first to her enemies in Arcadia and then back to face her brother. He would have preferred that she give up on Rangmere altogether. For a brief moment, he had even entertained the appealing dream of the two of them fleeing to southern Lanover and living a contented life as two regular commoners.

But he hadn't fallen in love with a commoner. He had fallen in love with a princess. And one who was born and trained with the steel of Rangmere in her veins. It had always been an empty and hopeless dream.

It wasn't the loss of such a future that tormented him now, it was the fear that he wouldn't be able to protect her from her brother. It made his senses extra sharp, but it also brought his gaze back to her face more frequently than he liked. Once again, he forced his eyes to return to the surrounding trees.

We will survive, he told himself grimly, *we will win. We have to.*

It was hard to make himself switch off when Evelyn woke to relieve him of duty. Eventually he managed it, though, and slipped into a light sleep. He stirred when Aldric replaced Evelyn but rolled over and quickly returned to slumber. He remained close enough to consciousness, however, that he was awake instantly when Aldric lightly touched his shoulder.

He could tell immediately that it was still several hours until morning and that something must be wrong. As soon as he sat up and saw the other man's face, he was sure of it.

Standing silently, he grasped the hilt of the naked sword lying beside his bedroll. Scanning the clearing, he could see no sign of a disturbance. He looked back at Aldric with a question in his eyes.

The Northhelmian put his mouth against Hans' ear and whispered, "Men, in the forest, I'm sure of it."

Hans felt a fleeting moment of relief that the trust he had placed in Aldric had not been misplaced. The emotion was quickly swallowed by the needs of the moment, however. His mind whirled as he formed a hasty strategy. There was no time for anything fancier.

"We need to flank them, take them out before they attack," he whispered back almost soundlessly, and Aldric nodded grimly. The other man was clutching a long dagger and seemed ready for action. He led the way across the clearing, carefully stepping around their sleeping companions.

When he reached Evelyn's bedroll, he paused and raised his eyebrows at Hans. Hans shook his head vehemently and gestured toward the other sleepers. Aldric seemed to understand and continued on without any further pauses.

Hans didn't dare wake the rest of the group, they were already pushing their luck to surprise their pursuers as it was. And he didn't dare take Evelyn with them. If Hans and Aldric failed, it would be up to Evelyn to protect the princess.

He felt slight relief when they entered the trees without eliciting any further sounds from the men Aldric had heard. He could only hope their counter-ambush remained intact.

Aldric led them unerringly forward, picking his way silently through the underbrush. Hans gripped his sword hard and followed, equally silent. At last Aldric stopped and gestured Hans to come up beside him. He had led them around so that they were now looking at the backs of three men, who were hiding in the trees a reasonable distance from the clearing. Their view of it was hampered by several thick bushes, and they didn't appear to have noticed that two of the sleeping group had disappeared. They were all dressed in the motley garb of a typical brigand, but Hans recognized their swords as standard palace issue weapons.

Sloppy, thought Hans, shaking his head. He would never have permitted his own guards to behave so carelessly. Even as he thought this, one of the men crept forward to a spot behind a tree and peered around it at the sleeping figures. His eyes narrowed, and he turned sharply toward his fellow soldiers.

Realizing that someone had spotted the empty bedrolls, Hans raised his arm ready to signal Aldric to attack. He was confident of the odds, even without knowing Aldric's skill level.

Before he could drop his hand, however, the man who had been observing the clearing turned his face upwards, as if he sought confirmation from the treetops. Hans frowned in confusion, and then a small flash of moonlight against steel showed through the leaves.

An archer!

Without pausing to signal to Aldric, Hans sprinted toward the tree, swinging himself into the lower branches before any of the soldiers could react. The man crouched above him already had an arrow on the string and was aiming down into the clearing. Hans didn't need to look to know who he was aiming at.

Reaching up, he grasped the man around one ankle, throwing off his balance just as he released the arrow. Giving a strong tug, Hans then dislodged the man completely. He fell to the ground with a thud, and Hans jumped down after him, dispatching him before he could struggle to his feet.

Looking up, he saw that one of the men was frozen, staring at his fallen comrade in astonishment. The other two, however, were closing in on Aldric who was desperately trying to fend them off with his dagger.

Hans rushed to his aid and managed to take one of the men by surprise from behind. He fell to the ground and didn't get back up. Now that the two against one odds had been reversed, it didn't take long to finish off the other man. As soon as Aldric was safe, Hans whirled around to find the remaining attacker.

He was gone, and now that the heat of battle was passed, Hans could hear the sounds he made as he burst into the clearing. For half a second Hans and Aldric exchanged stricken looks, and then they both took off running.

As he pushed his way through the underbrush, Hans reminded himself that Evelyn was a skilled guardswoman and that the arrow had given them warning. He couldn't allow himself to think that he might have failed and that Ava might be hurt or dead.

He cursed his carelessness and wondered what else he might have missed. Had there been more men? Would there be more attacks? Or had someone made a run back to Rangmeros? Nothing about the attack made sense. Konrad obviously wanted deniability in case he was unsuccessful but, even so, sending only four men made it a chancy business at best. Surely there was more to the prince's plan?

They would have to leave immediately and ride hard for the city. Their only chance was to get to the safety of the Magistrate's Guild before Konrad could spring whatever trick he had planned next.

When he pushed through into the clearing, the first thing he saw was Ava, standing upright, her knife in her hand. For a moment, the relief was so overwhelming that it erased all other thought from his mind. She was alive, and that was all that mattered.

Then his eyes skimmed over the arrow, which was buried sickeningly close to Ava's empty bedroll, and the body of the fourth man lying at Evelyn's feet.

"Apologies. That one got away from us. We've taken care of the rest, but we need to move, *now*. Our only chance is to be at the gates of Rangmeros when they open at sunrise."

CHAPTER 21

*T*here was a small pool of farmers still making their way through the newly opened gates when the group arrived at the walls of the city. Once again, Ava and Hans lurked at the back of the group, hoods up and faces down. Unlike the border, they weren't required to produce any papers to enter the city, and if Konrad had received word of their approach, they didn't want to be identified as the same group that had crossed the border a week ago.

Ava risked a brief glance up, but she didn't recognize any of the guards posted on the gate. She cast an inquiring eye toward Hans, but he shook his head slightly.

"I don't recognize any of them," he muttered. "They look alert enough, but they're not inspecting people too closely..."

Ava fought the desire to hold her breath, forcing herself to breathe deeply instead. When it was their turn to approach the gates, one of the guards stepped forward, his eyes examining the group closely. Hans reached under his cloak, and it was Ava's turn to shake her head subtly at him. Their only chance was to get out of this without a fight.

Just before the guard reached them, however, a guard on the

other side of the gates called to him loudly. An ornery farmer was arguing about some spilled vegetables, and the second guard wanted backup. From what Ava could gather, the farmer was blaming the guard for ruining his produce and demanding compensation. The guard who had been approaching their group sighed and redirected himself to the altercation.

Taking advantage of the opportunity, they rode quickly into the city. Once they were all safely past the gates, Hans moved to the front of the group and led them through the streets. The rest of the group formed up protectively around Ava so that she was shielded on all sides from interested eyes.

No one attempted to stop them or even paid them any notice. The city traffic was still light, given the early hour of the morning, and everyone they passed seemed intent about their own business.

An unexpected surge of affection and energy filled Ava as she traveled the familiar streets. She had never thought of herself as being attached to Rangmeros, but she now realized that she had missed the city.

Unlike Arcadie, which was arranged in giant circles around the palace, Rangmeros was a large square. The city had been built at the foot of a cliff, and the dark gray face loomed far above the buildings. The castle had been built flush against the rock, its back defended by solid stone, and the city jutted out from the castle, a giant square divided into six equal rectangles. Each district was named after a color and dominated by a particular segment of Rangmeran society. The Purple District, directly in front of the palace, was populated by the nobles while the Blue and Red Districts which flanked it were populated by the artisans and the military respectively. In front of these districts were three more, the Green, Yellow, and Orange Districts. They were more densely populated and were filled with merchants, shopkeepers, and laborers.

It was these districts Ava was riding through, but they

seemed as familiar as the castle or the Purple District. She was sure the city looked dark and gray to the Arcadians who were used to the bright and airy feel of their capital, Arcadie, but she found all the surrounding rock to be comforting. It felt like an extension of her beloved castle, all squared edges and gray stone walls.

Despite the names of their districts, the people too were dressed less colorfully and more practically than the people she had seen in Arcadie. But there was still the occasional window box of flowers or the flash of a red dress.

Hans led them to the Blue District where the great Hall of Magistrates stood. It was in this building that countless generations of princes had registered their claim to the throne. Even though he had no brothers to contend with, Konrad would still have completed this formality. Ava squared her shoulders; she would not be intimidated by her brother. Her right to rule was greater than his since, unlike him, she had committed no acts of treason.

She almost expected to see a wall of soldiers guarding the front entrance to the Hall, but there was no one in sight when they approached. As always, the great front doors had been thrown open at dawn so that any member of the populace could enter to register a dispute.

Evelyn volunteered to watch the horses, so the other five mounted the broad stairs leading into the Hall without her. When they reached the wide doorway, Ava paused and took a breath. She knew that once she stepped into the Hall, there would be no true rest until the Trials were over, one way or another. Hans stepped up beside her, and she smiled up at him as she took her first step into the building.

They found themselves in a vast marble lobby, the sound of their footsteps echoing coldly around the huge space. On either side of them, elegant staircases curved gracefully to a second level where Ava could see glimpses of a long row of office doors.

Across from the front entrance was a large mahogany desk occupied by a sleepy looking clerk.

He looked up at the sound of their approach and seemed mildly put out to have such early visitors.

"Good morning," he said, rather woodenly. "For civil disputes, please complete Form 4A, for trade disputes, please complete Form 3C, for…"

Ava cut him off with a raised hand. He stared at her, affronted.

"I have come to see the Head Magistrate," she said in a clear, ringing voice.

"Have you indeed? Well, for that you'll need to fill out Form 2B and place it in the left slot in the wall. Your request will be reviewed and, if approved, you will receive notification of the time and date of your appointment."

"I have come to register my claim to the throne," said Ava, ignoring this speech.

"Yes, well, as I said, you'll need to fill out form…wait, what did you say?" he asked, his mind catching up with his mouth. "Your claim to the throne?"

For a moment he stared at her, his eyes almost bugging out of his head, and then he breathed two words. "Princess Ava!"

Before she could confirm her identity, he had taken off running and had soon disappeared into the back portion of the building. She turned confused eyes on her companions.

"It seems that our friendly clerk is scared of ghosts," said Aldric drily.

"I can't say that I blame him," said Sarah. "I'd probably have been terrified in his place."

"You might have been shocked," said Mathilde, "but I'm sure you would have been a great deal more polite. When you're queen, Ava, you'll have to have a word with the magistrates."

Ava couldn't resist casting an amused glance at Hans who was looking down at her with equal humor reflected in his eyes.

"If I'm crowned queen, Mathilde," she said, "I'll give you full royal approval to whip all of my clerks into shape. I have no doubt you're capable of it."

To her credit, Mathilde recognized the humor behind Ava's words and laughed at herself.

"I'm much too busy cleaning up the Arcadian palace now that Alyssa's princess." She winked at Ava. "But I'll keep my eyes out for a suitable Rangmeran to take on the job for you."

Before Ava could respond to this rather terrifying offer, the clerk reappeared in the foyer. He had somewhat regained his equilibrium, and he offered Ava a small bow.

"If you would follow me, Your Highness. I will conduct you to the Head Magistrate now."

Ava nodded regally and sailed after him, her companions following at her heels. He led them through a small wooden door and down a long corridor. Thick, red carpet covered the floor, and large oil paintings, each depicting a previous Head Magistrate, decorated the walls.

The clerk led them all the way to the end before knocking on a large door. He didn't wait for a response but opened it and stood back, respectfully gesturing for them to enter. Through the door they found a large, plush office decorated in severe black and gold. An elderly man was seated behind a second large mahogany desk, but at the sight of them he rose to his feet.

Coming around the desk, he bowed low to the princess. Ava recognized him immediately as Lord Iver, the Head Magistrate. The title of lord was an honorary one, attached to his role, but she knew him well from court where he had been a frequent advisor of her father. She had always thought his advice sound and his judgments measured and fair. She was relieved to see that Konrad hadn't replaced him in her absence.

"Your Royal Highness," he said, carefully enunciating each word. "It is a joy to discover that you are still alive."

"I, too, am pleased at my current healthy state, Lord Iver."

He looked at her sharply. She had never been one to jest before, but the hint of a laugh was audible in her voice. It was an intentional effect. She wanted to make it clear from the beginning that she was a different person now.

"And what can I do for you?" he asked. "My clerk was spouting some nonsense about the Trials, but I'm afraid the young fellow is a little flighty."

"He reported me correctly," said Ava. "I have come to register my claim to the throne."

Lord Iver raised his eyebrows but said nothing, merely weighing the girl before him with his eyes. She was fully expecting some protest about the legality of such a move, but none came.

Instead he gave a small sigh.

"There is, of course, no law prohibiting such a thing," he said, and she felt her respect for his knowledge grow. "But since your own father is tragically no longer around to advise you, I must ask. Are you sure you want to do this?"

"I will make no public accusations until the Trials are complete," said Ava. "But in the privacy of this office, I will state that my brother is unfit to rule. This is the only avenue open to me, and I am determined to take it."

Lord Iver drew a deep breath and then nodded. "Very well. If you will please follow me."

He led her over to his desk, and she waited while he retrieved a large leather book with gilt-edged pages from a small dais against the far wall. Laying it flat on his desk, he handed Ava a long feather quill.

She leaned over the desk and stared at the page for a moment, the quill gripped so firmly in her hand she was a little afraid she would snap it. She easily recognized the strong, blocky hand-writing that spelled out her brother's full name. Drawing a deep breath, she wrote her own name beneath his. The ink was black and final, and she felt strangely glad knowing that she had passed the point of no return.

Once she had finished, Lord Iver made the required speech outlining the rules of the Monarchy Trials. She was familiar enough with the event not to need the summary, but she recognized the weight of tradition and silently allowed him to recite the words.

"The Monarchy Trials test the worthiness of all royal claimants to the throne. The Magistrate's Guild will set five trials to demonstrate the five required virtues of strength, resilience, strategic thinking, compassion, and intelligence."

Not surprisingly, compassion had been the only one of the five trials that King Josef had failed to win. Ava was hopeful that her brother would find it equally difficult. Which meant she only had to win two of the other three. Of course, the more trials that a competitor won, the greater legitimacy was attached to their rule.

"The trials will be completed here, in the Hall of Magistrates, and once the Trials have begun, no participant may leave the Hall until the completion of the Trials." This information was news to Ava, and she wondered why she had never heard it before. She had always imagined the Trials took place in the castle grounds. She disliked the thought of having to compete in such a cold and unfriendly place.

"Although the required virtues remain the same, each generation faces new and different trials. The five most senior magistrates will each be assigned one virtue and will be required to design a fitting trial. These five magistrates will act as judges. I will oversee them and will also have a vote. In the case of a tie, my vote will be weighted double."

He paused and cast an eye around the group.

"You have taken me rather by surprise, you know. We were not expecting to be called upon to oversee the Trials in this generation and have nothing prepared. I will, therefore, assign the date of the Trials to one week hence. We could not possibly prepare in any less time. The coronation is due to take place in nine days, however, so neither can it be left any later."

Ava nodded her acceptance of these terms and the date, and he gave her a small smile.

"Have you taken the glad tidings of your survival to your brother, Your Highness?"

There was sympathy in his voice, and Ava understood the subtle undercurrents of his question. He was one of the most intelligent men she had ever met, and he had yet to ask her how she had been mistaken for dead. She knew this omission meant he suspected her brother of foul play. His kind question was meant as both inquiry and warning.

She returned his look, openly displaying her gratitude in her expression.

"I have not. This was my first stop, but I intend to continue on to the castle. My companions will come with me, of course. Allow me to introduce Aldric, official representative of their majesties, the King and Queen of Northhelm; Mathilde, official representative of their majesties, the King and Queen of Arcadia; and Sarah, official representative of the traveling merchants, who are even now meeting in council."

Lord Iver's eyes widened, and he took a closer look at the individuals assembled in his office.

"A distinguished group." His tone expressed admiration for her strategy. "In that case, I will look forward to seeing you at court later this morning when I make the official announcement regarding the date of the Trials."

Ava gave him another grateful smile as the group made their farewells. It seemed she would have another witness to stand beside her.

CHAPTER 22

$\mathcal{A}$va had expected to feel nervous facing her brother for the first time since his failed assassination attempt, but after registering her claim, she felt unexpectedly emboldened. She even waved cheekily at the guards on duty at the castle gates. The men took one look at Hans and began to whisper excitedly among themselves. Ava had no doubt that news of her unanticipated return would be all over the castle within the hour.

She was still sure that Konrad would have kept the number of his accomplices small. So, while the guards who had attacked the merchant caravan were certainly aware of some part of his plot, she suspected that the majority of castle guards and all of the servants were ignorant of the true state of affairs. She hoped that at least some of them would be glad to hear that she was alive.

They dismounted in the castle courtyard, and several grooms rushed forward to take their horses. In fact, there seemed to be more of them than the six horses required, and they all kept casting covert glances in her direction. She smiled, turning so that they got a good look at her. Several of them gasped aloud, and she couldn't help chuckling at their shock. She revised her initial estimate down to thirty minutes. Gossip traveled fast in a castle.

Sure enough, there were footmen already pulling the castle doors open when they reached them, and a surprising number of maids seemed to be cleaning the large entranceway. She got no further than a few steps into the castle before her brother came rushing in from the opposite direction.

He looked exactly as she remembered him—a tall, masculine version of herself. His own gold curls were cropped short, and his blue eyes were colder than hers had ever been, but there was no mistaking them for siblings. Even while hurrying, he managed to appear both powerful and confident.

"Sister!" He threw his arms wide in greeting. "I couldn't believe the news until I'd seen you with my own eyes. What joyous tidings! What a miracle! But tell me, how are you alive?"

He came forward to embrace her, and she submitted for the briefest time possible. She understood that he was putting on a spectacle for the interested crowd, and she had no desire to play into his charade.

"Brother." Her voice was cold. "I only wish our father could have been so fortunate."

The briefest of clouds passed over his face, and she knew he understood her barbed reference. His smile faltered, but it was replaced by carefully practiced grief rather than the anger she knew he was truly feeling.

"I, too, wish he could be here to greet you," he said, his voice a perfect blend of sorrow and regret. "But I do not wish sadness to cloud this miraculous reunion."

His voice and face lightened. "You have returned in good time to attend my coronation, and I hope you will agree to stand beside me."

It was a weighted question, and Ava wondered how she would have answered if she had returned to Rangmeros without a plan.

"I am afraid that will not be possible, brother," she said. "I have come directly from the Hall of Magistrates where I have registered my own claim to the throne."

Konrad's subtle intake of breath, the only sign he gave of his shock, was lost amidst the general exclamations of the servants. Many of them had given up their pretense of cleaning and were now openly watching the scene playing out in front of them.

"Impossible, dear sister," Konrad said, and Ava was satisfied to hear a hardening of his voice that told her she had broken through his calm control.

"Indeed not." She kept her voice light and airy in comparison. "There is no law that says a princess may not register her claim. I have done so, and the Trials will take place exactly one week from today."

She could see a murderous gleam in Konrad's eyes, so she raised her voice as she introduced her companions. His eyes slowly widened with begrudging respect as she named each representative who accompanied her.

"Lord Iver himself will be here, later today, with the announcement of the Trials," she finished, and she could see the capitulation in Konrad's face. As planned, she had succeeded in making herself untouchable.

"I am pained that you would choose to put yourself through such an ordeal," said Konrad. "Especially when there can be no doubt of the outcome."

Hans shifted slightly behind Ava, but she didn't need the warning. She felt no temptation to challenge Konrad's assumption of victory.

"Nevertheless, Konrad, I will try," was all she said.

There was a long pause before Konrad spoke.

"You must be tired from your journey. I will have the house-keeper show you to some guest suites." He had returned to the role of amicable host. "But I hope, once you've rested, that you will join the court at an afternoon musicale I'm hosting."

"It would be our pleasure," said Aldric, speaking for the first time.

Konrad nodded once and turned, gesturing for the house-keeper, who had been lurking behind him, to come forward. She bustled toward the group and bowed low to Ava.

"What a pleasure it is to see you alive and well, Your Highness." She gave Ava a warm smile and received one in return.

Konrad had rapidly disappeared back into the castle, so Ava allowed herself to extend her smile to all the gathered servants.

"It is a very great pleasure for me to be back here with you all." She spoke loudly and was pleased to receive many answering smiles.

The servants seemed to gain courage from her friendly demeanor, and they approached her one by one to give their greetings and congratulations. It was a long process since no sooner had one servant departed than another appeared, as if by magic, to take their place. But Ava restrained any sign of impatience and greeted them all more warmly than she had done in years. She knew word of their interaction would get back to her brother, but she deemed that it was worth it. She needed to show the people of Rangmere that the new Princess Ava would be their champion and defender.

Her companions waited patiently throughout the process, and many of the servants greeted them as well. Some even went so far as to inquire after friends and relatives living in Arcadia or Northhelm or traveling with the merchants. The visitors were forced to admit that they had no knowledge of these people until a senior footman and a maid asked after their sister. The girl had taken a position as a maid in the palace at Arcadie, and Mathilde actually knew her.

This news was greeted with great delight and, within no time, the three were chattering away like old friends. Aldric looked at his wife with considerable affection and made no attempt to prevent the association. Ava was glad to see that he had no issue with his wife reconnecting with her servant roots. That was the sort of misplaced pride her father would have displayed.

When the stream of servants eventually dissipated, the housekeeper reappeared and led them all into the castle.

"Well, that was for the best," she said, "since it let me send some maids ahead to prepare your rooms." She looked toward Aldric and Mathilde. "Master Hans, here, told me that the two of you are married, so I've prepared one of the bigger suites for you. The representative from the merchants will have the one next door." She nodded at Sarah. "And you'll be in your own room, of course, Your Highness. The room is just as you left it, but I've had them add a pallet for your new guard."

It took Ava a moment to realize that she meant Evelyn. She expected the other girl to protest, but she gave no sign of discontent. Glancing at Hans, Ava realized that this was another effort on his part to protect her. Understandable, given what had happened the last time she had slept in that room. She was sure her brother wouldn't dare to touch her before the Trials, but she appreciated the gesture all the same. She would sleep better with the company.

The housekeeper had thoughtfully prepared the guest suites closest to Ava's own room, and when they arrived at the larger one, Ava told the housekeeper that she could direct the rest of the group from there. The woman departed with more protestations of joy and relief, and the group was finally alone again.

"None of them asked you how you were alive," said Aldric once the door had closed behind the housekeeper.

He received several confused looks.

"The servants, I mean," he clarified. "Konrad must have claimed to have found your body, I'm sure he even held a funeral. It's not as if you were missing or something."

"I'm not surprised," said Hans. "Konrad has a reputation for being a cruel man and a harsh prince."

"Yes, that much seems obvious," said Aldric. "Clearly the

servants aren't willing to risk challenging him. I think it will be easier to win the populace to your side than I had envisioned, Princess. I can't speak for the nobles, of course. Not until I've met them, anyway."

"I think it's time that I heard the rest of your story, Aldric," said Ava. "There's obviously more to you than a simple diplomatic attaché."

"That's true, Your Highness." Aldric smiled. "I was wondering how long it would take you to ask. I suppose no one liked to mention it to you considering I was a little involved with the business last summer."

Ava raised her eyebrows and waited for him to continue.

"Last summer I traveled to Arcadie with Princess Marie to take up a medical exchange. But that was only my cover. I was actually an intelligence officer."

"An intelligence officer?" asked Sarah, a little doubtfully. "That sounds boring."

"Not at all," said Mathilde, "that's just royal talk for spy."

"Oh," breathed Sarah, looking at Aldric with new respect.

"So, I do have some small training and skill in the art of observation which I'm happy to use for your cause." Aldric gave a small bow in Ava's direction.

"Well," said Ava, after a pause, "that does explain a lot, I guess. About then, as well as now. And I can use every tool I can get. So, thank you for your assistance."

"He's been training me, too," said Mathilde, pride in her voice. "And I've already got an in with the servants. You'd be surprised how much you can pick up from castle servants. They're a gossipy bunch." She grinned reminiscently.

"It seems Max and Alyssa chose more wisely than I realized when they sent you with me," said Ava. "But I think we'll all do better with some rest, so no spying until the musicale."

Aldric and Mathilde laughingly agreed with her demands but said that they would be visiting the Northhelmian and Arcadian ambassadors before they thought about rest. Ava heartily endorsed this plan, and they separated to their various rooms.

It was almost surreal for Ava to walk back into her old room and see that everything remained exactly as it had been before her flight. She couldn't help but feel that the room should somehow reflect the many changes that had taken place in herself.

All traces of her deadly encounter with Joran had been erased, and the room glowed as welcomingly as it had when she had come to bed that fateful night. The only difference was a pallet just inside the doorway and the tapestry on the far wall which had been rolled up and secured, revealing the wooden door behind it. Obviously, Hans felt that even such a flimsy barrier as a tapestry was more than he was willing to have between his door and her room.

She was tempted to cross over and open the door, just to see if his room looked as unchanged as her own, but she resisted the impulse. With all that had passed between them, it was doubly important that she respect his privacy. She was already taking enough advantage of his feelings.

Evelyn had followed her into the room and was looking around with a mildly impressed expression.

"Nice room," she said.

Ava looked at her and wondered whether she was being truly complimentary or subtly judgmental. She was used to being able to read people, but Evelyn had seemed different since the fight in the clearing, and she hadn't yet put her finger on the change.

"I've always liked it," she said eventually. "I used to feel safe here. That turned out to be an illusion, of course, but it was a comforting one for many years."

"Well, you're safe now," said Evelyn. "Or as safe as you possibly could be. Hans and I won't let anything happen to you."

Her voice was matter of fact, but Ava felt pleased at the progress her words represented.

"Thank you for sleeping in here with me," she said, adding as much warmth to her words as she could. "It means a lot."

"Anything to get away from Sarah's snoring." Evelyn flashed the tiniest of smiles, and Ava was surprised into a laugh. She knew from experience that Sarah didn't snore.

Definite progress then, she thought as she smiled back at her new guard.

Both girls took the opportunity to get some rest and were only woken by a servant bringing them lunch on trays. Hans followed behind the servant, and after she had left, he insisted on testing Ava's food.

"Don't be ridiculous, Hans." Ava crossed her arms as she watched him. "I'm not going to let you become my poison taster. You saw Konrad's face and, after all these years, you must know him almost as well as I do. He's not going to try to kill me with so many international witnesses present. Besides, he doesn't need to poison me, he's confident he can win. He's probably busy plotting some unfortunate accident during the Trials."

Hans nodded his agreement with everything she was saying and calmly continued tasting her food.

Ava sighed, leaned around him and took a hunk of bread. Dipping it into the aromatic stew, she took a big bite. He glared at her, but she just smiled up at him.

"Since you're not exactly an expert on poisons, I suppose we're just hoping that it's nothing slow acting?" she asked in a compliant tone that was contradicted by the twinkle in her eyes.

Now it was Hans' turn to sigh.

"You're impossible!" he said, and then belatedly added, "Your Highness."

"Not at all," said Ava. "I can assure you I have always been entirely possible. It's one of my greatest strengths."

Hans just rolled his eyes at her nonsense and took his own tray.

"Our strategy is sound," he said sternly, once they had all settled into eating, "but that doesn't mean you should take unnecessary risks. The danger is real, and if you present Konrad with enough of an opportunity, he might find himself unable to resist taking it."

His words sobered Ava and she meekly nodded her agreement.

When they had all finished their lunch, Hans placed their trays out in the hallway and firmly shut her door.

"If someone knocks," he warned her, "don't answer it. Let Evelyn or me do it."

Ava reluctantly agreed to this plan, and he retreated into his own room although he left the door between them open. Ava instantly had to fight the overwhelming impulse to peer into his space. She determinedly kept her eyes pointing in the opposite direction and was congratulating herself on her self-control when she met Evelyn's eyes.

The other girl was looking at her with an amused half-smile, and Ava instantly felt herself begin to blush.

Pull it together! She told herself. *You are not some besotted child. And you've been trained to hide your emotions.* It was one thing for Evelyn to see her feelings written on her face, but in a couple of hours she would be facing the court, and she would need her old control back. She took several deep breaths and managed to restore her calm expression.

"We should probably start preparing for the musicale," she said. She had barely gotten the last word out of her mouth when her door burst open.

In the space of a single breath Hans was back in the room. But when he saw who had come in, he relaxed, sighed and returned to his own room.

It was Sarah who had burst in, and she seemed oddly pleased with herself.

"Hi Eve, hi Ava." She had a big grin on her face.

"Here we go." Evelyn rolled her eyes. "What is it this time, cousin of mine?"

"Well," said Sarah, "I was sitting in my room—it's a lovely room by the way, Ava—and I got to thinking about the musicale this afternoon. And I realized that I don't have a single appropriate thing to wear. Sound familiar, Ava?"

"How could I ever forget?" Ava laughed. "You helped me in my hour of need, and I would be honored to return the favor now."

The dance she had attended as Anna felt like it had happened in another lifetime. For a moment, she remembered the sensation of Hans' hand as he placed a rose in her hair, but then she shook the feeling off. This was no time for distractions.

"Yes!" crowed Sarah rushing to Ava's wardrobe and throwing it open. "Yes, yes, yes!"

"You are utterly ridiculous!" said Evelyn as she watched her cousin with amusement.

"She is a princess, Evelyn," said Sarah as if she was explaining it to a simple child. "A princess! Which means that I am about to wear a dress made for a princess." She ran her hand along the dresses with a dreamy smile. "I always knew I was meant for better things."

Evelyn snorted loudly, snapping Sarah out of her reverie.

"You did not!" Evelyn said, bringing a healthy dose of reality back to the situation. "At least not all those years that you were getting into trouble for wading in the creek or coming home with skinned knees and dirt and rips and who knows what else from the crazy games we used to play with the boys."

"This is the problem with having a best friend who's also your cousin and has known you since you were born," said Sarah to Ava. "She's always trying to stomp on your dreams."

Evelyn snorted again, more loudly, and Sarah got a cunning gleam in her eye.

"Don't think you're getting out of it, Eve," she said. "You'll have to wear one of these dresses, too."

"Absolutely not!" Evelyn looked horrified. "I'll wear my guard outfit. I wouldn't fit any of Ava's dresses anyway."

"I'm sure I could find something that would fit you." Ava's offer earned her one reproachful glare and one grateful smile.

Deciding this was one conversation she would do best to stay out of, she left the two cousins arguing next to her wardrobe and walked over to Hans' open door. Carefully keeping her eyes from straying around his room, she informed him that she was just popping across the hall to talk to Mathilde and Aldric.

"I'll come with you," said Hans.

"You don't have to do that. It's literally across the hall."

"Nevertheless, I'm coming with you."

"All right, thank you, then." Ava's capitulation won her a surprised smile. Hiding a satisfied grin, she led the way to the guest suite.

Mathilde at first protested against the offer of a dress to wear, but Aldric reminded her that she was in Rangmere as a representative of King Henry and Queen Eleanor, and the way she looked would reflect on Arcadia. She quickly yielded once it was put to her in that light.

Returning to her room with Mathilde in tow, Ava informed Hans that the girls would need some privacy.

"I'll be ringing for a servant and then sending for a seamstress, so don't come bursting in here if you hear the door opening and closing a few times."

Hans opened his mouth to argue, but she shook her head sternly. "We need time to get ready, and Evelyn is here to protect us. We'll call for help if we need it. With so many of us in here, I hardly think we'll be taken by surprise."

Reluctantly Hans agreed and retreated from the room.

~

The following two hours, spent with the assistance of three seamstresses and two maids, turned out to be a surprising amount of fun. Except for the dance at the merchant caravan, Ava had never prepared for a party with other girls before, and she discovered that it was a great deal more enjoyable than preparing on your own.

There was lots of chatter and laughter and many compliments from the admiring servants who seemed to readily pick up on the atmosphere of merriment. Only Evelyn resisted, loudly declaring that she would stick with her guard outfit.

After listening to her protestations, one of the seamstresses declared that she had the very thing and disappeared from the room. She returned nearly twenty minutes later, reverently carrying a large parcel.

She unwrapped it and held up a long dress that had been made for a taller person than Ava.

"I had almost forgotten about this," the seamstress said. "It was made on commission, but the lady in question decided it wasn't what she wanted after all. It should be a good fit for you, Miss Evelyn, I think."

Ava could understand why the lady might have lost her courage, it was a dress unlike any she had seen before. It had been modeled on the uniform of a guard, and the severe bodice managed to look flattering and feminine while still clearly suggesting the tunic of a Rangmeran Royal Guard. The long skirt fell in graceful folds but had several long slits added for freedom of movement.

The seamstress showed them how the two layers of petticoats underneath had been slitted in different places to ensure that no flash of skin showed through as the wearer moved. It was a rather incredible garment, and it looked like it had been made for Evelyn.

Ava looked from the dress to Evelyn and was satisfied to see a gleam of desire in the other girls' eyes.

"It's perfect," she said. "You have to wear it, Evelyn. I'm making it a royal decree."

Evelyn put up a token protest and then agreed. Ava caught her stroking the fabric and smiled to herself. They would make an impressive group at the musicale, an effect that would only help Ava's cause.

When they were all finally ready, the servants broke into applause.

"Beautiful!"

"Stunning!"

"Magnificent!"

Ava couldn't help but smile at their dramatics. It made her a little sad, though, to acknowledge that she had cut herself off from this warmth for so many years. It reminded her of Hanna and the many laughs they had shared when Ava was a child.

The other girls felt none of her slight melancholy. Sarah, in particular, was lapping up the excessive praise like a satisfied cat. Even Evelyn allowed herself a large smile when she saw her reflection in the full-length mirror. She looked elegant and deadly, a perfect combination on the tall girl.

The servants were sent back to their usual tasks, and the girls went into the corridor to meet Hans and Aldric. Aldric was dressed rather severely in his Northhelmian diplomatic attire, and Hans was wearing his formal guard uniform. Ava had seen him wear it at many balls and royal functions, but it was the first time she had seen him in it since they had fled Rangmeros, and she had to fight another flush. He looked handsome and striking and even more deadly than Evelyn.

Ava had chosen to wear the most regal of her afternoon gowns, a full length dress of deep purple and gold. The purple made her blue eyes shine, and her hair managed to look more gold than the golden thread woven into the fabric. She had also placed a simple diamond tiara in her hair.

Hans came up beside her and spoke in a low voice.

"You look like a queen," he said, his voice slightly husky.

She looked up and met his eyes. "Let's hope the court thinks so, too."

"They will."

CHAPTER 23

*W*hether or not they thought she looked queenly, the waiting court certainly seemed impressed by Ava and her retinue. They had arrived at the musicale slightly late, a purposeful move by Ava, and a hush fell over the crowd as they were announced. It held slightly longer than normal as the assembled courtiers took in the appearance of the group in the doorway. Then someone clapped, and it unleashed a hubbub of noise and movement as everyone began to chatter among themselves, and a large part of the room surged forward to greet them.

Ava smiled a welcome to each person who approached them and had soon introduced her companions to a full two thirds of the Rangmeran court. Word of her return had obviously traveled quickly—she didn't remember musicales being so well attended in the past. She suspected that word of the Monarchy Trials had traveled equally quickly, but no one mentioned it to her.

Konrad had smiled and waved when she entered the room, effectively giving the impression that the siblings had already caught up and were on excellent terms. Ava wondered how many of the courtiers present were convinced. She noticed that

Princess Clarisse, her sister-in-law, was absent. She tucked the information away for further consideration.

She noted also that the Arcadian and Northhelmian ambassadors had chosen to attend and were among the first to greet her. Clearly Aldric and Mathilde's visits had been a success.

When the steady flow of greeters had dissipated, the group separated to mingle, eat, and listen to the music. It felt good to have a team and to know that she had extra eyes and ears working for her. Already she found herself wondering how she had ever managed alone.

As she made her way around the room, Hans followed her, always a couple of steps behind. They hadn't discussed it, but she knew it was a strategic move on his part, and she was impressed. She should have instructed him to do so.

Usually at such an event, Hans would have accompanied her and then stood against the wall, observing the party and watching for any sign of danger. The many personal guards of the musicale attendees were ringing the party in exactly such a way. Only the personal guard of the king followed him around an event, trailing two steps behind. Hans' initiative strengthened Ava's presence at the party.

Konrad, his own guard trailing behind him, hadn't responded to the sight of Hans. He'd obviously spent the morning regaining control over his emotions. It was a reminder to Ava about the strength of her competition. She would need every bit of her own strength and cunning to beat him.

She spent over an hour circulating through the event, mingling and regaining a feel for the Rangmeran court. The nobles were no more eager to mention the mystery of her survival than the servants had been. The less subtle among them were obvious in their avoidance of the issue. If the conversation strayed in that direction they looked nervously toward Konrad and then steered the topic down another track.

Overall, she thought that the tone of court was tenser than it had been under her father's rule. The Rangmeran courtiers had always known to tread carefully, but many of them seemed more fearful than cautious. It made Ava feel hopeful, and she was careful to ensure that the group around her was always the most light-hearted and lively group in the room. Her best chance was to show them that life under her rule would be a great deal less nerve-wracking than life under her brother's.

After two hours, she grew tired. She had forgotten how taxing it was to interact with such care all the time. She excused herself from the group surrounding her and stepped back into a shadowy corner of the room. From her secluded vantage point she watched the ebb and flow of the event, paying careful attention to who sought out her brother and who avoided him.

After a couple of minutes, a servant approached her bearing a tray with a drink. She expressed her appreciation, but the servant demurred, pointing toward her benefactor. Aldric was standing next to the buffet table and smiling in her direction. Somehow, she wasn't surprised that he had been the one to notice her hiding spot and to know that she was in need of refreshment.

The drink was cool and sweet and reminded her that there were advantages to not being on the road. She was musing on the many other differences between life at court and her life for the past couple of months when a voice spoke behind her.

"Death becomes you, Princess."

She turned around slowly and nodded a greeting to the man who was hidden even further in the shadows than she was. He was tall and thin and dressed with understated elegance. His outfit proclaimed that he was wealthy enough not to have to advertise his affluence on his person.

"I thought everything became me, Lord Adelmar," she said, smiling with mock flirtation at the noble who was old enough to be her father.

"Forgive me, Your Highness," he said with a small bow and an amused smile, "you are, as always, entirely correct."

"And you are, as always, entirely too kind, my lord."

He grinned at this sally, and she felt pleased with herself.

"On the contrary," he said, "I'm beginning to fear that I have never been kind enough. I must be losing my touch. Your," he paused, as if searching for the right word, *"resurrection*, has taken me entirely by surprise."

"Oh come, Lord Adelmar," said Ava, "you'll have a hard time convincing me that anything has ever taken you *entirely* by surprise."

He conceded the point with an elegant gesture of his head. "The Monarchy Trials, at least, were an inspired move. I almost begin to believe you might have a plan to win them."

Ava's senses heightened, and she felt her mind launching into a higher gear. He was the first person to mention the Monarchy Trials, and his choice to do so was as telling as everyone else's omission had been.

"I always play to win, Lord Adelmar," she said lightly. "You should know that."

"Indeed, but it seems I've underestimated you, and that's not something I'm prone to doing." His eyes strayed from hers and followed Aldric's progress around the room instead. "One day you'll have to indulge an old man with the story of how you won over the Arcadians. I confess I wouldn't have believed even *you* were capable of such a thing."

"Why, only a moment ago you confessed to underestimating me." Ava gave a small laugh. "And you always struck me as someone who learns from their mistakes."

The noble's eyebrows rose, and she continued in a harder tone.

"I have also learned from my mistakes, and it has made me stronger. I will achieve what I set out to achieve."

"I greatly look forward to seeing you do just that, Your Highness," he said with another small bow. "And I thank you for a most elucidating conversation."

She allowed the gracious smile to return to her face.

"As always, there is nothing I would rather be doing than conversing with you, my lord."

He smiled again and bid her a short farewell.

Ava watched as he quietly made his way out of the room. *Interesting*, she thought, *very interesting.*

Allowing her eyes to skim across the room, she found herself once more caught by Aldric's gaze. He was looking at her with interest and the slightest of questions. She raised her shoulders in the most infinitesimal of shrugs. It seemed Aldric had already managed to identify the key players at court. She was once again impressed with his skill.

The courtiers were firmly divided into two groups. One group flocked to court to socialize and seek advantageous marriages. They preferred not to risk getting on the bad side of their monarch and chose to remain out of matters of state. The other group were focused on politics and came to court in order to influence the king toward their own preferred policies.

The political group was made up of several factions, but Lord Adelmar was the undeniable leader of this set. Even those in other factions respected his wealth, intelligence, and influence. If he threw his support behind Ava, it would be a severe blow to her brother. And an encouraging vote of confidence for her. Lord Adelmar wouldn't make the mistake of backing the loser.

She was buzzing from the aftermath of their conversation, and it was hard to insert herself back into the inane chatter of the milling socialites. She quickly signaled to the rest of her companions, and they formed up around her in short time. When they left the event they once again traveled as a single bloc. The message was loud and clear, and Ava felt satisfied with her return to court.

They all made their way to Aldric and Mathilde's suite to debrief and strategize.

"Thank you, Hans," said Ava as soon as they were safely inside. "I should have told you to walk behind me."

"That's what I'm here for, isn't it?" He smiled at her. "To think of the things that you forget?"

"We make a good team," she said and then quickly turned toward Aldric when she realized how her words could be construed.

"And thank you, Aldric, for the drink. I sorely needed it."

"In recent months, I've had plenty of experience with these sorts of events, Your Highness," he said. "It required no great skill to discern your need."

"And what did you make of my court?"

"An interesting dynamic." He pursed his lips. "I suspect that your brother has been overconfident and has overplayed his hand. He didn't expect any competition and seems to have made no effort to endear himself to court. The effect of your presence was like a breath of fresh air in a suffocating room. I couldn't help but notice a glaring absence, of course."

Ava nodded. "Princess Clarisse."

"What is she like?" asked Sarah.

"She's..." Ava paused, considering her answer. The truth was that she had hated the other princess from the moment she had laid eyes on her. King Josef had always taught Ava to value her beauty and the advantage it gave her, so it had been a blow to find herself supplanted: no longer the most beautiful princess at the Rangmeran court. It didn't matter that the Lanoverian princesses were famous for their beauty. Ava had lost value in her father's eyes, and she found that difficult to bear.

It didn't help that the childish misconduct King Josef had blamed on Hanna had been connected with the Lanoverian alliance, or that, as Konrad's bride, Clarisse's beauty allowed her brother to gain another advantage over Ava.

Despite the way she had buried her emotions, there were some things that Ava had never been able to see clearly and her sister-in-law was one of them. It seemed rather strange to her now. Clarisse was stunningly beautiful, it was true, but she was dark haired and dark eyed, and her glowing skin was golden. She was altogether the opposite of Ava. They were so different there was no competition. Instead, standing side by side, they provided each other with the perfect foil. Together they would be a force to be reckoned with. Ava wondered why this perspective had never occurred to her before.

"Ava?" prompted Hans, gently.

Looking into his eyes, she wondered how much of her thoughts he was able to guess.

"She's very beautiful." Ava sighed. "But I confess, I've always found her difficult to read. She's never been particularly involved with the court. I guess I would describe her as... distant. Withdrawn."

"Is she the cold type, then?" asked Sarah.

"Nooo," said Ava. "Not cold exactly. More abstracted, I suppose. Like she isn't really present, her head always seems to be in the clouds. I don't think she ever adjusted to life in Rangmere."

"Is she delicate, sickly?" asked Aldric.

"Sickly? No, not particularly." Ava frowned at him. "No more than anyone else, I suppose. Why do you ask?"

"Apparently she hasn't left her room since the assassination."

"What?!"

"The official word is that she suffered minor injuries before Konrad was able to fight off their assailant, and she was so upset by the incident that she's refusing to leave her room until the assassin is found. Obviously, the court has no better read on her than you do since they're divided in their opinions on the situation. Some of them think it's quite likely she's still shaken from the attack, while others think she's just putting it on to be dramatic, and still others are whispering that maybe she actually sustained serious injuries. Though why Konrad would hide such a thing I couldn't guess."

"Something's wrong there," said Ava with certainty. "I haven't the slightest clue what it is, but I'm sure Clarisse wouldn't hide in her room like that. In fact, I would have expected her to be entirely unfazed by the incident."

"I'll see what I can find out then," said Aldric. "How did your conversation with Lord Adelmar go? Will he support you, do you think?"

"I think he's seriously considering it. What did Konrad make of our interaction?"

"Amazingly, I'm not sure if he even saw you." Aldric gave a short bark of laughter. "Or maybe not so amazingly. He was besieged by some rather insistent courtiers at the precise moment Lord Adelmar entered the room, and he was occupied with them until after the man left. Adelmar kept a low profile, I don't think many people saw him. He is obviously astute. Of course, the support of court will do you no good unless you can win the Trials."

Ava nodded gravely and took a moment to think. The others waited in silence.

"You're right, of course," she said at last. "And it's clear that no one wishes to be caught speaking to me of the Trials or even acknowledging that they're going to take place. So, I'll spend my time continuing to win over the court and the populace, and I'll need you all to do some research for me."

"You want to know what we're likely to face at the Trials." As usual, Aldric was a beat ahead of everyone else.

"You all heard Lord Iver. The five most senior magistrates will be allocated a virtue and told to design a trial. The trials themselves will be planned in the strictest secrecy, so we need to find out who the five magistrates are. From there we can begin making educated guesses as to the nature of their trials."

"The servants will know," said Mathilde. "Give me tomorrow, and I'll get you the information."

They spent a little longer discussing their various impressions of the court, but nothing more of significance came out. Until they knew which magistrates had been assigned which trials there was little they could do. When Sarah yawned, setting off a chain reaction that had them all joining her, Ava ordered everyone to bed.

"Tomorrow will be here soon enough. For now, we'll all be better off in our beds."

The next morning, Ava woke early, feeling refreshed and rejuvenated. She was back in her element and was delighted to find that the challenge and excitement were overruling the stress of facing Konrad in the Trials.

Evelyn woke instantly when Ava quietly slipped out of bed but looked much less pleased about facing a new day.

"You're almost as bad as Sarah," she muttered sleepily. "What are you getting up for?"

"Sorry to wake you," said Ava.

"That's all right." Evelyn shook herself. "One way or another this will all be over in a week, and then I'm going to sleep for two days solid before Sarah and I re-join the caravan."

"If I win," said Ava generously, "you can sleep for a week."

Evelyn snorted in amusement as she climbed into her clothes.

Ava was also scrambling into her dress and had only just finished when there was a light tap on the wooden door leading to Hans' room. She called out permission to enter, and Hans strode into the room, looking as if he'd been awake for hours.

"I thought I heard you two moving around. What's on the schedule for today?"

Ava shook her head at him. "Do you ever sleep, Hans?"

"Of course!" He looked confused. "Insufficient rest can lead to inattention at a crucial moment."

"Oh, Hans." Ava shook her head at him. "You're much too good a guard!"

"I didn't know such a thing was possible," he said, sounding amused.

"Well, when I win the Trials and am crowned queen, I'm hardly going to keep you on as my personal guard. You're far too skilled and valuable for that. But how am I ever going to replace you?"

"Replace me?" He looked as if he'd never considered the matter.

"There's plenty of time to worry about that after we win," said Evelyn, and Hans seemed grateful for her intervention.

"Very true, so what are you planning for today, Your Highness?"

"I thought we'd moved beyond the 'Your Highness' stage," said Ava, ignoring his question for the second time.

"Now that we're back at court, it would be inappropriate for me to call you anything else," he replied, a little woodenly.

Ava sighed. "Very well then. Today I would like to go out into the city and try to gauge the mood of the populace. Mathilde will want to stay here to talk to the servants, so I won't disturb her or Aldric, but we should see if Sarah wants to come with us."

"She will," said Evelyn. "She'll love it."

Her prediction turned out to be accurate. Sarah showed great enthusiasm for the idea and spent a full ten minutes deciding which of her dresses would 'send the right message'. In the end, Evelyn was forced to choose one for her. Ava was rather amused by the entire process, but Evelyn and Hans seemed to find it incomprehensible.

"You don't understand," said Sarah. "It's easy when you have a uniform to wear every day."

"Maybe you should join the guard then," suggested Evelyn drily.

Hans gave a bark of laughter and then looked guilty.

Sarah, however, was entirely unfazed.

"I'd make a terrible guard, as you very well know," she told Evelyn before shooing them all out of the room so she could get changed.

Hans was still chuckling to himself over the idea of Sarah as a guard. Ava was glad to see that their return to the castle hadn't caused a complete reversion to the perfect, wooden guard. She hadn't realized how much she had grown accustomed to the new, more relaxed, more fun Hans until he had disappeared.

"Where are you wanting to go first?" he asked, pulling her out of her reverie and making her realize she had been staring at his face.

She repressed a slight flush. "I'm not really sure."

"What about the Square of Fountains?" he asked. "Many of the town women do their washing there, and there are always a lot of children around. It would be the perfect place to showcase the new, approachable Princess Ava."

Ava nodded an enthusiastic agreement, impressed with the idea. Hans really was wasted as a personal guard.

hen Sarah finally emerged, the four of them made their way out of the castle, exchanging gray stone walls and floors for gray cobblestones and houses. The sun shone warmly in a blue sky, however, and the air hinted at summer. Leftover spring flowers hung from window boxes, and the populace filled the streets, enjoying the weather.

Hans insisted that they ride, and they attracted more attention riding through the streets than they would have done walking. People came out to stand in the doors of their homes and shops and call a welcome to Ava. She smiled and waved and called greetings back and felt wholly delighted.

Konrad will hate this when he hears about it, she thought. *He's been milking the people's sympathy, but now his plan has backfired.* A beautiful princess, seemingly returned from the dead, attracted a lot of attention and popularity. More so than Ava had ever received before her 'murder'.

The Square of Fountains took up a full city block, roughly in the middle of Rangmeros. Local women filled the square, using its many fountains to do their household laundry. Children ran between the women, playing games and splashing through the water. It was a pleasant scene despite the occasional childish fight or mother calling reprimands to her boisterous family.

Hans helped Ava to dismount, and Evelyn secured their horses to one of the larger fountains where they could drink from the water. A hush rippled across the square, and then a small girl gave a loud shriek.

"It's the princess!"

Everyone laughed, breaking the tension. Ava made sure her own musical laugh could be heard across the general hubbub and saw many smiles directed toward her in response.

Most of the women returned to their washing; it was a large job for many of them, and they couldn't afford delays. The children, on the other hand, had broken off their games and were gathering into a small mob a safe distance from Ava.

She smiled encouragingly at them, and one young boy worked up the courage to come forward and give her a small bow.

"Welcome back," he said and then seemed pleased with himself for delivering his short message successfully.

"Thank you." Ava knelt down to his level. "I'm very happy to be back with you all."

He nodded and backed away, his place taken by an even smaller girl whose peers had pushed her forward to present Ava with a single flower. The princess accepted the offering with thanks.

A second girl, no older than three, stepped forward next. She had two brown braids and large brown eyes that seemed to take up her whole face. She pointed at Ava accusingly.

"You were dead!" she said in her small piping voice. "Are you a ghost?"

A woman, presumably her mother, gasped in horror and left her washing to rush toward the child. The rest of the children watched with wide eyes, evidently impressed with the young girl's bravery and wanting to hear the answer. Several of them looked poised for flight.

Ava laughed again and held out her hand to the girl.

"I'm not a ghost. Here, take my hand and feel. I'm quite solid, I promise. It was just a misunderstanding. I was never dead at all."

"Oh!" said the girl, seemingly happy with this simple explanation. She toddled forward and lightly touched Ava's outstretched hand. She then gave her the briefest of smiles before rushing back to the safety of the crowd of children as fast as her little legs would take her. When she reached them, she was besieged by questions, and Ava could hear her high voice assuring the others that the princess was definitely not a ghost.

The rest of the children seemed happy with this testimony and surged forward as a group, surrounding Ava. The mother of the little girl had returned to her washing, but all of the gathered women were watching warily to see how Ava would respond. When they saw how she continued to engage with the children, they relaxed.

Hans seemed equally wary of the crowd around Ava, but he was soon surrounded by his own small throng. This one was made up of young boys who wanted to show off their budding skills in strength or combat. Every time Ava looked over at him and his small court she had to suppress a chuckle. He was attempting to maintain his usual vigilance and focus, but he also seemed rather pleased with the children's admiration.

"I have an excellent idea," said Ava, once all the children had spoken to her. "Hans and Evelyn, why don't you organize the children into two teams for a game of quickball?"

Before Hans could protest, something he clearly wanted to do, there was a great cheer from the crowd of boys surrounding him. Quickball was a common Rangmeran game and was highly favored by those children who had aspirations of becoming a guard. It required strength, athleticism, and precision and was considered early practice for the fighting arts.

Ava had never played it herself, it wasn't the type of game that was approved for princesses, but she had often seen the younger trainee guards playing it in one of the smaller castle courtyards. Konrad had occasionally joined them in his adolescence, and he had been a champion at the game. As a child, she had wanted to join them and had always secretly thought she would be rather good at it.

One of the children produced a ball, and they began to form themselves into two teams. Several of the girls, who had been shyly eyeing Evelyn, sidled up to her and expressed their desire to be on her team. She smiled broadly at them and began to take charge of the children.

"And I'll teach the rest of you how to make a special flower crown, if you like," said Sarah brightly to the remaining children. Several of them looked relieved to have an alternative option, and she was soon surrounded by her own small mob.

Ava watched it all with satisfaction as she drifted toward a group of women. They were keeping half an eye on their washing and the other half on their offspring but they greeted her with a formality that hid an underlying warmth. When Hans began to shake off the children in order to follow her, one of the burlier women called out to him.

"Go on, have a game with the children. We won't let anything happen to your princess."

He still looked reluctant, but Ava gave him a pointed look, and he returned his attention to the excited children.

"He's a good one, that Hans," said one of the women.

"Aye," agreed another. "I knew his family, back before they moved to Northhelm, and you couldn't have found nicer people. It was a real shame what happened, if you'll pardon my saying so, Your Highness." She gave a small bob in Ava's direction. Her tone suggested that the princess' presence was an afterthought, but Ava suspected they were, in fact, testing her.

With this in mind, she forced down the emotions that leaped

up at the mention of Hanna. She would deal with them later, when she was alone.

It was still hard not to glance toward Hans, however. The guilt of the secret she was keeping from him wanted to overwhelm her. And her fear of the moment when he discovered the truth and took off for Northhelm was even stronger. But these were the kind of weaknesses Konrad would exploit if he could discover them. Whatever the changes in herself, her role demanded she maintain a calm façade.

"I never met his parents," she said, in response to the comments, "but I was good friends with his sister as a child. I hear she's doing well in Northhelm."

"Is she indeed?" said a third woman. "Well, that's good to hear!"

All of the women seemed pleased with Ava's response, and she squashed down further feelings of guilt at misleading them into thinking she was still in friendly contact with Hanna.

The conversation moved on, and Ava found herself impressed with the subtlety of these women. Without ever saying anything that crossed the line or confronting Ava on anything, they managed to sound her out on a wide variety of issues, from taxation to working conditions and royal privilege. Ava, who had sat through endless meetings and councils with her father, had no trouble keeping up with this questioning. She even found herself enjoying it.

In the past, she had always approached an issue by asking herself what her father would do. Her end goal had always been to please him. But now she served a very different king, one who decreed that his kingdoms thrived when ruled by love. True love.

She still wasn't entirely sure what true love looked like, but she was enjoying working it out for herself. And she was gaining an entirely new perspective on the issues when she asked herself not *what would my father do* but *what would I do*? And more importantly still, *what would truly be best for my kingdom*?

As the women talked, Ava noticed that a rotation seemed to be occurring so that over the course of two hours, most of the women in the square had brought their washing to the fountain where she sat, perched on the rim. She doubted this was normal washing behavior, but she was glad to get the opportunity to hear from so many different women.

Meanwhile, the children ran up and down the square, screaming with excitement and exertion and swarming all over Hans and Evelyn whenever the game gave them an opportunity to do so. Both of the guards seemed to be enjoying themselves, grinning and spurring each of their teams on to greater feats.

Sarah seemed to be having an equal amount of fun. She was sitting on the ground, her skirts spread around her and her lap full of blossoms. Most of the girls surrounding her now wore simple flower circlets and, although her group was quieter, they were regarding her with almost equal levels of adoration. *I couldn't have imagined a more ideal team*, thought Ava.

Only when the children's game was reaching a climax did one of the women casually mention the merchant ban. She kept her voice light and her words incidental, but Ava was too well trained to miss the instant change in the atmosphere of the group.

Ah, she thought, *now we come to it.* This was the issue of greatest importance to the women of Rangmeros, and Ava could understand why. If the merchant ban remained in place it would be a serious blow to the Rangmeran economy, and few of these families would have the necessary reserves to weather the inevitable recession.

"I was there, you know," she said, "when Konrad's guards attacked the merchant caravan." She shook her head. "My two friends were nearly killed." She gestured toward Sarah and Evelyn. *Thank goodness these women don't know that was all my fault.* The thought was almost immediately followed by another. *I still can't quite believe they've forgiven me! They've all treated me far better than I deserve.*

The gathered women exclaimed in horror and shook their heads, tut-tutting sympathetically.

"So, do you know what the merchant council will rule then?" asked one of the bolder women.

"I couldn't say, unfortunately," said Ava. "I suspect it will depend..." she let her voice trail away, but her inference was clear, and she could see the comprehension in the faces around her.

Before any of the women could respond, the quickball game concluded, and the mothers were all mobbed by their children who were looking for either congratulations or commiserations.

It seemed that Hans' team had won but only by the narrowest of margins. Evelyn was already threatening revenge and, before they knew it, the group had promised to return the next morning.

Ava was well pleased. There would be a different group of women washing in the fountains the following day, and she would have a whole new opportunity to listen to their concerns and plant her own seeds. If the day went anything like this one, it would be time well spent.

Sarah teased Evelyn on her loss all the way back to the castle, and even Hans joined in for the occasional dig. Ava smiled absently, but her thoughts were elsewhere. She was wondering which of the courtiers it would be most fruitful to approach after the midday meal and, more importantly, what Mathilde and Aldric had discovered in her absence.

She felt that she was well on her way to winning over Rang-meros, but it would all be for nothing if Konrad won the Trials.

CHAPTER 25

*M*athilde and Aldric were nowhere to be seen when Ava returned to the castle, so she was forced to wait until after the evening meal to hear their report. She tried to use the time to visit her sister-in-law, curious about what she would find, but to her surprise she was turned away at the door of her suite. Apparently, she was still feeling too poorly for visitors. Even family. The whole thing was strange, but Ava could hardly force her way in.

She asked Aldric and Mathilde when she finally saw them if they had heard anything further about Clarisse, but they had nothing. Their day had been busy, however, and Ava had to restrain her impatience while Mathilde reported on the seemingly endless servants she'd connected with over the course of it.

Eventually Aldric gently cut her off, suggesting that they get to the important points.

"Oh, of course, sorry," said Mathilde. "We've managed to confirm that Hartmann has strength, Emmerich, strategic thinking, and Fastred, intelligence. The other two senior magistrates are Gumarich and Leuthar, but no one seems to know which trial they've been given."

"But you're sure of the other three?" asked Ava.

"It was confirmed multiple times," said Aldric. "We could give you the long and rather winding route the news took, but I think you have more important things to think about." He sounded amused, and Ava smiled at him gratefully.

"That's excellent work, both of you," she said. "The next step is to find out what sort of trials they're likely to set."

"There are rumors flying around, of course," said Aldric, "but nothing definite enough to report on. Hopefully we'll have more of an idea tomorrow, or possibly the next day.

It was more progress than Ava would have made on her own, but her gratitude didn't suppress her desire for more definite information. The names of the magistrates weren't enough to make plans on.

Much to her disappointment, Mathilde and Aldric had nothing to report the following two nights.

"There are just too many different opinions out there." Aldric shrugged. "It's taking us awhile to get to know everyone well enough to work out who has accurate information. I'm confident we'll have news on the strength, strategic thinking, and intelligence trials soon, though. It's the compassion and resilience ones that worry me. We still haven't been able to find out who's been assigned to them."

This discouraging news balanced out the excellent progress Ava was making in the Square of Fountains every morning and in the court in the afternoons. She was working tirelessly to win the people to her side and was increasingly confident that if she could win the Trials, her transition to power would be smooth and effortless.

It was a good feeling, like stretching long unused muscles. She had been trained for this role, despite never expecting to compete for the crown, and it felt good to put her training to use. On another level, however, it was quite ironic. When she was angling for the throne of Arcadia, Ava had never once wondered if she would make a good queen. But now that she was on the cusp of winning a legitimate crown, she found herself fighting against self-doubt.

Her most recurrent concern was Hans. Or more specifically, how she would ever cope without him when he left. Despite her resolution not to do so, she found herself relying on his solid presence and sound thinking both practically and emotionally. It was a dangerous path, but she told herself she needed all the support she could get if she was going to win the Trials.

On the evening of the fourth day after their return to the city, Aldric and Mathilde reported partial success.

"We don't have exact details, of course, but we've got some idea of what Hartmann, Emmerich, and Fastred's trials are likely to involve," Aldric said.

"Apparently no one gets creative with the strength trial." Mathilde grimaced. "It's basically the same every generation—a straight one-on-one physical fight. Some years with weapons, some years without. Most people seem to think Hartmann will only require first blood since you're a contender."

"As for Emmerich, we've been able to confirm that he's obsessed with chess. There's no doubt he'll base the trial on it, one way or another."

Ava could hear the hope in Aldric's voice when he added, "Maybe it'll be a straight chess game. That would keep things simple!"

"As for intelligence, apparently Fastred spends all his free time in the royal library. And one of his assistants has let slip that his trial will be knowledge based. Some of the other senior magistrates have been arguing that intelligence and knowledge are two completely different things, but he's refusing to budge. He says a good monarch is a well-informed monarch."

"Well," said Ava, thinking it all over, "that is very useful information indeed. I don't suppose you've heard anything further about the other two trials?"

"No," said Aldric with mild frustration. "No one can even confirm which of them was given which trial. They're by far the most tight-lipped of the magistrates."

"Well, we still have a couple of days," said Ava. "Who knows what will turn up? Keep collecting information tomorrow, and the day after we'll sequester ourselves and prepare for the Trials." It was strange to think that she only had two more days before the Trials. But, somehow, she suspected that no matter how many days she had, she'd never feel quite ready.

When she arrived at the Square of Fountains the next morning, there was the usual buzz of activity, but she found it unusually hard to concentrate. Her mind kept swirling back around to the coming trials, and she wondered if her time would be better spent in the library, cramming for the intelligence trial. Of course, the castle library was one of the biggest in the Four Kingdoms, and she had no idea which areas of knowledge Fastred would focus on, so it would probably be a futile exercise.

While the children swirled around her companions, clamoring for attention, Ava drifted back to the edge of the Square and watched the hubbub from a distance, trying to regain her mental focus.

"I heard you could be found here, Princess," said a voice behind her, and she once again found herself turning around to confront Lord Adelmar.

"I'm here every morning, Lord Adelmar," said Ava.

"Yes, word is getting around about that, you should be more careful."

"I'm not afraid of my brother." Ava allowed a bit of steel to creep into her voice. "I won't run and hide from him."

"So that's not what you've been doing for the last two months, then?"

Ava took a breath before replying, allowing any irritation she felt to drain away, just as she had been taught. Lord Adelmar's words were a challenge, but they were also a crucial piece of information. He either knew or strongly suspected that Konrad was behind their father's assassination and her own attempted murder.

"Of course not." Her tone was mildly chiding. "I was seeking allies."

"My mistake," he said lightly.

Silence fell between them, but Ava waited, curious to know what had brought him to find her. For several minutes, they both stood watching Sarah and Evelyn playing with the children. Hans had obviously noticed their conversation because he had detached himself from the crowd and was standing stiffly at guard, just out of earshot.

Finally, Lord Adelmar spoke.

"There is concern among some of the nobles that Prince Konrad has not demonstrated the restraint and patience required of a monarch."

Ava couldn't help an internal wry laugh at this backhanded reference to her brother's regicide.

"And there have been rumors..." he paused, but Ava remained silent. "Rumors that he further intends to upset the checks and balances that ensure our kingdom remains stable."

"That is concerning indeed, Lord Adelmar. And shows a lamentable lack of wisdom on the part of my brother." Ava shook her head. "It seems that his hunger for power has finally over-come him. A fatal flaw that I fear he inherited from our father. I suppose it was inevitable that one of his children would follow in his footsteps." She let the inference hang in the air between them.

"I'm glad to hear you say as much, Your Highness." He gave her a half bow. "I have long wondered what it would be like to be ruled by a queen."

Ava raised an eyebrow at him, and he smiled inanely. "Just an errant thought, Your Highness, pay it no mind. I actually came here for a bit of a gossip. Have you heard the news?"

"Which news would that be, my lord?"

"Oh, merely that I heard Gumarich was given compassion, and Leuthar was given resilience for the Trials." He wrinkled his nose. "Leuthar is too old school for my tastes. He thinks a monarch should be the strongest fighter in the clan. Lacking in creativity, you might say."

Ava was once again forced to conceal a laugh, this time at the idea that this piece of well-guarded information was common gossip.

As a senior magistrate, it was extremely unlikely that Leuthar maintained the ancient thinking of a clan member. Adelmar's exaggeration was clearly meant as a clue regarding Leuthar's trial. And she understood why he was concerned. With two strength-based, combat trials, Ava had a significantly reduced chance of leaving the Hall of Magistrates alive. Fortunately, she had no intention of completing those trials herself.

"How interesting," she said, in the same tone of voice she would have used to comment on the weather.

He seemed pleased with her calm response and guided the conversation into a rather random assessment of the various hospitals that were operating in Rangmeros. After musing for some time on their various conditions and who among the nobles chose to financially support them, he casually dropped a final name into the conversation.

"It's not well known," he said, his voice giving no indication that he was about to say something important, "but Gumarich is heavily involved, both practically and financially, with running two of the bigger ones. You could say it's his passion. He doesn't like to be seen as a philanthropist, though, so he doesn't let them make much noise about it."

After a couple of minutes of further chit-chat, he bid her farewell and departed, striding out of the square as if he owned it.

Which, Ava mused, *he quite possibly does.*

CHAPTER 26

*A*lthough Ava let Aldric and Mathilde know the basics of her conversation with Lord Adelmar, she canceled their usual evening meeting.

"Take the evening off," she said, "relax and get plenty of sleep. We'll all need to bring our sharpest thinking to our planning tomorrow."

She then took her own advice and went straight to bed where it took her two hours to unwind enough to fall asleep.

In the morning, she rang for the housekeeper and informed her that they would need all of their meals delivered to Aldric and Mathilde's guest suite. The woman's response seemed overly warm for such a simple request, and Ava couldn't help but feel that it was the housekeeper's way of wishing her princess good luck.

Once they had all gathered, Ava summarized her conversation with Lord Adelmar in more detail.

"Which means we have an idea of what to expect for each trial. Now we just have to decide our best approach to each one and decide which ones I will complete and which ones Hans will complete as my champion."

"You only have to actually win three, right?" Sarah sounded a little concerned.

"I'm afraid it's a little more complicated than that," said Ava. "Yesterday afternoon I went to see Lord Iver. I wanted to be sure that he wouldn't challenge the legitimacy of my use of champions. You may remember that we never actually discussed the precedent of Princess Clotilde."

"What did he say?" asked Sarah.

"He seemed familiar with her Trials and was expecting me to take that route. He warned me, however, that as well as winning a minimum of three trials, I am also required to win at least one of the trials that I personally compete in. If you remember, the law requires that I complete at least two myself."

"Konrad still seems confident of his victory," said Aldric. "That's the rumor around the palace, at any rate. There hasn't been even the slightest whisper of the use of champions. So, I think, miraculously, no one has made the connection with Princess Clotilde's precedent."

"The servants were all on tenterhooks the day after we arrived, wondering if the whole thing was going to be canceled." Mathilde began to gather up their breakfast dishes as she talked. "Konrad had a private interview with the Head Magistrate, and no one seemed sure what the outcome would be. It was pretty clear even then that everyone wanted it to go ahead, though. People are nervous to come out and say it, but none of them want to be ruled by Konrad."

"I can understand why," said Ava. "He was cruel even when we were children."

"It seems obvious that Lord Iver supports you, even if he hasn't said so publicly." Hans nodded his thanks to Mathilde as she took his plate. "He knows about the precedent, but he hasn't let on to anyone. If anybody got even a hint of Princess Clotilde, then word about the champions would be all over town."

"Yes." Ava began absentmindedly pleating her skirt with her

fingers. "His support and Lord Adelmar's are significant. Of course, Konrad's no fool. He'll be able to see which way the wind is blowing as easily as we can. And it will only make him more vicious and desperate to win."

She eyed Hans a little uncertainly as she said it, but he met her gaze with confidence.

"I'm not worried," he said. "Konrad and I are the same age, so he often trained with my group when I was a trainee guard. He's good but not as good as he thinks he is. It was well known among the trainees that it was a bad idea to defeat the prince. Those few of us who were capable of doing so, learned how to lose with subtlety."

Evelyn gave a snort of disgust.

"Typical royal entitlement," she muttered, reminding Ava that, unlike Sarah, Evelyn hadn't completely forgiven her for her behavior during the attack on the caravan.

"Maybe." Hans shrugged. "Dealing with Konrad was certainly one of the downsides of training with the Royal Guard. Of course, there were advantages as well. We didn't have to waste hours in the saddle every week which left more time for training."

Evelyn conceded the point with some grace, and Ava got the impression that the superiority of caravan guards versus royal guards was a topic they had discussed before. She forced her mind back to the problem at hand. For some reason, the thought of Hans training was quite a distraction.

"With Lord Adelmar's information, it makes most sense for Hans to act as champion in the strength and resilience trials," she said. "Which leaves intelligence, strategic thinking, and compassion for me."

"Actually," said Aldric, "I wanted to talk to you about that. Princess Alyssa specifically said that you're allowed to make use of more than one champion. And Lord Adelmar has tipped us off that the compassion trial is likely to have some connection with hospitals or at least public health. As you may remember, before I was an attaché, I was a doctor. I think it makes most sense for me to complete the compassion trial."

There was a moment of shocked silence.

"But Aldric, I can't ask that of you!" said Ava finally. "You only came as an international witness, and you've already done far more than that. There's no guarantee the trial won't involve some risk."

"I know that, of course," he said. "But the chances of the *compassion* trial involving physical danger seem very small. Mathilde and I have discussed it, and we think it's for the best. Plus, my monarchs sent clear instructions to the ambassador. They have thrown their full support behind you and expect me, as their representative, to offer any assistance I can. The rest of the kingdoms are well aware of what they'll face if Konrad becomes king."

"If you're sure your monarchs would approve of your involvement, I don't think I can refuse," said Ava. "It's the trial I've been feeling most concerned about. I have no medical training or experience whatsoever. Of course, neither does Konrad, so if you complete the trial as my champion, we'll have a significant advantage."

"If Lord Adelmar's information is correct, I feel fairly confident of success in the compassion trial." Aldric gave a small smile.

"My intention is to bring you all into the Hall of Magistrates with me as my team," said Ava. "It's the only way I can guarantee you'll be able to observe the whole thing. But I have no way of knowing how long it will last and, once you've come in with me, none of us will be able to leave. Not unless I forfeit the Trials altogether which is naturally not an option. So, if any of you would prefer not to come…"

There was a moment of silence as everyone looked around to see if anyone else was going to speak up. When no one did, Hans spoke for them all.

"We're coming with you. We haven't come this far to pull out now."

There was a general nodding of heads and murmur of agreement.

"Thank you," said Ava. "I would never have made it this far without you all, and if I succeed tomorrow it will be thanks to you. My victory will be your victory, and I swear that if I become queen, I won't let you down. I *will* be the ruler the High King requires—if it takes my whole life, I will learn how to love with the sincerity that is needed to see Rangmere prosper." Her eyes were shining with fervor, and she felt buoyed by their support.

"We do not doubt you, Princess," said Aldric with equal gravity. "If it is in our power to put you on the throne, we will do it."

It was hard to return to the minutiae of their planning after exchanging such solemn oaths, but Ava was determined not to leave anything to chance. All the known and suspected possibilities for each trial were discussed and examined, and a strategy was agreed on. Ava had half wondered if they would be finished by lunchtime but, somehow, they were still talking when the evening meal was delivered.

"Enough!" said Ava, when they had eaten. "We could continue all night with endless suppositions. I don't think there's any more to be gained from discussion. It's far more important that we all get a good night's sleep. Especially you, Aldric and Hans."

No one protested this pronouncement, and everyone began to say their good nights.

"The eyes of the Four Kingdoms will be on us tomorrow," said Sarah, once they had left Aldric and Mathilde's suite, "and I have no idea what to wear."

"Oh, for goodness sake, Sarah." Evelyn gave an exaggerated eye roll. "No one will be looking at what you're wearing!"

"They might be!" Sarah said. "I'm here as an official observer on behalf of the traveling merchants, after all. As merchants, we're known to have excellent taste. I wouldn't want to let anyone down." She attempted to look demure but failed to hide the mischievous sparkle in her eyes.

Ava expected Evelyn to protest further, but instead the taller girl just laughed.

"You wouldn't be the cousin I know if you didn't find some way to turn a serious occasion like this into a festival. Go on then, I'll come and help you choose what to wear." Turning to Ava she shrugged her shoulders. "There's no point resisting, she always wears you down in the end."

Ava smiled. "If you can't find something to wear, Sarah, you can always come and raid my wardrobe again."

"Don't tempt me!" said Sarah. "If I'm going to represent the merchants, though, I should do it in something of our own."

"You don't mind if I go with her, Ava, do you?" asked Evelyn. "I'll be along shortly."

"No, of course not," said Ava. "Take as long as you want."

The two cousins headed for Sarah's door while Sarah began to list the top contenders among her dresses. Ava watched them fondly as they disappeared into the room. There was no doubt her life had been more entertaining since they had come into it.

Before she reached her own room, a guard came hurrying down the corridor. He bowed to Ava, but his focus was on Hans.

"Captain, a word?" he asked.

Hans nodded but gestured for the man to wait. Opening the door to Ava's room, he checked that it was empty. Then he waved her inside before turning back to the man.

Ava walked inside, her good mood soured by the sight of the guard. What did he want with Hans? She recognized the man as one of Hans' old troop. Did he have them all on the lookout for trouble? Was Konrad plotting some sort of attack on her after all?

She could understand why he might be tempted. Almost idly,

she wondered what her father would do in her place. She considered the Trials. There was plenty of danger lurking there.

Then she considered her own assets. Aldric was trained as a spy. He knew how to enter a room unseen, and he had sworn to do everything in his power to put her on the throne. How hard would it be for him to sneak into Konrad's room and kill him while he slept? All her problems would be over instantly, and none of them would have to risk their lives at the Trials. It would be a neat solution and, after what had happened with their father, she doubted if anyone would raise much of a fuss.

Plus, said a voice in her mind that sounded uncannily like her father's, *if he gets caught, you can always put the blame on Northhelm.*

Even as she was thinking it, her gaze fell on her mirror. She staggered back in shock. Fur covered her skin, and claws erupted from her fingers.

She stared down at her hands. There was nothing but smooth, pink skin and soft, rounded fingernails. Relief!

What had she been thinking? She covered her face with her graceful, human hands and cried. How easily she had slipped back into her old mode of thinking. How quickly she had considered sacrificing a friend!

Hans strode into the room and paused. A second later he hurried toward her but stopped several steps away.

"Ava! What is it?"

She hated the care and concern in his voice. She didn't deserve it.

"I'm scared." She didn't look up from her hands.

"Don't be. We *will* win. I won't let your brother hurt you."

"Not of Konrad." Ava finally looked into his face. "Of myself. Of being swallowed up again by the wolf and losing myself. You wouldn't believe the horrible thoughts I have sometimes." She couldn't bring herself to admit to Hans what she had been thinking. It was hard enough just hinting at it.

Hans shook his head. "That isn't going to happen. You're

stronger than that, and you're changed now. It doesn't matter what you think, it matters that you reject those thoughts when they come. You choose not to act on them. Every time it will get easier until one day the thoughts won't come at all."

Ava looked at him, desperate for his words to be true.

"And every day until then," he whispered, "I will be here. Helping you to make the right choice."

Ava was suddenly aware that they were alone in the room together. Somehow, with just the two of them, the large room felt fuller than the guest suite had with six of them inside. Hans' presence filled the space, and Ava was unavoidably aware of every small movement he made. He took a step toward her and, before she could control it, a flush rose in her cheeks.

She looked down, trying to hide it.

"Thank you," she said. "For all your support. And for being willing to be my champion. I can see now that you're already my champion; that you have been for the last five years. I have no doubt that I would be dead right now, if it wasn't for you."

As she said the words, she realized how true they were. And she also realized something else. Tomorrow he would fight for her, and he might be injured or even killed. The thought was like a physical pain. She had been fighting her attraction to him for weeks, but it had turned out to be as irresistible as breathing.

Part of her mind still knew all the reasons they couldn't be together. That she was a princess who hoped to become a queen, while he was a guard. And, worst of all, that he loved her because of a lie. But in that moment, all she could think about was the Trials tomorrow.

Her heart beat sped up, and her breathing hitched. She couldn't bear the thought of harm coming to him because of her. And she couldn't bear the thought of letting him go out to fight without knowing how she felt.

She looked back up at him, and something of her emotions must have shown in her face. His breath caught, and he stepped forward so he was standing right in front of her. She mirrored his movement, bringing them close enough to touch.

She met his eyes and saw his love blazing in them, the warmth that was always there in the background leaping readily into full flame.

"Ava," he said, his voice a little ragged, and she had never been so enchanted by the sound of her own name. She took another, impossibly small, step toward him so that if he reached out his arms, she would already be enclosed within them.

"Yes?" she said, finding her voice.

"I told you once that I would never do this again but..." He paused to take a shuddering breath. "If you keep looking at me like that, I don't know if I'll be able to resist."

"Then don't," she said, and it was all the invitation he needed.

His arms wrapped around her, cradling her against his chest, and his lips came down softly onto hers. It was nothing like the kiss they had shared in the forest. That one had been wild and desperate, and she had responded out of her own aching need for love and acceptance.

This time she could feel the intensity of love and the sweetness of homecoming all the way down to her toes. She was instantly sure of two things. One was that, despite her determination to the contrary, she was wildly, madly and irrevocably in love with Hans. She had no need to spend her life searching for true love—it had been waiting beside her all along. The warmth and light of her love transformed the kiss and made their embrace in the forest seem like a pale shade in comparison.

She was certain that she had never wanted anything as badly as she wanted this kiss and the love of this brave, loyal, intelligent man. Which made her second realization all the more terrible.

In a few short hours, he would be going into the arena to face her brother. And she couldn't let him do it on the back of a lie. She could no longer excuse concealing the truth from him. She had told herself she was doing it for Rangmere, but Rangmere deserved better than a ruler who deceived the people closest to her. If Hans turned his back on her, she would simply have to find another way to win.

It was Hans who broke the kiss this time, pulling away just enough to rest his forehead against hers.

"Ava," he whispered again, and she was surprised to find that it was possible for her name to sound sweeter still. She held back a small sob.

Hans instantly picked up on her change of mood.

"What is it?" he asked, his eyes wild with concern.

She shook her head silently for a moment, gathering her thoughts, glad that he hadn't let her go.

"There's something I have to tell you," she said at last. "Something terrible."

"What is it?" he repeated, holding her tighter. She shivered, hating the fact that she felt so safe in his arms.

"You're going to hate me!" Her voice caught on the sob she'd been repressing.

"Impossible." His eyes bored into hers. "That will never happen."

"I've been lying to you." The words fell from her mouth like heavy stones. "I may have saved Hanna by sending her away with Ariana, but I was only saving her from myself. I'm the one who convinced her to join me in the first place, and it was my fault everything went wrong." The words began to come faster. "It was me my father was trying to punish when he made his judgment against Hanna. And, worst of all, I was glad to see her go. Glad that I didn't have any friends left to hold me accountable. To make it hard to control my emotions."

Fat tears rolled down her cheeks, and she waited to feel Hans' arms withdraw.

He didn't move.

"Is that what you've been holding in all this time? I could tell there was something." He sounded more amazed than angry.

Ava couldn't suppress a bubble of hope.

"I'm sorry," she said. "I know I should have told you the whole truth from the start. I was going to tell you eventually, but I had all sorts of excuses for waiting. I can see now that's all they were, though—excuses."

To her astonishment, Hans threw his head back and laughed. It was a light sound that carried a great deal of relief.

"My goodness, Ava," he said at last when his amusement had subsided. "Is that all? You nearly gave me a heart attack!"

"All?" asked Ava, astonished. "I'm responsible for destroying the lives of your entire family and leaving you stranded, all alone, in Rangmere. And I hid it from you."

She was relieved that he didn't seem devastated by her news, but she also felt a strange sort of frustration. Why couldn't he see how serious her actions had been?

Meeting her eyes, he slid his hands down her arms and firmly clasped her fingers in his. Then he smiled at her.

"I always knew what happened that day," he said. "My sister didn't keep any of it back."

"But... how could you have known?" she asked, her voice small. "How could you possibly love me if you knew the truth about me all along?"

"It was your father who was responsible for what happened that day. You were only a thirteen-year-old girl, and you were under immense pressure. Hanna understood that, and she made me understand it, even when I didn't want to." He smiled at the mention of his sister. "She was always good like that."

"Yes, she was," said Ava, still a little dazed at the turn the conversation had taken. Slowly the confusion cleared, and she felt delight build in its place.

"If only I had told you straight away! I've been tormenting myself with this for no reason!"

"Yes." Hans threw her a fond smile. "Let that be a lesson to you never to try to hide anything from me again."

"Yes, Hans," she agreed obediently, moving back into his arms and raising her lips toward his.

He lowered his head eagerly, but before he could meet them, the door behind them opened, and they sprang apart.

"Sorry, that took longer than I expected..." Evelyn looked back and forth between Hans's wooden expression and Ava's flaming cheeks.

"Oh," she said, "sorry. Do you want me to come back later..." again she trailed off, seeming unsure what to say.

"Of course not," said Hans, his voice brisk and professional, "now that you're here, I can safely retire for the night. I'll see you both in the morning."

He gave the smallest of bows in Ava's direction and strode toward his own door. Ava stared after him, struggling to recover from the surge of so many strong emotions. She kept her eyes trained on Hans' back even while she listened to Evelyn move toward her pallet and begin to unload the several weapons she carried on her person.

As Hans stepped through the doorway he looked back into the room and, after glancing in Evelyn's direction, he threw Ava a smile full of affection and a wink. And then the door closed behind him.

Ava wanted to laugh, but she wasn't entirely sure why, and she was a little afraid it might come out hysterical. Suppressing it, she quickly prepared for sleep, carefully keeping her eyes averted from Evelyn. When she slid into bed, she forced herself to lie still.

It was difficult to do when her whole body was singing with energy. She couldn't keep a smile off her face, and she kept thinking of how it had felt to have Hans' arms around her and to feel the glow of love returned.

For an entire hour she relived their conversation, basking in the relief: she had told Hans the truth, and his feelings were unchanged. With the weight of pending separation gone, her mind kept circling back to their mornings at the Square of Fountains and how he had looked surrounded by the children or intent on the game of quickball. Just thinking about him made her heart beat faster and her mouth curve up involuntarily.

But inevitably her thoughts swung back to the Monarchy Trials. In the morning, she would face her brother, and Hans would fight in her place. The thought brought reality crashing back down. She couldn't allow herself to get caught up in her feelings. Until it was all over, she had to maintain a razor-sharp focus.

It took all of her considerable determination and training to force the image of Hans' face from her mind and settle herself enough for sleep.

CHAPTER 27

*A*va woke well before dawn and was instantly far too awake to think of returning to sleep. Her first thoughts were of Hans and the feel of his lips on hers, but almost immediately her mind was consumed with the Trials. By the end of the day, one way or another, everything would be different.

She took her time getting ready, using the familiar routine to settle and steady herself. She was sure she had woken Evelyn with her movements, but the other girl continued to lie quietly on her pallet. Ava suspected that the merchant knew how much Ava needed the space and was giving it to her the only way she could.

When Ava was ready, Evelyn quickly roused and completed her own preparations. Despite attending merely as an observer, she secreted a larger number of weapons than usual around her person. It was a wise move, since none of them knew what the day would hold.

They had agreed to meet in the corridor outside their rooms at dawn, and no one was late. They had all already consumed a simple breakfast and were dressed for the Trials. Aldric carried his black medical bag which Ava had seen only once before.

They made their way through the surprisingly quiet castle corridors. Ava was used to seeing many servants up and about in the hour after dawn.

When they reached the entry foyer, the anomaly became clear.

What looked like every servant in the castle was formed into two rows, in some places several people deep. They created a corridor leading to the front entrance. When Ava appeared, the servants closest to her placed their right fists over their hearts in a gesture of respect. As their neighbors became aware of her arrival, they followed, and soon the entire room was full of saluting servants.

Tears gathered in Ava's eyes, and all lingering doubts were stilled. Her father had been wrong. No amount of power was worth cutting herself off from other people. And here was evidence that it was possible to rule a people by wielding love and respect rather than fear and cold strategy. It was a heartening show of support.

Raising her own fist to her heart, Ava stood for a moment, gazing out at the castle's inhabitants.

"Thank you," she said, her voice ringing through the large space, "I will not let you down."

And then she swept from the castle, her friends close on her heels.

She was still blinking away tears when she emerged into the city, and at first the streets seemed as strangely deserted as the castle corridors had been. But as she moved forward, people appeared in all of the doorways and windows lining the street. Unlike on her morning rides, they called out no greetings, instead they just stood there, fists on their hearts. Their message couldn't have been clearer. It wasn't only the palace; all of Rang-meros stood behind her.

Even as she put her own fist back over her heart, she found herself shivering. This wasn't just a few servants; it was an entire city. An entire kingdom. It was a burden they were giving her, and she was terrified of letting them down.

A presence moved to stand beside her, and warm fingers slid into hers. She didn't have to glance up to know it was Hans. The weight lifted a little. It was a burden she didn't have to carry alone.

No one in her small group reacted to Hans' actions, and Ava somehow doubted it was a real surprise to any of them. The people lining the streets, however, responded with subtle whispers and the rustle of small movements.

She wondered what they were thinking, and then decided she didn't care. In this moment, she needed Hans beside her. No one else's opinion mattered.

When they reached the steps of the Hall of Magistrates, Hans gently slid his hand from hers and took a small step back. She now stood alone, her friends a solid wall at her back. The huge doors were shut, marking the day as one unlike any other. Taking a deep breath, she climbed the steps and pushed them open.

Inside the large marble foyer was a small crowd of people, but they all fell silent at Ava's entry. Lord Iver stepped forward and bowed to her.

"Welcome, royal claimant." His words were heavy with tradition. "Do you hereby agree that you will abide by all rules laid down by the Hall of Magistrates for the conduct of the Monarchy Trials?"

"I do," said Ava.

"And do you hereby commit that if you win, you will rule Rangmere justly and fairly, but if you lose, you will relinquish all claim to the throne?"

"I do."

"Then I hereby declare that the Monarchy Trials are underway. Please follow my clerk." He gestured toward a young man standing behind him. When the clerk stepped forward and flashed her a sheepish smile, Ava recognized him as the one who had been manning the desk when she had registered her claim. She smiled at him broadly to show she harbored no ill will.

He looked relieved.

Ava didn't move.

"This is my team." She returned her focus to Lord Iver. "I formally request that they be granted entry to the Trials with me."

"Your team is recognized," said Lord Iver, equally formally.

Ava silently released a breath she hadn't known she was holding and turned to follow the clerk. The crowd fell apart before them, and she carefully noted who was present.

It looked like most, if not all, of the Rangmeran magistrates were there. The heads of all the major guilds were present along with representatives from each of the noble houses. Lord Adelmar was prominent, and he gave her a solemn nod as she passed.

As promised, the Arcadian and Northhelmian ambassadors had each brought along a small retinue. And Ava suspected that Max and Alyssa had been campaigning on her behalf since the Lanoverian ambassador was also in attendance. She bowed respectfully to Ava when the princess passed.

Once again, the clerk led them into the back section of the Hall. This time, however, they went through large double doors and emerged into an open courtroom. Both side walls were lined with tiered seats, and the middle area, which normally contained several desks and rows of chairs, was empty. Only the large throne-like judge's seat remained at the head of the room with its solid desk in front of it. Ava strongly suspected both would be too heavy to move.

The clerk led them across this room, their steps echoing loudly, and through another door at the back. This led them into a secondary foyer with a number of doors opening out of it. Gesturing toward one of them, he ushered them all into a small room. Several tables were pushed against a wall, and one of them held a tray with various fruits and pastries and a large jug of water.

"This will be your rest chamber," said the clerk. "For your use between trials. I'll call you when they're ready to begin."

"Is my brother here yet?" asked Ava.

"He is," said the clerk after a second's consideration. He was obviously unsure how much information he was allowed to disclose, so Ava refrained from asking any further questions.

When he had left, firmly shutting the door behind him, she took another deep breath and looked around at her companions.

No one said anything.

"Well, I guess this is it," said Sarah finally, wearing a shadow of her usual cheerful smile. "I, for one, will be glad to have this entire saga behind us."

"Yes, indeed," agreed Aldric heartily. "I was pleased to see the Lanoverian ambassador looking so friendly."

"You're forgetting," said Mathilde, "today you're a doctor not a diplomat."

"No, you're the one forgetting," said Aldric, with a fond smile. "I'm talented enough to be both at once."

Sarah laughed at their comfortable banter, and Ava found herself imagining what it would be like to wake up every morning next to Hans. To poke fun at him and laugh together at their inside jokes. It was an appealing picture, but it seemed impossibly far from her reality.

She looked up to find Hans' eyes on her. They were glowing with just a fraction of the fire of the night before, but it was enough to bring an answering glow to her own face. She gave the slightest shake of her head at him and turned to join Evelyn at the food table. She wasn't hungry, but if she was going to keep her head straight, she needed to distance herself from Hans.

"This is good," said Evelyn, her mouth half-full. She held part of a pastry in one hand. "You should have one."

Ava shook her head mutely, pressing her hand to her roiling

stomach. She had been able to get her breakfast down, but she couldn't imagine eating anything else now. She admired Evelyn's unflappable calm.

Before she could get too worked up, the door opened. Spinning around she saw that the clerk had returned.

"Please follow me for the draw," he said.

Filing after him, they all returned to the back foyer, and from there he led them into the converted court room. The seats on either side of the room were now filled with the people from the front foyer, and Lord Iver was sitting in the judge's chair. Five large chairs had appeared from somewhere, and Leuthar, Gumarich, Hartmann, Emmerich and Fastred were seated behind the table, two on one side of Iver, three on the other.

The section of seating closest to the judge's chairs on both sides of the room had been roped off. The clerk gestured for the six of them to sit in the roped off area to the judge's left. Sitting down, Ava looked across the room and straight into her brother's eyes. She had been mostly successful in avoiding him in the past week, so it was almost a shock to see him now.

The true shock, however, came when she saw who was sitting next to him. Princess Clarisse might be too sick to see her own miraculously returned sister-in-law, but she was apparently well enough to attend the Monarchy Trials. They were the only two people sitting in Konrad's section of seating, and Ava wondered how complicit she was in his plotting.

Looking at her as carefully as the distance would allow, Ava concluded that she did, in fact, look unwell. Her beautiful features remained unchanged, but her skin no longer glowed, and she looked as sallow as someone with such golden coloring could look. She kept her eyes trained on her lap and never once looked up to make eye contact with Ava.

Lord Iver stood, and the general murmuring of the audience quieted.

"The order of the trials will now be determined by draw," he said in a loud, clear voice. Another clerk brought forward a tray containing five identical pieces of wood. They were small and polished to a high gloss. Each one contained a symbol representing one of the five trials. The blocks were placed in a large velvet bag, and Lord Iver carefully shook the bag. He then reached in and drew out a block. There was a slight pause during which Ava attempted to read his expression.

"The first trial will be strength." His tone remained neutral.

Glancing at her brother, Ava saw a satisfied smile creep onto his face. He was looking directly at her, and she could read the murderous intent in his eyes. She swallowed, and he looked even more satisfied.

He had no way of knowing that her nerves were not for herself and was probably congratulating himself on the opportunity to knock her out permanently during the first trial.

While this silent exchange was taking place, watched with eager interest by all the spectators within view, Lord Iver had been drawing out the second block.

"The second trial will be compassion."

Ava refrained from glancing toward Aldric, but she heard Mathilde move slightly in her seat.

The rest of the blocks were pulled out quickly, and the remaining trials were announced as intelligence, resilience and strategic thinking. It was a beneficial order for Ava's team since it meant none of them would have to compete in two trials in a row.

Once the order of all the trials had been determined, Lord Iver resumed his seat, and Hartmann stood up to take his place.

"To demonstrate the virtue of strength, the two competitors will engage in armed combat. Each combatant will be permitted to use one weapon of their choice. The fight will continue until one combatant is disabled or concedes defeat. One minute's break will be called at every ten-minute increment from the beginning of the match. Upon hearing the gavel sound, both combatants must disengage. Failure to do so will result in the violating competitor forfeiting the Monarchy Trials."

Ava was sure Hartmann had included the rest break and the option of conceding defeat for her sake. She suspected many of the spectators were expecting her to concede well before the first break was awarded. She could see the smallest shade of disappointment in Konrad's eyes and felt certain he had intended to kill her in the strength trial.

Konrad stood up and removed his cloak. Underneath he was wearing simple clothes, similar to the outfits of the Royal Guard.

"I choose a sword," he said confidently.

Hans leaned over and whispered in her ear.

Standing, Ava announced that her choice was also sword.

"And for my champion," she said, in a clear, ringing voice, "I name my personal guard, Hans."

There was the briefest moment of shocked silence, and then chaos broke loose as everyone began to talk at once, exclaiming and asking their neighbors if such a thing was legal.

Konrad stood frozen for a moment longer than the crowd before letting out a snarl and vaulting over the railing that separated him from the floor. He approached the judge's desk with outrage visible in every line of his body. *He must be very angry, indeed,* thought Ava, *to lose control like that.*

"What is this nonsense, Iver?" he barked, loudly enough to be heard throughout the room.

Lord Iver replied in quiet tones that didn't even carry to Ava, who was sitting closest to the judging magistrates. After a glance toward the foreign ambassadors and Ava's own group, Konrad also lowered his voice. He was clearly still arguing, however.

Happening to glance up, Ava noticed that Clarisse was no longer staring into her lap. Instead she had fixed her gaze upon Ava, and if Ava hadn't known better she would have said it was hope she could see in her sister-in-law's eyes.

After several more minutes of quiet argument, Konrad stalked back to stand in front of his wife. He was no longer even attempting to conceal the murderous rage in his eyes.

Lord Iver stood up again and waved for quiet. When all the muttering and exclaiming had subsided, he addressed the crowd.

"The laws which govern the Monarchy Trials are ancient indeed. Although the provision is seldom used, the law does allow a royal competitor to choose a champion, or champions, from among their team. They may do so for a total of three of the five trials. If a competitor chooses this option, they are required, in addition to winning a total of three trials, to win a minimum of one of the trials in which they personally engage."

He sat back down, and the murmuring resumed although at a quieter volume than before. Ava could see many people in the crowd eyeing her companions, sizing them up and wondering who among them Ava intended to use as champions. She felt a glow of satisfaction. She could see a number of eyes resting upon her and knew that many in the crowd were reassessing their expected outcome.

Searching through the seats, she made eye contact with Lord Adelmar and received a subtle salute from him. His face said that he was impressed, and Ava knew that this was the kind of subtle maneuvering that Rangmerans loved. Far from losing points for weakness, she was gaining them for outsmarting her enemy.

And best of all, unless Clarisse had some sort of hidden skill, Konrad had no one in his own team to call upon even if he wanted to do so. He would have to compete against a fresh opponent in each trial, and she could see that the knowledge had shaken him.

While all of this had been going on, Hans had calmly removed his own cloak and the various weapons he had on his person. When he had finished, he gripped his sword and leaped over the rail. Once on the main floor, he laid it down and began a series of simple warm ups.

Looking at him, Ava glowed with pride. He looked strong and

capable and was possibly the calmest person in the room. She had already been surprised by how well known he was in the city, but after this she knew he would be famous.

Konrad also began to warm up, sizing Hans up as he did so. He was rapidly gaining control over himself, but Ava could still see hints of the anger. She hoped it was a good sign and would unbalance him a little. She was grateful for any small advantage, more for Hans' sake than her own.

After both men had warmed up, Hartmann stood up and requested them to assume fighting position in front of him. They each saluted the judges before settling into a crouch. They were positioned directly in front of Ava, and she could almost have reached out her hand and touched Hans' shoulder. For a brief moment, there was a lull as everyone held their collective breath in anticipation of the initial clash. Into this pause, Konrad spoke. His words were so quiet that Ava doubted even the judges heard him. He spoke to Hans, but they were clearly for Ava's benefit as well.

"You should never have come back," he said. "You should have stayed in the forest, where you were safe. Don't think I haven't seen the way you two look at each other. If I can't kill her, I'll just have to kill you instead."

The last word was barely out of his mouth when he surged forward, and the first clang of their blades rang through the great chamber.

CHAPTER 28

Konrad attacked with ferocity and skill, thrusting and lunging at great speed. He was clearly hoping that Hans had been thrown off balance by his words and that he could use that advantage to end the trial quickly. Hans, however, appeared entirely unperturbed. He parried Konrad with equal skill and speed, dancing just out of reach or meeting his blade with strength and precision.

Konrad seemed infuriated at his inability to land a blow and increased the intensity of his attack. No matter how fast he moved, though, Hans was always there, ready to block him. Ava could tell from Hans' expression that he was busy assessing his opponent, looking for patterns and noting any weaknesses for later use. They had agreed the day before that he would remain on the defensive at first, attempting to exhaust and frustrate Konrad.

At first their plan seemed to be working, but after several minutes of hard fighting, Konrad backed off, circling Hans and attempting to lure him into an attack. Hans refused to take the bait, but Konrad remained on the defensive anyway. He was a

263

master strategist himself and had no doubt recognized the danger of tiring himself out.

Several more minutes passed with only the most desultory of engagements between the combatants, and Ava began to wonder when the first ten-minute bout would finish. Before the gavel sounded, however, Hans moved forward in a lightning quick attack. Konrad, who had clearly not expected it, only just managed to parry him, stepping hurriedly backward.

Now that Hans had gone on the offensive, he didn't let up. His attacks came thick and fast, and it was soon apparent that he was the more skilled swordsman. Ava saw the realization flash in Konrad's eyes and couldn't help the surge of satisfaction that rushed through her.

Despite Hans' superiority, Konrad managed to hold him off, his parries becoming wilder and wilder. It was an even better beginning to the trials than Ava had hoped.

But just as she was thinking that Konrad couldn't last much longer, the bang of the gavel rang through the courtroom-turned-arena.

Hans instantly fell back, breathing heavily, and Ava felt a crushing disappointment. He had been so close to defeating Konrad!

Hurrying back to the rail dividing him from Ava, he accepted a water skin from her and tipped his head back to gulp down some water. Watching him, she felt a sharp pang and wished she were giving him a victory drink. Even with his superior skill, it was hard to send him back into danger a second time.

All too soon, the gavel sounded and he whirled back around, sword already raised, ready to fight again.

Konrad seemed to have rethought his strategy during the brief break, and he began on the offensive once again. He was obviously still thrown, however, because his first attack went completely wide. He only just managed to swing his blade back far enough to catch Hans a glancing blow along the arm.

Konrad's sword ripped Hans' sleeve, but it didn't have anything like the force it needed to disable him. Ava suspected he had only managed to cut him at all because Hans wasn't expecting such a wild and useless thrust.

As the match continued, Konrad seemed to settle, and his attacks returned to their previous level of accuracy. He kept the bout moving at a steady pace, neither retreating into defense nor attacking with particular speed. Ava wasn't sure what he was trying to accomplish, but she was soon distracted from speculating on his strategy by Hans.

Hans had shown no sign of tiring in the first ten-minute bout and had returned to the fight with apparent energy. But as the minutes passed, he started to flag, shaking his head as if fatigued and even losing his footing and slipping at one point. He managed to pull himself back up just in time, but Ava could see a flash of fear in his eyes. Her heart responded with a rush of fear of its own, and she had to remind herself to breathe.

It was now entirely apparent that the momentum of the match had switched. Konrad began to drive his attacks harder, and Hans was barely keeping up with his defense. Ava couldn't understand why Hans had tired so quickly, but she was too busy watching him, her heart in her eyes, to consider reasons and strategies. She had forgotten about their broader aim in the Trials. All she could think of was Hans and her terror that he might be killed.

As she watched, he slipped again, and this time Konrad was ready. He lunged forward, aiming for Hans' heart, but at the last minute, Hans was able to wrench himself around, causing the sword to plunge deep into his shoulder.

Time slowed. Hans fell, and blood blossomed on the floor around him. Ava screamed. And Konrad pulled out his sword, raising it to strike again. Before plunging it back into Hans, however, he paused, glancing back to see if Ava was watching. He clearly wanted to be sure she saw the killing blow.

But his pause cost him. Before he could bring his arm back down, the gavel fell, the sound ringing through the shocked silence of the room.

"Princess Ava's champion has been disabled. Victory in the strength trial goes to Prince Konrad."

Ava felt a distant gratitude to Hartmann, who must have been poised to intervene, but the majority of her mind was focused on Hans. She hardly even registered that they had lost the first trial. All she could see was the pool of blood that seemed to grow larger every second.

Konrad had fallen back a step, disappointment in his face. But as he stood there, watching his downed opponent, his expression transformed into one of satisfaction. After a moment, he turned on his heel and strode out of the room. As he left, he gestured to Clarisse, and she exited with him, presumably on the way to their own rest chamber.

Before Ava could force her frozen limbs to function, Aldric, Mathilde and Evelyn had leaped to their feet and hurried down to kneel at Hans' side. His face was white, and he didn't respond to their presence.

Mathilde produced a bandage from somewhere and pressed it to his wound. Somehow, she maintained the pressure while Aldric and Evelyn lifted him up and carried him out of the arena. No one from the audience moved to assist them, and Ava wanted to scream her frustration at them all. The saner part of her mind knew it wasn't their fault, however. They were as bound by the rules of the Trials as she was. Accepting assistance outside of her team meant forfeiting the Trials.

As they passed her seat, she leaped over the railing herself and rushed to help Aldric and Evelyn with their load. Sarah was trailing behind them, her face white. She didn't attempt to assist them, and Ava was simply glad the other girl had maintained consciousness.

As soon as they were inside the rest chamber, Ava leaped

forward and dragged one of the tables away from the wall. Aldric and Evelyn laid Hans on it while Aldric barked orders to Mathilde who pulled more bandages and various implements out of his medical bag. Evelyn had taken over the job of applying pressure to the existing bandage which was already soaked through with blood.

Sarah had taken up a position at the far end of the room and was averting her eyes from the proceedings. Ava knew she should also get out of the way, but she couldn't bear to leave Hans' side. She stood next to his head, brushing his hair back with her hands and whispering reassurances to him. His eyes were closed, and he gave no sign of having heard her.

She was aware of the flurry of movement from Aldric and Mathilde, but she kept her eyes averted, unable to bear the sight of Hans' wound. Her mind had stalled, playing the same scene over and over again. Konrad looking back at her, his sword raised, while Hans bled at his feet. How had everything changed so quickly?

"I can't get the bleeding to stop," muttered Aldric, and there was a desperate edge to his voice that made Ava shiver.

"We have to take him to hospital," she said. "Otherwise he's going to die!"

"We can't do that, you know we can't," said Evelyn, and her voice was gentler than Ava had ever heard it. "He wouldn't want you to throw away your chance to win the Trials, not even for his life."

"I can't let him die!" Ava focused her eyes on Evelyn.

"Aldric may still be able to save him," said Evelyn although there was more fear than hope in her voice. "But either way, you can't throw away your kingdom for one life, however important he is to you. Think of all the other lives that will be lost if Konrad becomes king."

In a deep part of her mind, Ava knew that Evelyn was right and that this was what it meant to be a ruler. She couldn't put her own desires above the good of her people. *This* was true love. If she hadn't been so heartbroken, she would have laughed at her naivety of the night before—thinking that she had no more to learn about love.

I didn't realize it could hurt so much, she thought.

Hans' eyelids fluttered, and she looked down at him with desperate hope.

"We can't leave." His words were slow and disjointed. "You must go on."

"I know, Hans," said Ava, letting her tears fall onto his face. He smiled up at her even as his eyes unfocused and he slipped back into unconsciousness.

Dimly Ava heard the distant sound of a slamming door and of running footsteps. But she was too focused on the pale face in front of her to even wonder who it was. Only when the door of their own room was violently thrust open, did she start and look around. A figure rushed into the room and then slammed the door behind them, leaning against it and taking deep gulps of air.

It took Ava a full second to register who it was.

Princess Clarisse.

All four of the girls in the room were staring at her, their mouths open. Only Aldric ignored her, too focused on his attempts to treat Hans' wound.

But it was to Aldric that Clarisse spoke, and her words jerked him out of his abstraction.

"You can't stop the bleeding, can you?"

Aldric stared at her.

"How do you know that?" he asked, his voice hard. "It doesn't make any sense. It's a clean wound, it should be simple enough."

"Poison," said Clarisse, and Ava recoiled from the word.

"When Hartmann called the break, my husband could see that he was losing. He was desperate, and he'd brought something with him, just in case. He wiped the tip of the blade in poison and then cut Hans' arm on his first thrust. After that it was just a matter of waiting him out."

The second bout now made sense, and if Konrad had been in the room at that moment, Ava would happily have run him through herself.

"But that's cheating, surely!" Sarah sounded horrified.

"If it can be proved, certainly," said Clarisse. "The rules stated that only one weapon was allowed. As I said, he was desperate."

"Forget that," said Aldric brusquely, cutting them off. "Do you know which poison he used? Do you know how to counter it?"

"I... I think so." She pushed off from the door and approached the table in the middle of the room.

Before she could say any more, however, the door opened again. Clarisse fell back, her hand rising as if to ward off a blow, but it was only the clerk who had shown them to the room. He looked around at them all with wide eyes and then swallowed visibly.

"I'm sorry," he said. "But it's time for the compassion trial."

Ava's eyes flew to Aldric's, and he returned her look grimly.

"I can go," he said. "We've already lost one trial. But if I do, Hans will almost certainly die."

"No," said Ava, shaking her head emphatically. "You stay with Hans. I'll go. I'll work it out somehow." Her doubt was evident in her voice.

"Are you sure?" he asked. "He might die, anyway, I can't guarantee anything."

"But you have to try. I'll just have to do my best."

"I'll go," said a resolute voice from Aldric's side.

"Mathilde!" said Aldric, but she gave him a stern look.

"We've already agreed this should be the safest trial. And I may not be a doctor, but I know a whole lot more than Ava. I've been an apprentice nurse for almost a year now."

Reluctantly Aldric nodded. "She's your best hope," he said to Ava.

"You don't need her here, to help with Hans?" asked Ava.

"No, I'll be all right. Evelyn and the princess will assist me."

The clerk cleared his throat.

"I'm sorry," he said again, "but you need to come now."

Mathilde ran to the jug of water on the table and poured some of it over her hands, washing off the blood. Wiping them clean on a cloth, she rushed back to stand next to the clerk.

"I'm ready," she said.

"Your Highness." He sounded even more reluctant than before. "I'm afraid that as the royal competitor, you have to come, too."

Ava nodded unwillingly and let go of Hans, bending down to brush a light kiss against his forehead.

"Don't you dare die," she whispered to him and then, louder, to the rest of the group, "I'll be back soon."

$\mathcal{K}$ onrad was already there, sitting alone in his section of seating and looking stonier than usual. Ava wondered if he knew where his wife was and guessed from the studied blankness of his gaze that he did. It was all she could do to restrain herself from shouting "cheater" in his face.

But, just as with the treason, no good would come of accusing him without proof. She had to trust that Aldric would be able to save Hans and that when he did, his testimony and that of Clarisse would be enough to have the first trial overturned and Konrad disqualified.

Most of the crowd looked relieved to see Ava appear, and many curious glances were cast at Mathilde. She looked terrified but determined, and Ava felt a rush of gratitude toward her.

"Are you sure about this?" she whispered to the Arcadian.

"I am," she said with certainty.

They had no sooner taken their seats, than Gumarich stood to his feet.

"What greater test of compassion can there be," he said, "than the care we show to those who are weakest among us? To the sick."

Ava felt momentary relief and cast a grateful glance toward Lord Adelmar. He had not led her astray.

"In order to demonstrate this important virtue, the competitors will be required to participate in a plague simulation. Would the competitors please join me on the floor?"

A table had been positioned in the middle of the courtroom, and a single chair had been placed on each side of it.

Ava stood and in a loud voice announced, "For my champion, I name Mathilde of Arcadia."

There was a murmur of voices and the rustle of craning necks as Mathilde stepped down onto the floor. Konrad eyed her with distaste but didn't attempt to protest.

Gumarich gestured for them each to take one of the chairs while he stood at the head of the table. Ava clenched both her fists in her lap. Her worries were only compounding, and she could hardly think straight between the tension she felt for Mathilde and the nightmare that was waiting in the room she had just left.

While Gumarich cleared his throat, she allowed herself to dwell for one moment on Hans and to wonder if he was still alive. But she was exercising every iota of her iron self-control to remain in her seat, and thinking about him didn't help, so she refocused on the trial in front of her.

"In order that the participants not be influenced by each other," Gumarich was saying, "they will write down their initial answers on paper. I will then ask them further questions verbally as directed by the previously prepared parameters of the exercise."

For a wild moment Ava wondered if Mathilde could write. Then she remembered that trainee nurses were required to both prepare and read medical reports on their patients.

"We will now begin. You are the ruling monarch of Rangmere." Gumarich read from a sheet of paper. "Reports have been brought to you of multiple new cases of plague in the Green District of Rangmeros. What do you do?"

Even though it was an imaginary scenario, it was close enough to reality that Ava couldn't help but wince. The Green District was densely populated, and the merchants who lived there were quick to demand assistance from their monarch while at the same time deeply resistant to new regulations. It was the sort of situation that every ruler dreaded.

"You will now have five minutes to complete your initial response on the paper in front of you. This response, and your subsequent verbal responses, will be assigned a score which will determine the winner of the trial. Your time starts now."

Gumarich stepped back from the table and consulted a large pocket watch that he held in his hand. There was silence from the watching crowd, and Ava could imagine the pressure of all those watching eyes.

She tried to think about what answer she would have given, but it was impossible to concentrate. Her thoughts kept circling back to Hans. So, she instead focused on Konrad's face as he deliberated over his answer.

She knew what his actual response would be. At the first report of plague, he would send a squad of soldiers to the infected households with orders to kill all the inhabitants and burn the house to the ground. But he wasn't stupid. He knew this was the *compassion* trial and, as little as he knew about that particular attribute, he knew enough to know it would be something other than his first instinctive response.

He was still thinking when Mathilde began writing, and he couldn't suppress a gleam of unease as he watched her moving hand. After another minute, he also began to write.

Ava forced herself to sit still, but it felt like torture, and she was starting to sweat beneath her dress. Several times she concluded that five minutes *must* have passed, but each time she looked at Gumarich, he remained frozen in place, eyes fixed on the pocket watch.

Finally, the time did pass, and Mathilde and Konrad were instructed to cease writing. Ava let out a sigh of relief and waited impatiently for the trial to progress.

"As the current front runner, I will ask you to read out your answer first, Prince Konrad," Gumarich said.

Konrad cleared his throat uncomfortably and read out what he had written.

Apparently, his response to plague reports would be to send doctors and nurses to the homes of the sick and to provide medicine and food from the palace stores to assist the families involved.

Ava almost snorted at the unlikely scenario he presented. She noted she wasn't the only skeptical one. There were raised eyebrows and amused looks all over the room.

Konrad noticed them, too, and his eyes narrowed. Most people immediately resumed serious expressions, apparently not confident enough in Ava's victory to risk annoying Konrad.

"I see," said Gumarich, his voice giving no indication of what he thought of this answer. He consulted the paper in his hand. Ava wondered how long he had spent coming up with every possible response and developing a scenario to fit it. He must have done a lot of study on the subject.

"This response is successful," he read, and Konrad began to smile, "for a time." Konrad's grin fell away.

"Soon new cases of plague are reported, and there are not enough doctors and nurses to attend them all. On top of this, the other inhabitants of the city have begun to complain that the hospitals are under staffed. What is your response?"

"Well," said Konrad slowly, clearly stalling for time. "In that case, I would have those who were ill taken to the hospitals, so they could be treated in one place. This would also allow the doctors and nurses to attend the other patients as well as the plague patients."

Ava shook her head. He was so far out of his depth, he had lost his head.

Gumarich once again consulted his sheaf of papers.

"All of the sick are moved to the various hospitals throughout Rangmeros," he read. "For a short time, this allows the doctors and nurses to successfully care for them all. However, soon the numbers of the sick grow. Within days, all of the hospitals are full to capacity, and some of the doctors and nurses also become sick. There is now no hope of keeping up with the new cases. The death toll rises, and the traveling merchants issue a merchant ban on Rangmere. Soon the other kingdoms follow suit with a general travel ban. Those citizens of Rangmeros who have not succumbed to the illness flee the city in terror. Some of them are, unknowingly, already carrying the plague, and they spread it to the other towns across Rangmere. Within the space of two months, both the population and economy of Rangmere are decimated."

He delivered the results of the scenario in the same flat tone he had used to announce the trial.

It was a devastating situation that he outlined, so Ava kept her expression serious, but inside she was smiling. Konrad hadn't even lasted five minutes before he had destroyed the kingdom. No doubt he was now cursing the entire trial in his head and resolving never to respond to any situation with compassion again. As if he even knew what the word meant.

Gumarich turned to Mathilde.

"Please read out your initial answer."

Mathilde cleared her throat and read in a loud voice.

"In the case of serious contagious illness, the wellbeing of the whole population must be considered while also taking into account the rights of the ill. At first report of plague symptoms, I would order large quarantine tents to be set up in the fields immediately surrounding the city. Twenty percent of the nurses and doctors from each city hospital would be sent to care for the sick in these tents. Anyone displaying symptoms would be transported to the tents in a covered wagon. Their house would then be marked with a yellow flag, and a guard would be stationed outside it to enforce a one-week home quarantine on the non-symptomatic members of the household. If any of them began to show symptoms, they would be immediately transferred to the tents.

"Those under home quarantine would be offered the option of accompanying their sick family members to the quarantine tents where they would serve as basic nurses and orderlies, fetching water and supplies and generally assisting the medical professionals. Anyone who recovered from the plague, and any healthy assistant who desired to leave the tents, would be required to pass a week in a separate quarantine tent to ensure they would not carry the plague back into the city."

Ava was impressed. It was a far more comprehensive response than she would have come up with, although she didn't think it would take much to beat Konrad. But the trials weren't solely about winning—Mathilde was making her look good which was also important. She could hear the approving murmurs running through the crowd.

"Quarantine tents are established outside the city, but they soon require more supplies than the hospitals have available," Gumarich read. "What is your response?"

"The castle servants would be instructed to conduct a stock take of the castle supplies and determine what provisions would be needed to supply the castle itself for one month. Anything excess to this would be sent to the tents. Messengers bearing certificates of health would also be sent to the surrounding towns and kingdoms to purchase supplies."

"With what gold are these supplies purchased?" asked

Gumarich, and for once he wasn't reading off his paper but was instead regarding Mathilde curiously.

"In order to support the sick, a voluntary contribution would be requested from the citizens of Rangmeros," said Mathilde after a moment's thought. "If this did not raise enough gold, a tax would be levied against all citizens. Everyone benefits from plague quarantine."

"Congratulations," said Gumarich after once again consulting his paper. "The plague is contained, and Rangmeros returns to normal functionality with only one hundred deaths to mourn."

He turned to the other judges.

"I do not believe a consultation is necessary," he said. "The scores are definitive. Princess Ava's champion is the victor."

Ava allowed herself a small smile which was mirrored across the room.

"But she locked the sick and their families away," said Konrad in disgust. "How does that demonstrate compassion?"

"As a ruler," said Gumarich, looking down his nose at the seated prince, "it is your responsibility to show compassion to all members of your kingdom and your job to know how best that can be done. Preventing the spread of plague—but in a way that allows for sufficient care of the sick—is the only valid compassionate response to such a situation. In fact, I want to congratulate the representative from Arcadia for such a thorough and exemplary response. She would be welcome in the hospitals of Rangmere at any time."

Mathilde flushed with pleasure and turned to beam at Ava, but her eyes quickly passed over her and stopped in the doorway behind the judge's table. Following her gaze, Ava saw Evelyn standing there, her hands still stained with Hans' blood.

CHAPTER 30

*F*orgetting all about the trial and Mathilde's victory, Ava leaped to her feet and ran to Evelyn's side. Mathilde was only steps behind her.

"Is he…" she couldn't get the final word out but let her eyes ask the question.

"We think he'll live," said Evelyn. "It was touch and go for a while, but Clarisse's information was invaluable, and Aldric has finally managed to stop the bleeding. He's awake too and asking after you."

Without a backward glance, Ava took off through the foyer and burst into the room where the others were waiting. The table had been pushed back against the wall, and someone had found several cushions which they'd laid out on the ground to make a more comfortable bed for Hans. There was blood everywhere, but everyone was smiling, even Hans, who was propped up slightly by even more cushions. He had a large bandage wrapped around his shoulder, and Ava was relieved to see that there was no blood seeping through it.

She rushed over to him and sank onto her knees.

Slowly he raised one hand and cupped her cheek.

"How did you go?" His words were slow and labored.

She smiled through tears and placed her own hand over his. "We won, of course."

He grinned back at her in response. "Of course, you did. I don't know why I even bothered to ask."

"Oh Hans!" It came out more like a wail than she had intended. "I'm so sorry!"

"What for? Nothing has happened that I wouldn't do over again." His face darkened. "Although if I can get my hands on that cheating brother of yours, that'll be the end of him, and you'll have no need to conduct a trial for treason, after all."

Ava shook her head at him. "You'll do no such thing, or someone will be trying you next. Once I've won, there will be plenty of time to see that Konrad gets justice."

Hans seemed satisfied with this, and Aldric interjected to say that he needed to rest. Hans smiled at Ava ruefully.

"Doctor's orders," she said with her own smile and helped him resettle himself on the pillows.

"So, what happened?" asked Sarah. "And don't just say you won! I want details."

Ava was so relieved to see Hans alive that she took great joy in narrating the entire trial with particular attention on Konrad's ineptitude and Mathilde's excellence. The others were all greatly impressed and showered praises on Mathilde who blushed and disclaimed.

"I was rather relieved when he announced the subject of the trial. Plague training is covered in the first year of nurse training. I kept imagining all these topics he could have brought up that I know nothing about. I think I got lucky more than anything else!"

By the time everyone was finished assuring her that luck had nothing to do with it, the clerk had returned to announce the third trial.

Ava had been so absorbed with Hans' recovery that she had almost forgotten the next trial was her own.

"Let's hope it goes as well for me," she said.

Aldric and Clarisse announced that they would stay with Hans, but the rest of the group wanted to come with Ava. As she passed through the doorway she glanced back and met Hans' eyes from across the room. He reached up and tapped his fist to his heart, and she felt a burst of courage. She could do this.

The table and chairs had been removed from the makeshift arena and had been replaced by two podiums that faced the judge's table. Fastred stood in front of them with his own sheaf of papers.

Ava didn't even have time to sit down before he called for the competitors to take their places behind the podiums. There was yet another rustle through the crowd when Ava herself stepped down onto the floor.

She could feel the rush of energy that came from being the focus of so much attention, and she was glad for it. She would channel it into her performance in the trial.

"A good monarch is a well-informed monarch," announced Fastred once they were both in place. "To demonstrate the virtue of intelligence, you will undergo a test of your general knowledge. If you look in front of you, you will see that you each have a gavel. I will ask a question, and if you know the answer, strike the podium in front of you with the gavel. You will then be given the opportunity to answer. If you are wrong, you will be instantly disqualified."

Wow, thought Ava, *he's tough.*

"If either competitor is the first to strike their gavel and give the correct answer three times in a row, they will be declared the victor."

So once again, rumor had been correct. This trial would be a straight test of knowledge. Ava gulped. For all the training she had received from her father, Konrad, as the heir apparent, had received still more. She picked up the gavel and felt its reassuring weight in her hand.

Using the techniques she had learned as a child, she pushed everything out of her mind except for this moment. When the first question came, she was ready.

The questions didn't follow a logical progression but instead jumped about between multiple topics, covering history, international relations, commerce, trade, and law. Sometimes the two gavels came down so quickly that Fastred had to call on the other judges for a ruling on which one had sounded first. Several times Ava managed to get two questions in a row, but every time she did, Konrad gained a fevered brilliance that ensured his gavel was the next to sound.

After forty minutes, the truly amazing thing was that there hadn't been a single question neither of them could answer. They seemed evenly matched, and Ava couldn't help but feel it was their father who was truly being tested in this trial. For all his faults, in this area he had excelled. He had produced two children with all the knowledge required to rule a kingdom.

But it had been an emotionally taxing few hours and with the focus on Hans' injury, Ava hadn't eaten anything since her breakfast before dawn. She could feel herself starting to fade, and the answers took a second or two longer to appear in her slightly sluggish mind. It was infuriating, but the harder she tried to think, the longer they seemed to take.

When Konrad got a particularly difficult question right, he threw her a triumphant smile. Seeing the expression infuriated her. It was a special one he reserved for her, and he had often flashed it at her behind their father's back when he had scored some imaginary point. All the injustices, not only of the last two months but of her entire life, came flooding back, and when Fastred asked the next question she didn't even hear it.

Konrad's gavel came hammering down, and his response was quick and sure. Two correct answers in a row.

She gripped her gavel tightly in her fist. She couldn't let Konrad get the next question, she just couldn't. This was the first trial where Ava herself was competing, and she had to show everyone, especially her brother, that she could beat him. She stared at Fastred as he consulted the paper in front of him.

Time seemed to slow down as he looked back up, and Ava held her breath, her hand poised, ready.

"In what year did King Christoph amend the treaty between Rangmere and the merchant council, and what was the amendment?"

Ava could recite the entire treaty, including the amendment, but when she tried to remember the year her mind froze. Had it been seventy-three years ago or seventy-four?

Konrad's gavel hadn't sounded yet, so Ava tried to prod her mind into action. It had been after the great drought but before the riots...seventy-four!

Even as her mind formulated the number, her hand flashed down. But the bang of her gavel wasn't the only sound ringing through the room. Konrad had also moved, and the noises had been so simultaneous, Ava had no idea who had been first.

She looked at the panel of judges and willed them to rule in her favor. She was completely sure of her answer now; the amendment had been made seventy-four years ago.

"Judges," said Fastred, "please give your ruling."

The other judges leaned toward each other and murmured quietly. Ava couldn't hear any of the words. The two gavels had fallen in almost perfect timing. Surely, they would find in her favor. She knew she shouldn't hope for preferential treatment, but she couldn't help it. She pinned her gaze on them and hoped they felt the weight of their decision. The future of their kingdom could be resting in their hands. Surely, they didn't want Konrad to rule them.

At last they all leaned back into their seats.

"Although in this instance it was extremely difficult to determine the order in which the gavels struck," said Leuthar, "we find in favor of Prince Konrad."

Ava stared at him in disbelief. She didn't even listen as Konrad gave the perfect answer she knew he would deliver.

The trial was over. Ava had lost.

A wave of fury rose up but instantly subsided into icy numbness. Ava had to remind herself that she wasn't that person anymore. She didn't need to bury her emotions. She would confront them, and she would use them to defeat her brother. There were two more trials to go. She still had a chance to win.

The crowd had responded to her loss with a heavy silence, and she felt many concerned gazes following her from the room. It was a relief to escape into the back foyer.

The result must have been evident in her expression because neither Aldric nor Clarisse asked her the outcome of the trial. Hans was unconscious again, but Aldric informed her that he was merely sleeping and that it was the best thing in the circumstances.

Ava had no wish to relive her failure, so she instead fixed her attention on her sister-in-law. Clarisse's beautiful golden gown was stained with red, and her hair had fallen from its immaculate arrangement, but she looked more peaceful than she had in the courtroom.

"I haven't thanked you," Ava said, "for bringing us the news that saved Hans. I tried to visit you when I got back to the capital, but you were too unwell to receive me."

"Quite the contrary," said Clarisse. "I've been in perfect health for months."

"Oh, I see," said Ava politely, although actually she didn't see at all.

The other princess chuckled darkly.

"I have not been ill or frightened or injured or any of the other things rumored about me since the attack. I have been a prisoner."

"What?" For some reason, this option had never occurred to Ava.

"I always expected to make a political marriage," said Clarisse, somewhat obscurely. "I have many siblings, and they had no other use for me in Lanover. My sisters thought me fortunate, to be marrying a prince who would one day be king. But I hardly need to tell *you* that Konrad is a cruel man."

Ava felt a sinking sensation in her gut. She had always known her brother's nature, of course. But in the two years since his marriage, she had never once put aside her resentment of his beautiful new wife to consider what effect his cruelty might have on Clarisse.

"He never abused me outright." Clarisse shrugged. "He knew I would have fled straight back to my family in such a situation, and he wouldn't have risked the fallout with Lanover. But he had a thousand small ways to make my life miserable and remind me who held the power within our relationship. I responded by disappearing into myself. I'm not quite sure where I've been living for the last two years, but it certainly hasn't been Rangmere."

Ava's guilt grew. Clarisse could have been a friend and a companion, but instead Ava had turned her back on her. She had left the other princess to deal with her new life and new family alone. And from what Ava knew of Lanover, Clarisse could hardly have been prepared for the royal family of Rangmere.

"And then came the night of your father's assassination.

Konrad never talked to me about it, he just assumed I had been cowed into complete submission. But killing his own father? That was beyond the pale. He must have been mad to suppose that I would accept it. He told me that his father was dead and that, as far as the court was concerned, we had also been attacked. It was quite obvious what had happened.

"Unfortunately, in my shock I was far from circumspect, and he realized that I didn't intend to go along with him. He immediately locked me in my room and stationed his own loyal guards outside the door. I have been stuck there ever since."

Ava shook her head, thinking of the guards who had turned her away from Clarisse's suite.

"Thankfully for me," Clarisse continued, "he was so certain of his victory today that he decided I should accompany him in a show of support. He figured if I didn't have the opportunity to speak to anyone, I couldn't do any harm. But when I saw him put the poison on his blade, I knew it was my one chance to escape him for good. As soon as we had returned to the room and his back was turned, I made a run for it. And here I am."

"We are glad to have you," said Ava, with feeling. "And I cannot apologize enough that you have suffered alone for so long. One day, when this is all over, I will tell you the story of what has happened to me in the last few months. I think it will explain a lot."

"I'll look forward to it," said Clarisse, in what Ava thought was a surprisingly forgiving tone. "If we both survive today, that is."

hile she had been speaking with Clarisse, the rest of her team had been deep in discussion at the other end of the room. When she glanced in their direction, they broke off their conversation and moved toward the two princesses.

"The next trial is resilience," said Evelyn, with a quick glance at the sleeping Hans.

Ava gasped. In all the chaos, she had forgotten that Hans was meant to be competing in the next trial. For a second she saw all hope of victory fade, and then Evelyn spoke again.

"There's only one option. I'll compete in his place."

It was the ideal solution. But then Ava's gaze was once again drawn toward Hans, and she remembered that was the old Ava.

"I can't let you do that." She shook her head. "We know it's going to be some sort of physical competition. There's every chance Konrad will try to poison you, too."

"Forewarned is forearmed." Evelyn shrugged. "I just have to make sure his blade never gets close enough to nick me."

Ava didn't want to question Evelyn's skill by suggesting this was easier said than done, but she was unconvinced by the other girl's words or her blasé attitude. She had to be at least a little nervous.

"You didn't even want to come to Rangmere, Evelyn," she said, instead. "You came to protect Sarah, not support me. I can't ask you to risk your life for me."

"You're not asking," said Evelyn. "I'm offering. You're right that I've resented you for what you did, but we've been traveling and living together for weeks now, and I can see that you really have changed. Besides," she grinned at Ava, "if it makes you feel better, I'm not doing this for you. Everyone in the Four Kingdoms will suffer if Konrad becomes king."

Ava could hardly argue with that.

"Thank you," she said. "I won't forget what any of you have done today."

"Make sure you don't," said Sarah with a wicked grin. "I have all sorts of requests I'm planning to make of my friend, the Queen. And they start with a gown as amazing as the one you gave Evelyn."

Everyone laughed, more loudly than the joke warranted. It was just like Sarah to try to relieve the tension with good-natured humor, despite her inevitable concern for her cousin.

The chuckles were still dying away when the door opened and the clerk reappeared. He didn't even have to say anything; they all knew the drill by this point.

Leaving Aldric and Clarisse, the remaining four filed out of the room.

When they entered the makeshift arena, Ava wondered if she'd stepped through the wrong door. The room looked completely different. The large open area in the center was gone and had been replaced with a complex obstacle course. Ava recognized many of the objects from the guard's training ground at the castle. There were hurdles and tunnels and climbing walls and other items Ava couldn't even name.

As well as the objects, the floor was also littered with rather reluctant looking clerks who were dressed in long quilted jackets and padded helmets. Some of them wielded lances, and others held balls the size of melons, similar to the ones used in quickball.

Evelyn paused for a fraction of a second before continuing on to their assigned seating. Once they were seated, Sarah leaned over to say something to her, and the taller girl smiled with amusement.

Once again, Konrad had beaten them back into the room, and the magistrates were quick to begin the trial. It was Leuthar who stood this time and announced the commencement of the resilience trial.

Ava stood and named Evelyn of the traveling merchants as her champion. Konrad looked contemptuous, and she guessed that he didn't think a girl presented much of a challenge. But Ava had seen Evelyn in action enough times to know that he was in for a surprise. She looked forward to seeing Konrad proved wrong.

"The two competitors will complete the obstacle course, beginning here and ending there." Leuthar pointed at the beginning of the course which was directly in front of him and the end of the course which was several feet to his right. The course worked its way down one side of the room and then back up the other.

"The competitors will compete the course one at a time, and the winner will be determined based on speed."

Ava heard Sarah breathe a sigh of relief and turned in time to see her pleased smile. It was a strange test of resilience. Once again Lord Adelmar had proven his value. Just as he had predicted, Leuthar had skewed his trial toward the skills of a warrior. Ava was simply relieved there would be no direct contact between Konrad and Evelyn.

"Each obstacle must be cleared, no obstacle may be bypassed," Leuthar continued. "To ensure that the second competitor receives no unfair advantage, they will have to wait in the back foyer while the first competitor completes the course. As the current front runner, Prince Konrad will perform first."

Both Konrad and Evelyn stood, and a different clerk appeared to lead Evelyn out to the back foyer. Konrad completed another warm up and took his place at the start of the course. He looked to Leuthar, waiting for the signal to begin.

Ava bit the inside of her cheek. Konrad had to be getting tired, mentally if not physically. Evelyn, on the other hand, was relatively fresh. Since many of the obstacles had come from the castle, though, Konrad presumably had more experience training on them.

"Go." Leuthar clicked the button of a stop watch, and Konrad took off.

He had taken three steps and was beginning to build some speed when the purpose of the clerks became clear. The one closest to the beginning of the course was carrying a lance, and he swung the long pole through the air at knee height, directly across Konrad's path. Konrad's gaze had been focused on the first obstacle, and he wasn't able to react in time. The lance hit him across the knees and knocked him off his feet.

Ava almost winced before she remembered who it was.

He was back on his feet within seconds and moving toward the first obstacle, but he was going more warily now. He leaped over the hurdle without interference and then approached the climbing wall behind it. Grabbing the swinging rope, he began to haul himself up the wall, hand over hand.

He had nearly reached the top when a ball came sailing through the air and struck him hard on the shoulder. He cursed and looked toward the thrower and so missed a second ball coming from the opposite direction. The second one hit him in the head and he fell, hard, onto the floor.

Shaking himself off he had to begin again at the bottom of the wall, and Ava could already see his tired muscles starting to shake. This time around he kept a wary eye out for balls, but none came.

Twice seemed to be enough to put him on his guard, and he was more prepared for the interference of the rest of the clerks as he completed the course. Twice more he was knocked down while scaling an obstacle, but he successfully jumped the next lance.

When he reached a strange, circular platform, he leaped onto it, and it immediately began to turn. As the spot he was standing on neared the opposite edge of the circle, he crouched, ready to leap onto an adjacent platform. His leap was poorly timed, however, and he wobbled, nearly falling off.

Ava gritted her teeth, willing him to fall, but he managed to regain his balance and, when two determined looking clerks appeared out of nowhere and leaped onto his back, he was able to throw them off. Ava could now understand the quilted jackets and padded helmets.

He completed the rest of the course without incident but was sweating and shaking at the finish line. Leuthar announced that Konrad's time was five minutes and seven seconds. He was directed to return to his seat while Evelyn was called into the room.

As she walked toward the starting line, Ava could see that the merchant was entirely focused on the course in front of her. Best of all, her gaze was darting back and forth between the various clerks, her eyes narrowed in concentration. Ava could only hope she was smart enough to see what was coming and prepare for it.

When Leuthar called 'go', Evelyn took off at a less headlong pace than Konrad had. Consequently, when the lance swung toward her, she was able to leap over it and continue without checking. Ava wanted to jump up and cheer, but she restrained herself.

When Evelyn reached the wall, she gripped the rope with the same confidence that Konrad had shown and began to pull herself up. She appeared fully focused on the top of the wall, and Ava found herself holding her breath and gripping her hands into such tight fists that her nails cut into her palms.

When the first ball came, it hit Evelyn in the shoulder as it had done for Konrad. Unlike Konrad, however, Evelyn looked, not at the thrower, but at the clerk lurking on her other side. When the second ball came, she was able to use the rope to swing herself wide. It missed her, and in the next moment she was up and over the wall and jumping down the other side.

"Yes, yes, yes!" said Sarah under her breath, and Ava would have smiled at the other girl if she could have torn her eyes away from Evelyn.

There was no question that without the two falls at the beginning of the course, Evelyn was making better time. She was clearly less tired and sore, and she seemed to tackle the obstacles with as much ease as Konrad had done.

Until she came to the two round platforms. She actually checked in front of them, gazing at them quizzically, and Ava suspected she had never seen one before.

Evelyn didn't pause for long, though. She stepped up onto the first one and rocked violently when it began to move. She managed to recover her balance, however, and quickly transferred her focus to the second platform. She was obviously picking up the idea quickly.

When the first platform had nearly completed its half turn, she crouched and at the correct moment leaped onto the second one. The transition was even smoother than Konrad's.

Before Ava could celebrate, however, the two clerks leaped onto Evelyn, and she crumpled under their weight, hitting the platform hard and then rolling off. Both clerks also fell, but they were quick to leap up and scurry away. One paused, clearly torn and wanting to help the prone girl, but after a moment he shook his head and departed. There was no doubt they had been forbidden to interfere in any way outside of their scripted roles.

Evelyn stirred and pulled herself back to her feet.

Ava and Sarah let out synchronized sighs of relief.

The fall meant Evelyn was forced to return to the start of both platforms, and she must have still been dazed because she mistimed the jump onto the first one and slipped off.

The third time, however, she made both jumps perfectly and was ready when the clerks attacked her. Dropping into a crouch and then springing up, she threw them both off without losing her balance.

Ava bit her lip and wished she had a watch with her. She had no idea how much time had elapsed, but it felt like an age since Evelyn had started the course. Of course, Konrad had messed up several of the obstacles and Evelyn only one. Still, it was impossible to know if she was running ahead of his time.

Leuthar's expression certainly gave nothing away, and Ava was starting to wonder if one of the criteria for seniority among the magistrates was the ability to keep a straight face.

As Evelyn sprinted for the finish line, Sarah reached out and gripped Ava's hand. She was holding on so tightly, Ava thought she might lose circulation, but she didn't care. She was glad for the contact.

When Evelyn pulled up in front of Leuthar, she bent over and placed her hands on her knees, panting heavily. Leuthar paused for a long moment, staring at his watch, and Ava suspected the staid man of relishing the drama.

"Five minutes and three seconds," he said at last, and Sarah jumped to her feet with a squeal of triumph.

Evelyn slowly straightened up, a restrained grin on her face. She strolled back over toward Ava, Sarah and Mathilde, and the three girls rushed down to the floor to congratulate her.

"That was amazing!" Ava glanced over toward Konrad. "I think my brother is still reeling from losing to a girl."

The two merchants shared a satisfied grin.

"I think I won *because* I'm a girl, actually," Evelyn said.

Sarah laughed. "Who knew those horrible boys would come in useful one day?"

"Boys?" asked Mathilde.

"When we were children traveling around with the caravan, Evelyn always wanted to be a guard. The boys wouldn't let her train with them, though, so she used to set up training courses whenever she could and practice on her own. Some of the boys thought it was funny to hide along the course and throw things at her or jump out and attack her. They always claimed they were helping her to train, but really they were trying to push her into giving up."

"I won them over in the end." Evelyn shrugged. "They all respect me now."

"And not just them," said Ava, nodding over Evelyn's shoulder at the murmuring crowd. "I think all of Rangmere will respect you now."

A flush crept up Evelyn's cheeks, and she smiled almost shyly.

"I'm just glad I won," she said. "I wasn't sure I was going to make it at the end there."

"Let's go and tell the others the good news," said Mathilde, leading the way out of the courtroom.

CHAPTER 32

*W*hen they entered the room, Ava's first thought was for Hans, but he was still sleeping.

"How did you go?" Clarisse was sitting at one of the tables drinking a glass of water.

"Evelyn won," said Mathilde, looking around the room, "but where's Aldric?"

"He's gone to see the judges, you just missed him," said Clarisse. "He wants to formally register our complaint. About the poison. He thinks they'll want outside medical confirmation before they'll progress it, but he figured it was best to at least register the complaint now."

"It doesn't matter at this point," said Ava.

"What do you mean?" asked Sarah. "If they disqualify Konrad from the strength trial, that means you've already won three. You'll be queen!"

"Except you're forgetting that I have to win one of my own trials," said Ava glumly. "So, either way, it still comes down to the strategic thinking trial. Whoever wins that will win the crown."

"But what if Konrad wins and then is disqualified from the

strength trial?" asked Mathilde. "Then neither of you will have qualified for victory."

"That's true." Ava frowned, trying to remember the tales she had heard in her childhood of the last few Monarchy Trials. "It's happened before, from memory, when there have been more than two competitors. In that case, they knock out the least successful competitor and run the whole thing over again in a week's time with all new trials. I suppose that's what they'd have to do if neither of us ended up winning."

"All over again!" Mathilde sat down hard in a handy chair.

Sarah looked almost as appalled as Mathilde sounded, but Evelyn just looked determined.

"It's not going to happen," she said. "Ava's going to win the final trial, and then she's going to be crowned queen, and then we're going to get rid of Konrad for good."

"Thanks for the vote of confidence," said Ava, strangely buoyed by the other girl's certainty. "I'm certainly going to give it my all."

The door opened again. Could it already be time for the next trial? But it was Aldric, not the clerk, who came into the room. He seemed moderately pleased and reported a receptive audience in Lord Iver.

"It was obvious to everyone watching that something strange happened in that second bout," he said. "But since I'm part of your team, they can't just take my word for it. Even with Princess Clarisse's testimony." He nodded at the princess. "And they'll want to speak to you when this is all over to confirm your story. Lord Iver also promised that once the doors of the Hall have been reopened, they'll have Hans examined by the most senior doctors in the city. Plus, they've already gone to Konrad's room to confiscate his sword for testing. Let's just hope he hasn't managed to clean all the poison off."

"Knowing him, he'll have done whatever he can to cover his

tracks." Ava shook her head in disgust. "Still, at least they took the complaint seriously."

"Also, I got a look at the courtroom," said Aldric. "They don't seem to be in a rush to clear all those obstacles away, and I didn't see any sign of a chess board. We may have been wrong about the final trial."

"Well, there's nothing we can do about that now." Ava was determined not to let fear undermine her courage. "I've spent most of my life training myself to think strategically. I just have to trust that it will be enough."

Remembering what had happened in the intelligence trial, Ava forced herself to go over to the table and choose something to eat and drink. The others were quick to follow her example, and they had just completed their simple meal when the clerk reappeared.

Ava was at the back of the group, and the clerk and all three of her companions had disappeared into the main arena when Konrad came striding out of one of the other doors. He checked for a moment when he saw her and then continued forward, not meeting her gaze.

On a whim, Ava stepped over to intercept him.

"Why did you do it?" she asked. "Why couldn't you have just waited?"

Konrad jerked to a halt and whipped his head up to stare at her. There was an almost manic glint in his eyes, and for a moment he looked strangely wolfish. She flinched, wondering if he would attack her. He made no move to do so, however, simply staring at her with his burning, inhuman eyes.

I guess I'm not the only one who Father turned into a wolf. She shuddered.

"I had to do it," he said, eventually. "He gave me no choice."

"How can you say that? I know he could be harsh, but you were his favorite."

"He was a fool." Konrad ignored her words, speaking in a

fevered tone. "He let you botch things in Arcadia, and then he did nothing to capitalize on their weakness."

"Arcadia was my fault, there was nothing he could have done."

"Of course there was." Contempt filled Konrad's face. "He should have led an attack while they were still recovering. I told him so at the time, but he wouldn't listen to me."

"What are you talking about? Northhelm would have stood with Arcadia. Possibly Lanover as well. We wouldn't have stood a chance against them!"

"Lanover is allied with us, not Arcadia, and you overestimate Northhelm's interest in them, too. Worst of all, you underestimate us, sister. As did Father. I have trained the best army Rangmere has ever seen. Father was an old, cautious fool, or he would have seen the inevitability of our victory. He was holding Rangmere back. As I said, I had no choice."

He stepped around her and disappeared through the door.

Ava stared after him, appalled. He was mad! There could be no other explanation. Twisted by their father into something worse than an animal. Drunk on his love of power and desire for domination, he was blinded to the reality of the other kingdoms' loyalties.

Many of his actions of the past few weeks suddenly made sense. How he had dared attack the merchants at the border, why he had sent only four men after them in the forest, and why his belief in his victory at the Trials had been so absolute. For all his strength and cunning, his mind was so warped, he no longer believed he could be beaten. Rangmere was large and strong, but it couldn't stand against the combined might of the other kingdoms. If Konrad won the trials, he would lead their kingdom into disaster.

She had to win. The alternative seemed doubly unthinkable now. She rushed forward into the arena.

The other three girls had already taken their seats and were looking around for Ava in confusion. As Aldric had reported, clerks were still busy clearing away the obstacles from the resilience trial, and nothing new had been set up.

The final magistrate rose, and Ava examined him for the first time. She knew this had to be Emmerich, but she didn't think she'd ever actually met the man before. He had a bushy white beard, quite different from the distinguished academic look that the other magistrates had perfected. He looked like Ava's childhood visions of a kindly grandfather. His mouth was surrounded by laugh lines, and when he spoke he sounded excited rather than serious.

"The fifth and final trial will test the competitors on their strategic thinking. Unlike the other trials, it will not take place here. Instead, it will be held in the library. The exit to the library has been locked. Each competitor must find one of the two hidden keys and then find the correct exit. The first to emerge from the library will be the winner of the trial, and therefore, the crown." He delivered the last two words in a loud ringing voice before beaming out at the audience. Some of the other magistrates had shown an inclination for the dramatic, but none of them came close to Emmerich.

Ava wondered what such a man would dream up for a trial. How hard could it be to find the library's exit? How many doors did it have? She had visited it once, when she had toured the Hall of Magistrates with her father, and she remembered it as a cavernous room, lined with bookshelves. The middle part of the room had been filled with rows of tables and chairs full of studious clerks. Would the key be hidden in one of the bookshelves? If so, the trial might last all night.

"I invite the competitors to follow me," said Emmerich, with no abatement of his good cheer.

Evelyn reached forward to grip Ava's shoulder in encouragement, and both Sarah and Mathilde patted her on the back as she stepped past them. When she reached the door of the courtroom, she paused to look back at the crowd.

This is it. I will see them again as their queen or possibly not at all. She had no illusions—if Konrad won, his first order of business would be disposing of his pesky younger sister.

As they followed Emmerich across the back foyer, Ava risked a quick glance at Konrad. He was staring straight ahead, his expression determined.

Emmerich paused outside one of the many doors coming off the foyer and turned to face them.

"I must ask you to remain here, Your Highness." He gave Konrad a small bow. "The door will be opened for you in exactly two minutes. I must also warn you, that the trial will be overseen by a number of my clerks. They have been instructed not to engage with the competitors, so it would be fruitless to seek their assistance. Now, if you will follow me, Your Highness." This time he addressed his words to Ava.

"Where's she going?" asked Konrad with narrowed eyes.

"I will conduct her to another door, a separate entrance to the library. But do not worry, both doors are equidistant from the exit, and neither location gives an advantage."

Konrad looked unimpressed, and Ava wondered if he had been hoping to sabotage her in some way. It seemed likely given his conduct so far.

Following Emmerich, she tried to imagine what might be waiting for her in the library. But all she could picture was the chaos the room would be in after she and Konrad had pulled all the books off the shelves in their search for the key.

After passing several doors, Emmerich stopped outside one that looked just like all the others.

"Here we are," he said, still cheerful.

"Thank you." Ava tried to suppress her nerves and wished she could have had her friends by her side.

"You're most welcome, my dear." Emmerich beamed at her. "Just wait here, and the door will open any minute now."

He turned to go and then paused, turning back toward her.

"Oh, and good luck," he said, "and may the best princess win!" With a wink he was gone, and Ava was left with a smile on her own lips.

Before it had died away, the door swung open, and she was confronted with yet another clerk. She was starting to wonder how many of them the Magistrate's Hall had and if they'd had to borrow some for the event.

Without saying anything, he handed her a slip of parchment and then stepped aside, giving her free access into the library. For several seconds, Ava stood there blinking stupidly and trying to work out what she was seeing.

Gone was the large room she remembered. Instead she was facing a long, narrow corridor, lined with books. She took several steps inside but was confronted with nothing but book-shelves. Walking along the corridor, she reached another wall of books. Glancing to her left and right she saw long, book-lined corridors stretching out in either direction. Not far down the left passageway, she saw an opening in the right wall through which she could glimpse more books.

Her eyes slowly widened. Emmerich had apparently trans-formed the enormous library into a giant maze, the corridors of which were created by bookshelves. She shuddered to think of the amount of work that would have gone into moving all the shelves into position. His words about finding the key and the exit now made sense.

She remembered the parchment in her hand and glanced down at it. The bookshelves were tall but didn't reach the ceiling, so there was plenty of light to see by. Several lines were written on the small scrap in an elegant calligraphy.

In two places I am hid,
   One to left and one to right.
   The third and fourth I never did,

On them your eyes will not alight.
So, if you follow as you're bid:
You'll find me hiding in plain sight.

A riddle! She read it through twice more, frowning with concentration. The first line seemed to refer to the two keys hidden in the maze. The second line also seemed obvious, one was hidden somewhere down the left path and one somewhere down the right.

The third line made no sense, however. No one had mentioned a third or fourth object. Out of old habit she held herself completely still while her mind worked furiously. Yes, the first two lines seemed to have a clear meaning, but this was a riddle. If the third line was incomprehensible, it must be because she had missed something in the first two.

"One to left and one to right," she muttered under her breath. "One to left and one to...oh!"

What if the second line referred not to the two door keys but to a different kind of key? The key to the maze. And what if the 'third' and 'fourth' mentioned in the third line were a clue? If she said it aloud, it sounded like 'one, two, left and one, two, right'. What if it meant that she should take a first and second left and then a first and second right?

It was as good a thought as any, so she decided to test it out. As long as she followed the pattern exactly, she could always find her way back if she hit a dead end.

Turning to her left she started off at a jog, ignoring the opening she had seen on the right. When an opening appeared to her left, she took it, still moving at a slow run. This corridor looked exactly like the last one, but this time she reached the end before she saw another opening in the wall of books.

Just like the first corridor, it wasn't a dead end but rather a perpendicular corridor. She paused for a moment to catch her breath and then hurried down the right-hand side. This corridor stretched on much longer than any of the previous ones, and the only openings she could see were to her left. Just as she was starting to doubt herself, an opening appeared to her right. She took it, her sweaty hand clutching the parchment in her closed fist.

She had now completed the instructions by taking two lefts and then two rights, but she was confronted with another long corridor of books with nothing to distinguish it from the others she had already encountered. She decided to start again with two more lefts.

She forced herself to slow down to a fast walk, pacing herself since she had no idea how many times she would have to walk around the maze. As she moved forward she kept her eyes peeled for any openings. The air was full of the musty smell of old paper, and she could see dust motes dancing in the golden beams of sunlight that were lancing down from the tall windows. She shivered at the thought of how much dust must have been disturbed when they relocated all the bookshelves.

Luckily her musings hadn't distracted her from her purpose because the next left was a narrow opening, nearly invisible among the monotony of books. She slipped through and was almost immediately confronted by another perpendicular corridor. Taking the left path, she soon found an opening to her right and took it. Not long after that, she found another opening to her right. This corridor stretched out long and straight ahead of her, so she broke into a light run.

The sound of a muffled cough broke the silence, and Ava jerked to a stop. The effect of the maze was so isolating that she had almost forgotten she wasn't alone in the room. Whirling around she looked behind her, but there was no one there. Slowly she turned in a complete circle, but still she couldn't see anyone.

She wondered if it was Konrad, on the other side of one of the bookshelves. As she was making one last circle around, her gaze strayed upwards, and she staggered back a step in shock. She could see the wall of the library behind her and, perched on the top of a bookshelf that was resting against the wall, was a clerk. He was looking down at her apologetically, and she guessed that he was the author of the cough.

Breathing deeply to calm her racing heartbeat, she continued down the book lined corridor. She passed several openings on her right but none on her left, so she continued on until at last she reached the end of the corridor.

It was a dead end. At first, she felt disappointed, but then she remembered the last line of the riddle. *You'll find me hiding in plain sight.* Maybe this was the hiding place for one of the keys after all.

She slowed down and examined the area carefully. Nothing stood out. It all looked exactly like the many bookshelf corridors she had already encountered. She glanced back down at the paper in her hand.

"You'll find me hiding in plain sight," she read quietly, but saying the words aloud didn't help this time.

In desperation, she considered pulling all the books off the shelves like she had envisioned before entering the maze. Looking directly in front of her, she ran her hand lightly along the spines at eye level. She wasn't paying close attention, she was mostly wondering if a clerk would rush over to stop her if she started manhandling the books.

But as her eyes slid over the spines, she gasped and stopped. Pulling a book off the shelf, she stared at it.

Plain Sight: A Medical History of the Human Eye was beautifully embossed across the cover. Flipping the book open, she found that a small hole had been cut into the pages, and resting inside it was a large brass key.

She grabbed it out of the book and slipped it into a pocket hidden in her skirts. Then she carefully closed the book and slid it back onto the shelf. Before it had fully returned to its place, however, she paused. A clue had directed her to this hiding place, but she had no idea where to go next to find the door.

Pulling the book back out again, she turned it over and shook it. A scrap of parchment slipped out and drifted down to the floor. Bending over she scooped it up in triumph. She was about to read it, when she stopped and tapped the cover of the book thoughtfully.

Running half way back down the corridor, she bent down and pulled a random book from one of the lower shelves. She carefully slid *Plain Sight* into the empty spot and ran back to put the other book where *Plain Sight* had originally been.

She smiled with satisfaction. If Konrad made it here, he would waste a lot of time trying to work out where the key was hidden. She just needed to get moving herself. She didn't want to linger if there was any chance Konrad was on his way.

Still clutching the scrap of parchment, she ran all the way back down the corridor and took a right. She walked several steps up this new corridor until she found an opening on her right and ducked into it.

She then smoothed out the parchment and found a second message.

Congratulations!
> **You're almost there,**
> **it won't be long!**
> **For my second,**
> **I don't belong.**
> **But other than that,**
> **I'm never wrong.**

She frowned, trying to puzzle out its meaning. Her heartbeat had picked up at the thought that she was almost there, and it took more effort than ever to calm herself down and focus on the words in front of her. She kept wondering if Konrad had found the other key and riddle, and if he'd already managed to decipher its message.

While she was still mulling it over, she heard the sound of running footsteps from the corridor she had just vacated. Moving quietly, she pressed herself against one of the book shelves and hoped that Konrad wouldn't turn down her corridor. She had no doubt he would relish physically wresting the key from her.

Thankfully the footsteps didn't slow, and she saw a glimpse of her brother as he hurried past the opening. She then heard him turn left into the corridor where she had found the key.

If she had thought her heart was beating fast before, it was nothing to the pounding that was now going on in her chest. Despite her precautions, she had mostly assumed that Konrad's instructions would lead him from his door to the other key. That the whole thing had been set up so they would never actually cross paths.

She felt desperate to get away from this part of the maze but didn't want to risk taking a wrong turn. She stared down at the riddle again and tried to force her brain to work faster.

When no solution presented itself, she pulled out the first bit of parchment to see if somehow the two riddles went together. But staring down at the first scrap, she got a shock. The words had changed! She was staring at an entirely different riddle.

How is that possible? she wondered. Casting about wildly for an explanation, she turned the parchment over in her hand, and there was the original message. Turning it back over again, she felt like a fool. She'd never even thought to check the back. Reading it over quickly she realized that it was instructions to the hiding place of the second key.

So, assuming Konrad had also received two riddles, there

were two possibilities as to why he had turned up at the same key as she had. Either they'd both just happened to decipher the riddle that led to the same key first, or he'd already found the other key and had decided his best strategy was to get his hands on both of them. If he had failed to find the second riddle or had been unable to decipher it, this actually made sense. Once he had secured both keys, he could take as much time as he needed to find the exit. He would hardly consider Ava a physical danger to him, even if she could find him.

She heard the distant sound of cursing and then a string of thuds that sounded like books hitting the floor. Ava was glad she'd taken the time to hide the *Plain Sight* book.

She stared back down at the riddle in her hand. Sooner or later Konrad would work out she already had the key, and then he'd come looking for her. She had to work out the clues now!

In the back of her mind, she was desperately hoping that she wouldn't be directed back past the entrance to the corridor where Konrad was apparently emptying bookshelves as fast as he could go. As long as it directed her to take a right first, she would be fine.

Be right, be right, be right, she found herself repeating over and over in her mind, until her eyes fixed on the word *wrong*.

If you're never wrong, she thought, *then you're right!*

She reread the riddle. If never being wrong meant making a right turn, then the one that didn't belong would be a left turn. In which case, the riddle was instructing her to turn right to start, then left and then all rights after that.

She was desperate enough to get away from Konrad that she didn't stop to think it through any further. The sound of flying books was still floating over the shelves, so she knew she was safe to step back out of her side corridor.

Assuming the instructions started from the hiding place of the key, she had already taken the first right. Which meant all she had to do from here was take the first left and then keep turning right until she hit a door.

She took off running.

Her feet were flying under her, fueled by equal parts excitement and fear, and she hit the end of the corridor quickly. Turning left, she continued on. The thud of falling books had ceased, but she couldn't be sure if that was because Konrad had stopped or she'd just passed out of hearing range. Somehow, she forced herself to move faster.

She almost missed the next right, sliding to a halt and changing directions at the last second. As soon as she'd recovered her balance, she was off running again.

The next wall she encountered wasn't covered in books, instead it was the actual wall of the room. Before Ava could celebrate this encouraging sign, she heard the sound she'd been dreading, running footsteps behind her. Konrad had heard her after all, and he was coming for her.

She turned to her right and ran along the wall of the room, desperately searching for a door. It was hard to be completely sure, but it sounded like Konrad's steps were only one corridor away. Just as she was starting to question how much longer she could keep up the pace, she spotted a square of brown wood in the wall.

The door! Pulling herself to a stop, her hand dug frantically around in her pocket. It felt like an impossibly long time but was, in fact, only seconds before she had pulled out the key and jammed it into the key hole in front of her.

Holding her breath, she twisted it around and heard a satisfying click. As she pulled the door open, she glanced to her left in time to see Konrad rounding the corner.

He let out a wordless yell of rage when he saw her, but she just smiled at him and stepped through the doorway.

CHAPTER 33

*S*he emerged into a large empty space and was enveloped by a reverberating cheer. It took her a moment to realize the door had exited into the courtroom.

She had won, and the crowd was shouting their approval.

She moved forward, away from the open doorway, and tried to grasp what had just happened. She had won. Rangmere was safe; she would be queen.

Despite all their planning and all their hopes, it was hard to believe.

She looked to her right and saw the rest of her team, standing next to the doorway. They had obviously been waiting there to see who would emerge. They were all smiling at her, and Sarah was actually jumping up and down and clapping her hands.

But best of all, Hans was with them, leaning on Aldric and smiling at her with an expression so full of pride that it made her want to run straight into his arms.

The crowd, however, had begun to climb over the railings. They were surging forward, clearly bent on congratulating their new monarch, and she realized that more personal conversations would have to wait.

Before the people could reach her, however, Konrad appeared in the open doorway. To her surprise he was smiling, although the expression looked strange on his face. He also moved toward her and, for one confused moment, Ava thought she saw a large silver beast instead of a man, his bright claws flashing in her direction.

Then from the corner of her eye, she saw Hans moving. He was coming at her far faster than someone with his injuries should have been capable of moving, and she half turned toward him, meaning to protest.

But before more than a syllable had crossed her lips, the flash she had seen formed into a dagger, and Ava realized her brother's true purpose. She gasped and reached down for her own knife, shock slowing her movements.

As Konrad reached her, he raised the dagger over his head, and someone in the crowd behind Ava screamed. She staggered back, sure she was about to die, and then he was lying at her feet in a pool of blood. It was far bigger than the one Hans had lain in, and with every second it got bigger.

Ava blinked down at it several times, too shocked to understand what she was seeing. She shuddered and looked up to see Hans staring at her with terror and relief, his chest heaving. His hand gripped his bloodied sword, and Ava realized what had happened. He smiled at her, his eyes full of love, and then he collapsed.

She cried out and stepped toward him, but Evelyn, who had been several steps behind Hans, managed to catch his head and arms before they hit the ground. She was straining to hold his greater weight, and Ava was relieved to see several members of the crowd break off and rush to help her.

Lord Iver, meanwhile, had stepped up to Konrad and knelt beside his still body. He examined him closely before standing up again.

"He's dead," he said loudly. "And as the victor of the Monarchy Trials, Princess Ava is our new monarch."

He was interrupted by a small cheer that was soon quelled by his stern look.

"To attack a monarch with the intent of physical harm," he gestured toward the knife at his feet, "is treason. As such, the law states that Prince Konrad is hereby stripped of his royal title. He will not be afforded a royal burial, and the kingdom will not hold a day of mourning. Which means," he allowed a smile to slip across his face, "we are free to celebrate the coronation of our new queen which will take place the day after tomorrow."

There were several calls of "hear, hear!" and several laughs. Ava felt too shocked to process everything that was going on. It seemed unreal to hear herself called queen and, as much as she had always disliked him, it seemed equally strange to celebrate while her brother lay dead at her feet. She was grateful when several clerks came forward and laid a length of black material over his body.

There were now people milling all over the floor of the courtroom. Aldric came pushing through the throng and was soon issuing orders for Hans to be carried to a quieter location. Ava turned, meaning to accompany them, but was prevented from doing so by the crowd around her.

Relief seemed to be the main emotion flowing from person to person, and Ava wasn't sure whether it was primarily aimed at her victory or the dramatic end of Konrad. Clearly any sympathy the people of Rangmeros had felt for him in the wake of their father's death had been worn away, and people had begun to fear his reign. Those present at the Trials were the head of Rangmeran society, and she wondered how many of them suspected her brother's involvement in the assassination.

All of this observation was happening without conscious thought. Instead, her mind was focused on Hans who was being carried out of the room. Her heart was screaming at her to go after him, but instead she was forced to smile and accept seemingly endless congratulations.

When the congratulations began to turn into subtle and not so subtle requests of the new sovereign, Ava decided she had had enough. She was just wondering how best to communicate this to her new subjects when she felt a light touch on her elbow. Looking over she saw that Lord Adelmar had come up beside her. The other people standing closest to her fell back a couple of steps, giving them room.

"You must allow me to congratulate you on making such excellent use of gossip, Your Majesty." His voice was as light as his touch.

Ava admired the adroit way in which he reminded her of her obligation to him.

"Thank you, Lord Adelmar," she said. "I always value good counsel."

"I've actually just been having a most interesting chat," he said, conversationally. Ava followed his gaze to where Princess Clarisse was standing. She had positioned herself away from the crowd but had still attracted her own small gathering of curious well-wishers.

"Perhaps you would allow me to escort you back to the castle in my carriage? I understand you walked here, and I fear that if you were to take to the streets now, you might not reach the castle before midnight."

When she looked at him curiously, he shrugged.

"News of your victory is already spreading through the city. You've made quite an impression on the local populace in the last week. I'm sure the people of Rangmeros will be as eager to convey their congratulations as this crowd is."

Ava couldn't suppress a shudder at the thought.

"Precisely," said Lord Adelmar.

Ava laughed.

"Remind me never to get on your bad side, Lord Adelmar," she said, "you're far too canny."

"Thank you, Your Majesty." He gave her a small bow. "I do my best."

With a look here and a gesture there, he parted an avenue through the crowd for them. Ava decided then and there to ask him to be her Chief Advisor. They would make a powerful team.

Evelyn and Sarah were waiting at the door.

"Aldric and Mathilde went with Hans," said Evelyn in response to Ava's questioning look. "But I knew he would never forgive me if I left you unprotected while he was unconscious."

"You are fortunate in your supporters, Your Majesty." Lord Adelmar gestured all three women to climb into his waiting carriage.

Once they were all settled, he signaled to his coachman, and they took off for the castle. For the first minute or so they rode in silence, Ava's thoughts revolving around Hans. She was desperately hoping that he had simply exhausted himself and not that he had suffered any serious relapse. They were so close to achieving everything they had set out to do, but she couldn't find joy in any of it when Hans' life hung in the balance.

A quiet throat clearing drew her attention back to Lord Adelmar.

"I hesitate to speak in your moment of triumph, Your Majesty," he said, although Ava noticed he didn't sound at all hesitant, "but you said that you value counsel."

"I do." Ava sighed internally. What could he possibly want that couldn't wait?

"Despite the impressive performance of your team in the Trials and your obvious grasp of political machinations, I fear that once the initial excitement dies down, there will still be those who oppose your reign. Rangmere, after all, is a kingdom that values strength, and we are used to having kings who are fighters as well as politicians." He paused respectfully, and Ava frowned.

What he was saying was true, of course, but she didn't know what she could do about it right now. She had hoped that such considerations could at least wait until after the coronation.

"What do you suggest I do, my lord?" she asked. "I can hardly transform myself into a warrior overnight."

"No indeed," he said with a quiet laugh, "please forgive me if you thought I was suggesting any changes needed to be made to your estimable person. It merely occurred to me that a kingdom can have both a queen *and* a king."

"Ah. So, you recommend I marry."

"As soon as possible." He gave a decisive nod. "Stop the talk before it can even get started."

"And who do you propose I ally myself with?" asked Ava.

"Well, that is entirely up to you, Your Majesty," he replied with what Ava suspected was mock humility. "I wouldn't presume to recommend a specific person. I would merely suggest that you choose someone who is well regarded for their combat skill. A hero would be best—the sort of person who would respond quickly and decisively at any hint of treason."

Ava almost let her mouth fall open at his words. He couldn't possibly be suggesting… could he? He looked back at her with a twinkle in his eyes, and an answering giggle came from the other side of the carriage.

They both turned to look at Sarah, and Lord Adelmar raised his eyebrows.

"I don't think we've met."

"You're the one who met Ava at the square two days ago, aren't you?" she asked. "Lord Adelmar, I think it was."

He nodded agreement and relaxed a little.

"And you are Sarah of the traveling merchants." He was obviously unwilling to be outdone.

"Why did you help Ava?" Evelyn narrowed her eyes at him.

"I found myself rather reluctant to swear fealty to her brother," he said equably.

"It seems to me you're pretty powerful around here," said Evelyn. "You didn't have a fancy to be king yourself?"

Lord Adelmar looked a little taken aback by the direct question, and Ava guessed that no one in Rangmeros would have dared to ask him such a thing. But it took him only a moment to regain his usual equanimity.

"Not at all. I assure you, such a desire has never occurred to me. To be a good ruler requires a level of self-sacrifice that I must admit I am far too selfish to desire. My interests are best served in the background."

Evelyn seemed to accept this answer and directed her attention to Ava.

"He's right you know. About the consort thing. A hero is just the sort of person you need." She tried to keep a straight face but was unable to restrain herself from flashing Ava just as wide a grin as Sarah was giving her. Their grins were so identical, in fact, that for one unusual moment they looked almost similar enough to be sisters.

Before Ava could reply, the carriage pulled into the castle courtyard.

"Let's hope his heroism hasn't cost this particular hero his life," she said a little darkly before jumping out of the carriage and hurrying into the castle.

She had been rather afraid that the servants would all be gathered in the entryway once again, but it was blessedly empty. She made it half way across the wide space before the housekeeper appeared from nowhere.

"They've taken him up to their guest suite," she said without Ava needing to utter a word. She flashed her a grateful look and took off up the stairs. She wondered a little ruefully if everyone in the castle knew how she felt about Hans and hoped the absence of celebrating servants didn't mean there was bad news waiting for her.

She paused outside the door of the suite to catch her breath. After a moment, she admitted to herself that she was scared to go in. Giving herself a mental shake, she opened the door and entered.

At first glance, the rooms appeared to be empty, but a small movement drew her attention past the open double doors and into the bedroom. To her relief it was Hans, and he was not only alive but sitting up on the edge of the bed.

She ran to him, crying in her relief.

He slid off the bed and onto one knee.

"My Queen." His voice was deep with emotion.

"No, Hans." She took his hand and pulled him to his feet. "Not from you."

"Why ever not?" He gently traced the outline of her face with his hand. "You've always been my queen, after all."

She leaned her face into his palm and shut her eyes. After a moment, she reopened them and looked up at him.

"Thank you for what you did back there. I was so afraid when you collapsed."

"Nothing like the fear I felt when I saw the knife in Konrad's hand. It gave me such a burst of energy, I didn't even feel my wound."

"What did Aldric say? It can't have been good for you!"

"I reopened my stitches," Hans admitted. "But I've now been stitched back up and fed all sorts of foul tasting concoctions that will apparently help with the blood loss. My nurses have been taking good care of me. They only left because they heard you were back and thought we might want a moment alone. And they were right." He flashed her a wicked grin before pulling her into his arms and pressing his mouth down onto hers.

She returned his embrace enthusiastically, being careful to

avoid his injured shoulder, and felt the flood of joy and triumph that had been missing earlier.

When they finally fell apart, she smiled up at him and was surprised to see a fierceness in his eyes.

"I don't care," he said, his voice rough. "I don't care that you're a queen now and I'm just a guard. I'm not letting you go. Not again."

She smiled up at him playfully. "Well, I guess in that case, it's a good thing I've just been told I need a warrior hero for my husband. Apparently, that's what the kingdom wants. For myself, I want a man who's strong and loyal and good. And, even more importantly, one who brings out the good in me. One who'll make me into a better queen. And I think you might be the only man for the job. What do you say Hans? Will you be my king?"

He stared down at her in wonder and then answered her question with a kiss.

EPILOGUE

*W*ith a kingdom-wide holiday already planned and the relevant international representatives present, Ava thought it made perfect sense to turn one royal celebration into two. The fact that she was finished waiting for her happiness had nothing whatsoever to do with it.

Hans made no objection to such a rushed wedding, in fact he brushed aside any suggestion that he wasn't well enough for the ceremony with scorn. Aldric had to make him promise to rest until the last possible moment and only seemed satisfied after Hans laughingly asked him to stand beside him at the wedding.

"I'm honored, of course," said Aldric, "and accept gladly. But don't think that means I'll be forgetting my role as your doctor. You'll rest until then if I have to hold you down myself!"

Hans agreed with all due solemnity, and Aldric was satisfied.

Sarah, on the other hand, was horrified.

"The day after tomorrow! That's not enough time to get a wedding dress ready! Let alone dresses for your attendants."

"Uh *huh!*" said Evelyn. "Now we get to the heart of it. And I suppose you're expecting to be an attendant?"

"Of course," said Sarah. "And I'm sure you and Mathilde will be as well. We did help win the Trials, didn't we?"

"Funny," said Evelyn, a little caustically, "I don't remember you competing in any of the trials."

"I was essential support personnel," said Sarah in mock outrage. "I even refrained from vomiting at all the blood."

Evelyn opened her mouth to reply, but Ava laughingly intervened.

"I will, of course, be having all three of you as attendants. Along with several other well connected noble girls of the court. And Princess Clarisse."

Evelyn shot her a questioning look.

Ava shrugged. "I'm hoping it will put all the murmuring to rest. Show the people that I trust Clarisse and that she had nothing to do with my brother's treachery. I gave her the choice of remaining or returning to Lanover, and she's chosen to stay in Rangmeros to support me."

"That's good of her," said Sarah. "But it doesn't address the more important matter: our gowns!"

Evelyn rolled her eyes, and Ava laughed again.

"Since the entire city seems to have thrown themselves into the planning with great delight, I now have a veritable army of seamstresses at my command. They may have to stay up all night to achieve it but, one way or another, you will all have dresses."

Sarah jumped in delight and immediately besieged Ava with questions about the color, cut and material. Her disappointment on learning that Ava had handed the whole project over to the royal seamstress was obvious. After a moment's thought, she declared her intention to go find the woman.

"Like the poor lady doesn't have enough to do," said Evelyn after Sarah had left. "For all Sarah's talk, she'll probably be quite helpful, though. She's good at this sort of thing."

"If I'd thought of it earlier, I would have made her my official wedding planner," said Ava.

"She would have loved that." Evelyn smiled. "But she'll enjoy being an attendant just as much. She's ridiculous sometimes, but she has a good heart. I know we bicker a lot, but it's all in good fun. Being raised in the caravan together, we're more like sisters than cousins, and everyone knows that even the best of sisters drives you crazy at times."

"I've never known what that's like," said Ava. "But, since you brought up the caravan, I've been wondering. How much do you like life on the road? Do you think you would ever consider settling down?"

"I've never really thought about it. Why do you ask?"

"Well, my personal guard is about to become my husband." Ava grinned at the thought. "Which means the position is open. And I can only think of one other guard I would trust in the role."

"Your personal guard?"

Ava was encouraged to see that Evelyn looked flattered.

"That's a significant promotion from caravan guard. Are you sure? I don't have any experience at court."

"I couldn't be more sure," said Ava.

"In that case, I'd be honored."

"Honored?" asked Sarah, popping back into the room unexpectedly. "Whatever for?"

"Ava has just asked me to be her personal guard. So, I'm going to stay in Rangmeros."

"Excellent," said Sarah a little absently.

Ava was rather surprised that the other girl wasn't at least a little disappointed to hear that her pseudo-sister wasn't returning to the caravan.

"Thanks for the congratulations," said Evelyn drily. "Let me guess, you're in the middle of hatching some scheme or other?"

"What, me? Scheme?" Sarah laughed. "Of course not! But in all seriousness, that's great Eve, it couldn't have happened to a more deserving person. Plus, it works out quite well since I've decided to stick around, too." She beamed at them both while Evelyn narrowed her eyes suspiciously, and Ava just blinked.

"I didn't like to mention it while we were fighting for our lives and all that," she continued, "but you've been seriously holding out on me, Ava!"

"What do you mean?"

"They might not *quite* measure up to your Hans, but your court is full of an uncommonly large number of handsome young men. There are a couple in particular that I have my eye on. I think one of them will do nicely."

"Do for what?" asked Evelyn in a resigned voice.

"Didn't I tell you I always knew I was destined for better things?" asked Sarah reproachfully.

Ava and Evelyn stared at her, and then both burst into uncontrollable laughter. Evelyn actually had to sit down she was laughing so hard.

"What?" Sarah watched them suspiciously for a minute, and then her own lips twitched. A few seconds later, she joined them.

As her laughter slowly subsided, Ava felt a glow of satisfaction. Her life couldn't have been more different than three months ago. And now these new friends were going to stay and continue to fill her life with laughter. It was a warming thought.

And who knows, she thought with amusement, *knowing Sarah, she'll probably convince some unsuspecting young nobleman to fall in love with her, after all.* There was no doubt the court would be a more cheerful, amusing place with her around. And a little light-hearted cheer was something the Rangmeran court sorely needed.

The changes in her life seemed even more stark two days later when she stood before the gathered court, and as many of the commoners as could fit into the great hall, and gave the solemn oaths of a Rangmeran monarch. When the crown was placed on her head, there was a great cheer, and she felt the weight of it settle, not only on her head but down into her soul. This was her kingdom and her people, and she would do everything in her power to protect and guide them.

Looking across at her new husband, she smiled to see the same determination on his face.

"A crown suits you," she whispered to him.

"I don't care about the crown," he whispered back. "I'm just glad that now, and for the rest of our lives, nothing can stop me from protecting you. So, watch out, Ava. While you're busy looking after the kingdom, I'll be here looking after you."

"I'm looking forward to it," said Ava, and the crowd cheered again to see the newlyweds smile at each other with so much love.

The post-coronation celebration had been quickly adapted into a wedding reception, and the party flowed out into the streets of the city and lasted well into the night. There was much jubilation and even talk of recalling relatives who had moved out of Rangmere.

"Just wait and see," predicted the older citizens. "Rangmere will prosper now that we're ruled by true love again. Just you wait and see."

The younger generations were perfectly happy to agree with their elders when it gave them an excuse to celebrate into the small hours of the morning. Impromptu bonfires and dances sprang up in squares all across the city.

In the castle, Ava and Hans were busy greeting their many guests. There were a couple of surprises among them, too.

The best one was Hans' parents.

Not having time to send for his family had been his only hesitation when Ava had suggested combining the wedding with the coronation, so he was overjoyed to see them rushing forward through the crowd as soon as the official portions of the day were over.

Apparently, they had only arrived in the city that morning although they had set out from Northhelm after they heard of Hans' disappearance.

"It took a while for the news to reach us and a bit longer to get everything ready for the trip," his father said. "We weren't sure what we'd find here, so we made Hanna stay behind."

"She'll be sorry she missed the wedding," his mother added, "but she can't be spared from the royal kitchens, anyway. You wouldn't believe the way she's rising through the ranks!" Her eyes glowed with pride.

"Of course, I'd believe it," said Hans. "Although given the state of things at the time, you two shouldn't have come, either. Who knows what Konrad would have done to you, if you'd arrived here earlier."

"We weren't just planning to rush in and announce ourselves." Hans' father shook his head. "Where do you think you got your smarts from, hey?"

"But we couldn't sit in Northhelm, knowing you were in trouble and too far away to help." His mother directed an affectionate smile toward her husband.

"Well, I'm just glad you were both here today," said Hans.

"So are we, son, so are we." His father clapped him on the back. "Although I think we're both still in shock. Here we were, rushing over to try to get you out of trouble, and we find you're a king! It's all a bit sudden."

"We had to take our time on the road because we weren't traveling alone," said his mother. "So, I'm doubly glad we made it in time. I imagine with all of this rushing around, you haven't had the chance to find a proper bride gift, either."

Hans shook his head and looked a little embarrassed.

Ava felt a sharp pang. She had been hoping that Hans had forgotten about the tradition that required a groom to present his bride with a gift on the morning of their wedding. The inequality of what they each brought to the marriage was already so stark, she didn't want it further emphasized.

"Well, we brought one for you, just like you instructed." His mother was smiling so broadly it looked as if her face might split.

"I asked you to bring a bride gift?" Hans looked as confused as Ava felt.

"You didn't know it would be a bride gift when you asked, of course. Just that it was something Princess Ava sorely needed."

"You brought her?" Hans' eyes lit up.

"Brought who?" Ava looked between Hans and his parents.

Hans' mother nodded at him, and he turned to Ava and took her hand.

"I'm sorry, my bride, that your present is a little late. I would have preferred to have it delivered to your room this morning, as tradition dictates. However, better late than never." His face broke into a grin almost as wide as his mother's. "You already have far more things than I could ever give you. And so, instead, I'm giving you something you've been without for far too long: the love and support of family."

Ava stared at him, her brow wrinkled, and then glanced at his parents, wondering if he meant her new parents-in-law.

And then she saw that there was someone standing behind them. The third person, who had previously been obscured by the crowd, stepped forward.

Ava stared in shock until the tears filled her eyes, and she could no longer see. As the first drop fell, familiar arms wrapped around her, and a familiar scent enveloped her. She and Hans had thought they had been married alone, without the support of family. But they had been wrong. They had both had family present that day.

~

When the tears and the hugs and the exclamations were finally finished, Hans explained just how he had managed to bring Ava the best bride gift she could have imagined.

"My parents wrote to me months ago to tell me they had met your grandmother in Northgate."

Ava stared at her grandmother.

"All these years I imagined you hiding in the Arcadian forest, but you were actually in the Northhelmian capital!"

"It was well known how much I loved the forest." Her grandmother shook her head. "My one goal was to make sure none of you ever found me.

"Your brother was far too much like my late husband." She shivered. "There was never anything I could do for him. And then you made it clear there was nothing I could do for you, either. You had made your choice and, once your mother was gone, I wanted nothing more than to forget."

"I was afraid that Father had killed you." It was the first time Ava had ever spoken her fear out loud.

"I'm so sorry, chicky." Her grandmother patted her on the cheek. "I can see now that I was blinded by my grief. I never should have abandoned you."

"No, no." Ava shook her head vehemently. "It's not your fault. None of it was your fault. I'm just glad to have you back."

"Well, your young man here…" She broke off to lean in and whisper in Ava's ear. "He's rather a fine specimen. Well done, my dear!"

Ava blushed and laughed.

Hans regarded them both with a raised eyebrow.

Her grandmother continued, entirely unfazed. "Your young man wrote me a very persuasive letter. It made me realize that I was being selfish hiding away in Northhelm. No matter how much I told myself I was free, your father was still the one in control. How was it freedom if I couldn't spend my remaining years in my own kingdom with my own granddaughter?"

"You never said a word!" Ava poked Hans in the chest.

"I didn't want to get your hopes up in case she refused to come."

"When the news came that you and your father were dead, I was afraid I was too late," said her grandmother. "But then these fine people persuaded me to hope." She gestured toward Hans' parents. "They wanted me to wait behind in Northgate while they came here, looking for information. But I was done with waiting."

"We knew that Hans would never have shirked his duty," said his father. "When his friends reported to us that he was missing, we guessed that you must be with him, Your Majesty. We couldn't dissuade your grandmother from accompanying us, so we all set out for Rangmeros to see if we could find your trail."

Ava shook her head. It was all a little too wonderful to believe. She gripped Hans' sleeve in one hand and held tightly to her grandmother's hand with the other. They were solid and real beneath her fingers.

Perhaps she could believe it after all. Her face broke into a smile.

The second surprise didn't appear until Ava finally had the chance to sit down with a delicious looking slice of cake.

"Ooh, that looks good," said a vaguely familiar voice, and then an arm snaked out and whisked the plate out of her hand.

Ava turned around, and the protest died on her lips. The being who sat down next to her had steely gray hair and wings, and the last time she had seen her they had been deep in a forest.

"Well," said the godmother after taking a couple of bites and smacking her lips appreciatively, "you've surprised me. And not many people end up doing that."

"Thanks...I think."

"Oh, it's definitely a compliment. You've turned yourself around and no mistake."

"Well, your High King had something to do with that."

"He usually does." The godmother chuckled. "Which is why I'm here, of course. I'm the official bearer of his congratulations. On the wedding and the coronation. We're all right pleased with how things turned out, in fact."

"I haven't forgotten that I owe him my allegiance. I'm already doing my best to learn about true love."

"I'm sure you are, my dear," said the godmother, although she looked a little distracted by the final few bites of her cake. When she'd finished, she set the fork down and pinned Ava with a piercing stare.

"He might be calling on you, you know. He told you that there's a darkness brewing in Northhelm. They'll need all the friends they can get when the time comes."

"Of course," said Ava eagerly. "Northhelm have given me their full support, and I'd do no less for them. Or for the High King, of course."

"I'm glad to hear that." The godmother got back to her feet. "And I never thought I'd say it, but I look forward to seeing you again. And gracing the Christenings of all your children, of course." She winked at the startled Ava and was gone.

"Well, that was unexpected," said a familiar voice behind her, and she welcomed the arms that slipped around her shoulders.

Leaning her head back against Hans' chest, she sighed. "It's been a long week, but I guess we've done things right."

He pulled her to her feet and spun her around, keeping her inside his arms and smiling down at her.

"Just you wait, my dearest wife." His voice lingered proudly on the word. "We're just getting started."

NOTE FROM THE AUTHOR

Want to read more about Ava and Hans' wedding? Want to see Sarah and Evelyn get their own happily ever afters? Turn the page for a sneak peek of the Four Kingdoms novella, *Happily Ever Afters: A Reimagining of Snow White and Rose Red*.

Thank you for taking the time to read my book. If you enjoyed it, please spread the word! You could start by leaving a review on Amazon (or Goodreads or Facebook or any other social media site). Your review would be very much appreciated and would make a big difference to me!

To be kept informed of my new releases and for free extra content, including an exclusive bonus chapter of the first Four Kingdoms novel, *The Princess Companion*, please sign up to my mailing list at www.melaniecellier.com. At my website, you'll also find an array of free extra content, including a prequel short story to *The Princess Fugitive*.

ENCHANTMENT

"*I*t wasn't an easy item for me to acquire." The strange man twirled the red jewel through his fingers in a casual manner. "The cost will be high."

"Whatever it is, I'm willing to pay it." The young man eyed the stranger before him with distaste. The man's leathery, wrinkled skin barely looked human. It was almost bronze in color, unlike anything he had seen before in the Four Kingdoms.

"I'm not talking about gold." The short man seemed amused by the younger man's disapproval.

"I will have that jewel, whatever the cost. Just as long as it does what you say it does."

"Of course." The stranger remained unoffended. "I, ah, *acquired* it from a godmother. You've seen its power for yourself. But are you sure you don't want to hear my terms?"

The young man shook his head. His eyes had drifted down and latched onto the gleaming surface of the gem. He didn't bother to look back up. He had already seen a demonstration of the jewel's enchantment, and he knew it was the only way for him to get what should have been his all along.

The many facets of the stone reflected the light until it bathed the entire clearing in a red glow. Still he kept his eyes fixed on it. First, he would claim his rightful place. After that, the possibilities were endless.

He could bide his time. Eventually the perfect opportunity would present itself, and Rangmere would be his to control. He just knew it was his destiny.

The stranger chuckled, but the young man, lost in the red radiance of his dreams, didn't notice.

SARAH

I twirled in front of the mirror and sighed in satisfaction. The pink silk swished around me in a luxurious swirl. It was definitely the most beautiful—and expensive—dress I had ever worn. In the back of my mind I kept calculating the cost of the gown and marveling at the sum. I hadn't grown up in a merchant caravan for nothing.

Thinking about the way the dress complemented my coloring made me think of my cousin. I looked at the closed door and sighed again, this time in exasperation. In another moment, it had changed into a giggle, however. No wonder she was late. It didn't matter that Evelyn's dress would suit her just as well, she was going to hate the pink. I grinned.

Only a royal decree, issued by Rangmere's new queen, had convinced Evelyn that she had to wear a dress instead of her guard's outfit. She had tried to use her new role of personal guard to the queen as an excuse, but Ava had overruled her.

"For this one day, you're off duty," the queen had said. "And I won't hear any more arguing about it."

Even Evelyn had subsided after that. Truth be told, Ava could be a little scary when she put on her royal manner. Sometimes she would get a certain look on her face, sort of cold and calculating, that reminded me she had once used me as a human shield, thrusting me into the reach of several hostile soldiers to cover her escape.

I knew she had changed—was doing her best to keep on changing—but she couldn't entirely erase the person she used to be. I don't think she even wanted to. On some level those attributes were necessary for a monarch, especially a queen. As long as they were properly balanced by a true concern for others.

So, I wasn't scared she would ever do something like that again, to me or to anyone else. But it didn't stop the occasional nightmare, or the shiver I got when she assumed her cold and queenly voice.

I shook off the thought. Ava had only been queen for two days, and Evelyn and I had helped to make that happen. Now was a time for celebration. I was wearing a dress that would have cost my parents an entire month of their earnings, and I looked incredible. I refused to think any but happy thoughts.

I returned to twirling in front of the mirror and imagining the look of horror that would soon be on Evelyn's face. The smile was back within seconds.

I was just wondering how I would ever bear to take the dress off when the door opened.

"Finally!" I turned around to confront the latecomer. But to my surprise it was Mathilde, not Evelyn, who was letting herself into the room.

"Still wearing it?" She smiled at me.

"I can't bear to take it off." I stroked the material lovingly. "How did yours fit?"

"As excellently as I can see yours does. They must have been up all night working on them."

"From what I understand, they had just about every seamstress in the city working shifts. They did a marvelous job."

"Oh, that's right, you talked to the head seamstress, didn't you?"

"Yes, I couldn't risk them putting us in something horrid." I scrunched up my nose at the thought. "I shouldn't have worried though, they'd already picked out the material, and it's perfect. They were friendly, too. The head seamstress is splendid and was even interested in some of my suggestions. The sashes were my idea."

I pointed at the light gold sash that highlighted my trim waist. It was the perfect complement to the deep rose of the dress, and I felt yet another glow of satisfaction. The Rangmeran court wasn't going to know what hit them.

I grinned. "She's offered to work with me to design some dresses when all of the excitement is over, too. I can't wait."

Mathilde glanced at the second, untouched dress lying across my bed.

"I take it Evelyn hasn't found the time to try her dress on?" Mathilde's voice mirrored my own amusement. "Has she even seen it yet?"

"I don't think so." I shook my head. "And don't you dare spring it on her when I'm not around. I have a score to settle with her. You wouldn't believe how she laughed at me yesterday! I think this dress is the perfect way to do it."

The smile crept back onto my face. I knew Evelyn thought I should take life a little more seriously, but I just didn't see the point. If I could simply choose to be happy and see the lighter side of things, why in all the kingdoms wouldn't I?

"I wouldn't dream of it," Mathilde said earnestly.

The Arcadian girl had been a good friend to me in the weeks we had spent as Ava's protectors. Now that Ava had succeeded in winning her kingdom, I wished Mathilde was staying in Rangmeros instead of heading straight back to Arcadie as soon as the wedding and coronation were over.

"You'll need to get back into your regular clothes now,

though," Mathilde continued. "We're all due in the gold sitting room for some sort of official pre-wedding lunch. Apparently, it's a Rangmeran tradition for the bride's party. You'd better bring both dresses. I think we'll all be getting dressed there, too."

With a sigh, I slipped out of the beautiful dress and into my regular clothes.

"I'll be wearing you again soon," I promised the dress as I laid it out on the bed on top of Evelyn's.

When I turned around Mathilde was laughing at me with her eyes.

"Come on, then," she said.

* * *

"So, I hear you've already got your eye on a couple of the young noblemen," said Mathilde, as we made our way through the castle.

I laughed. "Who told you that? Evelyn? Ava?"

"That's not a denial." Mathilde raised her eyebrows at me.

I smiled with self-satisfaction. "And why should I deny it? Clearly this court needs to be whipped into shape, and I'm just the girl for the job."

Mathilde chuckled. "Well, that's probably true."

"Of course it's true!"

I was about to launch into a more detailed explanation when we were accosted from a side corridor. Turning, I saw a group of young nobles approaching us. I recognized several of them as the richest and most popular young people at court, but I wasn't familiar with the one leading them. He was tall and broad-shouldered, and with his wavy dark-gold hair, just on the long side of short, he was exactly my type.

I privately admitted that, if I had seen him before, he would have gone straight to the top of my list of attractive Rangmeran men. I would have been astonished to find out that any fewer than half of the girls present were in love with him. And it was immediately obvious that despite his earlier absence, he was the leader of this particular set.

A challenge, then. I smiled.

He glanced condescendingly in our general direction. "We need food and drink brought to the small salon immediately." His tone was imperious and slightly arrogant, and I couldn't help my metaphorical hackles rising.

A challenge indeed, but not the one I had at first supposed. He was immediately transferred from the top of my 'fall in love with' list to the top of my 'teach a much needed lesson' list.

My narrowed eyes must have tipped him off because he gave us a more careful look, dwelling on the pile of fabric in my arms.

"Oh, apologies," he said, "I thought you were servants. We're having the most difficult time finding anyone." He flashed an unconcerned grin that was clearly supposed to melt us into little puddles at his feet.

I remained unmelted.

"Well, it is a rather important day," I said, my tone deceptively mild. "Perhaps the castle servants have something more important to do than wait on you."

He raised both of his brows and looked me over again. "You're two of the Arcadians, aren't you?"

"Arcadians?" I scoffed and turned toward my companion. "Come on, Mathilde, we don't have time for this. Ava is expecting us."

I sailed off down the corridor, trusting that Mathilde would follow me. When I didn't hear her steps, I glanced back and gestured for her to join me. Several of the noble girls were tittering behind their hands, but the mystery man was staring at my retreating form with curious eyes.

When I turned away again I allowed myself a smile. Overall, I felt that had been a success.

"Sarah, really!" Mathilde waited until we'd turned a corner

before tugging on my arm to slow me down. "Was that necessary? Do you even know who that was?"

"That," I said, "was a prime example of why the Rangmeran court is in such sore need of my influence."

Mathilde raised one eyebrow at me, and I burst out laughing. After a moment, she joined in.

"Sorry, Mathilde," I said when we both subsided, "I just couldn't resist. So, who was he?"

"His name is Miles, and he's Lord Adelmar's only son."

She gave me a significant look and I winced. No wonder the rest of them deferred to him. His family was easily the most powerful family at court after the monarchs. I had possibly bitten off more than I could chew.

I pondered for a moment and then shook my head. I might not be nobility, but I had been handpicked by the queen herself as an attendant at her wedding. How much harm could it really do if I played, just a little, with this particularly handsome and arrogant member of the court?

Read on in Happily Ever Afters: A Reimagining of Snow White and Rose Red

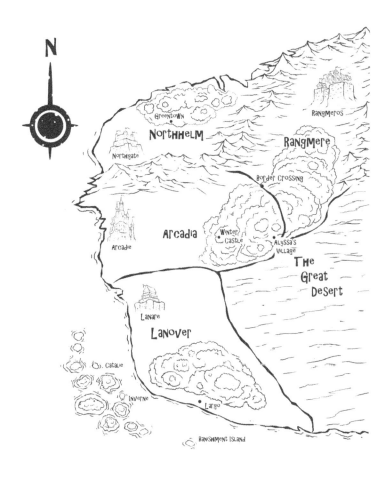

ACKNOWLEDGMENTS

My first book was dedicated to my parents because in the timeline of my life, they came first. But this book is for you, Marc, because you're the one who enabled The Four Kingdoms to happen. Thanks for helping to make my dreams come true!

Once again, a giant thank you goes out to my fantastic beta readers, particularly Katie, Priya, Rachel, Greg, Sea, Ber, and Steve. You guys took my first draft and helped me make it into something so much stronger. Your time and excellent feedback are so appreciated.

Another big thank you to my editors, Lyn and Dad, who went above and beyond to fit their fantastic editing services into my publishing timeline. As always, any mistakes are my own.

Thanks are also due to Karri for her beguiling cover image.

I also want to thank my family and friends for listening to me talk on and on about stories and writing and the publishing world and for giving me encouragement whenever I needed it. I couldn't make this author thing work without all of you to keep me sane! And it doesn't seem right not to mention the special little someone who is both my biggest distraction from writing and one of my biggest sources of joy. I love you little Adeline, regardless of your impact on my productivity!

And, of course, the final thanks goes to God, the source of my inspiration and strength.

ABOUT THE AUTHOR

Melanie Cellier grew up on a staple diet of books, books and more books. And although she got older, she never stopped loving children's and young adult novels.

She always wanted to write one herself, but it took three careers and three different continents before she actually managed it.

She now feels incredibly fortunate to spend her time writing from her home in Adelaide, Australia where she keeps an eye out for koalas in her backyard. Her staple diet hasn't changed much, although she's added choc mint Rooibos tea and Chicken Crimpies to the list.

She writes young adult fantasy including her *Spoken Mage* series, and her *Four Kingdoms* and *Beyond the Four Kingdoms* series which are made up of linked stand-alone stories that retell classic fairy tales.